ANGEL'S DAUGHTER

BOOK TWO OF
THE ANGEL TRILOGY

BY

B. J. SCOTT

authorHOUSE™

1663 LIBERTY DRIVE, SUITE 200
BLOOMINGTON, INDIANA 47403
(800) 839-8640
WWW.AUTHORHOUSE.COM

To Ann — Enjoy!
May You

B J Scott

First published by AuthorHouse 11/08/05

ISBN: 1-4208-7517-5 (sc)

Printed in the United States of America
Bloomington, Indiana

This book is printed on acid-free paper.

*For Martha Jack (1946-2004)—champion cyclist, musician, and friend,
who fought ovarian cancer for nine years before laying down her sword.
May we meet in Heaven.*

Acknowledgements

As with the first book, this sequel was a collaborative effort done with the assistance of several talented people, without whose help the final result would have been far less satisfying. Once again I am indebted to Dr. Richard C. Siebert, M.D., for insuring my medical information was correct. Sincere thanks go to my editor, Jeanette Lundgren, for her analysis and suggestions. Many thanks also to Maria Gerber, who proofread the final manuscript and found the flaws I could not. I am grateful for the resources of the public library of Santa Maria, California. Endless and heartfelt thanks go to all who read and loved the first book, giving me encouragement to write this sequel, particularly the Cover Girls of Arroyo Grande, California (you know who you are). And last, I am so grateful to my wife, Sherrie, who was the first to see these pages and give me a thumbs up or down, for putting up with being married to a writer. It isn't always easy.

Cover design and photography by B. J. Scott, © 2005. Digital enhancement by Arrow Camera, Santa Maria, California. Cover model: Shanna. Shanna's costume courtesy of the Great American Melodrama and Vaudeville, Oceano, California. Photographed at Avila Beach, California.

Lyrics to *Rose of Shannon* and all maps by B. J. Scott.

"A railroad, fellow citizens, is a machine, and one of the most beautiful and perfect of labor-saving machines. It well suits the energy of the American people. They love to go ahead fast, and to go with power. They love to annihilate the magnificent distances."

—19th Century Missouri railroad executive

1867
San Francisco, California

1.

The big copper-colored stallion pranced down the dirt street in brilliant sunlight, neck arched, feet lifting high, sunbeams chasing across its glossy, muscular flanks. Snorting as if to draw attention to itself, the horse seemed to carry its passenger with pride.

Regally upright aboard the broad back, Megan Daley gave up nothing to the magnificent horse beneath her. Her dark red hair bounced around her shoulders. Sunlight chasing across its broad waves highlighted the interwoven threads of gold. She wore a jacket and skirt of emerald velvet, a perfect compliment to her intensely green eyes. There was a teasing smile on her sensuous features as she surveyed her domain. Motherhood had stolen none of her arresting beauty; she still brought traffic to a standstill. She was the center of attention, as the Connelly women unfailingly were.

It was Megan's habit to ride into San Francisco each Saturday from her magnificent blufftop home overlooking the Pacific Ocean, leaving husband Alex and daughter Bridget to spend the day as they wished. She preferred shopping alone, and would always end her trip with lunch at her favorite restaurant.

Now on a sunny May afternoon, she gently guided her horse up to the front of the restaurant and dismounted. Her booted foot had barely touched the ground when a young boy bounded forward, all undisguised eagerness to serve, to take the reins of the big stallion.

"Afternoon, Miss Megan," the boy said brightly, doffing his floppy cloth cap. "Take your horse?" Though she was married and had a child, some people still called her "Miss Megan".

Megan flashed him a broad smile. "Of course, Jimmy. A little water for him, as usual, and make sure he's firmly secured to the hitching post."

"Yes ma'am!" Jimmy said. "I'll take good care of Shamrock, you can be sure of that."

"I know you will, Jimmy." Megan removed the shopping bag slung over her saddle horn and mounted the boardwalk in front of the restaurant. "I'll see you in a while." She glided into the restaurant, her passage recorded by every pair of eyes within fifty yards. Motherhood had done nothing to diminish her spectacular figure; generous breasts and hips were clearly evident beneath her fashionable attire. Even Jimmy, at age 12, couldn't resist an admiring shake of his head. As she approached the front door, it opened for her, and a smiling maitre'd beckoned her inside.

The numerous onlookers up and down the street slowly returned to their affairs, some men the target of frowns from their wives at their helpless stares of admiration.

One pair of eyes lingered longer than the rest on the door through which Megan had passed. Dark and malevolent, they belonged to a short, florid bullnecked man named Othniel Wanamaker. He stared at the door as if he could burn a hole in it with his vision. Finally, fists clenched, he turned away down the boardwalk.

Every Saturday afternoon, Megan made a visit to the same restaurant. And every Saturday, Wanamaker was there to stoke the fires of his rage. Two years had not dimmed the enmity he bore Megan Daley, nor diminished his desire for revenge. As if it were yesterday, he could still feel her hands on his, forcing them down on the plunger, setting off the blasting powder that sent his freight warehouse sky-high in a thousand pieces, to rain about him in flaming ruin. The fact that it had been *his* blasting powder, the same blasting powder he had planted underneath the trestle of the railroad Kathleen and her husband had built, mattered little to him. Nor did the fact that he had intended to blow the trestle to Kingdom come, and send the locomotive to the bottom of the ravine, along with anyone unfortunate

2

enough to be aboard it. The sad reality was that Pacific Freight, the mule-team freight business he had built from nothing, no longer existed. He had never recovered from the destruction of his warehouse. Shaken by the killing of his chief enforcer Martin Hofmeister, and the suicide of his confederate Ansel Platt in their failed attempts to destroy the Connelly women, he was a broken man. Wandering off to San Francisco, he had survived on the fringes of society for the last two years, his once-pressed clothes now shabby, his formerly clean-shaven face too often wearing a few days' growth of beard.

And so he watched her, hoping for some idea, some inspiration that would show the way to his revenge. It was all that kept him going. And on this spring day, he thought he had one. Reassuringly, he patted his pocket and felt the crackle of the newspaper page within as he scurried down the street to his appointment like a fat rat.

The three Connelly women wielded great power and influence in Central California, from the raw boomtown of San Francisco east to the Sierras. Kathleen, the matriarch and head of three business empires—cattle ranching, shipping, and railroad—still possessed the aristocratic beauty and fearlessness that had won her widespread admiration across the new, still wild state of California. Finally giving in to numerous requests, she had run for the state legislature, and won. There, her reputation and commanding presence were so respected she had been elected chair of the powerful Senate Appropriations Committee.

Her adopted daughter Danielle—orphaned as a French immigrant at age fourteen—had become a brilliant businesswoman whose judgment Kathleen trusted so completely she had made her CEO of all three of her companies. It kept Danielle busy, but she seemed born to the task.

Then there was Megan, whom Kathleen referred to as "my wild daughter". It was an apt description. Wherever she went, Megan drew a crowd. Her beauty stirred longing in men—all wanted her; none could have her. In women it produced suspicion; surely a woman so beautiful could not be trusted around their men—or any man. Megan did nothing to discourage the wagging tongues.

Many felt there was a fourth Connelly woman in the making—Megan's daughter Bridget. Though only five, she was visually a copy of her grandmother Kathleen, with raven hair and startling sky-blue eyes. And she had already started to display some of the same character traits—an utter fearlessness, and a steel-spined, unyielding determination to get what she wanted.

3

Kathleen had a sentimental attachment to gold mining, and so had not yet let go of her one remaining mine, though it barely made a profit. The family had invested cautiously in Colorado silver mines, which had risen to prominence as the California gold fields were fading. So far their investments looked good.

Their railroad, the Sierra and Western, which ran from Placerville to Sacramento, had been made possible by Megan's triumphant recruitment of two hundred Chinese laborers. It did a steady and growing business, and was poised for expansion. Too, with Sacramento now the western terminus of the transcontinental railroad, as had been predicted, their line would connect to it there, increasing its value even more. The railroad could yet become their largest operation.

But so far, it was the shipping empire that had truly burgeoned. Kathleen's flagship, her treasured 251-foot black-hulled clipper *Emerald Isle,* was still the fastest ship afloat. To this she had added over twenty other vessels of various sizes, from small coast-runner barks and side wheel steamers to fleet ocean-crossing clippers. Her vessels regularly made runs up and down the West Coast, north to Alaska and south to Panama and down the Pacific coast of South America. With the completion of the Panama railroad in 1855, it no longer made sense to risk runs around Cape Horn unless the cargo was too large to carry by rail. From California Kathleen's ships also sailed east to the Orient, ranging from China to Australia carrying a wide range of goods. The agreement Megan had worked out with San Francisco merchant Yuen Ling-Po for the railroad laborers had provided Kathleen with steady business sufficient to show a good profit, even with the twenty per cent discount Ling-Po received in exchange for the two hundred workers. And that ongoing agreement, profitable for both sides, had provided Kathleen and her family, through Megan, with unsurpassed influence and goodwill in San Francisco's Chinese community.

Megan finished her meal and went outside to retrieve Shamrock. Jimmy, sensing accurately the time she would be finished, stood stroking the big head, reins in hand. She gave him a generous tip and accepted his help in mounting. She had never cared for riding sidesaddle, and rode astride like a man, which only served to increase her slightly scandalous reputation among the cattier women who secretly envied her. "A proper lady rides sidesaddle," one had once sniffed haughtily at her.

"Yes, but I'm no proper lady," Megan had replied with a grin, then whirled her horse away.

"You can say that again," the woman said to herself.

Megan rode back home with her shopping prizes slung over her saddle horn. It was about forty-five minutes at an easy gallop to the bluff overlooking Pacific breakers. The late afternoon sunlight played off her long glorious hair as she loped Shamrock up the long driveway and slowed to a halt in front of the carved double doors. Their magnificent cut-glass oval windows made an elegant entrance to the Daley house. Not quite a mansion, it was still an imposing sight. The two-story Victorian encompassed about 4,000 square feet. There were big bay windows on either side of the entrance, and turreted towers at the east and west front corners. The house was situated with the entrance facing south, providing a view along the ocean shore from the porch that ran the entire width of the front.

The front doors burst open and a small hurricane in a frilly white dress sped across the porch and into Megan's arms. "Mama!" Bridget cried. "I missed you. Did you get me something?" Her black ponytail bobbed back and forth.

"Yes, but you shall have to wait until after dinner. What did you and Papa do today?"

"We went to Aunt Danielle's," Bridget said. "Do I really have to wait?"

"I think so," Megan replied, straightening up from their embrace as her husband came out to greet her. She dropped her bag and hugged him tightly. "Dear Alex. You're so sweet to indulge me every Saturday." She tousled his reddish-brown hair playfully.

Alex was tall at about six feet one, with a thick lock of hair that sometimes hung down over his smooth forehead nearly to the sandy-colored eyebrows above his dark brown eyes. He had pleasing, regular features with a hint of freckles, dominated by a strong, straight nose. But now he gave her a mock frown. "I don't like the sound of this. How much did you spend this time?"

Megan smiled sweetly and slipped an arm around his waist. "Oh, not so much. Don't fret. I'll make it worth your while—tonight." She knew, as usual, that he wasn't really upset with her. Megan had played such a vital role in bringing the railroad project into reality that no one in the family could deny her anything. Everyone was aware of the danger she had placed herself in to secure the Chinese laborers that had broken the boycott Pacific Freight had imposed through threats and murder. But no one knew the full extent of the price she had paid. That was something she kept to herself.

Alex had proven a worthy addition to the family. He had come back into her life in 1863, just two days before Danielle's wedding to Robert

Bradshaw. He had been lost to them since 1860, when Kathleen had banished him in a rage over Megan's pregnancy. Bridget was his, the product of a one-night liaison Megan, in one of her wild moods, had brought about. She had seduced him, pure and simple. Bridget, amazingly enough, showed no trace of his genetic contribution. If this bothered Alex, he didn't let on.

Since marrying Megan in a double ceremony with Danielle and Robert's wedding on the bluff near where their house now stood, Alex had shown he could succeed at any task given him. A top hand with animals, he had primarily been given responsibility for the acquisition and care of livestock for all the Connelly families, but Megan didn't hesitate to push for more when she talked to her mother. "He can do anything, Mother," she would say. "Just give him a try." Kathleen always promised to give it some thought. Though she was married to Ben, there was no doubt that Kathleen still called the shots for all of the family businesses. She was the unquestioned matriarch. Ben was content with that, pursuing his own construction engineering projects.

Somewhat to Kathleen's surprise, Megan and Alex had welded into a tightly bonded couple whose mutual admiration was clearly evident. Kathleen's soft spot for Megan's happiness, and her guilt over her banishment of Alex, had overcome her doubts about him.

As they glided into the parlor, which was decorated with abundant large ferns, Megan gave Alex a kiss as she slipped her arm from his waist. She put her shopping bag on the parlor table and brushed the hair back from her face. "So, what's happening at Danielle's?" she said. "Is she still upset about the last board meeting?"

"She's calmed down a little. But she thinks we need to keep our ear to the ground about what Eli Leatherwood may be up to."

"Hmph. I don't like the man," Megan said, pulling off her riding gloves and tossing them on a table. "Never did. If Mother's ever made a mistake, it was letting him on the board."

"Forget him for now. I've got great news," Alex said, holding up a letter. "Your mother's coming over next month. And she's staying for a while."

Megan brightened. "Wonderful! I can hardly wait."

Though Ben had designed and built magnificent blufftop homes less than 200 yards apart for Megan and Danielle and their families, he and Kathleen continued to live at their spacious mission-style ranch house outside of Sacramento. It was the centerpiece of the 20,000-acre Eire Ranch. Ben and Kathleen's immense spread was utilized mostly for raising cattle, but also contained significant acreage in grain crops. They traveled to San Francisco three or four times a year, including once each summer for a Board of Directors meeting.

The next evening, Danielle and Robert came striding over through the tall grass in the late afternoon sunlight. They often shared evenings with Megan and Alex on the front porch of each other's houses. Danielle moved with the easy grace French women displayed, a quality that had aroused particular interest in the hard-bitten frontiersmen of the new state. Too, her thickly accented English and serene gray-blue eyes never failed to enchant. When she was single, she had never lacked for male attention, though she was not beautiful. Megan welcomed them warmly and bade them sit with her on the porch. "Alex will join us soon," Megan said. "I think he's reading a story to Bridget."

Danielle and Robert sat on a large canopied swing near Megan. Robert's thick brown hair was, as always, parted down the middle, his smooth, handsome lawyer's face clean-shaven and tanned.

Megan smiled at him. "Still the handsomest lawyer in San Francisco, I think," she teased.

"Such flattery will do you no good," Danielle countered. "He's still dedicated to me."

Robert gave her a sly sideways look. "I don't know. *You* haven't called me handsome lately."

Danielle poked him. "I'm making sure you don't get a big head. Megan isn't helping." She smiled broadly.

Megan looked at her closely. "Hmm. I know that face. You look like you're bursting to tell me something. What are you hiding?"

Danielle blushed and ran a hand through her long, wavy chestnut hair. "I'm expecting."

Megan shrieked and sprang to her feet, leaning over to embrace her. "Sister! At last! Oh, I'm so happy for you. How wonderful. When is it coming?"

Danielle leaned into Robert in dreamy repose. "I'm not sure yet. Sometime in late summer or early fall."

"Well, it's been a long time coming. I couldn't be more pleased."

"Though we've been trying for a long while, the timing is good now," Robert said. "The delay has allowed us time to get the law firm strongly established. We're now the third largest firm in San Francisco, and closing in on second." Marrying into Ben and Kathleen's far-flung business empire, Robert had decided to specialize in corporate law, and had become the family attorney for all business matters.

7

Alex came out to see what the commotion was all about, carrying Bridget on his shoulders. Both joined the group on the porch. For a while, the adults were content to watch in silence as Bridget played in the tall green grass in front of the house, chasing her cat and rolling a hoop. Below them to the south, Pacific breakers rolled in in endless succession, their white foamy expanse peaceful and hypnotizing in the evening light. "Let's go down to the beach when Mother comes," Megan said.

"I'd like that," Danielle replied. "I wonder," she mused, "how many years those waves have been rolling in like that. Thousands? Millions?"

"Long before people were around, I'm sure," Megan said. "And they'll still be rolling in thousands of years after we're gone, I imagine. It kind of makes all our lives seem smaller."

Danielle grew silent again.

"Something else on your mind, sister?" Megan said, able to read Danielle well.

Danielle looked out to sea, a frown on her long Gallic features. "Eli Leatherwood."

Othniel Wanamaker paused at the entrance to the impressive three-story Market Street building. The front was all gray stone blocks and white marble. Above him, at the top of the stone steps, large brass-trimmed doors beckoned invitingly. Windows decorated with gold filigree gave a glimpse into the interior, where elegant chandeliers hung from the paneled ceiling. He pulled out his pocket watch. Right on time. He looked up the steps again. How he longed to walk up those steps, to throw open the doors like he belonged there! *Someday,* he vowed silently, *someday I'll walk through those doors like I own the place. Someday they'll notice me. Someday it'll be like before.* Then, his expression turning sour, he walked around behind the building and into the back entrance.

Once admitted inside the back door, he went up a flight of stairs to a second-floor office, where he knocked firmly three times on a closed door.

"Come in," he heard a voice beckon.

Wanamaker twisted the doorknob and fixed a smile on his face. It never hurt to put on a positive expression when meeting with Eli Leatherwood. He swung the door open and went in.

Elijah J. Leatherwood sat in a leather chair behind an elaborate oak desk. The desk boasted carved ornamentation at the front corners, and was polished to a high luster. The desktop was mostly bare, with a wooden tray holding a few papers on one side, and an elegant green-shaded kerosene lamp on the other. The man behind the desk did not look up at Wanamaker's entrance, but continued writing with a metal-tipped ink pen on a paper in front of him. Handsome in a decadent sort of way, he was dressed in an impeccably tailored pin-stripe suit, a white shirt with a starched collar, and a black silk tie at his throat. His hair, black on top and silver-gray on the sides, was cut with precision. The nails on his long fingers were buffed and flawless. There was nothing about him that was not precise, calculated, and perfectly in order.

Wanamaker shifted uncomfortably from one foot to the other. He always felt shabby and inadequate in the man's presence. And he always felt humiliated when Leatherwood made him wait, which was all too frequent. *Someday I'll make* him *wait,* he thought. *The tables will turn. Then we'll see how it is. I don't care if he is the biggest financier in San Francisco; he won't always be so high and mighty.*

Finally, Leatherwood put down his pen, looked up from his writing, and motioned Wanamaker into a chair. "Well, Wanamaker, what's on your mind for this week's appointment? Been out following Megan Daley again?"

Wanamaker's smile twisted and his eyes narrowed. "You bet. Saw her just a while ago."

"How'd she look?"

Wanamaker's expression turned sour. "Beautiful. Like always. People bowin' and scrapin' to do her biddin'. Like it is with all them Connelly women."

Leatherwood steepled his fingers together and looked at Wanamaker with curiosity. "I don't know why you resent that so much."

"I done told you," Wanamaker said, scowling. "And someday I'll have my payback."

"Ah yes, the warehouse incident. Well, payback is overrated. A poor way to motivate yourself." He smiled, eyes gleaming. "Now, payback with *profit*—that's something worth pursuing." He leaned forward, looking intently at Wanamaker. "Hmm," he mused, "I think there's something you want to tell me. Did you discover anything interesting?"

Wanamaker's look of self-satisfaction deepened. He reached into his pocket. "Damn straight I did. Look at this." He pulled out the newspaper and put it in front of Leatherwood. "Found it tacked to a wall in a shack, bein' used as insulation."

Leatherwood looked at the yellowed newsprint for a moment as if it were unsavory. "A piece of newspaper?" he said doubtfully.

"It ain't the paper. It's what's on it. Open it up."

Leatherwood reached out and gingerly opened up the folded paper, which crackled with age. It was an old edition of the *Alta California.* For a moment he was puzzled, then his eyes caught a series of headlines on the right-hand side.

HEIRESS FOUND DRUGGED IN
HOTEL LOBBY
OPIUM SUSPECTED
WEALTHY MOTHER ATTACKS
TWO CHINAMEN

His eyes scanned the story for a few minutes, then he looked up at Wanamaker. "The heiress was Megan Daley," he said.

Wanamaker oozed smugness. "That's right. She was still Megan Connelly then."

Leatherwood rested his chin on his fingers. "I'd forgotten about that, but I remember it now. That was back in '62. I heard Kathleen Connelly nearly tore the lobby apart trying to get at those Chinamen. Hmm. You know, that's the only whiff of scandal I've ever heard about with that family. Never did know just how Megan Daley got hold of the opium—or why."

"I heard she struck a deal with some Chinaman for all the workers that done built that railroad. It has somethin' to do with that. That's all I know."

"So," Leatherwood said, leaning back in his chair and folding his hands in his lap. "What's on your mind?"

"Wel-l-l-l," Wanamaker said slowly, "I figger I've uncovered somethin' I can use. That bein' Megan Daley and that opium. I've heard tell you try that stuff once and you never forget it. Could be she's still got a yearnin' for it deep down inside." He paused and leaned forward, piggish eyes closed to slits. "Maybe she should get some. It'd give me satisfaction to tempt her, maybe see her get hooked on it."

Leatherwood looked at him with an unreadable expression. "So that's it? You want to get some opium in front of Megan Daley and see what she does, see if she can be tempted into using it again? Maybe bring her down?"

Wanamaker nodded enthusiastically. "Yeah, that's it!"

"So what do you need me for? Don't I pay you enough to keep your eyes and ears open around town that you could afford opium? You can get it in any John Chinaman store in Chinatown."

"It ain't the opium. It's a good pipe I need. Somethin' real fancy, somethin' she just couldn't resist usin'."

"I see." Leatherwood turned in his chair to the window behind him, looking out across the San Francisco vista and over the bay for long minutes, saying nothing, lost in thought.

Wanamaker grew increasingly uncomfortable with the silence. He was beginning to wonder if Leatherwood had somehow dismissed him when the man finally turned around to face him again. The expression on his face made Wanamaker break out in a cold sweat.

"Oh, Wanamaker, you are such a despicable low-down cad. How could you even *think* of doing such a thing to that beautiful woman?" He leaned across the desk, eyes burning. "I like it."

Wanamaker let his breath out in a sigh of relief.

"Could be you've found the only weakness that family has," Leatherwood went on. "Kathleen Wilson's a regular Rock of Gibraltar. She can't be bought, influenced against her better judgment, or swayed one inch from her chosen goal. Lord knows I've tried. And that damned Frenchwoman—if she hasn't got a head for business! The greatest instincts for corporate structuring I've ever seen. No matter what I've thought up, she always seems to be ready for it, if not one step ahead of me. But Megan—"

Wanamaker leaned forward on the edge of his chair. "Then you'll help me get my revenge?"

Leatherwood looked at him in silence for a moment, then broke out in peals of laughter. "Wanamaker, you lack vision!" He fixed him with a cold smile. "There's potential here for infinitely more mischief than that."

Wanamaker shrank back and looked at him blankly. "There is?"

Leatherwood chuckled, a positively evil sound, Wanamaker thought, and over the next fifteen minutes proceeded to launch into a lengthy discourse that dazzled him with its scope and complexity. He could never have imagined that his proposal could have such far-reaching consequences. When Leatherwood at last seemed finished, Wanamaker was shaken. "You really think you can do all that?"

Leatherwood smiled. "Could be."

"My God," Wanamaker said, "if *any* of that stuff actually came to pass, and either Ben or Kathleen Wilson found out we were connected to it, we'd both be dead men."

"Well, then we'll just have to make sure they *don't* find out, won't we?" Leatherwood replied.

Wanamaker squirmed uneasily in his chair. The prospect of repercussions far beyond what he had thought to put in motion both excited and disturbed him. He knew Ben and Kathleen played for keeps when they were wronged. He would have to be careful, more careful than he had ever been. "So, how do we start?" he said.

11

Leatherwood smiled, a cold expression devoid of compassion. "With a gift."

The following Saturday, Megan made her customary ride into San Francisco, and as usual, ended her visit at her favorite restaurant. She ate a leisurely meal, then left her table for a moment and stepped outside to tell Jimmy that she would be leaving soon, after she had dessert, so that he could get Shamrock ready to ride.

Returning to her table, she sat down-and froze. A box had appeared on the table. It was elegant, long and narrow, and polished to a high sheen, with jade filigree inlaid on a hinged lid. There was a small white card attached to it with green ribbon. Puzzled, she looked around to see who might have left it. She saw no one she had not seen previously since she had been there. She called the waiter over and asked him, but no, he had not seen who had placed the box on her table. She thanked him and turned her attention back to the mysterious object.

It is certainly beautiful, she mused. She picked up the card, which was folded over, and opened it. There was elegant writing inside that said,

From an Old Friend

She put down the card, removed the green ribbon from the box, and slowly opened the lid.

And began to tremble.

Wanamaker watched from hiding as Megan burst through the doors of the restaurant and out onto the boardwalk. She appeared agitated, glancing up and down the street. Then she quickly strode to Shamrock, mounted, and galloped away. Jimmy was left scratching his head at her hasty departure. A few minutes later, a young busboy came casually out of the restaurant, and, unseen by anyone else, went around the side of the building, pulled the polished box from under his apron and hid it on the ground behind a loose piece of siding. Wanamaker waited a few minutes, then casually sauntered over to where the box had been left, picked it up, and walked off.

Megan tried desperately to calm herself on the ride home. Someone, for reasons she couldn't guess, was bringing an old nightmare back into her life. She had never given her family all the details about her negotiations with Yuen Ling-Po. The Chinese had built Ben and Kathleen's railroad from Sacramento to Placerville, in defiance of the scare tactics and even murder Pacific Freight had employed to intimidate white laborers in the

Sacramento area. She had negotiated skillfully to acquire the workers. Her family knew she had been required to smoke opium with Ling-Po to close the deal in good faith; they had found her passed out in the lobby of her hotel, accompanied by two of Ling-Po's guards. She had still been heavily drugged.

What she had never told them was the depth of the hold the opium had taken on her. There were times when she could still taste it on her tongue, could still feel the sweet smoke flowing into her body, could still remember the weightless bliss that had carried her away. It had been five years, and still she could not forget. Ever since, she had studiously avoided any forays into Chinatown, had removed herself from any circumstances where opium might surface. She knew how deep-seated the craving was, how strongly her body sometimes wanted it. And she kept it to herself, her only secret, one she dared not share with anyone. Now someone was placing temptation in her path again. *Why?* she pondered as her house came into view. She breathed deeply and tried to calm herself for Alex and Bridget.

Eli Leatherwood watched with amusement as Othniel Wanamaker fumed in frustration in the chair before his elegant desk.

"She didn't take the bait!" Wanamaker said bitterly. "She got up and left, in a hurry."

Leatherwood chuckled. "Wanamaker, it becomes more evident every time we meet why I'm where I am and you're where you are."

"I can do without the insults," Wanamaker replied sullenly.

Leatherwood gave him a sober stare. "I didn't get rich by being impatient. Patience is indeed a virtue. That's a quality you need to learn. No, I really didn't expect her to take the bait this time. But from the sound of things, you really got a rise out of her. She was agitated, from the report that busboy gave you. That's a start."

"So, what do we do now? Try next Saturday?"

"No, that would be too predictable. We'll wait two weeks, then try again. That'll keep her off balance."

"S'pose she goes to another restaurant?"

"Then you'll just have to know which one, won't you? And bribe another busboy." He reached forward and opened the polished box Wanamaker had placed on his desk. He opened the lid and smiled with satisfaction, lifting the opulent hand-carved opium pipe out of its case. "A beautiful piece of work, I must say. Had I the bent for opium, I'd find it hard to resist myself. I think next time we'll sweeten the pot a little, so to

13

speak. Now, if there's nothing further to report, I have business to attend to."

After Wanamaker shuffled out, Leatherwood leaned back in his chair and gazed out the window toward the harbor, reflecting on the opportunity Wanamaker had presented him with. Though financially successful, he lusted for power, for prominence. In fact, there was one position in particular he coveted—that of railroad baron.

He'd read of the heroic exploits of the Big Four—Stanford, Crocker, Huntington, and Hopkins. They had the contract to build the Central Pacific Railroad from Sacramento east across the Sierra Nevada Mountains, there to come together somewhere on the other side with the Union Pacific, which was building west from Omaha. The two roads were to meet at an as-yet-undetermined spot, where they would complete a glorious transcontinental line that would link the nation east and west— and profoundly transform it. He knew many people thought it couldn't be done, but he was sure it would be. And with his financier's knowledge of how the Big Four had structured their contracts, he also knew incredible wealth was coming their way, even if they were struggling now. The four men were as ruthless, rapacious, and greedy as they came. Just the sort of company he could relate to.

Yes, the railroad was the coming thing, and he wanted to be part of it. And now Wanamaker had unwittingly provided him with the possible means to do so. Because the Big Four weren't satisfied to be masters of the Central Pacific. They hadn't even gotten their road over the Sierras yet, and already they were angling to buy up every other railroad in California. Leatherwood knew Stanford in particular wanted a monopoly on the railroads within the state. He wanted them all. And he would get them. Except one. Leatherwood made it his business to know what was happening in the financial world, and he knew that Ben and Kathleen Wilson had steadfastly refused all offers from Stanford to sell their railroad. Small wonder. They had built it with their own money. No government loans of bonds, no land grants, no nothing. It was paid for, it made a profit, and most important of all, it was complete—unlike the other railroads the Big Four were after, which had hardly any miles of track laid.

Leatherwood knew what Stanford apparently didn't—there would be no budging Kathleen Connelly Wilson, nor her husband. But if he could find a way to get those two out of California for an extended period of time—well, anything was possible.

Grandiose visions danced through his head. If he could deliver the Wilsons' railroad to Stanford, what a reward could be his! He would hold out for president of the newly acquired railroad, of course. And then the Big Four would become the Big Five. Yes, his name would look good alongside theirs. And from there, the sky was the limit. After all, Stanford had already gotten himself elected Governor of California. Hell, even old Charley Crocker—whom an acquaintance of Leatherwood's had described as "a living, breathing, waddling monument to the triumph of vulgarity, viciousness, and dishonesty"—had been elected to the state legislature. Surely there would be a place for Eli Leatherwood there too.

It was two weeks before Megan felt like venturing into San Francisco again. She had kept herself busy at home, and when Alex occasionally inquired if there was anything wrong, she had sweetly said, "No". She decided to change restaurants for her afternoon meal, having been too upset by her experience to return to her favorite haunt. It wasn't the mysterious gift that scared her so much as the realization that the old desire still burned deep within. Even so, she couldn't countenance sharing her weakness with her family, not even Alex. It was a shame she didn't want to admit.

Cutting her shopping trip short, she decided on impulse to visit a restaurant on the waterfront, with a view of vessels anchored peacefully in the harbor. She looked out across the scene and could identify three of her family's ships riding at anchor. Somewhere out on the Pacific, there were over twenty more. They made up one of the largest shipping companies on Pacific waters.

She found a shady spot to tie up Shamrock, tipped an attendant to watch the big stallion, and went inside. After perusing the menu, she decided on a seafood dish, and ate a leisurely meal. When she was ready to leave, the busboy came to her table. He piled up her dishes, then paused.

"Ma'am, I was asked to give you this," he said. He pulled something from under his apron and hurried away.

Megan sat in shock, her face a mask of dismay. The box was back.

Suddenly galvanized with anger, she sprang up and ran after the busboy, who dove through the kitchen doors. By the time she got into the kitchen, all she could see was the back door to the restaurant swinging wide. She ran to the door, and saw the boy running furiously down the dirt street.

Megan sprinted around to the front of the building. "Give me the reins!" she shouted at the attendant. He did, and she vaulted into the saddle without using the stirrup. She dug in her heels and Shamrock erupted into motion. At the back of the building she spotted the boy a block away, running hard. He looked back and saw her, fright on his face

15

at the sight of an angry redhead on a huge stallion bearing down on him. Shamrock stretched out to top speed. The big horse ate up the distance with enormous strides, dirt flying from his hooves as he rocketed down the street. She gained ground quickly and was only twenty yards behind the boy when he swerved into an alley. Shamrock pounded up to the alley and she pulled him to an abrupt halt. The narrow space was full of trash. There was no room for her to pass. She could see no sign of the boy. He had either gone into a door somewhere or found a way through the debris. Disappointed, she turned Shamrock around and walked him back to the restaurant, where she gave the reins back to the attendant. She stalked inside and went straight to the manager. He knew nothing about the boy except his first name.

"I doubt you'll see him again," Megan said. "I'm sorry I rushed out so abruptly. I was upset." She returned to the table. The box was still there. *I don't want this thing to show up again next time,* she thought. *Maybe if I take it, this foolishness will stop.* She picked up the box, paid her bill and left.

In deep shadows across the street, Othniel Wanamaker fixed a look of smug satisfaction on his face and walked away.

Megan stalked into the house and threw her shopping bag into a corner. Fortunately no one else was home to see the scowl on her face. She stomped around, blowing off steam. After a while she returned to the parlor, pacing back and forth, staring at the shopping bag on the floor. After a few minutes of tormented indecision, she sat down and pulled the bag to her. Opening it, she pulled out the elegant box. She took it gingerly onto her lap, and, finally, opened the lid.

The same magnificently worked opium pipe lay within, nestled in blue velvet. About eighteen inches long, it appeared to be made of ivory, and was covered with detailed scrollwork swirling around inlaid pieces of jade and abalone shell. Sighing, she stroked its length. Her fingers caressed the small bowl fixed to the pipe a few inches from one end. She felt a faint stirring deep inside. Then a wave of nausea swept over her. There was something else inside the box. She could smell it. Lifting the velvet cloth, she saw what she knew was there—a ball of opium paste.

Trembling, unable to stop herself, she picked up the opium ball and held it under her nose. Suddenly she was back in Ling-Po's elegant parlor in Chinatown, drawing the smoke deep into her lungs, terrified but determined, and then *floating* . . . . Her face twisted in torment and she mashed the opium ball back into the case, then slammed the pipe in with it and closed the lid. She ran to the kitchen and rummaged about for some twine, then, finding some, wrapped it securely around the box. Stumbling out the front door, she ran with the box to the edge of the bluff above the beach about 100 yards away. By the time she reached it, her cheeks were wet with tears. Raging at her need, her face twisted into a mask of anguish, she flung the box off the cliff, saw it tumble over in the air and land in a patch of beach grass far below. Then she sank to her knees, sobbing into her hands.

Three days later, Megan and Alex walked over to Danielle and Robert's house. They all sat together on the front porch in the fading evening light. "Are you having morning sickness?" Megan asked Danielle.

"Yes," Danielle replied. "It's a bother. But I've waited so long to have it, it's still more exciting than bothersome. I don't mind."

"Oh sister, I'm so happy for you. Have you given any thought to a name yet?"

"Well," Danielle said with a grin, "Robert and I are wrangling about it, but I am determined that if it is a girl, she shall have a proper French name. If it's a boy, he shall have an American name. We agree on that much."

"Hmm," Megan mused, "I expect you'll be showing by the time of the stockholders' meeting this summer."

"Yes," Danielle replied. "I'm glad I won't be farther along than I am, though. Something tells me I'll need a clear head for this meeting."

"You expecting trouble?" Alex put in.

"There could be," Robert spoke for the first time in a while. "Danielle doesn't like the way Eli Leatherwood's been acting the last couple of meetings. He seems hostile to our best interests."

"I'm not sure I understand the concern," Megan said. "The man's a snake, but he owns only nine per cent of the railroad stock. Our families, counting Ben and Mother, still own an overwhelming controlling interest, 70 per cent."

"True," Danielle said. "But the railroad's the only family business not completely owned by us. Since we expect to expand with lines up and down the western slopes of the Sierras, and farther into the Sacramento Valley, it's more valuable than ever. And the transcontinental railroad's coming to Sacramento, no doubt about it. When our line links up with it, it will vastly increase its value. Ben and Mother own the shipping company and the cattle operation outright, so there's no danger there. But the railroad's going to become our most valuable holding, and it's the only place we're vulnerable at all. I can't discard the impression that Leatherwood has his eye on gaining a controlling interest in it."

17

"Never happen," Alex said. "Rich as he is, he couldn't swing that. We'll never sell our company shares anyway."

"No, but he could buy influence," Danielle said.

"I wish we'd never offered railroad stock to the public," Megan said.

Danielle sighed. "I know, so do I. But the fact is we needed a fresh infusion of capital at the time to finish it. Not doing so would have strained our resources to the point other operations might have been vulnerable." She turned and looked away, out over the vast Pacific, silent for a moment. Then: "I probably worry too much. By himself, Eli Leatherwood can't hurt us. But sometimes I get the feeling he's really just a front man for someone else. Someone powerful. Someone ambitious."

Megan suspended her weekly rides into San Francisco. When Alex asked why, she simply said she thought she had enough clothes for a while. Instead, she took to riding Shamrock along the high ocean bluffs near her house. Her mind whirled with conflict; she cursed the flame of desire that burned deep within her. When she finished her rides and turned Shamrock over to her stable hand, she would run into the house and scoop up Bridget, hugging the girl tightly, sometimes reluctant to let loose. "I love you, little one," she said. "I'll never fail you. I won't. I won't."

"Mama, are you all right?" Bridget said, her sky-blue eyes wide.

"Yes, I am," Megan said. "I'm just fine."

But she wasn't.

Three weeks after her last encounter with the box, she saddled up Shamrock and rode out alone toward the ocean. She gave the big horse his head and let him stretch out in long strides along the bluff top, the tall grass whipping at his legs. She exulted in the wind, her luxuriant coppery hair streaming out behind her. She let Shamrock run until he slowed of his own accord, then turned for home. The house was still a mile away when she stopped at the top of a path leading down to the surf. She sat in the saddle, staring down at the beach for a long time. From where she sat, she could just make out the patch of beach grass where the box had landed, at the bottom of the cliff below her house. After a while, she became aware her hands were twisting the reins tightly. She grasped the saddlehorn in a death grip, breathing heavily, trembling, and lowered her head to rest on Shamrock's neck. When she straightened up at last, there was anger and resignation on her face. Slowly, she turned Shamrock from the bluff top path and down the trail to the beach below.

2.

Megan approached the clump of tall beach grass warily, one foot seeming to place itself in front of the other on its own. She was at war inside, hoping the box wasn't there, even as she looked for it. Walking back and forth through the reedy grass, she couldn't see it. A couple of times she glanced upward apprehensively to see if anyone might be standing on the bluff top above, watching her. But there was no one.

She began to get angry as she poked through the grass. She was sure this was the spot. Just as she was about to give up, a flash of color caught her eye. Her heart thudded in her chest as she recognized the twine she had tied around the box. It was still firmly in place, she saw, as she picked up the box. She stared at it for long moments, emotions roiling in her head. For a fleeting instant she had the urge to throw the box as far as she could into the surf, but then she turned and stuffed it into her saddlebag. She mounted and rode away, a stony expression on her beautiful features.

Eli Leatherwood looked across his polished desk at Othniel Wanamaker as one might examine a newly discovered species of insect. There was caution along with the curiosity. "Wanamaker, you look nervous. That makes me unhappy. Are you losing the stomach for this operation?"

19

Wanamaker ran a hand over his face and grimaced. "Boss, you know how bad I want payback on them Connellys."

"Yes, I know. You don't talk about much else. As I've told you, you need to broaden your horizons, do something else with your life." He leaned forward over his desk and fixed Wanamaker with a chilling stare. "But since you've brought me this little opportunity, I expect you to play your part—or I'll be forced to decide you're no longer a team player. And that means I'd have to make sure you're kept quiet."

The nasty implications left hanging in the air caused Wanamaker to shiver. "Boss, you can count on me, really you can. It's just that—well, sure, I want to punish her. And her damned mother too, but—but I never figured on doing to her what you got in mind."

Leatherwood looked out the window, an expression of impatience on his face. "Are you with me or not?"

Wanamaker lowered his head, unable to look at the man. "Yeah, I'm with you. All the way."

"Good. Now, what do we know so far? We know she has the box. Or at least she took it home. What she's done with it is anyone's guess. We need inside information to see if she's taken the bait, or if we have to plant another lure. I happen to know she's got a stable near her house, with a full time stable hand to look after that big horse she rides around on. Think he'd be willing to cooperate if the price is right?"

Wanamaker shook his head. "Impossible. The Connelly women choose their employees real careful-like. They pay them good, and they inspire unquestioned loyalty. You won't get to him."

"Well, then we'll find some other way. Work on it. I provided her with a very small ball of opium. If she's smoked it, I don't imagine it lasted very long. She'll want more. But I don't think we can try planting a new box with another opium pipe in her favorite restaurant again. I doubt she'll go for that another time. Besides, time is short. No," he said, looking out the window, deep in thought, "we need to tempt her into making a trip to a place where she's vulnerable. I'm going to do a little checking around, and see if I can find out exactly who provided her with the opium that time three years ago. So if you'll excuse me," he said, rising, "I've got business in Chinatown. Maybe we can lure her back there. And then," Leatherwood said, a Satanic grin on his chiseled features, "we strike."

Megan gave no thought to bringing the opium pipe into the house again. Instead, after she rode home and had dismounted in the stable, she gave Shamrock over to her stable hand, and then waited until the boy walked the big horse outside for a cooldown. Then, unseen, she hid the box behind a bale of hay and went into the house.

For two days she stayed clear of the stable. But she didn't forget what was waiting for her there. She knew there was no reason she should feel the pull of the opium. She had everything a woman could want—wealth, power, family, admiration, beauty. She was the most fortunate of women, she knew that. Yet, deep within her was the hunger for a dangerous thrill, a risk-taking, that all she had could not extinguish. When, on the third day, she got a letter saying her mother would arrive the next week, she could deny it no longer. With Kathleen's powerful presence in the house, she would never make a clandestine trip to the stable. If she was going to do it, it would have to be now.

That evening presented the possibility. Bridget had gone to bed tired, and could be expected to sleep soundly. Alex, she knew, could sleep through an earthquake. She could risk an hour away from their bed. So she lay awake, pretending to sleep while she stared at the ceiling as Alex breathed softly beside her. In the dark room, she cursed her weakness, knowing she was about to fail her family, but unable to stop herself. *I don't deserve them,* she thought. She waited until three in the morning, then got up and went to Bridget's room. She stood looking down in silence at her daughter. The girl's glossy black hair spread over her pillow like a fan, except for an errant strand that lay across one smooth cheek. Tears rolled slowly down Megan's cheeks; her hands formed tight fists. *My daughter,* she thought. *How precious and perfect you are in sleep. No tantrums, no demands. Mother was known as The Angel of the Gold Rush. You are my own angel, but you are so much like her. Both of you are so determined, so resilient. And I am so weak. Oh, why must I need! Why are my right thoughts so easily broken? Daughter, please forgive me.* She turned away.

Drawing her robe tightly about her, she silently descended the stairs of the dark house. From a drawer in her sewing desk, she took a single long knitting needle, then retrieved a box of matches from the kitchen. She paused at the front door to light a lantern to guide her feet, then went out. The moon was full and the night air brisk; a slight breeze sent ripples through the long grass in the field around the house. She shivered and quickened her pace toward the stable. It was about seventy yards downwind from the house. Reaching the big doors, she eased one of them open and slipped into deep darkness. She heard the rustle of horses' feet as her entrance caused the animals to stamp nervously for a moment. They were not used to a visitor this time of night. She uttered soothing words as she held the lantern high, searching for the bale of hay behind which the box was hidden. She found it right where she had put it three days earlier. She sat down on the bale and, with shaking hands, tore the twine off the box. She opened it and lifted out the magnificent pipe, then the ball of opium paste. For long seconds she stared at them, breathing heavily. Then she retrieved the knitting needle from her pocket and skewered the opium ball with it. Ordinarily she would have used a small oil lamp to heat the opium until it was sticky, then place the ball in the small bowl affixed to the pipe, where it would stick as she held the pipe bowl over the lamp. The opium ball would blister and smoke as it was heated; she would draw the smoke through a hole in the bottom of the bowl, down the length of the pipe, and into her lungs. Lacking the oil lamp, she turned the wick up high in her lantern, and held the opium ball over the glass chimney with the knitting needle. She watched in satisfaction as the opium slowly began to heat and bubble. When it looked gooey, she reclined into a prone position, held the opium over the pipe bowl and drew in the smoke. It was less than satisfactory and she had to reheat the opium a couple of times, but it worked. The opium ball was very small, and it was quickly consumed. She lay her head down on the straw floor of the stable in dreamy repose. Her muscles were so loose she felt like she was going to melt into the floor. She could see a piece of the moon through the crack of the open door. The moon came down from the sky and sat next to her for a while, a luminescent eye that regarded her balefully. *You failed your family,* it said. *You're weak. Not like your mother.*

No one is like her, Megan replied. *No one else measures up to her. I don't even try. I know I failed. It's not the first time.*

It won't be the last, the moon said. *You're weak . . . .*

Go 'way, Megan said. *I don't need you to remind me. Go 'way!*

The moon rocketed away out the door. She lay for a while in limp surrender to the drug, letting it carry her on a warm river of joyous fulfillment. Disconnected fragments of thought came, circled around her mind, and went. At one point she was sure her body was going to float upward and bump against the stable roof. She clutched desperately at the straw to prevent it.

Because the opium ball had been so small, she was not under its influence for long. She didn't know how much time had passed when she finally raised herself to a sitting position. Groggily, she put the pipe back in its box and returned it to its hiding place. Then she casually wiped the knitting needle on her robe, picked up the lantern, and made her way back to the house. She put the needle back in her sewing desk, looked in on Bridget, who still slept soundly, then returned to her bed alongside Alex.

Someone was shaking her. She could hear her name being called, far away.

"Megan, wake up."

With some effort, she opened her eyes.

Alex was looking down on her, smiling gently. "Aren't you the sleepyhead this morning," he said. "It's nearly ten o'clock. I haven't seen you sleep this long in a while. You must have been very tired."

Megan sat up. Sunlight was streaming through the lace curtains. She rubbed her eyes. "Yes, I was. Sorry." She reached for her robe and pulled it around her.

"Hmm," Alex said, reaching toward her, "how'd you get straw on your robe?"

Megan momentarily stopped breathing. "I—I don't know. Housekeeping must be getting sloppy. I'll speak to them. Maybe Bridget brought it in. I think she was making a doll out of straw the other day. Now," she said, grinning at him, "is it too late for some breakfast?"

Four days later, on June 7th, Kathleen arrived. Megan was at her stable, leaning against the corral fence stroking Shamrock's big head. At a hello from behind her, she turned to see her mother striding toward her. She walked along the path worn in the tall grass between her and Danielle's houses. The narrow path forced Ben to walk behind her. Megan smiled broadly as she watched her mother approach. As always, Kathleen walked with an authoritative, confident stride. She had a regal bearing that demanded attention, and the gray hairs shot through her glossy black mane only increased her stature as a woman who commanded, if not universal affection, a healthy respect. *She's as commanding as always,* Megan mused. *I wonder the grass doesn't part for her, like Moses's Red Sea.* She ran to meet her mother, and threw her arms around her. "Oh Mother, I missed you so!" she cried. "It's been since Christmas this time. That's too long."

Kathleen pulled back and studied Megan closely with extraordinary sky-blue eyes, the same eyes that had convinced Northern Paiute Indians years earlier that she was an evil spirit, the same eyes that stopped most people in their tracks.

As so often happened, Megan was, at close range, momentarily hypnotized.

"Megan, are you well?" Kathleen asked.

Megan was flustered, if only for a second. "Of course, Mother, I'm fine. Why?"

Kathleen cocked her head to one side like a bird sensing a worm underground. It was an old gesture that told Megan her mother was probing for something. "Oh, I don't know," Kathleen said. "Something about you seems—different. Well, I suppose that tells me it has indeed been too long. I stand reprimanded."

Megan turned her attention to her stepfather. "Hello Father," she said, embracing him tightly. "I love you," she whispered.

Ben lifted her off the ground and then set her gently back down. "You're more beautiful than ever, if that's possible," he said, smiling.

"Oh, all right, I'll fix your favorite meal. Please, come into the house," Megan said. "Are you stabled over at Danielle's this time?"

"Yes, it was her turn," Kathleen said. "We'll be staying there for a bit, then come over here. We'll relax for a few days. Then it will be time to start preparing for the stockholders' meeting in July."

Mother and daughter walked off toward the house, arms around each other's waist. Megan glanced sideways at her mother, searching for some sign of the fragment of vulnerability that had surfaced the year before. The previous summer, Kathleen's father died in his sleep at Eire Ranch. True to her promise to him, she had taken his body back to New York, and there laid him to rest beside his beloved wife, and Kathleen's mother, Maggie. Megan had been there when he passed away, and it was the only time she could remember seeing her mother cry. It hadn't happened when the Indian, Two Moons, had stolen Megan. It hadn't happened when Danielle, as a teenager, was nearly spirited off by a French couple who wanted to raise her as a proper French girl. And it hadn't happened when Kathleen lay near death with Two Moons' arrow in her chest. But that night, a small ghostly shadow of little-girl Kathleen had surfaced, had broken free from some deep prison to manifest itself on her body, her face, for a brief time. For a while, Kathleen had not been a fortress, a bastion of strength and emotional self-sufficiency. For just a little while, she had *needed*.

Now, as Megan looked at her mother, it was clear that the weakness had been forcibly reburied, the chink in the wall sealed up.

Othniel Wanamaker jutted out his lower jaw in vexation. With his puffy cheeks, it made him look a bit like an impatient goldfish as he regarded the boy across the table. They were alone in a quiet corner of a waterfront restaurant. It was the same boy he had bribed to present Megan with the box the second time. His name was Hiram.

"Boy, don't get greedy on me," Wanamaker groused. "I can always find somebody else."

Hiram grimaced and ran a hand through his sandy hair, his freckled cheeks turning red. "It ain't the money, mister, really it ain't. It's just that Megan Daley almost ran me down last time. It was just luck I stumbled into that alley where her horse couldn't go. I don't cotton to crossin' them Connelly women. I've heard people who do end up dead." He paused, looking especially pained. "From what you told me, it's a wonder *you* ain't dead."

Wanamaker leaned back, chin up and thumbs under his suspenders. "Well, I ain't. That's because I know how to handle 'em. And if I can handle *them*, I can sure handle you." He paused and looked sharply at the boy, letting the implied menace sink in. When he thought it had, he said, "Now, this is real simple. All I want is for you to tag along on the next delivery of hay to Megan Daley's stable. It's all been arranged."

"How?"

"Never you mind. The less you know, the better for all of us. You help unload the hay. Mind you work hard at it. Look like you belong. Before you leave, slip this"— he produced an envelope from his coat pocket—"into one of her saddlebags."

"How'm I to know which saddle is hers?"

"Ask the stable hand, if he's there. If he ain't, look for a saddle that's kinda reddish, with a silver saddlehorn. I don't reckon there'll be two of them."

Hiram looked like he wanted to be somewhere else. "What's in the envelope?"

"That ain't for you to know! Like I said, the less you know, the better. Open it and you'll regret it."

Hiram took the envelope and got up to leave. "I'll be takin' payment now."

Wanamaker slid a twenty-dollar gold piece across the table. "And when you're back in town, lay low until I call for you again."

"You better keep the money comin'," Hiram said. "I ain't been able to find a job since I had to run out on the last one. Word gets around fast in this town, I guess." The boy shuffled out.

Wanamaker watched him go with a sour expression on his face. Then he poured himself a fortifying shot from the nearly empty whiskey bottle in front of him. This stage of the operation was risky. There was a chance the letter would be discovered by someone else. And if it was read, the whole operation would be over.

The boy was right, word did spread fast in the raw frontier town— whether it was true or not. Good thing, he reflected, that the letter couldn't be traced to him. He had set the wheels in motion for a dangerous game, and he was caught in the middle. The Connelly women and their husbands were on one side, and they were lethal when they were aroused. On the other side was Eli Leatherwood, and that, well, that was a deal with the devil if ever there was one. For the first time, he began to regret his thirst for vengeance.

If Wanamaker could have seen Eli Leatherwood at that moment, he would have been vastly amused. Because that man was himself feeling the fear of the consequences of what he had set in motion. For Eli Leatherwood was face to face with someone whom he feared every bit as much as Kathleen Wilson.

He shifted nervously in the big leather chair, acutely aware of the elegance of the office in which he sat. All around him was polished brass, lush carpeting, crystal, and carved wood. It was the sort of surroundings he would normally be comfortable in; it suited his refined tastes. But there was one thing that looked out of place, and it unsettled him greatly—the man behind the desk before him.

The big man scowled at him. He had dark hair, and a short chin beard on an otherwise clean-shaven face. Dark eyes burned beneath black brows. He was wearing a black suit over a black vest and white shirt, with a black bow tie around his thick neck. "Well, are things proceeding according to plan?" he asked.

"So far, so good," Leatherwood replied. "We know—" He stopped at the big man's raised hand.

"You know I don't want any details," the man said. "I don't want to know how you plan to get the Wilsons out of state for a while. Just that you can do it. Still think you can?"

"Yes," Leatherwood replied. "And are you still willing to provide funds to grease whatever wheels need it to help make it happen?"

The big man's scowl deepened. "Eli, I want the Sierra and Western railroad. It's the last—and best—piece I need to rule the coming railroad boom in California."

"But no federal land comes with it," Leatherwood said. "It's land-poor. The Wilsons bought a narrow right of way just wide enough for the roadbed."

"Yes, but as I've said before, the road is finished and it's profitable. Acquiring it would not only give the Central Pacific an additional source of income, which we badly need at present; it would also legitimize our operations here. That would win us favor with the federal government when it comes time to ask for more funding. And we need all the help we can get. Besides, geographically, the Wilsons' line is ideally placed to expand south along the western flank of the Sierras, and from there into all of southern California. In fact, I happen to know they're going to announce plans to do just that at their upcoming stockholders' meeting."

"Your sources are good."

"I depend on it," the man said. Then he swiveled his chair to the side and stared out the window. "Besides," he said, "Kathleen Wilson's opposed me once too often from her seat in the Senate. She allied herself solidly with the good citizens of Placerville when they introduced that proposition in '64."[1]

"No surprise there," Leatherwood said, "since her railroad runs right to Placerville. What else would you expect? When defeat came, she accepted it graciously."

"Well, she and the Placerville crowd fought us without quarter as far as it went," the big man groused. "She's chummy with Wells Fargo, who've contributed big sums to her railroad trying to extend it through Placerville over the Sierras to Washoe. And she's entirely too friendly with the *Alta California*."[2]

"All things you'd take advantage of if you were in her place," Leatherwood said.

"Well, I won't take it." Leland Stanford turned back from the window and skewered Leatherwood with a chilling glare. "You brought this deal to me, Eli. You thought it would work, if you could get the right backing. I'm skeptical that it will, but I'll do my part. However, my capital and influence are not limitless. You have the seat on the Wilsons' Board of Directors. Make sure you do *your* part. And Eli," he continued, "should you fail, we never met. I'll leave you to twist in the wind by yourself."

Leatherwood was sweating beneath his carefully groomed and poised appearance. He knew Stanford meant it. But he wasn't ready to wilt yet. Gathering his courage, he leaned forward in his chair. "Leland, I'd advise you to back off on that talk. You need me. I know things you don't know."

Stanford regarded him coldly. "Such as?"

---

[1] In the California legislature and the Nevada Constitutional Convention of 1864, propositions were drafted and lobbied for that would have awarded several million dollars to the railroad company that first reached the California-Nevada border. These attempts to influence the continental railroad to use the Placerville wagon road route over the Sierras instead of the Central Pacific's Dutch Flat wagon road were both defeated.

[2] A San Francisco newspaper noted for its hostility to the Central Pacific Railroad in the early 1860s.

27

Leatherwood fought to remain calm. What he knew was the fact that Ben and Kathleen didn't own *all* of the land their railroad ran across. There had been two parcels they had had to settle for five-year leases on, thanks to Wanamaker's efforts to sabotage their project. And those leases were about to expire. What he didn't yet know was the status of the Wilsons' efforts to either renew the leases or acquire the parcels outright. But he also knew Stanford would squash him like a bug if the former governor perceived him as a liability, and he needed some leverage for survival.

"I think it wise to hold some information in reserve," he told Stanford, trying to read the big man's expression. "You just remember that when you get your hands on that railroad, I expect to be named president of the line."

The late afternoon July sun shone warmly on the three Connelly women as they strolled along the beach below Megan's house. As sometimes happened on beach walks, their husbands had walked ahead so they could be free to talk man talk. Kathleen was content to let them go. "They don't see each other often enough," she said, eyeing the men walking about fifty yards ahead. "Let them have some time together." She winked at Megan. "Later we'll find out what they're talking about." A few yards ahead of the women, Bridget danced on the sand, daring the seawater to wet her toes as it surged up the beach and flowed back. Walking between her daughters, Kathleen spread her arms and embraced them both, smiling with delight as the surf foamed about their feet. "I can't imagine anything more wonderful than this moment," she said, "walking through the surf with my daughters. I *do* miss the beach so much, living over in Sacramento."

"You should move here, Mother," Megan said, swinging her feet back and forth as she walked, scribing wide arcs in the sand with her toes.

"So you keep saying," Kathleen replied. "But whatever would we do with that enormous house? Besides, it's usually a little too cool for me here. You'll just have to come visit more often." She looked to her right at Danielle. "Danielle, you're definitely showing now."

Danielle patted her expanding abdomen. "Yes, no doubt about it. The morning sickness has slacked off, and I'm just happy to watch my belly grow. Soon Bridget will have a playmate."

"Well, you always were too thin. The baby has put a little meat on your bones, and I like what I see."

They walked along in silence for a few more minutes. Then Kathleen said, "Tomorrow we'll start fleshing out proposals for the stockholders' meeting. It's less than three weeks away, and the Board of Directors meeting two days before that. We'll want to firm up our ideas before then. Danielle, how's Robert's presentation on the proposed expansion coming along?"

"It's shaping up well. He'll be ready, never fear."

Kathleen was silent for a moment. Then she said, "I'd like him to be prepared for the unexpected, in case we're confronted with a power play from Leatherwood."

Megan broke in suddenly. "Mother, could you please move over to my house early? I know you were going to wait another week. But it would be good to have you there now. Please?" She looked at Danielle. "Danielle, would you let her come a week early?"

Danielle recognized the earnest pleading in her sister's eyes. "Yes, yes of course. I don't mind. Oh," she said, looking away, "you'd better see to Bridget. She's getting a little far from us."

Megan strode away to her daughter. Kathleen and Danielle watched her closely as she went. Danielle frowned slightly. "What was that about?"

Kathleen's blue eyes were fixed on her younger daughter as Megan chased Bridget through the sea foam. "I don't know. But something's not right. I sensed something—I don't know what—as soon as I got here. I'm beginning to feel guilty for being away from you both so long. It really isn't that far to come. I'll see if I can talk Ben into staying longer. If there's something going on with her, I'll find out. You can fool me when you really want to, Danielle. But she never could."

Hiram wiped damp hands on his pants as the buckboard loaded with hay made its way up the last few yards of driveway to Megan's stable. He hadn't said two words to Reno, the boy beside him who was driving the buckboard, since the trip began.

The boy, a few years older than himself, had looked at him curiously a time or two, then was content to drive in silence. Now as they pulled up to the barn, he spoke. "Dang, Jimmy would go and get sick on me when I need him for this delivery. If you're going to fill in proper for him, you'll need to buck your share of bales, boy. We're here," he said, pulling back on the reins. "Fetch a little water for the horses, while I see who's about." He jumped down and went into the barn, returning in a minute. "Looks deserted. That stable hand of hers oughta be here, but we're a tad early. Come on, let's get to it."

Hiram tied the horses to a hitching post, and they set to work unloading the hay bales. It was a far cry from busing tables in a restaurant, and he nearly staggered under the weight of the first bale.

"Dang, boy," said Reno, "you oughta see your face! It's red as a whorehouse lantern. Why, I'd think you never lifted no bale before."

Hiram said nothing, plodding into the barn with the bale, cursing the day he met the shabby little man who got him involved in this crazy business. He made several trips, peering into the darkened interior each time in search of Megan's saddle. On the fourth trip in, he spotted one that matched Wanamaker's description. It looked like no other in the barn, and he decided that had to be it. But it was toward the back, several yards away from where they were stacking the hay. How was he to get to it? He had to think of something fast; there was only one more bale to be brought in.

"I'll take the last bale," he told Reno.

"Suit yourself," Reno said, climbing up on the buckboard seat.

Panting, Hiram staggered into the barn with the bale, mind racing furiously. As he slammed the bale down, inspiration came to him. Slowly he walked back to the barn entrance.

"Come on, boy," Reno urged. "I got a cold brew waitin' for me."

"I—I gotta go," Hiram said, looking embarrassed.

"Hmph. Well, all right, just be quick about it. Go on out back a ways from the barn, into the tall grass. Mind there ain't no womenfolk around to see you."

Hiram wordlessly ducked into the barn, went straight to the saddle, and took the letter from his back pocket. It had suffered from the rough trip out on the buckboard, but he couldn't help that. He chose one of the saddlebags, lifted the flap, and put the letter in. Then, heart pounding, he ducked out the back entrance of the barn and relieved himself. He walked quickly back into the barn, buttoning his pants as he went. He was four steps in when he stopped dead, breath catching in his throat.

Sky-blue eyes such as he had never seen regarded him coolly. They were set in a face of refined features and smooth alabaster skin. Though he had never met her, he knew immediately who stood in front of him.

"Lost your way, young man?" Kathleen said.

"Uh, no, I ah," he stammered, then turned red when he realized his hands had frozen on his trouser buttons.

Kathleen smiled. "It's all right. Nothing wrong with it. Now, you'd better get along."

"Ah, yes ma'am," Hiram replied hastily, and beat a quick retreat out the door and up into the buckboard seat.

Kathleen followed him out. "It's a warm day," she said to Reno, "perhaps you and your assistant would like to stay for lemonade on the porch."

"That's mighty kind of you, ma'am, it really is," Reno replied. "But we gotta get back right away. Maybe next time."

"Very well," Kathleen replied. The buckboard turned from the barn and rolled away. She followed it with her gaze.

Hiram was sweating, and not from his recent exertion. He could feel her eyes on him as they drove away.

Reno looked over at him and chuckled. "Well, I see she had the usual effect on you. That was the Angel, in case you didn't know."

"I know who it was," Hiram replied morosely. "Ain't no one else looks like that." Like many people, he had heard plenty about the Angel. Some of it seemed pretty fantastic, and he wasn't ready to believe all of the tales. He had heard she had crossed Carson Pass with her daughter in the dead of winter and survived, the first woman to do so. He had heard an Indian tried three times to kill her, and the third time he had put an arrow in her chest, and she not only didn't die, she killed *him*. That other men who had crossed her were dead by her hand.

"Ain't she somethin'?" Reno said, interrupting his thoughts. "You know, the Indians thought she couldn't be killed. I think that's a bunch of superstitious hogwash myself. Still, it makes me a little uneasy to be around her. That's why we didn't stay for the lemonade."

When Hiram got back to town and gratefully said goodbye to the hay-hauling operation, he looked up Wanamaker. He had to wander the docks for a couple of hours to find him, but when he finally did, he didn't waste any time saying what was on his mind. "I'm through, mister. Don't ask me to do no more of this."

Wanamaker regarded him through slitted eyes. "Why, you look plumb spooked, son. What's got into you?"

"The Angel was there."

Wanamaker turned a shade paler under his two-day growth of beard. Nervously he ran a hand over his chin. "She was, huh? She didn't see you plant the letter, did she?"

Hiram wrung his cap nervously. "I really don't know, mister. I don't know what she saw. All of a sudden-like, she was just *there,* like she popped out of a wall."

Wanamaker poked Hiram on the lapel of his jacket. "Now you look here, boy. Don't you go buyin' into any of that superstitious nonsense. She's as mortal as you or me."

"All the same, I ain't havin' nothin' more to do with this business. I don't fancy meetin' her again."

31

"All right," Wanamaker said, backing up a step. "Then you lay low and keep quiet 'til this is over. There'll be money to see to it. You got that?"

"Yes sir." Hiram started to turn away. "I'd stay clear of that lady, mister." With that, he melted into the crowd.

The Connelly women and their husbands gathered in the conference room of Danielle's blufftop home on a Thursday afternoon. Because Danielle was Chief Financial Officer for all operations, and her husband Robert was Chief Legal Advisor, business meetings were always held in their home, where there was a room reserved for such matters. They were gathered to discuss strategy and proposals for the upcoming stockholders' meeting.

Even though it was Danielle's house, the seat of honor was reserved for Kathleen. Ben had never cared for business affairs, and was content to let Kathleen be the acknowledged matriarch while he went about his own projects.

It would have been hard for it to be otherwise. Kathleen naturally dominated any gathering she was part of. Her regal bearing radiated control and commanded respect. People listened when she spoke, and, when push came to shove, deferred to her wishes. It unfailingly turned out to be the best course of action.

Kathleen had done her best to raise her daughters to be like her. It was ironic that her adopted daughter, Danielle, was more successful in that than Megan, the child she had borne. Danielle was a natural corporate leader, with an astute command of facts and figures, and vision usually one step ahead of the competition. She had constructed strong businesses that had unfailingly shown a profit, and Kathleen had come to have limitless respect for her business acumen.

Megan was another matter. A strikingly beautiful, impetuous, woman-child, she had never shown an interest in affairs of business, even though as Kathleen's daughter she was one of the principal owners of the companies. She was usually content to go along with whatever the others decided. Her inspired and expertly negotiated deal with the Chinatown merchant Yuen Ling-Po, that had provided the manpower to turn a railroad dream into reality, seemed to have been an isolated contribution. Since then she had been content to fade into the background—as much as that was possible for a woman of such arresting appearance. Instead, she relished the role of wife, mother and wealthy socialite.

Now as the meeting was about to start, she customarily excused herself, saying she wanted to go riding.

"I wish you'd stay," Kathleen said. "I value your opinion, you know. And you and Alex do own twenty per cent of the businesses."

"I know, Mother. But I trust Alex's judgement. Let him represent me. Besides, Shamrock needs a run. Bridget is down for her nap, so now's a good time."

Kathleen turned to Megan's husband. "Alex?"

He nodded. "It's all right. I'll brief her later."

Megan walked out, and Kathleen watched her go with regret. "I keep hoping she'll change and want to be part of this, but I guess it's just not who she is. Well, to business. What's first on the agenda?"

Megan strode to the barn, eager to be astride her big stallion. Her stable hand was off duty, so she set about the task of saddling Shamrock herself. After bringing him in from the corral and giving him a thorough brushing, she set the saddle blanket on his broad back and then hoisted the big saddle on. She reached under his belly to grasp the belly band, then brought the end of it up through the saddle ring. She wound the band around through the ring several times, then, checking to see the horse wasn't swelling up his belly as he sometimes did in hopes of keeping the band loose, she cinched it up. Once it was tight, she stepped in front of the horse. She leaned down and grasped one foreleg at the knee and pulled gently. Shamrock obediently shifted his weight. She pulled the leg up, stretching the horse's belly skin forward to insure no loose skin was caught under the belly band. Then she repeated the procedure with the other leg, checking the bottom of each hoof as she did so to insure Shamrock's feet weren't caked with mud. Then she checked his hind feet. Satisfied, she took the bridle and tapped the bit gently on Shamrock's teeth until he opened his mouth and let her slide it in. She gently maneuvered the bridle over his ears, and pulled the forelock of hair out from under the band across the top of his forehead.

She led the horse out into the sunlight and was about to mount when she noticed the flap to one of her saddlebags was unfastened. She pulled down on the strap to pull it through the buckle, and heard a faint rustle of paper. Curious, she opened the saddlebag.

There was a letter inside. The envelope was expensive paper, but it was wrinkled and bent, as if it had spent some time in someone's back pocket. Her name was written on the front. A premonition made her heart start thumping. After a moment's hesitation, she tore open the envelope. There was a short message inside, written on fine rice paper in a familiar hand, the same writing she had seen on the note in the box containing the opium pipe.

Honorable Megan,
I hope the gift pleased you. If you would like more,
come to the address on the card. It is best you come alone.
Your Friend,
Yuen Ling-Po

There was a card enclosed on which were Chinese characters; below that was written a street address in English. She had not kept the card Ling-Po had given her that dark night three years before, when he had pulled her off a dangerous Chinatown street just before she was going to be set upon by two muggers. So she couldn't be sure the address was the same. It didn't seem familiar.

Megan was puzzled. Though her family did a steady business with Ling-Po, shipping his goods to and from the Orient under the contract she had negotiated, the old trader himself had studiously avoided any direct contact, preferring to conduct business through intermediaries. He had doubtless received a firsthand report of how enraged Kathleen had become when she found Megan deep in the bonds of opium after smoking it with him to close their deal.

That had been fine with Kathleen, who had frostily declared she had no wish to meet him, and besides, didn't want his blood on her hands. Ben knew she wasn't kidding, and made sure Kathleen steered well clear of any dealings they had with his organization.

But now he was making an overture to her. Why? It didn't make sense. She couldn't imagine he would endanger his shipping contract by risking Kathleen's wrath. Their business negotiations had been concluded with honor for both sides; there could be no imbalance there. She felt ambivalent about him. On the one hand, she had never quite come to terms with the fact that he had exposed her to opium, and with the subsequent yearning it had ignited in her. On the other, there could be no doubt that he had saved her from a possibly horrible street crime when she had foolishly put herself in a vulnerable situation.

She paced back and forth, turning the letter over in her hands, while Shamrock obediently shadowed her footsteps. For three years she had successfully hid her desire for more of the drug. *They can't know about this,* she thought. *I can't chance one of them coming across something like this letter. Whatever he wants, I can't allow Ling-Po back in my life. I have to sever the connection once and for all.* She was going to have to see him one more time. And she was going to have to go alone.

She worked Shamrock hard that day, flying fast along the bluffs, red hair streaming out behind her, grass whipping around the horse's feet.

When they rested, she spent long moments staring out at the white sea foam, breathing deeply of the salt air, trying to wrap her soul around the vibrancy of being young and alive, to feel complete and satisfied, to strengthen her resolve against needing anything more. She thought of how dear Bridget and Alex were to her.

She waited until a week before the stockholders' meeting, then decided it was time to put an end to the threat. There was no way she was going after dark. She would go in the middle of the day, when plenty of people would be around. She took Bridget over to Danielle's, as she often did when riding into town. Alex was gone off somewhere with Ben and Kathleen, so the house was empty.

She wasn't going unarmed. She didn't have a gun, but Alex did, and he had made sure she knew how to use it. She went upstairs to their bedroom and retrieved the big .44-40 pistol from its bedside table drawer. The drawer had a hidden locking mechanism that prevented Bridget from opening it. She checked the cylinder to make sure it was loaded. It was. Slipping it into her purse, she went downstairs, out to her stable where Shamrock had been readied by her stable hand. Saying she would be back in no more than three hours, she rode off.

She walked Shamrock all the way into town, resisting the big stallion's desire to run. He was a bundle of nervous energy beneath her, as if he could sense her tension. *He knows something's up,* she thought. *I don't know how, but he knows.*

In San Francisco, Shamrock's feet lifted high as she rode down the dirt streets, comforted by the number of people milling about. As she entered Chinatown, it didn't take her long to realize the address she had been given wasn't the same one where she had last found Ling-Po. *Maybe he's moved,* she thought. No, that was unlikely, given the size and elegance of the elaborate living quarters he had taken such pains to conceal. Then a chilling thought occurred to her. *Maybe it's not him at all. Maybe someone else is using his name to attract me for some reason.* She reached down and reassuringly patted her purse, feeling the hard steel of the pistol within. *It's probably not true. Why would someone do that? Then again, I don't know why* he *would do it. Well, I've come this far, and I know how to use this pistol. There's plenty of people around. I'm going to see this through.*

After a couple of turns, she came to the street listed on the card, and found the address in the middle of the block. She slowed to a halt in front of the building, a nondescript structure that housed, according to the sign on the front in both Chinese and English, a general store. She could see a variety of canned and packaged goods, and some hardware, through the dusty windows, along with small signs and cards with hand-lettered Chinese characters. Megan knew Chinatown stores could be a front for almost anything, and didn't let the plain storefront fool her. She felt safer on Shamrock, so didn't dismount, but could see no movement inside through the windows. She noticed a broad alley to her right, and walked Shamrock over to it. It was wide and clean, leading to a large dark opening at its back that she thought could be the front of a receiving warehouse for the store and surrounding buildings. She saw no movement there either. She glanced around at the streets, which contained a few Chinese who seemed to be ignoring her. Taking a deep breath, she squeezed her legs into Shamrock's side, urging him forward at a slow walk. She brought the purse up closer to her hand. The dark, silent space loomed ahead. She came to a halt ten feet from the entrance. There was still no sign of life. She was about to turn away when a small Chinese man emerged from the black interior, walked a few steps toward her, and bowed low. He was dressed in the dark, pajama-like clothes and cloth shoes common to the Chinese, with a small round hat atop his head.

"Welcome, Honorable Megan," he said, smiling.

"You know me?" Megan said.

The little man looked up at her, displaying yellowed teeth in a broad grin. "Certainly, Missy. Who does not?"

She frowned at him. "You are not Yuen Ling-Po. Where is he?"

The man's smile grew even broader. "I am here in his place, Missy."

Megan was beginning to smell a rat. She fished the card out of her saddlebag and thrust it at him. "Did he send me this card? Or did you?"

The man looked at the card. "The Honorable Ling-Po most certainly sent it, Missy."

She regarded him coldly, a current of fear causing her neck to tingle. "I don't believe you."

The little man bowed again. "As you choose. I mean no harm. Perhaps you would care to partake of some most excellent *ah-pin-yin*[3] while you are here?"

"No," Megan said severely. "I'm through with that. And I'm here to tell you I don't want any more of these messages or gifts in my life. Stay away from me, I mean it. If there is any more of this, you will suffer dire consequences. Do you understand?"

The man was all fawning compliance. "Of course, Missy. As you wish."

---

[3]   opium

"Good. Now, I'll be on my way." She turned Shamrock around— and saw to her dismay that high gates had been silently shut behind her, blocking off the alley from street view. She thrust her hand into her purse, pulling out the pistol, ready to draw aim on the little man. But when she turned back, he was gone. Fighting rising panic, she turned Shamrock around in a circle, looking for a target.

Suddenly four men waving blankets erupted through the gate and ran toward her. Before she could stop him, Shamrock shied away and bolted into the darkened interior at the other end of the alley. Coming in from bright sunlight, Megan could see nothing inside. She whirled Shamrock around in a circle, knowing as long as she was still on the big stallion, she had a chance. She could sense the movement of running figures around her. Shamrock neighed in fright and confusion. She had the gun in her hand, but couldn't see well enough to take aim at anything. Abruptly she felt hands on her left leg, pulling her down. She thrust the gun across the saddle and fired.

A deafening roar filled the room, she heard a moan, and the hands fell away. Her eyes had adjusted to the dark now, and she could see four men circling her, and one on the ground, his chest a mass of blood. "What do you want?" she shouted.

"You, Missy," one said.

"Let me out, or I'll shoot you all," she answered.

"Can't do that," the same man said. He threw a wadded up blanket at Shamrock's head, causing the horse to back up in fear. Megan fired at the man, but missed. Shamrock reared up at the gunshot, and her head smashed into an overhead beam. She tumbled to the ground, unconscious.

The men came at her. But Shamrock wasn't budging from his fallen mistress. He stood near her prostrate form, ready to charge anyone who dared approach. One man, thinking he could scare the horse off with shouting and arm waving, ran at him. Two hooves smashed into his chest, and he flew backward, dead.

"Light the torches!" one of the others shouted. Two flaming torches were quickly produced. The men carrying them advanced slowly on Shamrock.

"Easy!" another said. "We can't let the horse get away. Just back him off her."

Shamrock didn't budge for a moment, but then the fire waving a few feet from his muzzle became too much, and he whirled from Megan, running out into the alley. To the dismay of the men, though, he didn't stop there. Running hard at the gates, he smashed through them and raced

37

out into the street, reins trailing from his bridle. In moments, he was out of sight.

"Damn!" one of the men said. "This ain't good. If the horse heads home without her, it'll raise the alarm. We gotta move extra quick now. Get her in the wagon and get down to the docks, fast."

In less than three minutes, the arena in which Megan had fought so desperately was empty. There was seemingly no trace of her, of the men who had captured her, or the bodies on the ground.

Othniel Wanamaker was waiting at the docks as the wagon carrying a concealed Megan arrived. "You're way early. What happened?" he said to the wagon driver.

"Change of plans," said the man. "She didn't go for smokin' opium again. We had to get rough."

Alarm spread across Wanamaker's face. "What do you mean?" He reached into the wagon and pulled back the canvas cover of a box. "Damn! What did you do? There's blood on her head! I said she was to be brought unharmed."

"Best we could do," the man said sourly. "She's still breathin'. Considerin' where she's going, what does it matter?"

Wanamaker got close to the man, furious. "It matters!" he shouted. "She won't bring a good price if she's hurt. Dammit, you bungled the job." He paced back and forth on the dock in anger. "Well, there's nothin' for it now. Get her on board, quick-like. The sooner we all disappear, the better."

The man looked at the unconscious Megan, an evil leer spreading across his face. "By God, that's one fine-lookin' woman. Never been close to somethin' that beautiful. Wouldn't never have no better chance to jump her bones." The two thugs with him gathered closer, smiling in agreement.

"Any man who touches her won't live until sundown," sounded an iron voice behind them.

Wanamaker and the three men turned. The men he had hired were low-class brutes and gutter brawlers, but fear gripped them as they stared at the figure regarding them coldly.

The man was tall and solidly built. He was wearing a heavy seaman's coat, and there was a red silk bandana around his neck. A strong scar ran across his ruddy face from his left temple down to his jaw line. He had gray eyes, curly black hair, and a gold earring in one ear. A strong nose with an arched bridge sat above a mustache that flowed into a goatee. One huge hand rested on the hilt of a dagger that was stuck under his broad belt.

As he looked at the men gaping at him, a cruel smile twisted his lips. "I made a deal for a woman in top condition. If you've hurt her beyond repair, I'll hunt you down one at a time and cut out your liver."

Wanamaker was shaking despite his best efforts not to show it. If he'd made a deal with the devil in the person of Leatherwood, this had to be one of old Lucifer's disciples. "This here's Cap'n Parmenter," he told the three men, who had backed off from Megan a couple of paces. "Now no more talk. Get her on board."

Megan never felt herself lifted from the cart in the covered box, and taken onto a fast opium clipper at dockside. And she never felt the ship raise anchor and slowly sail from the harbor, out into the vast Pacific.

3.

Danielle answered the knock at her door to find Alex standing there. He looked worried.

"Is Megan here?" he said.

"Why, no," Danielle replied. "I haven't seen her since this morning. I thought she was at home. Could she still be out riding?"

"I don't know, she could be. Guess I'll check with the stable hand."

"I'll come with you," Danielle replied, drawing a shawl about her shoulders.

They strode quickly across the grassy meadow separating Danielle's house from Megan's stable. When they got there, they found the stable hand, Robby, cooling his heels on a bale of hay.

"When did Megan leave?" Alex asked.

"Four hours ago, Mr. Daley," Robby replied, getting quickly to his feet and brushing a loose shock of hair away from his forehead. "She's overdue. I been waitin' for her to come back so's I could go home."

"How long did she say she'd be gone?" Danielle put in.

"Three hours, ma'am. But she's not always back when she says."

Alex moved closer. "Exactly what did she say about when she'd return?"

Robby appeared to think for a moment. "Well, she said she'd be back in no more than three hours. She seemed real certain about it, Mr. Daley. So she's an hour overdue."

Alex looked at Danielle, then out across the bluff toward the city. After a few moments of searching the distance, he turned back to her. "I've got a bad feeling about this. Go get your mother."

Danielle hustled away as Alex turned back to Robby. "Saddle my horse."

Danielle was back in ten minutes with Kathleen, accompanied by Ben. "Robert is staying with Bridget," Danielle said. "There's no need to alarm her at this point."

"I agree," Alex said. "Megan will probably be along any minute."

Kathleen looked closely at his face, blue eyes searching. "You don't really believe that."

Alex was grim. "No."

Kathleen crossed her arms and began to pace back and forth, shooting Robby hateful looks every time she turned. "You should have said something sooner, young man."

"Don't get on him, Kathy," Ben said. "Let's stick to thinking about Megan."

They stood in the waning afternoon light while Alex checked his horse's saddle strap. He was about to mount up when he heard Kathleen gasp. He turned to see her face suddenly gone pale as she looked out across the blufftop.

"Dear God," she said. "It's Shamrock. And he's riderless."

The big copper-colored stallion loped up to the stable, reins trailing in front of his chest. He obediently came to a halt before the group, sweat glistening on his flanks.

Alex took the reins and examined the horse. "He's been running a while," he said.

Kathleen put a hand to her mouth, tears glistening in her eyes. Danielle looked at the ground in silence.

"Maybe she's been thrown off somewhere," Kathleen said faintly.

Alex blew out his breath. "Could be. But Shamrock's never thrown her. He might throw me, but not her. I swear this horse is dedicated to her. Robby," he said, turning to the stableboy, "did she say anything about where she was going?"

"No sir," Robby said, looking miserable.

"Let's have a look in her saddlebags," Alex said. "Maybe there's something in there that will help." He lifted the flap of one saddlebag and found it empty. He walked around to the other side and searched in that one. His hands closed on something. He brought out an envelope made of expensive paper. With a glance at Kathleen, he opened it. There was a short letter inside written in an elegant hand. He read it silently, puzzlement spreading on his face. Then he handed it to Kathleen.

She read it as Ben and Danielle looked over her shoulder. When she looked up, her eyes were wide with shock. "What is this gift?"

"I'm going to look for her," Alex said, mounting his horse. "I don't know what that Chinaman is doing poking his nose back in her life. But I'm going to find out."

"The letter makes reference to an address on a card. But there's no card," Kathleen said.

"Megan must have it," Danielle said.

"Alex, you can't go into Chinatown at night," Kathleen cautioned. "There's only a few hours of light left. It's not going to help her to take a risk like that."

"Like hell," Alex replied. "Megan could be hurt or in danger. This is no time to be cautious."

Ben reached up and put a hand on the saddle horn. "Kathy's right, Alex. We don't need to be worried about both of you. Let's go into Chinatown together tomorrow, with some firepower."

Alex looked down, teeth clenched. "No. Mount up and ride with me. Robby, you too. We'll spread out and search until dark. Then we'll come home."

Kathleen sighed heavily. "Thank you, Ben. Danielle, go tell Robert what's going on. I'm going in the house and search through her things. Maybe I'll find some clues there. No one is going to get any sleep tonight. Except Bridget, I hope."

Kathleen stood on the porch of the house, watching the men ride off. She clutched at her stomach, where an icy ball of fear had settled. Try as she might to dismiss the notion that this was anything serious, her motherly instincts told her otherwise. With leaden feet, she turned and went into the house.

She began rummaging through drawers, under beds, in closets, finding nothing that raised an alarm. After a half-hour of searching, she stood in the middle of the parlor, frustrated and weary. Then her eyes fell on Megan's sewing cabinet, the one place she hadn't yet looked. She walked over and pulled open the top drawer, which was full of spools of thread, buttons, knitting needles, and yarn. She picked through the contents, and was about to close the drawer, when one of the needles caught her eye. Something was different about it. She picked up the needle and held it near a lamp. At first her mind didn't register what had attracted her attention. Then it leaped out at her.

Near its end, one of the needles was discolored, as if it had been exposed to heat or flame. Gingerly, she brought the needle near her nose. A pungent odor assaulted her nostrils. And at once she knew. She squeezed her eyes shut in pain. "God help her," she said softly. "She's used opium again."

An hour after dark, Ben, Alex, and Robby were back. Kathleen went out to the porch at the sound of the approaching hoofbeats, holding a lantern. The men didn't have to speak for her to know. Their grim faces told her everything.

"Nothing," Ben said, dismounting and embracing her. "Not a trace."

Kathleen melted into his arms and began sobbing. "I found something," she said.

They all gathered in the parlor while she showed them the knitting needle. Robert had joined them while Danielle stayed home and did her best to comfort Bridget.

"You're sure?" Alex said, pacing back and forth.

"Yes, reasonably sure," Kathleen said. "I sensed something was amiss when I first got here. Now I know what it was."

"But why?" Alex said, slapping his thigh. "Why now? After five years?"

"I don't think any of us have ever appreciated what she went through to get those two hundred workers to build the railroad," Kathleen said. "She was willing to risk addiction to opium. I've heard that some people, once exposed, never completely get over it. I'd be willing to bet she's harbored a desire over the years for more." Kathleen sighed. "She certainly kept it a secret. Sometimes I wish she wasn't so much like me, so damned resolute."

"But she is," Ben said. "She's proven that for sure."

"Yes," Kathleen said. "And I'd say this knitting needle probably tells us what that gift was that the letter mentioned. It must have been opium."

"When I get my hands on that Chinaman, I'll wring his yellow neck," Alex said bitterly. "I'm going upstairs to look around the bedroom myself."

"Let's not jump to conclusions," Robert put in as Alex mounted the stairs. "I just can't imagine Yuen Ling-Po risking his contract over this.

Though he always does business through intermediaries, his relations with us have always been above board. This just doesn't fit."

"Maybe it wasn't him," Ben said.

They all turned to him in puzzlement. "What are you suggesting?" Robert said.

"That maybe someone used his name to lure her," Ben replied.

"But for what purpose?" Robert said.

"That I just don't know. But we're going to start with Ling-Po tomorrow."

Alex came down the stairs, interrupting them. Kathleen was startled at his expression. "Alex, what is it?"

Alex looked at them bleakly. "My gun is gone."

No one was asleep when the sun rose the following morning. Robert had gone home to be with Danielle, and Kathleen had gone with him to comfort her granddaughter as best she could. The little girl was distraught for a while, then began to exhibit a stone-jawed look of determination Kathleen knew all too well as nothing more than a reflection of her own personality.

"Get her back, Grandma," Bridget said.

"We will," Kathleen said, stroking the black hair away from the girl's face. "I guarantee it."

Before the sun had cleared the horizon, Alex, Ben, and Robert were saddled up and prepared to leave. They were about to do so when they saw Kathleen riding across the meadow toward them.

"You really didn't expect to go without me, did you?" she said as she rode up.

"I'd considered it," Ben said.

"Not on your life," Kathleen said. "It's time I met Ling-Po. One way or another, he's the one who started this." She spurred her horse up beside them as they started to move out. "I just don't understand," she continued. "If she took the gun, she must have figured she was going into a potentially dangerous situation. Why, oh why did she go alone? Why didn't she tell us?"

"And admit she'd used opium again?" Ben said. "That she had a weakness?"

"Well—yes. Why not?"

"Because she's your daughter, that's why. She wants to be like you. When did you ever admit to a weakness?"

Kathleen had nothing to say.

They all rode off toward San Francisco. Robert knew the city well, and guided them to Ling-Po's Chinatown lodging. By 9:30 they were dismounting in front of the nondescript storefront.

Kathleen looked at it dubiously. "This hardly looks like the home of a wealthy man."

"Wait until you see the inside," Robert said. "You may be surprised."

"Providing we *get* inside," Alex said.

"We will," Ben said, putting his hand on his pistol. "We're not taking no for an answer. Check your guns. But Kathy, try to control yourself."

Kathleen shot him a look of vexation, but said nothing.

They walked up to the door, and Ben rapped on it sharply. There was no response from inside for about thirty seconds. Ben was about to knock again when a hand pushed aside the filmy curtain covering the glass panel, and the wrinkled face of an old Chinese woman scowled murderously at them.

"Go!" she said. "Closed. Go!"

Ben pulled his pistol and put it in front of her face, the end of the gun barrel resting on the glass. "Open up. Now."

The old woman's eyes went wide, and after a moment's hesitation she disappeared. A few seconds later the door opened. A small, Chinese man stood before them, dressed in dark pajama-like clothing. A straggly gray chin beard reached to his chest. Though obviously much older than they, his eyes sparkled with alert intelligence. He gave them a shrewd look of appraisal, and when he saw Kathleen, he bowed low.

"You are the Venerable Kathleen," he said, smiling.

"Yes," Kathleen replied. "And you must be Yuen Ling-Po."

"The very same," the man replied. "Please forgive bad manners of ancient crone. She always in foul mood. To what do I owe honor of visit?"

"We need to talk," Ben said. "It's very important."

The old man bowed low again. "Of course. Please come in at once." He motioned for them to follow him. They all went in as he led them down a dingy hallway, then turned up a narrow flight of stairs, and opened a door at the top.

In other circumstances, Kathleen would have been stunned at the opulence of the room she now entered. Magnificent Oriental artifacts were everywhere, along with beautiful furniture and carpets. It was clearly the home of a wealthy man.

Ling-Po motioned them to take seats, which Kathleen did while the men stood. "May I offer you tea?" he said.

45

"There is no time," Kathleen said. "My daughter Megan, whom you know, is missing." She took the letter from her pocket. "We found this in her saddlebag yesterday. I also found evidence she's used opium again."

Ling-Po took the letter and examined it for long moments. When he looked up, his face was sober. "I know nothing of this."

Alex took a step forward, but Ben put a hand on his arm. "This is Megan's husband."

"I am very sorry," Ling-Po said, bowing in Alex's direction. "I have much respect for the Honorable Megan. This news distresses me greatly. But I truly know nothing of this matter. How may I be of assistance?"

Kathleen rose and walked over to stand in front of the Chinese man. Her blue eyes bored into him. "You started her on this road. Were it not for our mutually beneficial business arrangements, which she initiated at great risk to herself, I would have settled with you long ago." She leaned forward slightly, trembling with rage. "Find her, Ling-Po. Find her, or I swear by all that's holy, I will bring the wrath of God down on you and this house. I will destroy you. Never doubt it."

Eli Leatherwood turned from the view outside his window and looked with discomfort at Othniel Wanamaker. The disreputable little man was a blight on his otherwise elegant office, a shabby blot perched in the leather guest chair like a lumpy weasel. For the umpteenth time, he regretted doing business with such riffraff, at the same time he acknowledged the advantage. "The deed is done, then?" he said.

"She's away," Wanamaker answered. "Sailed last night. There were complications though."

Leatherwood felt a sudden chill. "I don't want to hear that."

Wanamaker pursed his lips and shrugged. "Can't help it. There were. We were hopin' she'd do opium again and pass out, makin' it easy. But she wouldn't go for it. She fought."

"And?"

Wanamaker sighed noisily. "Two men dead. She shot one; her horse killed the other. The horse got away."

Leatherwood was silent for a long moment. "Who were they? Anyone that can be traced to us?"

"No. Just street garbage. They never met me." He paused, then continued. "There's more. Somebody bashed her on the head, or she hit her head on something. When I saw her, there was blood behind her right ear. She was still breathin', but I don't know how bad she's hurt."

"My God," Leatherwood whispered. "I never figured on that."

"Well, ya shoulda!" Wanamaker nearly shouted. "You ain't dealin' with refined gentlemen. What's done is done."

Leatherwood shot him a withering glare. "Indeed. This had better be worth it. Did you plant the clues around Chinatown as I instructed?"

"Yeah, I did. Now, if you don't mind, I'm gonna disappear for a while. This whole thing turns my stomach."

"The price of revenge, my friend." Leatherwood watched him go, a sour expression on his face. So Megan was indeed gone. It had actually worked. And the clues had been left to make sure Ben and Kathleen Wilson knew where she'd been taken. Oh, Kathleen would pursue her hotly and bring her back, he was sure of that. Nothing could stand against that woman when she was determined. Megan would be a little the worse for wear, but she'd come back, no doubt. And while the Wilsons were gone, business would be left in the hands of that damned calculating Frenchwoman and her husband. His sources had told him she was pregnant. Maybe she'd be a little less rational, Leatherwood speculated, a little less orderly in her thoughts. And just maybe, then, the Wilsons' railroad and all its potential would pass into the hands of the Big Four, and himself.

Yuen Ling-Po looked up at Kathleen with glittering eyes in an otherwise expressionless face. No one had spoken to him like that since he had come to America. But he was a superb judge of character. He knew she meant every word. "I will do everything within my power, Mrs. Wilson. I will not rest until I have found her." He rose, walked a few steps away, and turned. "I will send searchers into the streets immediately. And one more thing. I will put Hsien Lu at your disposal for as long as you wish. He is the best I have."

That evening, Kathleen slumped into a parlor chair in Danielle's house, exhausted with worry. Except for Robert, they had all returned home after four hours of riding the streets of San Francisco, looking for something, anything, that would help. Robert had remained in town, determined to use his legal connections to dig for information.

Kathleen was in the chair only a few seconds before Bridget crawled into her lap and buried her face in her neck.

"Grandma, I want Mama," the girl said. "When will she be back?"

Kathleen put a hand to her mouth, fighting for control. "Soon, dear. We'll have her back soon."

Danielle made a move to lift Bridget away, but Kathleen waved her off. They were interrupted by the sound of hoofbeats outside, followed by a gentle knock. Ben went to the door and opened it. After a moment, he called to Kathleen.

She went to the door and saw a muscular Chinese man with a smooth face and a shaved forehead. His body looked rock-hard. He was somewhat taller than the average Chinese, and his black hair was tied in a small ponytail at the back. He gave Kathleen a faint smile.

Kathleen's eyes shone with tears, and her lip trembled. "Shen Lu," she whispered, pronouncing his name as westerners did. "Dear friend." She stepped forward and embraced him.

"It has been long, Venerable Kathleen," Hsien Lu said, returning the embrace.

"Too long, for someone who saved my daughters' lives." Hsien Lu had been assigned by Yuen Ling-Po to protect the Connelly women during the dangerous building of the railroad to Placerville several years earlier. He had run a saber through the back of Wanamaker's enforcer, Martin Hofmeister, as the man was strangling Megan after knocking Danielle unconscious.

"Master Ling-Po has instructed me to be at your disposal for as long as you wish," Hsien Lu said. "I was greatly saddened to learn of Honorable Megan's disappearance. I will not rest until I learn what has befallen her."

"Come in and have some tea," Kathleen said. "Then we will see to your quarters while you're with us." They went inside, and over tea, Kathleen told him what little she knew. They had been talking for nearly an hour when Robert arrived. He gave Danielle a long hug and kiss as he entered. Danielle buried her face in his shoulder as her body shook with sobs. After a minute she composed herself and pulled away, wiping her cheeks.

Everyone looked at Robert expectantly as he thrust his hands into his pockets and paced the room. "I went to the police," he said. "I was hoping to learn of anything unusual. I did. I don't know what it means yet, but there could be a connection."

They waited in silence.

"Two bodies were found in the bay this morning. They apparently hadn't been in the water long, and were found close together. The police don't know who they are, but they say that's not unusual. Disillusioned gold seekers are constantly wandering into town from the gold rush country."

"Any indication of how they died?" Alex said.

"One of them was shot. The other had a crushed chest. The marks on his body looked like hoof imprints."

48

The atmosphere in the room was heavy with quiet. Kathleen finally broke the silence. "Ben, what do you think?"

Ben sighed. "Could be there's a connection. If it *was* Megan and Shamrock, they must have put up a hell of a fight. But if so, it just deepens the mystery. Why was she lured? Why did someone want to get at her bad enough that two men died? On the other hand, let's not jump to conclusions. This may mean nothing."

"No," Kathleen said, rising and pacing back and forth. "It's her."

No one doubted her for a moment. They had all come to trust Kathleen's intuitive feelings for anything involving her daughters.

None of them made it to bed that night except Bridget. Everyone else napped and fretted restlessly on chairs and sofas, unable to sleep for long. Kathleen was up in the pre-dawn hours making coffee. As the sun came up, Ben, Alex, and Hsien Lu rode out to the city.

The Chinese vendor pushed his two-wheeled cart down a mostly deserted Dupont Street in the early morning light—pots, pans, kitchen utensils, opium pipes, and other miscellaneous items gently swaying. He was headed in the direction of the bay, hoping to secure a prime spot on Market Street from which to accost passersby. He hummed softly to himself as he strode along, the chance of pleasant weather evident in the clear sky overhead.

The old song on his lips choked off as his throat constricted at sight of the solitary figure walking toward him. It was not someone he wanted to see. Nervously he looked around, hoping to spot someone else that might be the target of the man's attention. But there was no one else nearby. There could be no mistaking it; Yuen Ling-Po's feared right-hand man was coming straight at him.

He knew Hsien Lu's reputation all too well. The saber tucked into his sash was not for show. Ling-Po usually sent him to ferret out information no one else could; he was not a man to be denied. The street vendor had heard some strange things in the past twenty-four hours; he wondered what information Hsien Lu might be seeking. Hoping desperately to avoid him, he put his head down, pushed the cart harder, and pretended not to notice.

He felt the cart come to an abrupt halt against something very solid.

"Old Fong."

Fong looked up and bowed a quick, nervous bow, feigning surprise. "Honorable Hsien Lu!" he said in Chinese. "I did not see you coming."

"The evidence suggests otherwise."

There was no warmth in the voice. The old vendor could feel sweat breaking out on his brow. He bowed again. "To what do I owe the honor of this encounter?" he said.

"I seek information," Hsien Lu said. "I know little happens in the streets that escapes your notice. Two men were found floating in the bay yesterday morning. It appears they did not die a natural death."

"I know nothing of this matter, Honorable Hsien Lu."

"Hmm. Have you heard anything unusual in the last two days?"

"No. Well, there was one strange thing. I heard there was a disturbance of some sort at Lee's Market on Kearney Street. It is said there were gunshots, and a horse running wild without a rider."

"Anything else?"

"No, Honorable Hsien Lu."

"Very well. One more thing. Do you know of the woman Megan Daley?"

"Who does not? She is of surpassing beauty. She is the daughter of The Angel herself."

"Yes. Well, that will be all for now. I may have need of you later."

"Of course, Great One."

Hsien Lu stood in the alley next to Lee's Market, senses probing. There were the prints of horses' hooves in the dirt all about him, but that was to be expected. He looked intently into the dark opening at the end of the alley. All was quiet. Slowly, he walked toward the opening, and then was inside. It seemed to be some sort of dirt-floored storage area or warehouse. No one was about. He walked around in the open space, shoes sifting the dirt as he stepped. He bent down at sight of a dark patch in the soil. He sniffed at it. It could have been blood. He stood up and continued his inspection. After a few minutes, his eyes caught a faint gleam. Bending down, his fingers plucked an object from the soil. He turned it over in his hand, examining it closely for a moment. It was a pearl stickpin, the kind a woman of considerable means might wear. He put it in a pocket. He was about to resume his search when a sharp voice from behind interrupted him.

"Who are you? What do you want here?"

Hsien Lu turned slowly, a look of cold menace on his face.

The stocky man before him paled at recognition of his visitor, his mouth open in soundless dismay.

Hsien Lu advanced on him, one muscular arm on the hilt of his saber. "What happened here two days ago?"

"Nothing! Why does Yuen Ling-Po send his assassin?"

"You lie." Hsien Lu glared at him murderously. He began to draw his saber.

The man sank to his knees, quaking with fear. "No, I swear by my ancestors!"

Hsien Lu reached down with powerful arms, lifted the man into the air, and pinned him to the nearest wall. With one hand, he withdrew his saber and put it under the man's throat. A thin trickle of blood appeared. "Your head will roll down Telegraph Hill within the hour if I do not hear the truth," Hsien Lu said. "What do you know of the disappearance of Megan Daley?"

"Nothing!"

The saber blade began to slide across the man's neck.

"Wait!" the man pleaded, eyes bulging. "I wasn't here. I was paid!"

"To do what?"

"To—to go away for a while. So they could use this place. Please, let me go!"

Hsien Lu ignored the request. "Who paid you?"

"I—I don't know. He didn't say his name. You must believe me!"

Hsien Lu eased his saber from the man's neck. "What did they do with her?"

The man rubbed his neck gingerly. "She is gone."

Hsien Lu's eyes narrowed into slits. "What do you mean?"

The man looked as if he were about to cry. "She is gone! She was taken out on *Red Rover* two days ago."

Hsien Lu couldn't hide his astonishment. "She was kidnapped? Put on a ship?" He grabbed the man's shirt and pulled him close. "How do you know this?"

"They told me!" the man wailed. "I didn't even ask, and they told me."

"Where is she bound?"

The man's knees gave out, and he sagged in Hsien Lu's arms. Hsien Lu let him sink to the ground.

"She is bound for Hong Kong," he said sadly.

Not knowing where Ben and Alex were, and feeling a sense of utmost urgency, Hsien Lu rode as hard as his horse was willing back to Danielle's house. He reined to a dusty halt at the front door, vaulted out of the saddle, and ran up to the front door. Not standing on ceremony, he thrust it open and went inside.

"Kathleen!" he called. "Please come at once."

51

Kathleen, Danielle, and Bridget came running from the back of the house. "What news?" Kathleen said.

"Let us go to the parlor," Hsien Lu said. "I think you should be seated."

They went quickly into the parlor and took seats. Hsien Lu drew the pearl stickpin from his pocket. "Does this belong to Honorable Megan?" he said.

Kathleen put a hand to her mouth, eyes brimming with sudden tears. "Yes. I gave it to her."

Hsien Lu looked at Danielle. "Honorable Danielle, I suggest you take Bridget from the room."

Danielle looked at Kathleen, who nodded. Bridget protested momentarily, but Danielle prevailed and the two left. Kathleen looked at Hsien Lu, her smooth face pale as death.

"Venerable Kathleen," Hsien Lu said. "I have grave news. Megan has been taken from the country."

Kathleen slumped in her chair, drained of all energy. She clung to Ben's hand as he bent over to comfort her. Too exhausted to cry any more, she didn't have the strength to stand. Ben and Alex had returned about two hours after Hsien Lu, and heard the news. Ben had said nothing, but Alex had nearly gone crazy.

"This can't be happening," he said, slamming his fist into the wall in frustration. "How can I have neglected her so? How could I let her go into town alone?" He turned to Kathleen. "How is it you could see something was wrong and I couldn't?"

"She's my blood, Alex. I just knew; I can't say how. But please don't torture yourself. I know the depth of your love for her. I lay no more blame on you than on any of us. If any of us failed her, we all did."

"But why did they take her? *Why?*" Alex said.

Kathleen shook her head sadly. "That I don't know. But by God, I will."

Robert spoke up. "Hsien Lu, you say the name of the ship she was taken on is *Red Rover*?"

"Yes."

Robert looked at Ben. "I know the ship. It's an opium clipper owned by Jardine, Matheson and Company, one of the original Hong Kong trading houses. And it's fast, I'm sorry to say."

"I remember seeing it in port," Ben said. "The captain's name is Parmenter, or something like that."

"That's it," Robert replied. "And he's as bad as they come. Ruthless and unprincipled."

"He's a dead man," Alex said.

Danielle moaned. "Will we ever see her again? What can we do now?"

Kathleen rose unsteadily, a look of determination etched on her face as if in stone. She took three steps to the window and looked out to sea. "We go after her."

Ben, Alex, and Robert sat in the parlor late that night, planning. Ben had ordered Kathleen to bed with Bridget. He was the only person who could order her to do anything. She had numbly complied.

"Thank God *Emerald Isle* is in port," Alex said. "She's still the fastest ship afloat. If we can sail soon, we might catch *Red Rover* at sea before she reaches Hong Kong."

"Unlikely," Robert said. "Even though the routes are well established, variations in the trade winds cause course deviations at times. It would be a miracle to actually find and overhaul her at sea."

"Then we'll go for a miracle," Alex said.

"We're going into pirate waters," Robert said. "And we don't know but what we may encounter hostilities in getting her back. We may find it dangerous to have to depend on a fair wind to set sail from Hong Kong. Maybe we should take one of the steamers, even though they're not as fast. One of them's in port too."

"No," Ben countered. "I'll take my chances with *Emerald Isle*. She's bigger, and we're going to take every able-bodied fighting seaman we can lay our hands on. We're also going to turn her into a floating arsenal, and I want all the space I can get. Now, I'm going to give you both your assignments. Start immediately. Nobody sleeps. We sail in two days."

4.

Megan struggled to consciousness, fighting to open her eyes. Her head throbbed. She slowly reached a hand above her right ear, and felt some sort of padding over her hair. Puzzled, she pressed on it, and cried out as her head exploded in pain. She gritted her teeth, struggling to sit upright. Swamped by a wave of dizziness, she flopped back, moaning.

"I'd take it easy for a few minutes," she heard a voice command her.

Megan summoned what little strength she had and forced her eyelids open. Gradually a figure came into focus. A big man dressed in a seaman's coat and calf high boots was grinning at her. He had curly black hair and a prominent scar that ran from his left temple to his jaw line. There was no trace of humor in his cold gray eyes.

Megan regarded him in bewilderment. "Who are you?" That was as far as she got before memory burst in her mind and her eyes went wide. She suddenly had a mental picture of the pistol blazing in her hand, and Shamrock rearing. "Where am I?" she croaked.

"About a half-day's sail out of San Francisco," the man said.

She was suddenly aware of the rolling deck underneath her feet. "My God, I'm at sea! What have you done?" She struggled again to sit up, and this time succeeded, clutching her head in both hands as a surge of nausea nearly overwhelmed her. She stood unsteadily and staggered to a small open porthole. Pressing her face to the opening, she saw nothing but rolling gray swells. Horrified, she turned on the man. "Who are you? Why have you done this?"

The man got up and leaned against the hull. "Captain Tobias Parmenter at your service. You're aboard my ship, the *Red Rover*."

Megan was beginning to recover from the shock, and anger swelled within her. "Why?"

The man smiled again, an expression registering frigid amusement. "You have no idea how much you're worth."

"What does that mean?"

"You're being sold to a Chinese lord. For a lot of money."

Weak-kneed, Megan crossed the deck and sank back down on the pallet she had been laying on. "Impossible. I've got a child, and a husband."

There was no answer.

She put a hand to the bandage above her ear. When she brought it down, there was a trace of blood on her fingers. "What happened to my head?"

"Your head hit something, or somebody knocked you out with a sap; I don't know which. That wasn't part of the plan, as I understand it. It was hoped you'd give in to temptation and smoke opium again."

"Not a chance."

He ignored her retort. "Then, when you were passed out, it would have been much easier to get you aboard on the sly. I'm sorry it didn't turn out that way. I didn't want you hurt. I bandaged your head the best I could, but you're going to have to rest up for a while. You're much too valuable."

Slowly she raised her face. "I don't think you know who I am."

Parmenter snorted. "No, they didn't tell me, and I didn't ask. Does it matter?"

"It will to you."

"All right, I'll bite. Who are you?"

"Megan Daley. My maiden name is Connelly."

Parmenter's eyes widened ever so slightly. He was silent for a moment. "Then your mother is—"

"Kathleen Connelly-Wilson. Some call her The Angel. And she'll come after me."

Parmenter turned his back to her. He didn't speak for nearly thirty seconds, looking out the porthole. "No matter," he finally said over his shoulder. "*Red Rover* is a fast ship. And we have a good head start."

"It won't be enough," Megan said. "My family will come after me on *Emerald Isle*. She's the fastest ship afloat. Nothing can outrun her."

Parmenter grinned wolfishly, revealing uneven teeth. "You really think they can find and overtake us on the high seas?"

Megan rose unsteadily, Irish fire blazing within her. "Yes, I do. Keep a sharp eye astern, Captain. If you see three tall masts on the horizon, you're a dead man."

* * *

The light from rows of torches glowed on the black waters of San Francisco Bay where *Emerald Isle* lay dockside at Pier Six. It was three a.m. two days after the decision to sail was made. The fore and aft cargo gangways were down, and crowded with a steady stream of foot traffic. A prodigious cache of supplies continued to flow onboard and down into the ship's vast holds. *Emerald Isle* could carry 650 passengers, but for this voyage, most of the hold space would be taken up with supplies.

Ben stood on the foredeck looking over the scene, two days' growth of beard on his weary face. When word had gotten out about Megan's kidnapping, there had been no shortage of volunteers for the rescue mission. Together with *Emerald Isle's* captain, Theophilus Rowan, he had chosen two hundred of the toughest fighting sailors in the city. The rest of the volunteers had been pressed into service carrying aboard the several tons of food, water, and miscellaneous necessary items for the voyage. Robert had been in charge of rounding it all up, and had done well. Ben hadn't seen him for almost twenty-four hours, but the results of his efforts were evident as the holds swelled to fullness.

Alex had been charged with weapons acquisition. The first day, he had rounded up seventy barrels of gunpowder, eight twenty-pounder cannons, and, with unexpected good fortune, two sixty-eight pounder long toms. The latter had been expensive, but Ben had given him a blank check. He had also purchased ten thousand rounds of ammunition, but it had yet to be delivered. Now, in the middle of the night, Ben saw Alex returning, at the reins of a freight wagon as it appeared out of the darkness and rolled rapidly down the pier. Alex pulled the two-horse team to a halt at the foot of the fore gangway and jumped down.

Ben went to meet him. "What luck?"

Alex was already walking to the rear of the wagon. "Take a look." He grabbed a large canvas and threw it aside.

Ben stepped closer and whistled in appreciation. The multiple barrels of two big Gatling guns softly reflected the torchlight. "Where in hell did you get these?" he said in wonderment.

"From Fort Gunnybags. They were left over from the second Vigilance Committee. They're on loan, but I'm not sure they'll ever see San Francisco again." He turned his face toward the harbor for a moment, rage settling on his features, and slammed his fist against the side of the wagon. "I'll fire them until the barrels melt down if I have to to get her back."

"It could be a long voyage," Ben said. "We'll need these in good shape, so we'll keep them belowdecks until we're close. Then we'll bring them up and lash them into place."

"How close are we to sailing?"

"A few hours. Providing the ammunition you were promised gets here, I plan to hoist anchor and sail with the outgoing tide at morning."

"It can't come soon enough," Alex said. "Don't let me interrupt you any further. I'll see that these get below."

As dawn broke over the harbor, the last supplies were secured in the holds. Another large freight wagon pulled up at dockside with the promised ammunition.

Numb with fatigue, Alex trudged down the gangway to greet the driver. "You get all ten thousand rounds?" he said.

"Closer to twelve thousand," the man answered. "There was a last-minute gift. Your mother-in-law's got a lot of friends in this town."

"No surprise there. Good work. Get this below. My brother-in-law will see you're all well paid tomorrow. Or I guess it's today now."

As the ammunition was being brought aboard, a carriage pulled up carrying Kathleen, Robert, and Danielle, with Danielle holding Bridget on her lap. They quickly stepped down and strode up the fore gangway. Ben and Alex saw them coming and met them at the top.

Kathleen embraced her husband tightly, then raised a face taut with exhaustion. "You look like you're ready to fall over," she said, eyes full of concern.

"You've looked better yourself," Ben replied. "There'll be time to rest as soon as we sail. Then we can turn things over to the crew. You have all your personal stuff?"

"Yes. But before we depart, there's something you'd better hear from Danielle."

Danielle came forward and put a hand on his arm. "Ben, there's a connection here to the stockholders' meeting. I'm sure of it."

Ben was so tired he didn't grasp what she was saying. "What?"

"I couldn't stop thinking of something Hsien Lu said the other night," Danielle continued. "He said the man at Lee's Market was *told* what happened to Megan, where she was being taken. He said he didn't even ask, but they told him anyway."

Ben wiped a hand across his face, trying to concentrate. "What are you saying?"

"Ben, without that information, how long might it have taken for us to discover what happened to her?" Danielle said, soft gray-blue eyes shining in the morning light. "If we had ever found out at all?" She tightened her grip on his arm. "Someone *wanted* us to know what happened to her. Someone *wants* us to go after her. The stockholders' meeting is only days away. Someone wants as many of us out of town as possible when the meeting is held; I'm convinced of it."

"This could be Leatherwood's doing," Robert put in. "He could be planning some sort of power play at the meeting."

"If he *is* involved, he'll have his tracks incredibly well covered," Kathleen said. She sighed heavily. "There's nothing to be done about it now; we have to go." She turned to face Danielle. "Daughter, you've got a good head on your shoulders. And Robert's the best lawyer in town. You two are going to have to hold down the fort while we're gone. Do the best you can and don't worry about the results. If something bad happens, I'll see to it when we come back." She glanced down at Danielle's enlarged stomach. "And take care of yourself—and that baby. I expect to see another grandchild some time after we return."

They embraced for long moments. "I won't let you down, Mother," Danielle whispered.

Captain Rowan approached them. He was a big barrel-chested man with a full, short white beard. "The tide's turning, Mr. Wilson," he said, touching the brim of his hat. "We're ready to sail. All ashore what's going ashore."

Kathleen knelt and embraced Bridget, fighting back tears. "As God is my witness, granddaughter, we'll bring your mother back. You mind your aunt now."

"I want to go, Grandmother," Bridget said, black hair falling around her face.

"I know," Kathleen said, smiling. "I know." She rose. "Danielle, guard her with your life." She turned to Ben and spoke in a low whisper. "Danielle doesn't look good. I'm worried about her. It took her a long time to get pregnant. I wish I could be here to see her through it."

"Do you want to stay?" Ben said.

Kathleen sighed. "No. Robert will take good care of her. Let's hoist anchor."

Danielle, Robert, and Bridget sat in a carriage above the Pacific shore, watching *Emerald Isle* move out to sea. As the long black hull cleared the harbor headlands, more sail was being added, and she began to gain headway.

Danielle turned to Robert, eyes wet. "It's such a long way," she murmured. "Such a long way to go."

"Godspeed, *Emerald Isle*," Robert whispered, barely audible above the faint roar of the waves breaking on the shore below.

"The next time I see that ship," Bridget said, jaw set in determination, "Mama will be on it."

They watched for a long time as the ship slowly receded over the vast water, stared until their eyes ached, strained to catch a last glimpse of the giant clipper ship as it slowly disappeared into the morning mists.

* * *

The second day out from San Francisco, Parmenter came to Megan in the cabin she was confined to, and told her she would be allowed on deck. "If the weather turns foul, you'll go below," he added. "And don't get any ideas about jumping overboard. Try it, and you'll be in chains for the rest of the voyage."

Megan regarded him venomously. "Why should I? You'll never get me to Hong Kong. My husband will cut your throat first, after *Emerald Isle* overtakes us."

Parmenter laughed. "You cling to that hope, Missy. It'll keep your spirits up."

Megan paced back and forth. "I hope you don't think these clothes I'm wearing are going to last for weeks. I need something else to wear. Is there anything on board fit for a woman?"

"Yes. I've got a whole trunk full of clothes I've picked up over the years. Some of them are bound to fit you."

"Why is it you have women's clothes?" Megan asked suspiciously.

"Some of them belonged to former mistresses of mine." He cocked his head and eyed her speculatively. "Sailing's a lonely occupation. One needs company."

Megan shuddered. "I would never put on anything that belonged to your mistresses."

"Suit yourself. But if I were you, I'd keep that fine dress you're wearing in reserve. I want you looking your best when we arrive."

Some of the clothes in the trunk Parmenter brought did indeed fit her, although most were too small in the bust. Some were Asian style; some were Western. She would have nothing to do with the Asian clothes, though she would have looked incredible in them. After putting on her first selection, she tentatively emerged on deck. She had removed the bandage from her head and cleaned the dried blood from her hair. Her head still ached and was very tender above her right ear. She had found a sash among the clothes and fashioned a scarf from it, which she wrapped around her head, covering the injured spot.

A stiff breeze greeted her, blowing loose hair about her head. The initial seasickness she had felt the first day had abated, and she walked over and leaned against the railing, watching the blue ocean slide by.

Parmenter spotted her and came over. "You look real good," he said.

"Go to Hell," she replied sullenly.

"Ever the Irish spitfire, huh? That Chinaman's going to like your spirit. Chinese women are tame."

Megan looked around the deck. Crewmembers shot her sideways glances, never staring directly at her but checking her out all the same. "I wonder what these men would say if they knew what you're planning to do with me," she said.

"You'd better hope they don't find out," he said, grinning at her. "They think you're my woman. If they knew you weren't, it could be a lot harder to keep them off you. They might consider you fair game."

Megan squeezed her eyes shut and bit her lip. She was in the middle of the vast Pacific, the only woman on a ship with thirty men, most of whom looked like the type she would hope never to encounter on the street. She was left with the unsettling thought that Parmenter, verminous scum that he was, might be the key to her safety.

The days stretched into a week, then two. Megan fought desperately to keep her hope of rescue alive. But as the leagues continued to slide under *Red Rover*'s keel, her spirits sank.

* * *

Danielle looked around the big conference table in her home at the twelve members of the railroad's board of directors. It was two days before the stockholders' meeting. Except for Kathleen, all members were present, as expected. Robert sat next to her. As Chief Operating Officer, Danielle commanded the chair at the head of the table. She had carefully examined the faces before her as she told them of Megan's kidnapping, and the unplanned but necessary absence of Kathleen, Ben, and Alex. To a man, they had expressed shock and sorrow at the news. If any of them had a hand in Megan's disappearance, or knowledge of who might have done it, their reactions didn't betray them. Her gaze bored into Leatherwood. His sorrow seemed genuine, but she gave it no credence.

"Rest assured, gentlemen," Danielle continued, "I hold full executive powers, and voting proxy for all family members. At the stockholders' meeting, it will be as if they were all here."

"This will be a regular meeting then, lassie?" said Ian MacLendon, a gruff Scotsman who had made a name for himself in banking. "In your mother's absence we can still present proposals to the membership for a vote?"

"*Oui*," Danielle replied, slipping into French as she still did at times, usually when she was tired.

"You look a little pale, lassie," MacLendon replied. "The wee one's not giving you too much trouble already is it, with weeks yet to go before it enters the world?"

"I am a bit tired, yes," Danielle said, feeling Robert reach over and tenderly grasp her hand under the table. "I haven't been sleeping well since Megan was taken."

"I'm sorry to hear it, lassie," MacLendon said. He paused, as if considering the wisdom of his next words, then continued. "And I'm sorry to give you this news now, but Governor Stanford has asked me to present another offer to the stockholders at the meeting."

Danielle put a hand to her head. This was the last thing she wanted to deal with during Megan's disappearance, but the timing didn't surprise her. The Central Pacific Railroad's Big Four, Stanford in particular, had made their desire to acquire the Sierra and Western Railroad clear over the past several months. They had already made a merger offer, which had been swiftly rejected by the board. This was followed by a buyout offer of cash and Central Pacific stock, which was also rejected. But in both of those instances, Kathleen had been present. Her calm wisdom, and the sheer power of her presence, had discouraged serious consideration of either one. Few people doubted her, and fewer still would go against her wishes. But now she was far out at sea, the date of her return unknown. This wasn't a good time for another buyout offer—and Danielle knew that was exactly why it was being presented.

She frowned at MacLendon. "I can't stop it from being presented to the stockholders," she said. "But it will go nowhere. The family will never agree to it. *I* will never agree to it, no matter how generous the offer." She stopped, putting a hand to her stomach, a look of distress on her face. *"Mon Dieu,"* she gasped.

Robert leaned over and put his arm around her. "I want you to go lie down right now," he whispered in her ear. "I'll get the housekeeper to attend you. I'll take the meeting from here."

"Very well," Danielle replied. Robert helped her slowly to her feet. "Gentlemen, I must take my leave of you," she said. "I wish to be well rested for the meeting two days hence. Robert will assume control of the rest of this one." She stepped around her chair and walked slowly out of the conference room, steadying herself with a hand on Robert's arm.

Eli Leatherwood's gaze followed her until she was out of sight.

* * *

The sharp black bow of *Emerald Isle* knifed through the Pacific waters, sheets of spray exploding into the air every time the ship fell in its undulating motion. Her three tall masts were heeled over slightly as a fair wind drove her onward through smooth seas under a clear sky.

Kathleen stood at the bow of the ship, as far forward as she could get, her body pressed against the rail. She had been there almost constantly since the ship's departure from San Francisco three days earlier, staring at the horizon ahead. No one dared suggest she should give it a rest, though Ben had kept a close eye on her.

"You be not a sail, Madame," said a gruff, though warm, voice behind her.

She turned, ebony hair wafting around her head in the breeze, and saw Captain Rowan smiling at her.

"What?" she said, bringing her mind back to the ship around her.

"She's flyin' every square yard of canvas she'll hold," he said, glancing aloft at the taut sails. "You can't make her go any faster by standing here at the bow the entire journey."

"I wish I were," Kathleen said, returning her gaze to the open sea.

"What's that, Madame?"

She spread her arms wide. "I wish I were a sail. I wish I could stretch my arms out and catch the wind and send us racing toward Hong Kong. I wish I could send us flying westward, like a flying fish." She lowered her arms. "But I can't." She was silent for a moment. Then: "I just keep hoping I'll see sails ahead. Once yesterday I thought I did. But it was nothing."

"I'm sorry, Mrs. Wilson. She's doing twenty-four knots, as fast as I've ever known her to go. But *Red Rover*'s got a four-day jump on us. I don't think we'll see her before she reaches Hong Kong. Now, I think we're in for some rough weather ahead. I think you should come below."

Kathleen nodded but she didn't move as Rowan walked off. Large raindrops began to patter on the deck, increasing in intensity until her black hair was plastered on her forehead, and water ran off her hands. She was dimly aware of Ben's arms around her as he gently lifted her up and carried her below.

Emerald Isle sailed on, her 251-foot black hull a long dark line on the endless sea.

* * *

Megan fell into a dispirited listlessness as the weeks went by, and the chance that rescue would overtake *Red Rover* before she reached Hong Kong grew ever slimmer. She became more and more fearful of the crew, some of whom had begun to eye her with a hungry look. She kept as far away as possible from them when on deck, and increasingly kept below in her cabin. Parmenter kept her well fed, and she had found a small cache of women's toiletries that allowed her to keep feeling reasonably feminine, although the realization that they had doubtless belonged to one of his former mistresses caused her to view them with distaste. She washed herself and her undergarments in seawater at night, her skin chafing at the salt residue it left. She was sick with longing for Alex and Bridget, and prayed daily on her knees. *Alex . . . Mother . . . Ben . . . where are you?* Tears fell to the deck, and she wished she had her *An Paidrin Beag* wrist rosary with her. She still had trouble believing this was happening. There had to be more to it than Parmenter's greed. Someone else had set her up, and it wasn't Yuen Ling-Po. She had no idea who it might be, or why.

The weather at sea grew increasingly humid. Though she had never been to the Orient, she feared the change meant they were nearing land. The fear was confirmed one day when Parmenter approached her on deck as she stood at the rail.

"We should sight land tomorrow or the next day," he said, not bothering to look at her.

She shuddered. "I can't believe an old, established shipping company like Jardine, Matheson would be a party to this," she said. "You'll lose your job when they find out."

Parmenter chuckled. "It doesn't matter. I'm sailing to the South Seas anyway, as soon as I'm rid of you. When we reach port, nobody but us and one or two crewmen are going ashore until the deal is sealed. By the time my employer finds out, I'll have disappeared. I've been sailing the world for thirty-some years. I've had enough. And you," he said, turning to her with a nasty grin, "you're my retirement."

She suddenly couldn't stomach standing next to him, and turned to walk away. But she didn't get more than three steps. About fifteen crewmen were massed amidships, not twenty feet away. They were staring at her with an intensity that made her shiver.

Parmenter turned and saw the men. He came forward to stand beside Megan. "You're not at your stations," he said coldly.

One of the men took a step forward. He had shaggy hair and was missing several front teeth. His eyes, narrowed to slits from years of squinting in sunlight reflected off the sea, were set in a craggy face. "There's some of us want a sport with the woman, Cap'n," he said in a gravelly rumble. "You be knowin' what we mean."

Terrified, Megan stepped behind Parmenter.

Parmenter took a step forward and put a hand on the pistol he kept stuck in his belt. "I told you when we sailed, and I'll tell you again. Any man who makes a move on her will catch a ball between the eyes."

"It ain't fair, Cap'n," the man growled. "It be a long voyage, and you be keepin' her to yourself. And there's some of us never bought that story about her bein' your woman."

"You'll be in port in a day, two at the outside," Parmenter replied. "There's no shortage of whores in Victoria."

The man sneered at him. "They be not so fair as this one." He took a step forward. "No, not so fair. We ain't never seen one like this." The men behind him stirred menacingly.

Parmenter drew his caplock pistol.

"You got but one shot in that pistol, Cap'n," the speaker continued. "Use it and you be shark bait. We want our turn with the woman."

The group of men shuffled a step forward.

Parmenter raised the pistol and pointed it straight at the man. "If I go into the sea, one of you will go with me. Who wants to be the one?"

No one said anything.

"Well," Parmenter said, "any of you think it's worth it?"

Silence.

"You've got ten seconds to disperse and get back to your stations. Otherwise, I'm going to pick one of you and fire." He cocked the pistol. "And you all know I'll do it. Get back to your stations. Now."

The men stood their ground for a few seconds, then, amidst muted grumbling, slowly turned and walked away. The one who had spoken turned back after a couple of steps. "You best be keepin' a sharp eye,

Cap'n. Think you can stay awake until we reach port?" Then he walked off.

Megan's knees gave out, and she collapsed to the deck in fear.

Parmenter reached down and roughly lifted her up. "Get below, double quick. And stay there."

When dark fell two hours later, Parmenter came to her cabin. He found Megan on the deck, huddled against the cabin wall. Her arms were clasped tightly around her, and she was shaking. Her head jerked up at his entrance, fear still on her beautiful features.

Parmenter scowled at her.

"You almost aren't worth the trouble," he said. "I think I'm going to ask more for you than I planned."

"None of this trouble would be happening if you hadn't kidnapped me," Megan said, pressing tight to the wall. "Damn you! Damn you for the danger you've put me in."

He crossed the cabin, reached down, and jerked her to her feet. He gripped her arms tightly and brought his face close. "You don't seem very grateful for me keeping the crew off you."

Megan went wide-eyed in shock. "You think I should be *grateful?* You bastard!" She swung both hands at his face, raking her nails across his cheeks and drawing blood.

"Bitch!" he roared, and slammed her into the wall. He grabbed her hair and forced her head back, then drew his knife and brought it close to her face. "If you weren't worth so much, I'd carve you like a Christmas turkey."

Megan gasped, dazed and fighting for balance. She could feel his hot breath on her face. "Please—"

"You know," Parmenter said, "as long as there aren't marks on you that show, you ought to bring full price. So I think I'll do what I've been wanting to do for weeks." He swung his foot at her legs, and she collapsed on the deck. He was swiftly astride her.

"No!" Megan screamed. "No, please!"

"Yell all you want," Parmenter said, face twisted into a mixture of lust and hate. "Nobody's going to hear you."

She twisted and struggled to get at his bloody face, but he grabbed her arms and forced them over her head, where he held both wrists in one powerful hand. With his other hand, he tore her clothes open.

And then brutally raped her.

* * *

Ben sat at a table in a cabin built into the aft end of *Emerald Isle*'s vast hold. With him at the table were Kathleen, Alex, and Hsien Lu. A single lantern hung above the table from an overhead beam, gently swaying as the huge clipper ship made its way through the Pacific waters. Spread on the table before them was a map of Hong Kong Island and its surroundings.

"Hong Kong is actually the name of the island, not a town or city," Ben said. "As you can see, it sits very close to the China coast. Trading ships put into port at Victoria, which is around the far side of the island, facing the coast." He pointed to markings on the map indicating a settlement at Victoria Harbour. "That's where the Jardine, Matheson and Company headquarters are, and that's where *Red Rover* will drop anchor."

"Can we be sure?" Kathleen asked. "Suppose Parmenter decided to put in somewhere else on the island, to get Megan ashore without the authorities knowing about it?"

"That's a chance we're going to have to take," Ben said. "We can't afford to take time to check every inlet and cove. Besides, *Emerald Isle* is just too big to do it. No, I'm guessing Parmenter will put in exactly where he's supposed to, to make it look like business as usual. And we need to get there as soon as we can."

"What happens once we drop anchor?" Alex asked. "What's our first move? We don't know Victoria at all."

"But Hsien Lu does," Ben replied. "Like the back of his hand. He's going to go out scouting at once, to see what he can find. He has a talent for getting the information he's after. Perhaps a white woman will attract attention from someone. If she's taken ashore at Victoria, he'll find out about it. We'll wait for his first report."

"No," Kathleen said. "I will not sit around and wait. I suggest we go straight to the colonial governor and talk to him. If Megan's sold to a Chinese lord, maybe he can suggest whom it might be."

"Why not go to the American Consulate?" Ben said.

"No," Kathleen replied. "Hong Kong is a British colony. Let's go straight to the governing authority."

"I'm with her, Ben," Alex said. "There's no way I'm staying on board waiting. Whoever's got Megan might decide to take her inland into China. That would complicate things even more. We've got to try to find her before someone is tempted to take her off the island."

"Who is the governor now?" Kathleen asked.

"William Mercer is the acting administrator of the colony," Ben said. "He hasn't actually been named governor, but he's filling the position."

"Good," Kathleen said. "Captain Rowan has informed me we should be in Victoria Harbour in three days at most. As soon as we can get ashore, we'll pay a visit to Mr. Mercer."

* * *

Danielle looked around the large ballroom in the St. Francis Hotel in San Francisco. It was crowded with over three hundred stockholders. There was a quorum, though by the thinnest of margins, and with more than enough shares present to vote on any matter put before them. The meeting had been in progress for just over an hour, but she was already tired. The stress of Megan's kidnapping weighed heavily on her. She hadn't slept well ever since Megan had been taken, and her doctor had strongly advised her not to attend the meeting. She had curtly told him that was out of the question.

Robert had also come down hard on her to stay at home in a prone position. "You don't *have* to be there," he said. "I can vote your mother's proxies for you."

"Mother entrusted me with this meeting, and whatever it might bring," Danielle replied. "I've never let her down, and I don't intend to now. I'm going."

Robert had taken hold of her shoulders and brought his face close to hers. "Are all Frenchwomen so stubborn? Now, I could order you to stay home, but I don't want to. I love you too much to force you. But you're carrying our first child, and it's more important than you being at the meeting. You're tired, and you've been having some discomfort with the pregnancy. I wish you'd take the doctor's advice."

Danielle looked at him, features twisted with the agony of choosing between two equally unpalatable options. "I've never missed a meeting. And something's afoot at this one. There's no telling what Leatherwood's got up his sleeve, with Mother and Ben out of the country."

"But it isn't Leatherwood who's going to introduce the buyout proposal from Stanford. It's MacLendon."

"Of course. Leatherwood will never come at us directly. If we dig deep enough, I'm sure we'll find he maneuvered MacLendon into doing it somehow. Robert, I'm going."

Robert sighed. "All right. I know the women in this family. When your minds are made up, there's no dealing with it." He drew closer and lifted her gaze to meet his. "But you hear me good. If I think you're in distress, I'm taking you back to our room in the hotel right away."

Danielle nodded in silent assent.

Now, as the meeting was in brief recess, she attempted to gather her strength and hide from Robert the increasing pain in her belly. The minutes of the previous meeting had been read, the officers and committees had presented their various reports, and old business had been taken care of. When the meeting reconvened, it was time for new business. First on the agenda, MacLendon would outline the buyout proposal from Stanford. Danielle would vote the majority of shares against it for the family, and that would be that. Then Robert would outline his proposal for continued expansion of the Sierra and Western southward down the western flank of the Sierras and out into the Sacramento Valley.

Danielle poured herself a glass of water and mopped her forehead with a handkerchief. Though she had not been pregnant before, she knew something wasn't right. She promised herself she would return to her hotel room and lie down at the earliest opportunity. She looked up as Robert returned to her table, and forced a smile.

Robert didn't buy it. "You're perspiring," he said, taking his seat next to her. "I'm taking you out of here right now."

"No," Danielle replied. "It's just a bit hot in here, that's all. Now, it's almost time for your presentation. Go to it."

Robert gave her a long look as the meeting was gaveled to order. "All right," he said as he slowly got to his feet. "But I'm sending for the doctor." He stepped to the big doorway of the ballroom and whispered to one of the attendants, who quickly took off down the hall. Then he slowly made his way to his seat as the crowd gradually fell silent.

MacLendon skewered the crowd with his gaze, eyes agleam. "Fellow citizens, a railroad is a machine, and one of the most beautiful and perfect of labor saving machines. It well suits the energy of the American people. They love to go ahead fast, and to go with power. They love to annihilate the magnificent distances. I tell you, the transcontinental railroad is destined to become the greatest industrial entity in world history! And *you* can be a part of it. I don't see profit for the Sierra and Western in remaining independent any longer," he advised the crowd. "As you know, the Central Pacific has already locked up the California traffic in mail, government supplies, and troops, in exchange for the free land they are being given. And what land! Why, between 1850 and 1860, 20 million acres of public lands were given to the transcontinental railroad. *Think* of the potential wealth! And the Central Pacific is getting $16,000 for every mile of track laid in California, and $48,000 per mile to build through the Sierras. And as you know, Governor Stanford persuaded the legislature to donate millions in state bonds to the Central Pacific. I tell you, the nation has never seen anything like it. And it never will again. Bonds! Land! Traffic! Imagine the potential, ladies and gentlemen!"

MacLendon was waxing eloquent, and Robert, knowing full well the high-flown oratory the man was capable of, shook his head in disgust. Nothing of what the Scotsman was laying out was new.

MacLendon began to pace back and forth, hands gripping his lapels, elbows flapping with enthusiasm. Then, for effect, he adopted a sober expression. "The good citizens of Placerville lost their battle in '64 for the transcontinental railroad to follow *their* wagon road route through the Sierras to the Nevada silver mines. Instead, it went to the Central Pacific's Dutch Flat route. Most unfortunate. But a sign, I tell you, that Providence is with the Central Pacific. The train is pulling out, ladies and gentlemen. Get on board! Now, as to Governor Stanford's most generous offer . . . ."

MacLendon had finally come to the point, and Robert listened closely. His back was to Danielle, and so he did not see her eyes widen in shock as she put a hand between her legs and slowly raised it, blood-covered, in front of her pale face. Nor did he see her head slowly sink to the table as she lapsed into unconsciousness.

* * *

Megan gripped the sponge with trembling hands and ran it down her legs, trying to see through tears that wouldn't stop. Sobbing quietly, she cleaned herself from neck to toes with seawater as best she could. She scrubbed on and on, until her skin was red. But she couldn't clean off what Parmenter had done.

He had at last rolled off her and wordlessly left. She had retreated into silent shock. After awhile, she pulled her torn clothes together and rolled onto her side. There she remained, still as death. It was an hour before she could summon the strength to rise, pull the bucket of seawater to her, and mechanically go through the motions of washing.

She had been fearful of such an attack for days, if not from the beginning. To that end, she had stolen a bottle of vinegar from the galley. It was tall, with a long neck, and only partly full. Now she filled it up with some of her precious remaining supply of drinking water, and mixed the contents. She was terrified that Parmenter's seed might take root within her. And she knew it might already be too late. But she had to try. She lay down on the floor close to a bulkhead, and, bracing her feet against it, raised her hips as far off the floor as she could. With shaking hands, she inserted the long neck of the vinegar bottle into her vagina and watched its contents slowly drain into her.

She kept herself elevated as long as her muscles would allow, which wasn't long. Then she sank back to the floor, numb. Her legs and hips ached from having Parmenter's weight on top of her. Slowly, she became conscious of her hair being tangled. She crawled to the small chest containing the toiletries, and retrieved a hairbrush. Leaning against a wall, she brushed her hair with long, slow strokes. She continued to brush long after the tangles were gone.

Sometime far into the night she crawled to her sleeping pallet, curled up tightly clutching the thin blanket, and fell tearfully into an exhausted slumber. She did not see the green hills of Hong Kong rise ahead of *Red Rover* in the dawn light, nor did she stir when the ship dropped anchor in Victoria Harbour.

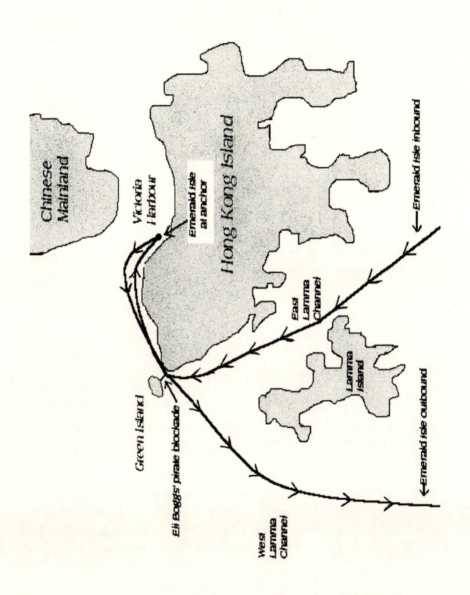

Chinese Mainland

Victoria Harbour

Emerald isle at anchor

Hong Kong Island

Emerald isle inbound

East Lamma Channel

Lamma Island

Green Island

Eli Boggs' pirate blockade

Emerald isle outbound

West Lamma Channel

5.

Hong Kong is an archipelago of 235 rocks and islands which sit beside a mountainous peninsula. To the south and west is the coast of China. Hong Kong Island itself consists of treeless, scrub-covered granite hills which rise rapidly from the harbor. Between the hills are sharp-sloped valleys. Eighty per cent of the barren island is too mountainous to farm. Hong Kong is hot and humid in summer, and burdened with overcast skies for weeks at a time. Damp and all-pervasive mists beset the island, and it is often assaulted by summer typhoons.

Hong Kong fell under British control in 1841. The town of Victoria grew rapidly, and many major trading houses established large headquarters there. Swift clipper ships came and went carrying cotton, sugar candy, rattan, salt, and tea. Much of the inbound traffic was smuggled through Chinese customs. It was not unusual to see British warships and opium clippers in the harbor.

As the damp dawn mists began to clear in Victoria Harbour, an old Chinese fisherman mending his nets at the edge of the pier beheld a most curious sight. A small skiff slowly emerged out of the shroud of fog. He saw that it was being rowed by a foreign devil, while two other figures, as yet indistinct, sat in the stern. As the skiff gradually drew nearer to the pier on the calm water, he could see that one of the figures in the stern was a man, and the other was a most extraordinary-looking white woman.

The fisherman's hands never stopped moving as the mending pawl worked its way back and forth through the net. He had learned it was not profitable to involve himself in the affairs of the *gweilo*[4]. Still, from beneath his large conical bamboo-weave hat his gaze was locked on the skiff and its occupants. The woman was most arresting in appearance. She wore fine Western dress, which he knew she would soon discover was much too heavy for the climate. Her complexion was pale, and her long hair was the color of dark flame. She held her hands in her lap, and the old fisherman noticed her wrists were bound. As the skiff reached the pier, he could see that her gaze was downcast, and she appeared very sad.

The oarsman took a rope and tied the skiff to the pier pilings, then ascended a ladder to the top. The woman slowly rose, prodded by the man in the stern beside her. Climbing carefully with her bound wrists, she too ascended the ladder, followed by the man. Once all three were on top, they went into a large warehouse at the back of the pier, and were lost from view.

The old fisherman looked at the door through which they had gone for a moment, then shrugged slightly and continued his mending. The ways of the foreign devils were often strange. But it was not his affair.

Megan stood in the dimly lit warehouse, eyes on the rough plank floor. Piled high around her were bales of cotton and tea. Before leaving the ship, Parmenter had ordered her to once again don the dress she was wearing when she was kidnapped.

"I want you to look your best," he said. But he hadn't hesitated to bind her wrists. "I'm not taking any chances with you," he told her as he fastened the rope firmly.

But all the fight was gone out of her. She was crushed with grief. Parmenter had defiled her, and she knew that deep inside, she would never be the same. Rescue hadn't come. Her mother hadn't come. Alex hadn't come. She was thousands of miles from her home, surrounded by evil people who looked on her as a commodity. And there was no one to help her.

"What do we do now?" the seaman who had rowed the skiff asked Parmenter.

---

[4]   ghost or devil man; foreigner

"We wait," Parmenter replied. Upon entering the warehouse, he had found a worker. A few whispered words had sent the man off at a trot. "I expect Yang will be here soon to see his prize. He'd better be. We can't hang around long."

"Lord Yang doesn't jump for you, Cap'n. No disrespect."

"True enough. But he wants this one bad," he replied, looking at Megan.

They waited about half an hour, and then there was the sound of carriage wheels and footsteps on the pier planking outside. In a moment, the warehouse door opened, and a Chinese man came in, accompanied by several attendants. He was short by Western standards, about average for a Chinese man, and appeared somewhat beyond middle age, but trim and hard. His face and head were clean-shaven. Dark eyes looked out with a penetrating gaze from beneath full eyebrows. He radiated authority and command as he eyed Parmenter.

"So, Captain, you have at last brought me what I desire," Zhao Yang said. "Let us see if you have earned your price." He walked forward and looked at Megan. His expression darkened when he noticed the ropes on her wrists. "Why are her hands bound?" he demanded angrily.

"She's trouble," Parmenter said. "She'll fight if she gets the chance."

Yang looked more closely at Parmenter's face and saw the scratches across his cheeks. "Yes, I see. We will discourage her from such behavior." He continued his examination of Megan, slowly circling her in the dusty gloom. "She is most beautiful, by Western standards. I'm sure she will be helpful. But she doesn't look well. Is she in good health? Did you beat her?"

"Nay, Lord Yang. And she was well fed. Her health is good, but I fear she wasn't used to being at sea for so long. Her color will soon improve."

Yang resumed his slow walk around Megan. For nearly a minute he said nothing.

Parmenter grew restless. "Yang, I can't be hangin' around here too long. We need to conclude our business."

Yang stopped and turned to him. "I will pay your price."

Parmenter stopped leaning against the cotton bale he had been resting on and stood up to full height. "Well, price has gone up by ten per cent. She was extra trouble; I damn near had a mutiny on my hands."

Yang's eyes narrowed. Though he gave no sign, one of his attendants put a hand to the hilt of the sword stuck in his sash. "That is not my problem," Yang said coldly. "I am already paying you enough to retire in luxury. I do not renegotiate agreements." He turned and beckoned to another assistant, who sprang forward with a box in his hands.

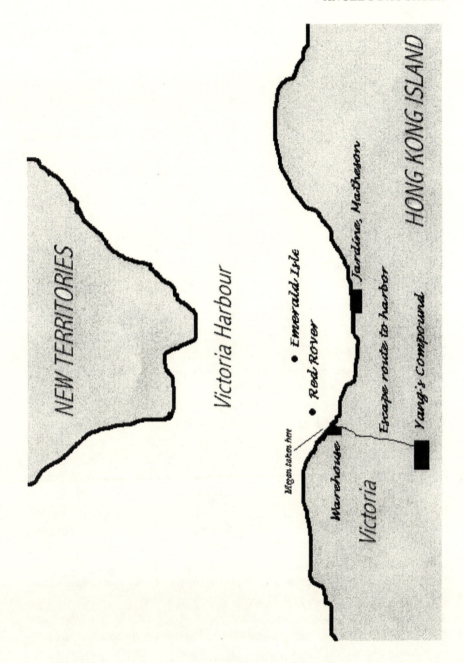

"Here is payment as agreed. I suggest you take it and return to your vessel, before I decide you no longer have need of your head."

Parmenter stepped forward and took the box. He turned, set it down on a bale of cotton, and opened the lid. After examining the contents for a few moments, he turned back to face Yang. "Take the wench, then." With that, he motioned the seaman out the door, and followed him, box under his arm.

Yang turned to his assistants and barked an order in Chinese. Two men came forward. One drew a knife and cut Megan's bonds, which fell to the floor. Then each of them took an arm, and she was led out the door to an enclosed rickshaw. She stepped up into it, and the rickshaw began to roll along the pier, and then away from the waterfront up a long dirt street. None of her captors looked at her, and thus did not see the single tear roll down her cheek.

* * *

Robert's first inkling that something was very wrong came from the faces of the stockholders in the front row, who went wide-eyed with surprise. He turned quickly and saw Danielle's head resting on the table, her arms limp at her sides. He rushed to her and put a hand on her cheek. She was burning up with fever. Then he saw the blood on the floor. "We're in recess!" he shouted to the audience. He embraced Danielle and lowered her gently to the floor.

A stretcher was sent for, and arrived within minutes. Robert recruited two of the stockholders, and Danielle was lifted onto it with infinite care. Robert walked close by her side as she was carried out of the room.

Confusion reigned in the ballroom in the wake of their departure. Eli Leatherwood let the crowd stew for about five minutes, then strode to the speaker's platform and raised his hands. "Ladies and gentlemen," he called loudly, "it's unfortunate Mrs. Bradshaw has been taken ill, but we have a meeting to continue, and a serious proposal for your consideration. I suggest we set a time limit, say forty-five minutes, for her or Mr. Bradshaw's return, and then, if neither one has rejoined us, consider proceeding without them. May I see a show of hands of those favoring this proposal?"

There was a buzz of conversation, then most of the crowd slowly raised their hands in assent, some with considerable reluctance.

Leatherwood tried to hide the feeling of smug satisfaction that came over him. "Very well," he told the assembled mass. "I am loath to carry on without them, but I'm sure you'll all agree on the necessity of attending to business. Few of us could afford to stay over for another day in the city if we were forced to continue this meeting until tomorrow. If Mr. or Mrs. Bradshaw has not returned after forty-five minutes, I'll send a messenger to Mr. Bradshaw's room requesting instructions. Fair enough?"

The lack of dissent told him he'd won the point, at least temporarily.

The stretcher carrying Danielle had not quite reached her hotel room when the Frenchwoman's eyes flew open and her mouth went wide in soundless surprise as she felt her insides twist into a knot. She reached up and clutched Robert's coat as he walked by her side. "Oh! *Mon Dieu*, the baby's coming!" she gasped.

The stretcher-bearers hustled her into her room and gently transferred her to her bed, just as the doctor came walking rapidly up the hallway.

"She's going into labor!" Robert said.

The doctor, a middle-aged man of medium height and heavy build, hustled to Danielle's bed, drew up a chair, and put his hands on her swollen stomach. For long minutes there was silence in the room. Danielle turned her head slowly from side to side as Robert attempted to cool her with a wet washcloth.

Finally the doctor turned and looked up at Robert. "If the baby's determined to come, there's nothing I can do to stop it. I did feel a contraction. The next hour will tell the tale. I'm going to give her some laudanum, which should relax her and may slow down or stop any further contractions. If we keep her down on her side, they may stop."

"What should we be doing?" Robert said.

The doctor rose, ran a hand through his thick silver hair and took Robert aside. "I think she needs a lot of rest and no two ways about it. I know the load she's been carrying, what with her sister being taken, and the big meeting going on downstairs. All that worrying probably brought this on. I'll wager she's exhausted. Plus, she's got a fever. I'm going to give her some quinine for the fever. I have to tell you, there's a slight risk there. Quinine could further stimulate contractions, and if she does deliver, the baby will be sedated too, from the laudanum. That could be dangerous. But we need to stop these contractions. Do I have your okay to go ahead?"

Robert blew out his breath in a sigh of helplessness. "I trust your judgement, Doc. Give her the smallest dose you can get by with."

"Okay. Afterword, I want her in bed for at least forty-eight hours. Make sure she drinks lots of water. If the contractions continue, or if there's any bleeding, get hold of me pronto, and I don't mean maybe. You will *not* let her back in that meeting." He turned back to Danielle and sat on the edge of her bed.

"I'm going to give you some laudanum to relax you and diminish the chances of any further contractions, and just a little quinine for the fever.

And I'm ordering you to get a lot of rest. You've been carrying far too great a burden for a pregnant woman."

After administering the promised medications, the doctor left, and Robert sat by Danielle's bedside, lovingly wiping her face.

After a while, she slowly opened her eyes and turned her head to meet his, managing a drowsy smile. "I'm sorry," she whispered. "How long have I been away from the meeting?"

Robert looked at his watch. "About an hour and a half."

Danielle's eyes widened in alarm. She tried to rise up, but Robert pushed her back down. "You've got to get back!" she gasped.

"It's all right," Robert soothed. "Now that you're awake, I'll get back down there and leave you in good hands." He motioned to a woman seated in a nearby corner. "Mrs. Jensen here will see to any need you'll have. She'll send for me if necessary. Don't worry about the meeting; they don't have a quorum with us gone. Leatherwood can't push anything through in our absence."

"No," Danielle rasped, this time succeeded in lifting up and grabbing his coat. "You've forgotten. They *do* have a quorum." She paused, breathing heavily and fighting to clear her head. "At a stockholders' meeting, the quorum is established once, at the beginning of the meeting. After that, no matter how many people leave, the quorum stands. If Leatherwood reconvened the meeting . . . ." She paused, pulling on his coat, her intense gaze burning into him. "You've got to get back there!"

Eli Leatherwood had waited precisely forty-six minutes before sending a messenger out of the meeting to ostensibly ask Robert for instructions. What the rest of the crowd didn't know was that the messenger had been told to go nowhere near Robert and Danielle's room, but to simply disappear. After twenty minutes more, Leatherwood pointedly looked at his watch, then got up at the head of the room and raised his hands for silence.

"Ladies and gentlemen," he intoned soberly, "the day grows late. The messenger has not returned. Can we really afford to wait any longer? We don't know if this deal will still be good tomorrow. What do you say, should we re-convene and vote on this most generous offer?"

There was a chorus of agreement, but among the noise a few grumbles could clearly be heard.

"I don't like going against the Angel," one stockholder said.

"Amen to that," said another. "Mrs. Wilson's always been real square with us. It ain't right to cross her."

"Yeah," said another. "Kathleen Wilson would never go for this."

"I understand your concerns, gentlemen," Leatherwood said soothingly. "But we don't know that. Everyone stands to profit from this proposal, most of all, as majority stockholders, the Wilsons. I'm not sure she would reject this new offer. It's considerably better than the last. Why, she might even be disappointed in us if, in her absence, we let this deal get away. I have it on good authority the offer is being made for a limited time only. Can we really afford to let it go? No one knows when the Wilsons will return. Now, you're all being offered an excellent price for your shares, *and* the opportunity to become part owners in the Central Pacific, the most dynamic enterprise the west has ever seen! Ladies and gentlemen, there was never anything like the transcontinental railroad, and there never will be again. Now's the time to join up, and take advantage of the growth to come. What do you say, should we, as Mr. MacLendon said, *get on board*?"

There was more discussion, and plenty of misgivings expressed, but in the end, a vote was taken on Stanford's offer. And, by the narrowest of margins, greed carried the day. By the time Robert returned to the meeting, the Sierra and Western Railroad had become part of the Central Pacific.

* * *

The rickshaw carrying Megan rolled along the dirt street underneath gray skies. The humidity was oppressive. Megan could see that the one in which she was carried was following one carrying Yang. After about a block they turned uphill, but the pace did not slacken as an additional man joined the first one in pulling the long poles protruding from each rickshaw. The rest of the men jogged along on either side. They proceeded up the hill for about ten minutes, twisting and turning along various streets. Megan quickly became disoriented in the unfamiliar surroundings. In the few times she looked up, she noticed that people they passed on the streets bowed respectfully. She knew some of them noticed her; she was sure of it. But there was no visible reaction on their faces.

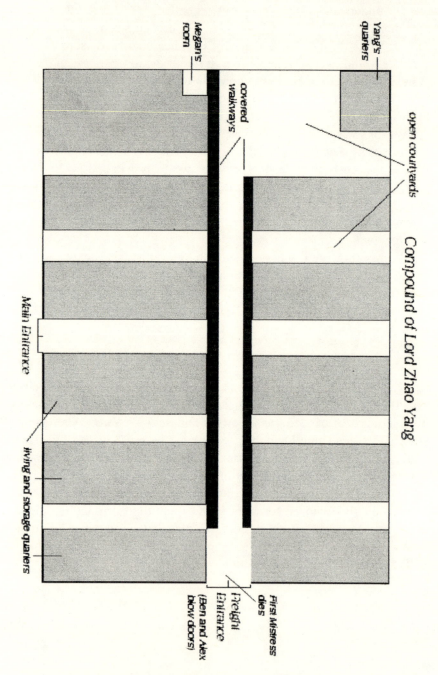

The rickshaws at last came to a halt on a hill high above the harbor. Megan was ordered out, helped to the ground by the men who had flanked her on the rickshaw seat. She stood in the street, feeling abandoned and lost. She noticed that they had come to a halt in front of the entrance to a large walled villa. Yang barked orders to his assistants, then ascended the low stone steps to the large wooden doors and went inside.

The two men who had ridden with Megan led her up the steps and inside, where they entered a spacious waiting room. There they halted while the rest of the men walked off down a hallway. Megan stood silently, nearly sick with fear.

They waited for long minutes. The men with her said nothing. Finally Megan heard the sound of approaching footsteps from the hallway. A group of about ten Chinese women appeared before her. Three were regally dressed, while the others were clothed very plainly. It was clear she was seeing women of high station and their servants.

The well-dressed women looked at her with seeming amazement. They circled around her, gesturing and chattering in Chinese. After a minute or two, one of them, a tall, imperious-looking woman, sharp-featured and older than the rest, issued an abrupt command, and then turned her back and stalked off down the hallway, accompanied by the other well-dressed women. Megan was poked and prodded into motion by the remaining servants, and swept along down the dark hallway.

As they emerged from the hallway to walk along long covered porches, Megan had the impression that she was being held in some sort of large complex consisting of a series of rectangular buildings connected to each other in a manner that formed several interior courtyards. The two courtyards she saw in her swift passage were bare, devoid of ornamentation except for large paper lanterns hanging from the roof eves. Her gaze swept across the tile roofs to adjoining buildings, then a stern reprimand in Chinese from one of the women unmistakably warned her to keep her eyes down.

After about five minutes of walking, her escorts ushered her through a doorway, where the procession came to a halt in a small room. The women began chattering animatedly among themselves, poking and prodding at her. Then they began trying to unbutton her dress at the top. Distraught, Megan clutched her dress tightly beneath her chin and pushed their hands away, bringing a sharp scolding. The women were berating her like harpies when two of the elegantly dressed women returned.

Silence was immediate. The five women who had escorted Megan bowed to the two, then, at a sharp command from one of them, backed away from her.

The two well-dressed women halted a few feet away from Megan and stared at her as she stood, head down, clutching her dress tightly. Then they began to circle her, eyes roving over every inch of her body.

81

When they had completed a full circle, they stopped. The older of the two approached closer. "What is your name?" she said.

Megan looked up in surprise. "You speak English?"

"Yes. I am Second Mistress. Obey me. You will answer the question."

Megan's lip trembled, then she said softly, "Megan. My name is Megan."

The woman's eyes narrowed. "What does it mean, this *May-gan?*"

Megan looked at her in confusion. "It—it doesn't mean anything. It's just a name."

The woman turned to the other woman who had arrived with her, and they chattered in Chinese briefly. Then she turned a disapproving gaze back to Megan. "Your clothes are unacceptable. You will take them off."

"But—" Megan protested.

"Take them off! You must be prepared for Master Yang. We will give you proper attire. Now do as your are told, at once."

Megan hesitated, then, sensing it was a hopeless situation, dropped her arms. The servant women who had escorted her quickly rushed in and began removing her clothes. The other well-dressed woman with whom Second Mistress had spoken, who appeared very young, came forward and spoke to her in a softer voice.

"I Third Mistress," she said. "You not be alarmed. We give new clothes. Ones you have offend nose and must burn. You—" She stopped, eyes wide. The chattering servant women had grabbed hold of Megan's chemise at the shoulders and carelessly ripped it open. She stood naked from the waist up.

The Chinese women stared in silent astonishment. They had never seen such a body. Megan's big globes mocked their comparatively flat chests. There was a slight chill in the room, causing her nipples to become erect.

After a few moments, they seemed to recover and drew closer, staring at her breasts in wonder and chattering rapidly in Chinese. Embarrassed, Megan tried to cover herself with her arms. The servant women tried to pull her arms away, poking at her breasts. She twisted away from them, crying in protest.

Suddenly there was a loud command in Chinese from the other side of the room, and all the women sprang away from Megan. The tall, imperious-looking Chinese woman Megan had seen at the entrance walked in. The woman who had identified herself as Third Mistress leaned toward Megan and whispered, "It is First Mistress. You no anger her!"

There was complete silence as First Mistress walked slowly toward the group. All the women bowed to her. Megan remained turned away, arms clutched against her chest. First Mistress walked up to her, a severe look on her Oriental features. With a wave of her hand, she made the other women back off. She barked a command at Megan.

"She wishes you turn around," Third Mistress said.

Megan slowly complied.

First Mistress motioned for Megan to drop her arms. When Megan did so, the woman's eyes widened in wonder. She leaned forward, staring at Megan's large breasts. Then, apparently unsure they were real, she reached out a hand and squeezed the left one.

Megan brushed the hand away.

First Mistress slapped her.

Suddenly furious despite her circumstances, Megan balled up her fist and slugged her as the other women gasped in horror.

First Mistress went down hard on her back. "Cow bosom slut!" she screeched in Chinese. Stumbling to her feet, she came at Megan, fingers outstretched to claw and scratch.

No longer intimidated, Megan snatched up a bamboo pole leaning against the wall nearby and brandished it in both hands, ready to swing it at First Mistress's head. The two glaring women circled each other.

They circled for several seconds when a shout from the back of the room froze everyone. All the Chinese women turned and bowed low. Lord Yang stood in the doorway. He frowned angrily at the women. "What is this?" he said sternly, walking up to them.

"Fourth Mistress is disobedient," said First Mistress, still bowing.

He looked at her with contempt. "What do you expect? She is *yi*[5]. She knows no better." He brusquely ordered First Mistress and Second Mistress to stand erect. "You will teach her. You will prepare her. Treat her harshly and you will answer to me. Is this clear?"

"Yes, Master!" First and Second Mistresses said in unison.

"See that it remains so," the man said. For the first time, he set his gaze solely on Megan. Clasping his hands behind his back, he walked slowly around her, eyes roving up and down. Megan stood silently with her head down, knowing she did not dare resist this man as she had the women. She was ashamed of her nakedness, but there was nothing she could do. After a few tense moments, the man spoke to one of the servant women, who then lifted up the pieces of Megan's ruined chemise and thrust it at her. Megan clutched it to herself, covering her breasts.

---

[5]   uncultured

"There is no need to shame her," he said. "Little can be expected of a barbarian until she is properly taught. First Mistress!" he said, turning to the tall woman.

She bowed. "Yes, Master."

"This room is unfit for removing her clothes. Take her to your quarters and see that she is washed and dressed. Take Third Mistress to assist you."

"Yes, Master."

He turned to go. "Prepare her and see that she is well fed and rested. I will receive her tomorrow morning first thing. Second Mistress, you will accompany me now."

"Yes, Master!" the women chorused. Megan was left alone with the First and Third Mistresses. First Mistress looked at her with undisguised contempt, then turned on her heel and walked off.

"Come," Third Mistress said.

Megan followed her. They walked past another empty courtyard, down another covered walkway, and entered a room behind First Mistress. They came to a stop in the center of the room.

First Mistress looked at Megan as if finding her unworthy of her attention. "Third Mistress, you will bathe her. I will select new clothes for her to put on when she is clean." With that, the woman turned and walked out of the room.

Third Mistress approached Megan and gave her a faint smile. Megan could see that she was very young, probably still a teenager. Her face had a soft beauty Megan desperately wanted to find comfort in.

"You new Fourth Mistress of House of Yang," the girl said. "It is great honor. Master Yang go to great expense to select you."

"What—what happened to the last Fourth Mistress?" Megan inquired softly.

Third Mistress hung her head and looked at the floor. "She disobedient. They hang her. Very sad."

Megan's lip trembled and tears streaked down her cheeks. "I—I can't be Fourth Mistress," she sobbed. "I have a young daughter. And a husband."

Third Mistress gave a tight-lipped grimace. "You be wise not to speak of such things again. Master be most angered. Your place here now. Do you understand this?"

After a moment, Megan nodded.

"Now," the woman said, "I prepare bath water." She brought a large shallow pan from one corner and set it in the center of the room. Then she retrieved a bucket full of water from the same corner, poured it into the pan, and motioned for Megan to step out of her dress and into the pan.

Heartsick, Megan loosened the remnants of her dress and let it and her chemise drop to the floor.

The young Chinese woman gasped at sight of the silky red delta of hair between her thighs. "You different," she murmured in amazement. "Chinese women are not so. Are there many women like you among *gweilo*?"

'What does that word mean?" Megan said.

"It means foreigner, devil man."

"Yes, there are plenty others like me."

"Aiee," the woman breathed softly, shaking her head in amazement. When Megan was standing in the pan of water, Third Mistress brought over a large sea sponge and proceeded to give her a thorough sponge bath. The water was cold.

Megan didn't resist, but after a few minutes, she said quietly, "My mother and husband will come for me."

"What was that?" Third Mistress said, stopping briefly.

"My mother is coming for me. She will come to retrieve me."

Third Mistress reflected for a moment. "She is powerful woman, your mother?"

"Very powerful. She commands great respect among men, great influence among many people. She gives no quarter to those who wrong her. Men who tried to kill her in the past are dead. She is to be feared," Megan said, feeling bolder. "She will slay those who have wronged me. When she arrives, nothing will stop her. She will come like the hurricane."

"What is hurr—hurri—?"

"A great storm. She will come like a great storm."

Third Mistress's expression sobered and she said nothing more, finishing the sponge bath in silence.

First Mistress arrived with some loose-fitting simple garments that she ordered Megan to don. Then Third Mistress took her out the door, down to the other end of the building, and into an unoccupied room. It was furnished with a sleeping mat and two tables made of bamboo, plus a large chest along one wall. One of the tables held a small oil lamp, which flickered in a slight current of air coming in the window. A sturdy bamboo latticework covered the window, which was flanked by shutters. Two paintings of Oriental scenes adorned the walls. The floor was covered with bamboo mats. "This room yours for now. Later you be moved to room closer to Master Yang."

A servant woman entered with a tray containing three covered dishes, a cup, and a teapot. She set the tray on one of the tables, bowed, and departed.

"Here is food," Third Mistress said. "You must eat, then rest. Master Yang will see you in the morning." She turned and went to the door, where she paused. "Please, Fourth Mistress, you not think of escape. There are guards, and you surely fail. I not want see you punished. Soon you see it is honor to be part of this great house." With that, she went out, silently closing the door behind her.

Megan sank down on the sleeping mat, numb, and buried her head in her hands. Quickly the tears came and her body shook with great sobs. Ignoring the food, she curled up into a fetal position and clutched a pillow, pretending it was Bridget. "Mama," she cried. "Alex. Please come for me. Please."

But in the morning she was not taken to see Master Yang. Second Mistress came into the room and roughly shook her awake. "Wake, barbarian woman. Master has been called away on urgent business. He may be gone for some time. But we must begin your education while he is gone."

Megan groggily rose to a sitting position.

Second Mistress regarded her with pursed lips. "I do not know why Master desires a *gweilo* woman. It is an insult to have you here. I do not think you can be taught to act properly. You will only bring disgrace to the house."

"Then let me go," Megan said.

"Hold your tongue. That is one of the first things you must learn. You will obey the Master, First Mistress, myself, and Third Mistress, in that order. You must not question what you are told to do. Your duty is only to obey. Do you understand?"

"Perfectly."

"Good. Now, you may use this basket"—she plopped a dark basket in front of her—"to relieve yourself. Then you will come with me. All the Mistresses eat together." She turned and lifted the covers on the food dishes. "You did not eat last night. You will do so this morning. Disobedience will not be tolerated!"

Emerald Isle sailed into Victoria Harbour at midmorning of a beautiful July day. She dropped anchor not far offshore, dwarfing most of the other ships around her.

Kathleen stood on the foredeck, gaze roving around the harbor. She strained to see into the last remnants of morning mist that hid some of the ships from view. The harbor was full of ships—British warships, paddle steamers, and opium clippers. She caught a whiff of what smelled like rotting vegetables on a faint gust of air. She wrinkled her nose and looked questioningly at Captain Rowan, who had walked up to join her.

"Opium," he said. "It can smell like that. One of the ships nearby probably has a hold packed with it."

"Have you seen *Red Rover* yet?" she said.

"No, but it's a big harbor."

They stood looking out across the harbor, and were joined by Ben and Alex, who had been searching from the starboard rail. The last of the morning mist faded away.

"There!" Alex shouted, pointing ahead and slightly to port.

"I see her," Kathleen said. *Red Rover* was resting at anchor about three hundred yards off. No crew was visible on her deck.

"We've got to get over there," Kathleen said.

"You're not going," Ben said. "It could be dangerous. Captain Rowan, lower a boat. Give me two men on the oars, and Alex and I will go over. Alex, arm yourself. Kathleen, while we're gone send a messenger ashore to inquire about an audience with Mr. Mercer. If we can, we'll depart as soon as we return."

Kathleen wasn't happy, but she complied. Rowan produced a small boat and two burly seamen. The boat was lowered over the side and they rowed off toward *Red Rover*. When they reached the sleek hull, all was silent above. No one answered their call. One of the seamen tossed a lightweight boarding ladder over the railing, and they climbed up to the deck. As they began to walk forward, a man emerged from belowdecks.

He stopped and stared at them. He had shaggy hair and squinty eyes, and was missing several front teeth. "Who be you?" he said. "And what's your business on this ship?"

Ben put a hand on the butt of his pistol. "Where's Parmenter?"

The man rubbed his chin, appearing to be shaking off sleep. "I don't know. He left the ship at dawn when we made port and ain't come back."

"When was that?" Alex said.

"Two days ago this morning."

Alex looked at Ben. "We gained two days on her on the open sea. It wasn't enough."

"Every day helps," Ben said.

Alex turned back to the man. "Was a woman brought in on this ship?"

The man gave him an evasive look. "What sort of woman?"

Alex took a step forward, towering over the man. "A white woman. With red hair."

The man crossed his arms over his chest and hesitated for a moment. Then he spoke. "Aye. She was aboard. Who be ye?"

Alex was shaking with anger. "I'm her husband. Where is she?"

"I figgered someone would come after her," the man said. "It were plain she weren't no willing passenger."

Alex stepped forward, grabbed the man by the shirt, and shook him like a rag doll. "Where is she?" he shouted.

"Gone!" the man said. "Parmenter took her with him. What he did with her after they left the ship I don't know. Lay off me!"

Alex pushed him back roughly. "Was she mistreated during the voyage?"

"Not by the crew, by God," the man said, straightening his clothes. "As for what Parmenter did in her cabin, I can't say. But I do know the morning he left with her he had some wicked scratches on his face."

Alex looked at Ben, rage twisting his features.

"Does Jardine, Matheson know about this illegal use of their ship?" Ben asked.

"They do now," the man said. "They be lookin' for Parmenter too. But I don't expect they'll find him."

Ben put a hand on Alex's shoulder. "Let's get back to the ship."

Back on *Emerald Isle,* Ben broke the news to Kathleen. "Megan was taken ashore at dawn two days ago by Parmenter. From what we've learned, she didn't appear injured."

"Probably not," Kathleen said, voice heavy with bitterness. "Parmenter would want to keep her in good shape so she'd fetch the best price."

"Captain, are the men battle-ready?" Ben asked Rowan, who was standing nearby.

"Aye, Mr. Wilson, that they are. Armed to the gills, weapons primed, and hungry to spill some blood to bring Miss Megan back, if they have to. They seem very dedicated to her."

"She's well loved," Kathleen said. "There are men below who'd give their life for her. Let us pray they don't have to."

"Bring the Gatling guns up on deck," Ben told Captain Rowan. "We don't want to cause a stir just yet, so keep them covered. Now that we're in port, we won't need to lash them in place. Let's keep them mobile in case we need to move them about the deck."

They sat discussing strategies and opinions for another hour, and then were interrupted by the return of the messenger Kathleen had sent to Governor House to inquire about an audience with William Mercer. The young man handed Kathleen a note written on official-looking stationery.

Kathleen broke the wax seal on the note and opened it. She read in silence for a few seconds, her expression darkening. "He can't meet with us until tomorrow," she said, looking up. "Eleven o'clock."

"We'll have to go with that," Ben said. "Let's not try to push things yet."

"I'll push them all the way to Peking if I have to to get my daughter back," Kathleen said with barely controlled fury.

"The pushing can come when we know more," Ben replied. "But that doesn't mean we have to sit and wait today. Let's go ashore and make a little visit to Jardine, Matheson, and Company. Hsien Lu will come with us and begin poking around on his own."

They all went ashore less than an hour later. Hsien Lu went off, with the understanding he would not return to the ship until he had news of Megan. The other three went in search of *Red Rover*'s owners.

They found the headquarters of Jardine, Matheson and Company along the waterfront on Des Voeux Road. It was a large rectangular building, three stories in height. The bottom floor had a façade consisting of a series of arched openings which were filled by barred latticework. The top two floors boasted roofed verandahs all around, the roofs being supported by white columns done in the Doric style. The building was topped with a tiled roof.

During the meeting with Jardine, Matheson officials, it soon became clear that they were caught as much off guard as anyone by Parmenter's actions, and were equally in the dark as to where he might be.

"Rest assured, we're looking for him, Mrs. Wilson," one of the officials said. "We'll do our best to make sure he doesn't ship out on one of our vessels. And we'll solicit cooperation from our competitors for the same. But Parmenter may very well be already off the island. He's got a lot of options."

"Undoubtedly," Kathleen said. "But in any case, he's not our immediate concern. Wherever he is, wherever he goes, his time will come."

That night, Ben and Kathleen stood at the rail onboard the ship, looking at the dim lights of Victoria visible across the water. Kathleen leaned tight against her husband, head on his arm.

"She's out there somewhere, Ben. I know it."

"Can you feel her presence, like you did with Two Moons years ago?"

Kathleen leaned forward, elbows on the rail. "No, not yet. I'm just going on a mother's intuition right now." She turned her face to him, eyes wet. "Oh, Ben, this is the second time she's been taken from me. It's just not fair. I miss my girl so much." She wrapped her arms around him and didn't seem to want to let go.

He held her in silence for long minutes. Then he gently pushed her back and lifted her chin up. "I love you, Kathleen. More and more each year. I swear I'll move heaven and earth if I have to to get Megan back for you. And for me. I'll never give up." He bent down and kissed her tenderly, hands stroking her ebony hair.

She returned the kiss, then started trembling and broke away. She forced a grin, and fished in a pocket of her coat, withdrawing what looked like a bracelet. "Look, I brought Megan's wrist rosary. When I see her again, the first thing I'll do is—" She broke off, and put a hand to her mouth. "I, ah—it's late. I'm going below and give this rosary a workout." She stretched her face up to his and kissed him again briefly. "I love you. I'll see you later."

A heavy blanket of humidity cloaked Victoria under gray skies the following morning as Ben, Kathleen, and Alex rode in a rented carriage toward the Governor's residence. Kathleen took in the unfamiliar passing scene in silence. She saw small mirrors hanging outside shops and restaurants, and now and then small shrines of stones adorned with ribbons, red paper, and candles. She couldn't guess their purpose.

The dirt streets thronged with Chinese—merchandise hawkers with pack ponies, boys riding water buffaloes, coolies carrying bundles or pots slung on long poles across their shoulders, and countless others going about a dozen different things. The coolies wore wide-brimmed, bamboo-weave hats with conical tops, and were dressed in knee-length skirt-like garments belted at the waist.

She noticed the bigger, fancier buildings were a mishmash of foreign styles—Indian, British, Italian, and others she didn't recognize. Captain Rowan had told her these were residences of wealthy Britons, who were fond of imitating other cultural influences.

The carriage rolled up at last to an imposing building, and they stepped to the ground. They entered through ornate polished doors, and were received by a liveried servant. After a wait of about ten minutes, they were ushered into the Governor's office, precisely at eleven o'clock.

William Mercer came to Hong Kong when he was only twenty-two. He had studied law without taking the bar exam, and was the nephew of Sir John Davis, who served as Colonial Governor from 1844 to 1848. In 1847 he replaced J. W. Hulme as Chief Justice of the Supreme Court in Hong Kong, and later served as Colonial Secretary. Described as "gentlemanly and scholarly" by his peers, he nevertheless had not been appointed Governor of the colony, a title he dearly wanted.

Ben, Kathleen, and Alex found themselves facing a tall man with a full beard, heavy eyelids, and a long straight nose. He greeted them warmly and bade them be seated.

"I am familiar with your company, Mr. and Mrs. Wilson," he began. "Your ships often grace our harbor, although I am delighted to see that this time you've brought your magnificent flagship. She is certainly a most beautiful vessel."

"Thank you, Mr. Mercer," Kathleen said. "I fear we must attend to the purpose of our visit quickly. We are here on a matter of great urgency. My daughter Megan was kidnapped in San Francisco and brought here on a clipper ship owned by Jardine, Matheson, and Company."

Mercer's eyes widened. "You're sure of this?"

"These facts are well established, Mr. Mercer. We have learned she was taken ashore three days ago from *Red Rover* by Captain Parmenter. We believe the purpose of this crime is to sell her to a Chinese lord. That has probably already happened."

Clearly taken aback, Mercer rose slowly and walked to a large window that overlooked the harbor.

"Can you give us some idea about who might wish to buy her, Mr. Mercer, and why?" Kathleen said.

Mercer stared out at the harbor scene for a long silent moment before turning back to them. "There is no shortage of candidates," he said. "A Triad lord would certainly have the resources. As to why, I cannot guess."

"What are Triads?" Ben said.

"Criminal societies. They've been here almost since the beginning. Some of the Triad lords are very wealthy. And they are quite formidable." He turned back to the window.

91

"The Chinese," he continued, "are a contemptible lot. There is nothing to admire in their culture, not one thing. And they have an arrogant conviction that every Chinese ever born is superior to every foreigner. Dealing with them is a constant headache. They have an ancient custom of selling girls as servants. The practice is called *mui tsai*, which means 'little sister'. It brings money to poor families with numerous girls to support. There is also considerable traffic in kidnapping girls for transport to other parts of the Orient. What the purpose of that might be, I will not speculate on in your company, Mrs. Wilson. But it would appear one of the local lords has decided to take their customs a step further."

'What can you do for us, Mr. Mercer?" Alex said.

"I see that *Red Rover* is still in port," he replied. "I will have every crew member questioned at length to gather what information we can. I will marshal what forces I can spare to join in the hunt for Captain Parmenter. But I fear my resources are indeed limited. The financial state of the colony is in decline."

"We appreciate whatever effort you can mount," Kathleen said.

"I should warn you, Mrs. Wilson, gentlemen," Mercer continued. "Though our Captain Elliot declared in 1841 that protection would be given to all foreigners, and we try our best to honor that, Hong Kong and the surrounding waters are dangerous places. Piracy is an everyday occurrence. There is one pirate, an American named Eli Boggs, who is particularly troublesome. He has a fleet of about thirty armed junks. And Victoria is dangerous at night, though I am pleased to report we installed gas street lighting this past January. Outside the city it is unsafe even in the daytime. No European ventures abroad without a revolver. Since you are unfamiliar with the area, I suggest you let me investigate. If I can find out who is holding her, I will lend my full authority toward negotiating for her release."

Ben rose, anger evident on his broad face. "We didn't come to negotiate."

"Negotiate!" Kathleen said, cheeks flushed with outrage. She rose and stood by her husband. "Mr. Mercer, we came prepared for whatever is necessary to get my daughter back. There are two hundred fighting seamen on *Emerald Isle*, armed to the teeth and spoiling for a fight. We also carry ten cannon, including two sixty-eight pounders, and two Gatling guns. We're prepared to use them. If it will help, we may well lob a few cannon balls onto Jardine, Matheson's second floor verandah." She rose and went to the door. "We are deeply grateful for whatever assistance you can provide, sir. But we intend to move aggressively on our own. Time is not on our side."

Two days had passed, and Yang did not return. Megan was ordered this way and that. The servants deferred to her, though with obvious distaste. It was clear none of the women shared the Master's desire to have a barbarian in the house. Megan often complied sullenly with the teachings they attempted to impose on her, and the obviously irritated First Mistress sometimes berated her lack of progress, particularly in learning dining protocols.

"Stupid woman!" she said one day. "Master is foolish; you will never be an acceptable mistress. Your barbarian manners are offensive. Try harder!"

The shock of the rape had abated somewhat, and Megan's Irish temper was beginning to reassert itself. Several times she stifled the urge to strangle the imperious woman, but more often than not, the rebukes brought her near tears.

As time passed, Megan fell into increasingly prolonged spells of depression. She ate little of the strange food they put before her, though she was constantly pushed to eat more. Most nights she cried herself to sleep. Hope withered within her. Desperately she clung to the one positive in her captive life: it soon became evident she had a sympathetic friend in Third Mistress. Megan observed that although the girl often talked of the honor of belonging to Master Yang, she didn't seem to believe it herself, and was not entirely happy with her lot. Despite Third Mistress's sometimes-imperfect grasp of English, the two women fell into girl talk in idle moments. Megan figured she would learn all she could from the teenager, hoping to glean some information that would aide in her escape.

"How is it you and the other mistresses speak English?" she said one day.

"Master learn English to help him in his business. He command us to learn also as matter of prestige. First and Second Mistresses speak well. I not speak so good yet."

Megan smiled. "You do very well. I have no trouble understanding you."

Third Mistress smiled back. "You are kind, for barbarian."

Megan was puzzled. "Why do you say that? Did you think we are cruel?"

"Oh, Fourth Mistress! I did not mean to offend. Please forgive me. It just that we are taught that foreign devils are—are—"

"Uncivilized? Ill-mannered? Ignorant heathens?"

Third Mistress hung her head. "Yes," she said softly.

Megan put a hand on her shoulder. "It's all right. We are told the same about you."

The girl looked at her with mild astonishment that someone could contemplate such a thing. After a moment, she seemed to recover and said, "Fourth Mistress, tell me about mother."

"My mother? Why?"

"I know little of your world," the girl said. "I want to know what women like there."

Megan smiled. "Well, I'm not sure telling you about Mother will help you know what Western women are like. Because she's like no other woman I know." She paused in reflection for a moment. "It's hard to know where to start. She came to America as a young married woman from a country called Ireland, in 1847. She had a husband named Terry." Megan paused and looked down. "My father."

"Fourth Mistress, I not want to cause pain."

"I was very young when we came to America," Megan said, waving a hand. "We moved west in search of gold in 1849. We were nearly to the gold fields when my father was killed by an Indian."

"Indi—what is In-di-an?"

"Savage people that lived in America before white people came. They fought us hard to keep their land. And they lost." She sighed, and continued. "Just after my father was killed, the same Indian who did it stole me from my mother. My mother went after him with no weapons. She didn't need any. She had herself. She went to his camp and dared him to either return me or kill her. He was afraid to try. I think she scared him. He was afraid she might be a demon—an evil spirit. But in the years that followed, he tried twice more to kill her, and failed. The last time, she killed him, even though he put an arrow in her chest. She refused to die. Later, two other men who tried to harm her and her children were also killed. She destroyed the property of still another." She turned and looked at the teen girl. "My mother does not forgive those who wrong her or her family. When she comes for me, those who have done this will pay."

Third Mistress was silent, eyes big with wonder.

Hsien Lu spent his first day in Victoria reacquainting himself with the town. He had first come there as a boy of about ten—he wasn't sure of his age—when he had no longer seen any reason to stay at home. His father had succumbed to opium addiction, and his mother had sunk into a torpid listlessness. Hsien Lu thought perhaps he could find work among the foreign devils who were increasingly numerous along the coast of China, and send some money back home.

He had indeed found work, starting out at the lowest possible position with the powerful merchant Yuen Ling-Po. He had exhibited unswerving loyalty and fearlessness, and Ling-Po had rewarded him with the best training in hand to hand combat. When Ling-Po decided it would be better to emigrate to America, Hsien-Lu had gone with him. He had sent money home until receiving word his mother had passed away five years after he left. Over the ten years since he had left home, the slender boy had been transformed into a thickly muscled man with formidable fighting skills.

He found Victoria had gained little in class in his absence. He passed squatters' huts, rundown theaters, schools, opium dens, duck pens, pigsties, and gambling halls. He saw little that looked familiar. Then it occurred to him that the best place to start would be where Megan was most likely to have been seen when she was brought ashore.

In the early morning of the second day, he walked along the waterfront, looking at *Red Rover* riding in the gentle harbor swells. It made sense that Parmenter would want to ferry Megan ashore as quickly as possible, and so choose the shortest route from ship to shore. He identified that spot and headed for it. Once there, he strolled up and down, taking in everything carefully. On his second pass through the area, he spotted an old fisherman seated at the edge of the pier, legs dangling over the water, a net in his lap in the process of being mended.

He knew fishermen were creatures of habit, and also that anything unusual in the harbor would most likely not escape their notice. He approached the man and greeted him.

The old man did not even look up, but continued his mending. But when he heard the metallic rasp of a saber being withdrawn from its scabbard, he stopped. Glancing up, he turned pale. He knew a dangerous man when he saw one, and the frowning visage on the heavily muscled warrior before him made his heart start pounding. He sprang to his feet, surprisingly quick for one of such advanced age, and bowed. "Greetings, Honorable Stranger. Please forgive my rudeness."

Hsien Lu let the saber slide back into its scabbard. "Old One, I seek information. Were you at this spot two mornings ago, about this time?"

"Yes, Honorable One."

"I am Hsien Lu."

"Yes, Honorable Hsien Lu. I was here."

"Did you observe anything unusual?"

"Indeed I did, Honorable Hsien Lu. Very early, just as the morning mists were lifting, a sampan carrying three foreign devils appeared. It was rowed to the pier, there," he pointed to a spot about thirty yards away.

"Was one of the foreign devils in the sampan a woman?" Hsien Lu said.

"Yes, Honorable Hsien Lu. A most beautiful woman with hair the color of flame."

Hsien Lu's heartbeat accelerated. "What else did you notice?"

"Her wrists were bound. She climbed the ladder with some difficulty."

"What then?"

"The two foreign devils with her took her into that warehouse," he said, pointing to a large nearby building. "After that I saw them no more. I left to fish."

"Very well," Hsien Lu said. "You have been most helpful." He turned to go, but the old fisherman took a step forward.

"Might this information be worth something, Honorable Hsien Lu? Might there be a reward for my sharp eyes?"

Hsien Lu paused. "There may be. But I can make no promises."

The old man bowed enthusiastically and returned to his net mending.

Hsien Lu approached the warehouse door. It was locked, but he broke the lock with his saber. Quietly opening the door, he stepped inside.

The warehouse was deserted. Shafts of sunlight coming from high openings in the wall illuminated isolated spots in the otherwise gloomy interior. He could make out the dim shapes of barrels and bales of cotton. Slowly he walked around, eyes scanning walls and floor. He was about to leave when he caught sight of something to one side, next to a bale. He walked over and knelt down, reaching to pick it up. There were two objects, and as he lifted them he saw that they were short lengths of rope. There was still a knot in each piece, and they had been cleanly cut apart. It was the kind of rope one might use to bind someone's wrists.

Two hours later Hsien Lu was back aboard *Emerald Isle* showing the rope segments to Kathleen, Ben, and Alex.

"I think these were used to bind her wrists," he said. "I found them in the place she was last seen by the old fisherman."

"Why would Parmenter do that?" Alex said. "Did he think she was dangerous?"

"Megan is intelligent," Kathleen said. "She wouldn't needlessly endanger herself if she knew the situation was hopeless. But she will fight if pushed hard enough, no matter what the circumstances. I think she fought him. I think he was forced to bind her wrists."

"I'm afraid to think what he did that caused her to fight," Alex said.

"So am I," Kathleen said. She rose from her seat and strode to the railing, looking out across the harbor vista. "Keep fighting, daughter," she whispered.

6.

After five days, Lord Yang returned late in the afternoon. He came immediately to Megan's quarters, accompanied by First Mistress. It was obvious he wished to see what progress had been made in transforming Megan into something he regarded as civilized.

"She is stubborn," First Mistress said. "I do not think she can learn. She clings to the barbarian ways." It was obvious the woman, considerably older than Megan and with a rather severe face, was jealous of the new arrival.

"She will learn," Yang said. "You will see to that. Now, even though she is ignorant, I wish to receive her in my bedchambers. Prepare her, and bring her there tomorrow afternoon at three o'clock."

"Yes, Master," First Mistress said coldly.

Megan felt like a piece of meat.

First Mistress left with a promise to return the next day to begin the preparations. Megan sank down on her sleeping mat in despair. She was still there when Third Mistress came in to inquire about her an hour later. She could see that Megan was despondent, and asked why.

Megan told her. "I suppose you think this is an honor too?" she said.

98

Third Mistress sat down beside her. "Megan," she said softly. It was the first time the girl had used her name. "It is way of things here. You must accept it."

"Is he gentle?"

Third Mistress hung her head. "Not always."

"I'll kill myself before I let him touch me." It was a notion that had visited Megan several times in the past week as she increasingly despaired of Kathleen's ever finding her.

Third Mistress's eyes grew wide with horror. "No, you must not! You bring great disgrace on you, on all of us."

"Oh, but it's not a disgrace to hang a woman because she was disobedient!" Megan shouted.

Third Mistress sank to her knees, pleading tearfully. "Please, Honorable Megan! You must not speak of this. We all be in danger. Please, I beg you, let us talk of something else!" Distraught, the girl seemed to have momentarily forgotten that her station was superior to Megan's. Her face twisted in fear, cheeks wet with tears.

Megan took pity on her and pulled her up from the floor. "Very well. Dry your eyes." She used the sleeve of her garment to wipe the girl's cheeks, and bade her sit next to her on the sleeping mat. Megan put a comforting arm around her. "Tell me," she said, "how you came to be here."

Third Mistress stopped crying. She was quiet for a moment, and Megan had the impression her thoughts were in a place and time far away. The girl raised her face, and stared at the wall in front of her. After a few moments, she began speaking. "I am last of five children. Others were boys. They marry, bring dowries to family. I was—was burden." She looked down. "Father say times hard. Father say—father say they no can afford me. But they could afford daughters-in-law." Her lip trembled, and Megan feared she might start crying again.

"Father meet Master Yang. I was fifteen. Master see me. He want." Her voice got very quiet; Megan could barely hear her. "Father say he sell me to Master. Mother, she cry. But Master offer good price. Father take money, bring me here. I never see family again."

Megan was sorry she'd asked.

The girl spoke again, barely audible, her face partially hidden between her arms. "Honorable Megan, this talk not make me happy. I stop."

"Yes, that's enough."

The girl suddenly lifted her face to Megan, anguish written on her features. "Honorable Megan, your powerful mother really come here?"

"Yes, she really will. No force on earth can stop her if she knows where I am."

Third Mistress looked directly into Megan's eyes. "Honorable Megan, you must obey rules of house. First Mistress jealous of you. She mean sometimes, but mostly fair. Obey her. It is Second Mistress you must fear most. She of noble family. She think it not right she not First Mistress. She always plotting, planning. And she make poisons just for fun. She very bad woman. Stay away from her."

Third Mistress rose to her feet. "I go now," she said, wiping her cheeks. "Rest well, and talk no more of killing. Tomorrow First Mistress prepare you for Master." With that, she was gone.

Megan sat in silence for a while. The hour was late, and she was tired. She sat with her chin on her knee, thinking. *I don't know if Mother can find me,* she thought. *Does she know where I am? I can't hold out much longer. Oh, Bridget, my daughter, I love you! Alex, I love you!* She rose and went to the window, looking out into the darkness through the latticework that held her in. *I won't be defiled again. I won't let that heathen have me. Tomorrow morning I'll take the knife I stole from the kitchen and slash my wrists.* She sank onto the mat and curled up into a tight ball. Wrestling with sleep for a long time, she finally succumbed out of weariness in the small hours of the morning. Her slumber was filled with bad dreams, and twice she awoke in a cold sweat.

Hsien Lu roamed the streets of Victoria on his third day of searching. He had started out from the waterfront warehouse, which he had learned was owned by Jardine, Matheson. Walking up and down the rutted dirt streets under gray skies, his penetrating gaze skewered passersby. Most stepped aside to avoid him as he methodically worked his way back and forth up the slope from the harbor. He stopped occasionally and questioned people he came across—coolies, merchants, young boys driving livestock—but no one had seen a red-haired woman being brought through the streets.

Or at least they claimed they hadn't. After numerous inquiries, it became evident to Hsien Lu that some of the Chinese he encountered *had* seen something. Their claims of ignorance were offered entirely too quickly. He decided it was time to apply a little more pressure.

He didn't want to threaten to lop off heads just yet. That would attract attention. He decided instead to resort to that most common of Hong Kong motivators, money. Kathleen had provided him with a handsome sum for just such a purpose, and now he reassuringly patted its bulk deep within a pocket.

Sunlight was fighting its way through the overcast as he spotted a merchant who had set up his stall on a side street, accosting passersby with a nonstop pitch. Pretending to be attracted to the merchant's wares, Hsien Lu ambled over and poked at various items on the table.

The merchant grinned, all fawning servility, displaying big yellow teeth. He bowed slightly. "Astute One, you obviously know superior wares when you see them," he said. "What do you seek today?"

Hsien Lu said nothing, continuing to casually examine this and that, taking his time.

The merchant began to do a little nervous dance behind the table. "Fine cloth?" he suggested. "Pottery? Barbarian trinkets? Knives?" He leaned closer and whispered conspiratorially. "Guns?" He glanced up and down the street. "I can acquire such things for you."

Hsien Lu picked up a teapot and handed it to the man, as if deciding to purchase. "I seek information."

The merchant took the teapot and payment from Hsien Lu and wrapped it in rice paper without missing a beat. "Information can also be had," he said, concentrating on his wrapping. "For a price."

"Price does not concern me," Hsien Lu said, "though I will not be taken advantage of."

The merchant bowed again. "Of course, Honorable Warrior. Information is kept inside. Please follow me." He motioned for Hsien Lu to follow him into the interior of the building behind him.

Hsien Lu followed him inside. No one else was about. The merchant bade him take a seat in a bamboo-weave chair beside a scarred wooden table, then set about retrieving teacups, and poured tea for both of them.

"Now," he said, sitting, "what information may I provide you with?"

Hsien Lu picked up his teacup, swirled the lightly colored liquid around a moment, and then, taking a sip, put the cup back down. He looked the merchant in the eye. "Several days ago, a white woman was brought ashore from a ship in the harbor. She was a prisoner. Her wrists were bound. She was taken into a warehouse owned by the English company, Jardine, Matheson. From there her path is unknown. It is believed she was, or will be, sold to a local person of wealth and influence, perhaps to become a mistress. Did you see her, or do you know of her passing?"

The merchant took a slow sip of his tea. "I may know of her."

"Either you do, or you do not," Hsien Lu said. "What will sharpen your memory?"

"Such information is dangerous to possess," the man said casually.

Hsien Lu glared at him. "Withholding it could be dangerous as well. You could lose your head."

The merchant feigned calm, but beads of sweat broke out on his forehead. "You place me in a difficult position. If I tell you, or I do not tell you, I could lose my head. I have no wish to meet my ancestors just yet."

Hsien Lu retrieved the cloth sack of gold coins from his pocket, and, placing it on the table, opened it. The gold gleamed invitingly in the dim light.

The merchant's eyes widened. "You know," he said, pouring more tea in both their cups, "I have been thinking of retiring to the mainland."

Hsien Lu picked two coins from the pile and shoved them across the table at the merchant.

He didn't hesitate to pocket them. "I did not see her," he said. "But I know where she is."

Less than half an hour later, Hsien Lu stood in the street, casually observing the high walls of the compound belonging to Lord Yang. It was a huge complex, stretching at least two long blocks up and down the slanted street, and fully as much deep. Guards stood outside the entrance. The merchant's tongue had loosened considerably when given half the contents of the sack of gold coins. Yang's status as a feared Triad Lord had kept gossip to a minimum. But there had been quiet talk in the neighborhood, behind closed doors, of the passage of the white woman. It had been impossible to get Megan into the compound without notice, and it was known in the neighborhood that she was there. Now Hsien Lu appraised the formidable walls before him, and the alert guards outside the entrance. If Megan was still inside, getting her out would not be easy.

First Mistress came to Megan's room early. As usual, she looked surly.

"It must be tough, being jealous of a barbarian," Megan needled her, spoiling for a fight.

"Silence," First Mistress said. "You will speak when I tell you to."

"Go to Hell," Megan said sweetly.

First Mistress didn't respond. She went back into the outer hallway and barked a command in Chinese. Four servant women entered. First Mistress gave them orders and then turned to Megan.

"I refuse to take part in preparing you for Master Yang. Let the servant women see what they can do with you. If you are found unsuitable, it will please me."

"Why must you hate me?" Megan said in frustration. "I didn't want to come here!"

"But you *are* here," First Mistress said frostily. "And you will never take my place. I will see to that." She turned on her heel and left.

Megan was left with the servant women, who stripped her, washed her, and dressed her in a silk robe. They combed her hair carefully and made a try at applying some pale makeup, but it looked hideous on her, and they swiftly removed it. After fussing with her for nearly an hour, they were interrupted by the arrival of Second Mistress.

Second Mistress examined Megan with a critical eye. It was the first time Megan had seen her since her arrival four days earlier. She was under no illusions that the Chinese woman was any less hostile to her presence than First Mistress. Now Second Mistress circled her, looking her up and down. Finally, she spoke sharply to the servants, who scurried out.

Second Mistress turned to Megan. "Well, barbarian woman," she said coldly, "Master Yang still wishes to bed you. Do not think your cow bosoms will attract him. You will never be the equal of a Chinese woman. He will grow tired of you and your barbarian manners."

"Good," Megan said. "Then I can go back to my family."

Second Mistress smiled a chilly smile. "No. You belong to Master Yang, to do with as he pleases." She went to the door. "I will send Third Mistress to bring you to Master Yang. This is a duty more fit for her." With that, she went out and slammed the door.

Megan heard the *thunk* of a bar being levered into place, locking her in the room. It was not the first time they had done so. She didn't care. She didn't intend to be alive long enough to be shown into Master Yang's quarters. This was it. No more waiting and hoping. No one had come for her. They didn't know where she was, and couldn't help her. She would not allow herself to be violated again. Reaching under her sleeping mat, she pulled forth the kitchen knife she had stolen. She sank to the mat, legs underneath her, and drew back her left sleeve. She rested the knife blade on the pale underside of her wrist, feeling its sharpness. But before she could bear down, she heard the sound of the bar being withdrawn from her door. The door swung open just as she hid the knife under her robe.

Third Mistress entered. The young teen girl looked at Megan with a sober expression. "Fourth Mistress, it is time. Master Yang wait." She stood there expectantly.

Megan rose and followed her out the door, hand over the slight bulge in her robe caused by the knife handle. She walked silently behind Third Mistress, eyes seeking an escape. After a few minutes, they entered an area of the compound Megan hadn't yet been in. As they neared the end of one of the long covered porches, Megan saw her chance and ducked through a doorway. Swiftly she slammed the door shut behind her, and levered an interior bar into its brackets. She heard Third Mistress scream and pound on the door, and then a moment later the sound of swiftly fading footsteps. Wasting no time, she retreated from the door and withdrew the knife. She leaned against the wall near the room's one window, breathing heavily. Once again she drew up her sleeve. Trembling, she put the knife to her wrist. She bore down and saw a trickle of blood ooze out and drip to the floor. She raised her chin and drew in a deep breath, gathering strength to cut deeper. As she did, her gaze fell upon the open window. Through it, she could look out down a hill to the harbor below, not half a mile distant. For a moment, she was saddened by the thought that the last thing she would see was a foreign land, so far from her home and family. But something about the scene was prodding at her tortured mind. She stared harder—and froze. Her eyes widened and her breath suddenly caught in her throat. Then she gasped out a single word: "Mother." Down below, riding serenely in the gentle swells, sails neatly furled, was the familiar shape of *Emerald Isle.*

The door behind her shook with a thunderous blow, then burst inward, ripping the bar brackets from the wall. Two burly Chinese men rushed in and angrily seized her. One tore the knife from her hand. Behind them Megan could see Third Mistress, cheeks wet with tears.

Third Mistress entered, saw the blood dripping from Megan's wrist, and became even more distraught. She turned and spoke in an urgent tone to a servant woman who hovered outside the doorway. The woman rushed off and returned a moment later with a strip of clean cloth. The men released Megan but hovered close to her, scowling. First Mistress grasped Megan's arm and wound the cloth around the cut. The blood stopped dripping.

Third Mistress raised her face to look at Megan. "I tell you not do this," she said, voice full of fear. "You shame us. Now Master beat me!" But her face registered consternation as she saw that Megan was smiling at her, eyes gleaming. "You crazy!" she hissed.

Megan grabbed the girl by the arm, causing Third Mistress to jump in alarm. "No," Megan whispered. "Don't worry. My mother is here. Her ship is in the harbor."

Third Mistress began to tremble. "Your mother here?" She pulled away, wide-eyed. "She kill us all!"

"No," Megan said. "Only those I point out. And Yang's first on the list. Prepare yourself, little one. All Hell is going to break loose."

Third Mistress looked ready to dissolve into tears again. "Please, you come now. Master Yang in a rage!"

Megan followed docilely, her mind whirling. So her family was here. How long had they been here? Did they know where she was? There was no way to tell. She had to stall Yang, but how? As she followed Third

Mistress, flanked closely by the two scowling Chinese men, the glimmer of an idea began to form.

In the morning of their fourth day in port, Ben and Alex went to see William Mercer again. Kathleen remained on the ship at Ben's suggestion.

"Diplomacy is not one of your strengths, Kathy," Ben told her. "Let Alex and me handle this visit."

Kathleen was predictably unhappy, but relented.

Mercer's secretary told them he was busy; they would need to make an appointment.

"We'll wait," Ben said.

The secretary gave them an acid look, but let them wait. After an hour, they were shown in to see Mercer.

"It's good to see you again, Mr. Wilson, Mr. Daley," Mercer said, offering them a seat. "Have there been further developments regarding Mrs. Daley's whereabouts?"

"Yes," Ben said. "We have reliable information she's being held inside the compound of one Lord Yang."

Mercer paused, left hand stroking his beard. "Yang. I'm not surprised."

"You know him?" Alex asked.

"Yes," Mercer said, slowly striding to the window. After gazing out at the harbor scene for a moment, he turned back and looked at them. "Prominent Triad lord, opium merchant, friend of pirates, and all-around scoundrel. If Mrs. Daley is there, you would do well to extricate her at the earliest possible opportunity."

"That's what we intend to do," Ben said. "Do you know anything about the interior of his compound?"

"Unfortunately, no."

"Is he well protected?" Alex said.

"Quite," Mercer said. "He's got a sizable security force. And they're loyal, especially so in a place like Hong Kong where money can buy allegiance. You likely won't turn any of them."

Alex jumped to his feet and began pacing. "We've got to do something, fast."

"I will lend you what resources I can, gentlemen," Mercer said. "Please keep me informed of your plans. But our first effort had better succeed."

Alex felt a chill settle over him. "What do you mean?"

"Wealthy Triad lords like Yang have estates on the mainland as well. If he gets wind of an effort to retrieve Mrs. Daley, he may take her there. If he does, she will be beyond the reach of any force I can assemble."

Back on *Emerald Isle*, Ben relayed the news to Kathleen and Hsien Lu.

"I want her out *now*," Alex said.

Kathleen put a hand on his arm. "I understand fully, dear. But we can't simply go charging in there, guns blazing, much as I desire to. We need to plan our entry, and especially our exit."

"How can we?" Alex said. "We don't know what's on the other side of those walls."

"We need to make contact with someone on the inside," Kathleen said. "A servant, perhaps." She turned to Hsien Lu. "Dear friend, this is a task I must entrust to you. I want you to scout the walls of the compound. Make note of the smallest details. Look at entrances, guard schedules, comings and goings of people, everything. See if you can pick out someone coming from inside with whom we might make contact."

Hsien Lu gave her a sober look. "My Lady, I will not fail."

Megan was led by Third Mistress and her strong-arm escort to Master Yang's quarters. It was a large and lavish room, dimly lit by the glow of colored paper lanterns hanging from the ceiling. A big Western-style bed dominated one corner underneath a window letting in a broad shaft of sunlight. Bamboo-lattice screens with landscape scenes painted on them stood at various places around the walls. A large, luxurious rug lay at the foot of the bed. A lacquered tea table and elegant chairs sat to one side.

Third Mistress entered first and bowed low, then moved to the side. Yang dismissed the guards with a wave. He stepped forward, clearly unhappy. "Why was there a delay?" he asked Third Mistress in Chinese.

Third Mistress trembled and spoke in a halting voice. "Master, Fourth Mistress, she—she try to cut herself." The scared girl raised Megan's left sleeve to reveal the bloody cloth wrapping on her wrist.

Yang's eyes narrowed to slits and his jaw clenched. "She is not seriously injured?"

"No, Master," Third Mistress gasped, cringing in fear.

"Incompetent girl!" Yang snapped. "How could you let this happen? You will answer to me later. Begone."

Third Mistress bowed again and quickly shuffled out, tears streaking down her cheeks.

Megan stood alone before the Triad lord. The silk robe she had been dressed in was truly elegant. It was colored a brilliant shiny blue. Rampaging dragons masterfully embroidered in gold thread faced each other on the front. Megan's coppery-red hair glowed softly in the lantern light.

Yang approached to a few feet away. "Magnificent," he said in a barely audible voice. "You are breathtaking." He put a hand under her chin and raised her face, revealing her emerald-green eyes. "No Chinese woman is like this. I have long dreamed of such a moment."

Megan fought to keep her composure. "Why have you brought me here?" she said in a small voice.

Yang clasped his hands behind his back and walked around her. "For two reasons. One, it is well known that those who understand the *gweilo* best profit most. I hope that you will be able to instruct me in the ways of foreign devils, so that I may expand my businesses. And two, I simply wish to experience the moment of clouds and rain[6] with a barbarian woman, fresh from the West. It should be most delightful. Yes, you are so different. I will enjoy conquering you." He stopped and held out a hand. "Come, sit on my bed."

Megan moved forward on leaden feet, mind racing. She had to say something fast, or it would be too late. Numbly, she sat on the edge of the big bed. "Master Yang, how can you do this? I have a husband, and a young daughter who needs me."

"That is not my concern. You are mine now. I paid handsomely for you. Now, remove your robe. Or would you prefer I do it for you?"

Megan was down to her last card. "Master Yang, I am unworthy."

Yang frowned at her. "What do you mean?"

Megan bit her lip, hoping her words would be enough. "I am defiled."

Yang's eyes widened. "By whom?"

Megan hung her head, tears squeezing from the corners of her eyes. "Parmenter. He attacked me just before we reached port."

Yang raised her head, examining her face. "Yes, I can see by your expression it is true." He scowled murderously. "If he ever shows his face in Hong Kong again, his head will grace my wall." He turned from her and began to pace. "You must be examined by my physician. And you must be formally cleansed. And then"— he stopped pacing and looked at her—"then you will lie in my bed. Be sure of that."

---

[6]   sexual climax

"Yes, Master," Megan said, nearly weeping with relief. She had bought some time. Whether it would be enough, she would know soon.

"There is another matter," Yang said. "Someone is looking for you. There is word on the streets that a powerful man who carries a large saber has been questioning many people about your location."

The words struck Megan's mind like a bolt of lightning. *Hsien Lu!* she thought. *It has to be. He's here. Praise God.*

Yang was speaking again. "I will not take chances with you. You are too great a prize. I have another estate on the mainland, in China. I will take you there, far from the reach of others."

Megan's hopes were suddenly punctured. She sat despondently on the bed for a few minutes as Yang summoned an escort, then accompanied the men back to her quarters. She heard her door being secured again, locking her in. She didn't doubt they would watch her every move now. *I've got to get word to the ship*, she thought. *But who can do it?* It took only a moment for the answer to become obvious.

Hsien Lu stood casually in the shadow of a wall, observing the entrance to Yang's compound. He had been around the entire perimeter, making note of every detail he could discover. On the far side of the compound there were two massive wooden gates at an opening for the delivery of supplies. They were guarded as securely as the entrance. They were the only openings in the high walls.

He had watched the comings and goings of people at both entrances for a while, looking for a likely prospect to make contact with. Now, in mid-afternoon, he observed a young girl come out the main entrance and walk quickly away in the direction of the harbor. She looked supremely unhappy. He decided she was as good a prospect as he had seen, and fell in behind her several yards back. The girl never slowed her rapid pace, and was at the harbor in fifteen minutes. Several times she glanced back as if to see if anyone was following her.

Third Mistress was scared. She had come to Megan the next morning. Megan had become enraged when she showed the barbarian woman the marks on her back left by the bamboo-stick beating she had been given. When Megan had asked her to make contact with someone on board *Emerald Isle*, she had at first refused. If she was caught, her fate would likely be the same as the former Fourth Mistress suffered. Then she surprised herself by summoning some small reservoir of bravery from deep inside.

"I will go," she said. "If Master kill me, he kill me. I not care now. He beat me once too often. But, Honorable Megan, your mother scare me also." Megan's descriptions of her mother made the foreign devil woman sound somewhat supernatural, possessed of unusual powers—and the capacity for wreaking vengeance on those who wronged her.

"What if she angry with me?" the girl said. "Maybe she kill me for belonging to Master!"

"No," Megan said gently, putting a comforting hand on the girl's arm. "She will not. Just tell her I send my love to Bridget. That's my daughter. That will be enough."

As Third Mistress walked out onto the pier, she slowed in awe at sight of the massive bulk of *Emerald Isle* floating in the harbor. The long black hull looked menacing. She could see several cannon, and a large number of men milling about on deck. She had to make contact with someone aboard. But how? Suddenly she sensed that someone was behind her. She turned slowly, and gasped.

A powerful-looking man with a large saber in his sash stood a few feet away. It was the very man she had been told to watch for. Suddenly weak-kneed, she bowed low. "Honorable Hsien Lu?" she murmured.

She heard the man step closer. "Yes. How is it you know my name?" he said roughly.

"Honorable Megan has sent me," she said. "Please, I must speak to the mother of Honorable Megan!"

Hsien Lu could hardly believe his good fortune. "Then we must go to the ship at once."

"No, I cannot," the girl said, anguish on her features. "Someone may see me go to the ship. If Master Yang finds out, he will kill me. This will not help Honorable Megan."

Hsien Lu was silent for a moment. "You have come this far. You must go one step farther. Come, time is short."

"Shorter than you know, Honorable Warrior. Master Yang prepares to take Megan to China. You will not rescue her there."

Hsien Lu was sobered by this unexpected news. "Get in the boat," he said. "Now. We must hurry."

Feeling her life was most likely forfeit no matter what she did, Third Mistress meekly descended the ladder on the side of the pier and boarded a small skiff with Hsien Lu. She kept her head down as he rowed with powerful strokes across the harbor. In minutes they were at the ship.

Despite her fear, she gazed in wonder at the immense black hull that loomed over her. Hsien Lu secured the skiff and boosted her up the rope ladder to the deck. She looked up at the gigantic masts soaring far overhead, and knew she was in the grasp of foreign devils now. She stood on the deck, miserable, as the *gweilo* men stared at her. Hsien Lu trotted off and returned, took her in tow by the arm, and led her down a flight of stairs belowdecks.

She was ushered into a large room. There were two men and one woman inside. There was no doubt in Third Mistress's mind who the woman was. She was dressed in black, and had glossy ebony hair framing an elegant face with smooth pale skin. This could only be the powerful devil woman. As the woman rose from her chair and approached, Third Mistress could see her eyes were an incredible sky blue. Their glacial gaze bored into her, and she fell to the deck, quaking in fear. "Great Lady, do not slay me!" she wailed.

"Get up, child," Kathleen said. "What is your name?"

Third Mistress rose, trembling and sniffling. "Great Lady, I am Li Fanfan."

"What do you know of my daughter?" Kathleen said.

The words came out in a stumbling rush as Li Fanfan suddenly forgot much of the English she knew. "Great Lady—"

"I'm Kathleen."

"Venerable Kath—Kath-a-leen, Megan send me. She say—she say she send her love to Bri—Bri-Bri-jet. She say this make you believe me, so you not punish me."

Kathleen smiled. "Child, why would I do that? Come, sit down."

Li Fanfan quickly took the offered chair and was introduced to Ben and Alex. She turned back to Kathleen. "Venerable Kathleen, I must be quick. It is great risk for me to be here. You must hurry. Master Yang prepare to take Megan to house in China."

Alex rushed up to her. "When?" he said.

"I not know," Li Fanfan said, looking miserable. "But Master know someone looking for her. He take her soon. Please, you hurry!"

Kathleen leaned forward. "Tell us everything you know."

Hsien Lu escorted Li Fanfan most of the way back to Yang's compound, but left her just out of sight of the front entrance, not taking any chance on her being seen with him by the guards. Kathleen had given him definite instructions to see to her safety to the fullest extent possible. Once she was back inside though, her fate was out of his hands, at least temporarily.

Aboard *Emerald Isle*, Kathleen, Ben, and Alex pored over the map of the compound that Li Fanfan had hurriedly drawn for them.

"Megan's room is a good distance from the freight entrance," Ben observed. "Once we get inside, we'll need to be able to go straight to it. There won't be any time for wrong turns. In a place that big, we could get lost easily. I hope the girl will meet us to open the gate as agreed, and lead us to it."

"I'm convinced she will," Kathleen said. "She wouldn't have committed herself this far if she wasn't intending to follow through."

"As long as she isn't discovered," Alex said.

"That's why we won't wait for her to open the gate," Ben said. "If she doesn't do it at the agreed-on time, we proceed on our own. She knows that."

"I'll pray for her," Kathleen said. "She's a brave girl. I hope this doesn't cost her her life."

Alex studied Ben's face. "What's bothering you most about this operation, Ben?"

"Just about everything. But it's not our movements inside the compound," Ben said. "I'm counting on the element of surprise. That, and the superior weapons we'll be carrying. It's getting back to the ship that worries me. The compound is a good half-mile from the harbor, probably more. We could encounter hot pursuit from Yang's security force long before we reach it. If people on the street decide to join them, we could be fighting hand to hand just to reach the pier. I don't like it. We need more speed."

"Any solutions come to mind?" Alex said.

"Yes. We come in mounted."

"Horses?" Kathleen said with a dubious look. "How many horses do you suppose are on this island? Not many, I'll wager."

"Maybe not," Ben said. "But we have to try. That's where Mercer can help us. If there are any horses here, the English will have them. And Mercer can get them. I'm going over to his office now, let him know our plans, and ask him for forty horses. Alex, I want you to inquire among the crew. Finding skilled riders among a bunch of sailors won't be easy, but get the best ones you can."

"I'm going into the compound with you, you know," Kathleen said.

Ben looked at her. "No you're not. I don't want your safety on my mind. Here you'll be surrounded by well over one hundred heavily armed men. No one will be able to get at you. I know you want to have a direct hand in bringing Megan out; that's how you're made. But you let me handle this my way. We won't come back without her. That I promise you. We go in at dawn day after tomorrow."

First Mistress looked at Third Mistress with suspicion. "Where did you go today? I know you went outside. This was not something we discussed."

"I did not require your permission to go into town before, Honorable Lady."

"No, but your trips have been regularly scheduled. This trip was not."

"I needed to buy a new kitchen knife to replace the one stolen by Honor—by the barbarian woman. It was soiled by her blood."

"That is the concern of the kitchen staff, not you."

"And—and I also wished to purchase some fresh herbs for a headache remedy. I heard that a new shipment arrived just the other day."

First Mistress regarded her with contempt. "I don't believe you. Do you think I have not noticed that you are friendly with the barbarian woman? Do you think I have not seen that you treat her as an equal? You are helping her plot something."

"It is not so, Honorable Lady."

"You are lying to me, you country peasant. You are planning something, I know it. If I discover you are deceiving me, you will pay dearly. You are not to see her again until I give you permission." With that, she turned abruptly and left.

Third Mistress sagged against a wall, weak with fear.

In the pre-dawn darkness, twenty-seven sailors from *Emerald Isle*, skilled riders all, gathered at the harbor. There each one received the reins to a horse from the handlers Mercer had sent to meet them. The handlers were to stand by at the docks to receive the horses upon their return. Mercer had been able to provide only thirty of the requested forty horses; Ben, Alex, and Hsien Lu mounted up on the other three.

Each man was armed with pistols and rifles, and Ben had a sizable cache of blasting powder strapped behind his saddle. He felt insecure on the small English riding saddle, but it would have to do. There was no conversation. When everyone was mounted, they moved out at a walk up the deserted dirt street.

The freight entrance had been chosen because it was located on a less-traveled street than the front entrance, and it offered a more direct route to the harbor. As the mounted group padded slowly through the streets, the recently-installed gas lamps barely revealed them. They encountered no foot traffic; it was considered unsafe to be about at that hour. The loose dirt muffled the horses' footsteps.

In fifteen minutes they were around the corner from the compound entrance. Everyone dismounted and held their horse's reins firmly. All was accomplished without talking. Hsien Lu crept silently to the corner and peered around it. He turned back to Ben and signaled that the usual number of guards—four—was present.

Ben pulled out his pocket watch and held it up to read in the dim lantern light. It was less than five minutes until the time Li Fanfan was to open the door. Time to take out the guards. Ben signaled to Hsien Lu.

Hsien Lu left his side and glided like a ghost through the darkness, approaching the door in a roundabout way to within a few feet of the guards. In movements too swift for Ben to follow, Hsien Lu's saber flashed. All four guards were down before they could put up a fight. Two of them were unconscious. The other two would never rise again.

Inside the compound, Third Mistress walked hurriedly down the hallway leading to the courtyard in front of the massive wooden doors that hung at the freight entrance. She glanced nervously from side to side, knowing the trip was fraught with peril. She really didn't expect to make it all the way. But suddenly she was there. She looked at the huge doors for a moment, then walked toward the large sliding bar that secured them. Five feet from the bar, she froze in fear, heart pounding.

First Mistress emerged from the shadows at one side. "So," she said, "it is as I suspected. You have plotted with the barbarian. You have betrayed us. But you will not succeed." She started walking toward Third Mistress.

Li Fanfan backed away in terror, unable to speak.

"Those who plot against us will pay with their lives," First Mistress said, taking a large knife from the folds of her garment. "Starting with you, traitor!"

Outside in the street, Ben looked at his pocket watch, then at the sky. The first hint of daylight was visible over the harbor. He looked at the massive doors again. There was no sound, no movement.

He turned to a man behind him. "It's time," he said. "The girl didn't show. Blow the doors."

7.

Megan was shaken awake in the pre-dawn darkness by Yang, who was accompanied by two thuggish-looking guards. She looked up at them in disoriented fear. "What is it?" she said.

"We are leaving for the mainland," he answered. "Now." He jerked her to her feet. "There is activity in the streets. I'm not waiting to find out what it is."

Megan had not been allowed to see Li Fanfan since she had sent the girl to try to make contact with someone on *Emerald Isle*. She didn't know if the effort had been successful or not. But the obviously forced separation made her fear the worst. The girl must have been caught, and her faint hope of timely rescue gone. "No!" she screamed, twisting in Yang's grip. "I won't go!"

Yang cuffed her across the face and threw her into the arms of the two thugs. Dazed, she struggled to break free. Yang shouted orders in Chinese and the men began to drag her out of her room. They had gone two steps when the walls shook from a tremendous explosion somewhere in the compound.

The men froze and Yang went wide-eyed in shock. "What was that?" he said.

Megan glared at him with grim satisfaction from behind the red hair that had fallen in front of her eyes. "That would probably be my husband."

First Mistress advanced on Li Fanfan, knife held high, smiling in demonic satisfaction. "Master Yang will reward me handsomely for this," she said.

They were her last words. A stunning blast blew in both giant doors. The right-hand door, weighing at least a ton, ripped from its hinges and smashed into First Mistress, driving her off her feet. The door crashed to the ground on top of her. First Mistress was dead.

Li Fanfan stood speechless in shock as a mass of mounted men swarmed through the opening. She didn't recognize Ben until he dismounted and was right in front of her.

"Are you all right?" he said.

She nodded, too shaken to speak.

"Take us to Megan," Ben said.

Li Fanfan gathered herself and took off at a run, with Ben, Alex, and several of the other men close behind her. All around them was confusion. The halls and courtyards were filled with shouts and the sound of running feet. Gunfire erupted behind them, but Li Fanfan kept running at top speed. In a little over a minute, they were at the door to Megan's room.

The room was empty.

"She gone!" she cried to Ben in dismay. "Master Yang take her."

"Take us where you think he might be," Ben said.

"Come!" she shouted, sprinting away. Ben, Alex, and the others followed her, guns drawn. They ran along the covered porches beside courtyards now filled with frightened servants milling in confusion. Screams punctuated the night. Glowing lanterns bobbed in the darkness. Ben and Alex quickly became disoriented.

"Lady, I hope you know where you're going," Ben shouted above the din.

"Down here!" Li Fanfan cried, making a sharp turn toward Master Yang's private quarters. Ben, Alex and the others were right on her heels.

Alex couldn't keep silent any longer. "Megan!" he screamed.

Megan's answering shriek cut through the bedlam. "Alexxxxxx!"

They turned a corner—and came face to face with Megan, held firmly between her two captors. At sight of the intruders, they threw her aside, drew swords, and charged.

Ben and Alex took quick aim and blew them off their feet.

Megan got up and sprinted into Alex's embrace. "Alex, I love you," she sobbed.

He wrapped his arms around her and lifted her off the ground. "I feared I'd lost you lass," he said, face buried in her hair.

Just then a small, shaven-headed Chinese man poked his head through a doorway.

Li Fanfan spotted him. "Master Yang!" she cried.

Ben took two big steps forward and seized the man by his shirt, nearly jerking him off his feet. "You're coming with us," he said. Then he turned to Li Fanfan. "Take us back to the gate."

Li Fanfan took off, running as fast as she could. Alex took Megan by the hand, and they followed. Ben prodded Yang in the back with his pistol, keeping close behind with the other men. At several points guards armed with pikes and swords assaulted them, but warning shots close over their heads kept them at bay. Even so, by the time the fleeing party finally burst into the courtyard before the ruined gates, a screaming throng was hot on their heels.

The courtyard was in chaos. Hsien Lu was leading the invasion force in holding off Yang's security guards. The acrid smell of gunpowder was heavy in the air. Screaming combatants surged back and forth in the darkness. None of the guards had modern firearms, but some of them, armed with pikes, charged anyway, only to be cut down in a hail of gunfire. Frightened horses, barely under control, stamped the earth and pulled at the reins held by their dismounted riders. Alex ran to his horse, Megan in tow, and vaulted into the saddle. He pulled Megan up behind him. Ben reached his horse, picked up Yang, and threw him over the saddle. He was momentarily grateful for the flat English riding saddle as he mounted quickly behind him. "One wrong move from you and I'll put a bullet in your head," he told him. Two guards, pikes lowered, ran screaming at him. Hsien Lu charged them and chopped the pikestaffs in half with two savage strokes. The men fled in terror.

"Hsien Lu, mount up!" Ben said.

The guards had retreated over the bodies of a score of their number back to the edge of the courtyard. Hsien Lu reached his horse and jumped into the saddle, brandishing his saber as he took a turn around the enclosure to keep the guards at bay.

"Go, to the harbor!" Ben shouted at Alex.

Alex guided his horse around the fallen gates in the dim light, and had just reached the opening when Megan spotted Li Fanfan huddled against a wall to one side.

"Honorable Megan!" she called. "Please take me with you. Please!"

Megan didn't have to hesitate. "Hsien Lu!" she shouted, pointing at the girl.

Hsien Lu spurred his mount to her and swept her up on the run with one brawny arm. Then they galloped through the ruined entrance and into the street.

A red dawn was breaking over the harbor as the mounted rescue party thundered toward the water. The streets were filling fast with confused townspeople, awakened by the explosion and gunfire. The horses swept down the hill at top speed, scattering villagers as they went.

Megan hung on tightly to Alex's waist. Behind her she could hear an increasing uproar as Yang's security force reorganized itself. She knew the villagers would rally to Yang in short order if they realized what was happening, and prayed the harbor would be gained first. Otherwise they might never make the ship.

The horses rounded street corners at breakneck speed, spurred relentlessly by their riders. Megan looked to her left and could see Li Fanfan hanging onto Hsien Lu like a little rag doll, face a pale mask of fear. It must have been her first time on horseback.

Villagers were beginning to pour out of side streets and run at them. Word of the invasion had spread. The horses smashed the attackers aside as they pounded for the waterfront. The lead riders fired into the semi-dark, dropping some of the figures. But their path to the harbor was rapidly constricting.

Then suddenly they were there, rounding the last corner and sprinting out onto the pier, horse hooves thudding on the pier timbers. The group reined to a halt and jumped to the planking. Mercer's horse handlers were there as promised, and mounted as quickly as the rescuers dismounted. Then they spurred their horses away into the darkness. In less than thirty seconds, every horse had disappeared.

The rescuers ran for *Emerald Isle*, which had been pulled up to the dock. Kathleen and Captain Rowan had made good use of their time. Nearly all of the approximately 170 men left on board lined the port railing at dockside, armed with as many weapons as they could carry. The big Gatling guns had been uncovered and positioned astern, gleaming menacingly in the dawnlight. A narrow gangplank provided a twelve-foot gap between ship and dock. *Emerald Isle* strained at her lines in response to the sails that were filling with the morning breeze.

Alex and Megan sprinted across the gangplank, with Ben right behind, pushing the stumbling Yang with a vengeance. The rest of the rescue party swarmed across in single file. Last were Hsien Lu and Li Fanfan.

At the railing, Kathleen's immense relief at seeing her daughter again was chopped off abruptly by a terrifying sight at the foot of pier. She rushed to the top of the gangplank and flung herself at Megan. "Get below, daughter. We've got company." She turned to Ben, grabbed his arm, and whirled him around. "Look!"

A low rumble of sound suddenly exploded into a roar as a seething mass of yellow-skinned humanity erupted out of a side street and spilled out onto the pier, brandishing pikes, lances, swords, knives, and torches, and shrieking like demons from Hell. The horde surged forward down the pier toward *Emerald Isle*.

"Cast off all lines!" Captain Rowan shouted. The gangplank was rapidly pulled on board. The giant clipper ship began to drift slowly away from the dock. Most of the men at the railing were forced to abandon their positions and see to putting on more sail.

The horde of Chinese reached the spot where the gangplank had been. The gap was already too broad to jump, and they stood at the front edge of the pier brandishing their weapons and screaming with ferocious bloodlust.

"Kathy, you get below too," Ben ordered. "See to Megan and the Chinese girl."

Kathleen quickly obeyed.

Ben took Yang by the collar and shoved him to the port railing. Then he drew his pistol and put it to the Chinese man's head in plain view of the mass on the pier.

A fearsome silence quickly descended over the crowd. They stood glaring out at the ship for long seconds.

"Hold your fire," Ben called to the men at the railing.

"What do you think they're going to do?" Alex asked.

"I don't know," Ben said uneasily. "But they'll do *something.*"

As if in response, the Chinese horde suddenly turned almost as one and bolted back down the pier, where they sprinted along the docks and began jumping into every vessel they could find.

Now the sun had cleared the horizon, and the waterfront was crawling with Chinese for blocks. Confusion reigned, but Ben knew it wouldn't last. He turned Yang over to one of the seamen and went forward.

Emerald Isle's vast bulk slowly began to gain headway as the sails filled and it moved away from the pier toward the open sea. But Ben could already see the ship was going to be cut off. Junks and sampans were furiously raising sail and moving to intercept them. "We're not going to make it untouched," he said to Rowan, who had joined him at the rail.

"Aye," the captain said. "That seems certain." He looked aloft. "The men are spreading the canvas as fast as they can. We'll do our best."

Emerald Isle's sleek hull cut the water toward the narrowing gap to freedom. In less than five minutes the nearest junk was only one hundred yards away off the starboard rail. Ben could see the mouths of small cannon bristling from the sides of the junk.

"We needn't fear the cannon," Rowan said. "They're pretty much useless. They can't be aimed, and Chinese gunpowder is better suited for fireworks."

As if to emphasize his words, a puff of smoke appeared on the side of the junk, followed simultaneously by a sharp report and the whistle of a cannonball as it passed overhead through the rigging.

"A few holes in the sails is about the worst we'll suffer, unless they get lucky and strike a mast," Rowan said. "And the closer they get, the more useless their cannon. They can't be depressed. You can see how high that ball flew." He gave Ben a grim look. "If they close with us though, there'll be a battle. Now if you'll excuse me, I'll see to *our* cannon."

Rowan left and walked amidships. He gave orders and the starboard Long Tom thundered, with deadly results. The cannonball smashed into the nearest junk just above the waterline. Even if the junks had been far more substantial than they were, they could not have withstood a weapon that could hurl an iron ball with a muzzle velocity of 1,000 miles per hour. The junk cracked open like an egg, then split in two and sank, sending Chinese sailors scurrying to swim clear.

Rowan could see that the junks astern were not going to catch *Emerald Isle*, so he gave orders for the Gatling guns to be carried to the bow. The transfer took several minutes. The starboard Long Tom continued to thunder away, with the twenty-pounders on that side also scoring some direct hits. The men armed with rifles and pistols withheld their fire until closer targets presented themselves.

That was all too soon in coming. The cannoneers couldn't destroy all the junks. The whole harbor seemed to have come alive in pursuit. Two junks and three sampans managed to get through the gauntlet of cannon balls and closed on *Emerald Isle*'s bow. That was their mistake. Alex and one of the other seamen opened up the big Gatling guns. With a roar, twin streams of big shells spat forth and began shredding the approaching boats, their crewmen screaming and jumping into the water.

Emerald Isle swept faster across the harbor, a swath of flaming scrap and boatless sailors in her wake. Still the Chinese came on. Cannonballs from the junks continued to whistle overhead through the rigging, causing no real damage. Finally two of the junks managed to close on the clipper ship's hull. Archers on board the junks prepared to shoot fire arrows into *Emerald Isle*'s sails. Riflemen at the railing cut loose with a tremendous volley and blew them off their feet. Some fire arrows were launched and found their mark. Crewmen scrambled into the rigging to smother the flames.

"Stand by to repel boarders!" Rowan yelled.

The junks slammed into the big black hull. The Chinese were screaming in fury, some of them swinging grappling hooks, others waving pikes and swords. Some of the grappling hooks took hold, but Hsien Lu, saber flashing, ran along the railing, chopping them loose almost as fast as they landed. Still, some Chinese gained the rail and others climbed the superstructure of the junks and leapt toward *Emerald Isle*, braving the fusillade of gunfire.

Vicious hand to hand combat erupted on the starboard railing. Hsien Lu waded in, swinging his saber in deadly arcs. Heads and limbs tumbled into the water as he worked with deadly purpose. The fighting was too close for rifles and cannon. But the clipper ship's crewmen were giving a good account of themselves at close quarters. Bodies surged back and forth over the railing, wrestling and screaming. Slowly the tide of battle turned in *Emerald Isle*'s favor, and the boarders became fewer. At the bow, Alex and the other seaman continued to tear apart everything in range of the Gatling guns. Smoke from burning junks and the heavy smell of gunpowder drifted over the ship.

Then the last of the boarders were thrown over the side and left behind. The seamen on board shouted in triumph.

"Another hundred yards will do it," Rowan shouted to Ben. "We'll be clear."

But two large junks were moving into *Emerald Isle*'s path. There was no room to maneuver to either side. "No where to go," Ben yelled back.

Rowan turned to the helmsman. "Ram them!" he shouted. The big clipper ship swept forward under full sail, continuing to gain speed.

"Can we roll over them?" Ben asked.

"I don't know," Rowan answered. "Maybe not without damage to the hull. But we've got no choice." *Emerald Isle* surged ahead, now less than fifty yards from the blockading junks.

"Brace for impact!" Rowan shouted above the din. But one of the junks suddenly blew skyward in a tremendous blast of smoke and flame, then descended in fiery remnants which quickly sank. Ben looked behind him. One of the British warships across the harbor had opened up with their cannon, and scored a direct hit on the junk's powder magazine. As they watched, another cannonball whistled overhead and tore away the superstructure of the remaining junk, cracking the hull. Seconds later, *Emerald Isle*'s long bulk smashed into the junk, driving it under and sweeping over the shattered remains as it gained open water at last.

Captain Rowan stood in the stern, looking with grim satisfaction at the carnage in their wake.

Ben joined him. "We're clear," he said.

"Aye," Rowan said. "And none too soon I'd say. Thank God Mercer decided to take a hand in freeing us. Without that warship's intervention I don't know if we'd have been able to clear those last two junks."

"Where are we headed?" Ben said.

"South and then east toward the East Lamma Channel. Soon as we clear Green Island, we'll be there. Shouldn't take long, the old girl's flying now. The only thing that concerns me is the looks of that sky eastward. It's bloody red. Could be a storm brewing."

"We'll face that when it comes, if it does," Ben said. "I'm going below to see to Yang." He left and descended belowdecks where Yang was still being held under the watchful eye of the seaman Ben had left him with.

"He hasn't taken that smug look off his face since we left," the seaman said to Ben.

Ben stared hard at Yang, who only smiled back at him. "I ought to break your neck right now," Ben said. "If I find out you've laid a hand on my daughter, I'll use your body for a barnacle scraper. But I reckon my wife will want a piece of you first."

"I did not touch your daughter," Yang said calmly. "But she was bought and paid for in an honorable transaction. The price was quite high."

Ben snapped. He took two steps forward, lifted the seated Yang by the shirt, and slammed him against a bulkhead. "My daughter was not for sale! There is no honor in the buying and selling of human beings."

Yang's expression never wavered as Ben thrust him into the chair again. "It is the way of things," he said.

"Not where I come from," Ben said.

"No?" Yang said, grinning. "I have heard of the slaves in your country, bought and sold."

"Yeah," Ben said, "and we just fought a civil war in which tens of thousands of our best young men died to free them." He clenched his jaw in disgust. "What am I talking to you for, you opium-trafficking scum. There's no reason to keep you alive now."

Yang's eyes glittered. "You dare to condemn me for trafficking in opium? When it was barbarian traders who pushed it on *us?*"[7]

"Yeah, and you were first in line to take advantage of the demand," Ben said.

Yang's eyes glittered. "You think you're free, don't you? You think you have escaped. In truth, I admired this ship from the moment you dropped anchor, and thought of how I might acquire it. It could not be done in the harbor, though your recent activities gave me a fair opportunity. Now you have broken through my preparations. Or so you think. Soon you will be in sight of Green Island. Then you will see what I have arranged for you."

Ben stared at him for long moments. "Whatever it is, you won't live to see it." He motioned to the seaman who had been guarding Yang. "Bring him on deck."

Topside, Ben found Kathleen, Megan and Alex standing with Captain Rowan. He joined them, with Yang brought along behind. Megan turned and glared murderously at Yang, arms folded across her chest. She had already discarded her Chinese garb for Western dress.

Kathleen regarded Yang with a frigid stare that made even Ben pause. He could see she had vengeance on her mind. He turned to Rowan. "How much maneuvering room is there in the passage between Hong Kong and Green Island?" he said.

Rowan looked at him with curiosity. "Enough. Why?"

"Something's up. I think this Chinese snake's got a reception planned for us."

Rowan frowned. "We'll know soon."

Black clouds were massing in the eastern sky when Green Island became visible, and the sea was starting to chop. Rowan stood on the forecastle deck looking ahead with a spyglass, Ben and Kathleen beside him. Megan, exhausted, had gone below with Alex. Yang was back on the quarterdeck, guarded closely by the seaman.

"There's something in the sea ahead, sure enough," Rowan said. "But whatever it is might be the lesser of our problems."

"What do you mean?" Kathleen said.

---

[7]   Widespread opium addiction in 19th-century China was directly attributable to British tea and silk merchants. Eager for a market to offset the tremendous imbalance of trade goods flowing out of China, and British money flowing in, they aggressively introduced East Indian opium to the Chinese population, even fighting several small wars to keep the supply lines open. Some American traders later joined in the trafficking.

"The barometer's dropping like a rock, lass. We're in for a real blow. I can't put off bringing in the sails much longer."

Ben took the spyglass and looked ahead again. A dark line on the sea gradually took shape. It was a line of junks, strung out across the strait between Hong Kong and Green Island. There must have been nearly thirty of them. "Get Yang up here," he ordered a nearby crewman.

The man trotted astern and brought Yang back at gunpoint in three minutes. The little Chinese man's smirk had only increased.

"Who is that out there?" Ben demanded.

"A most useful associate," Yang said. "Your American pirate, Eli Boggs."

"He's a bit out of his territory," Rowan said. "You can usually find him farther west, preying on traffic in the Pearl River. Didn't expect to see him out here."

"It looks like he's forming a blockade," Ben said, peering through the scope again. "Are all those junks armed?"

"Count on it," Rowan said.

"Can we sail around them?" Ben said.

"Not an easy proposition in these rough seas," Rowan said. "Too close to shore for safe maneuvering. And conditions are only going to get worse."

Kathleen spoke up. "Can we sail to the south, around the other side of Green Island?"

"Not my first choice, lass," Rowan said. "I'd like to be as far as I can from land when this storm strikes. I don't want to chance being driven aground. In fact, I think we'll bear southwest now toward the West Lamma Channel. It's broader." He gazed ahead. "Providing we can get through yon line of junks."

As they watched, dark smudges of smoke appeared far ahead along the line.

"What's giving off the smoke?" Ben said.

"Most likely fire rafts," Rowan said, "barges loaded with firewood, straw, saltpeter, and sulfur. They're sometimes used on rivers as a blockading tactic, set afire to block a ship's path. I'd never expect to see them out in open water. I don't know how much of a threat they'll be here in the Channel. It seems like a stupid move to me, but then whoever said pirates were smart?"

"Smart enough," Ben said. "These people have had entirely too much time to plan."

"Aye," Rowan said. "Perhaps Yang had them signaled from Victoria Peak or some other high point."

The wind began to rise, vibrating the shroud lines and stays. The sea grew rougher. "Let's go astern," Rowan said. "I want to be near the helm. I suggest you all get below."

"Not yet," Kathleen said, eyeing the darkening sky.

They all walked astern, Rowan instructing the crew to prepare *Emerald Isle* for the oncoming storm as they went. When they reached the quarterdeck and turned around, they were stunned at sight of the distant sky eastward. A malevolent black wall of cloud was bearing down on them, stretching from sea to infinity above. The wind increased to a shriek, buffeting them as they held onto the shroud lines. The seas were rolling now, the clipper ship heaving its way ahead toward the channel and the junk blockade.

Yang's laugh startled Kathleen. She turned to see him staring at the oncoming fury, and heard him mouth two words.

"Tai fung."[8]

Yang turned and looked at her. "You see?" he yelled over the rush of wind. "Even the elements conspire against you! I have prayed to the sea gods, and their wrath is upon you."

Kathleen looked questioningly at Rowan. "Sea gods?" she shouted to be heard over the wind's roar.

"Aye," Rowan shouted back. "They've got a slew of 'em. Gods for every purpose—water gods, mercy gods, kitchen gods, monkey gods, sea gods—you name it."

Yang stood smiling in smug triumph as the wind bore down on them like an express train.

Kathleen couldn't restrain herself any longer. She walked up to him. "There is but one God," she shouted, leaning close to his face. "And I am the instrument of His justice." With that she turned her back to him and took a few steps away. Black thunderclouds were boiling out of the eastern sky. The sea was turning to roiling mountains of water. Kathleen stood with her feet apart, braced against the onslaught. She raised her fists high and looked skyward, ebony hair swirling about her head.

"Bring it down!" she screamed. "Bring it dowwwwwn!"

A blinding flash of light singed the air, followed by a staggering clap of thunder that shook the ship. The clouds ahead seemed to funnel downward toward the sea. The people huddled on *Emerald Isle*'s deck could see light reflecting dimly off something moving in the sea ahead.

Out of the blackness a gigantic wave swallowed the horizon. It rose higher, a one hundred-foot wall of water headed straight at them—and

---

[8]   Typhoon; literally, "big wind".

at the line of junks. In seconds it broke above the junks. Yang gaped in horror as millions of tons of black water came down on Eli Boggs' pirate fleet, driving it under in a thundering crush of devastation.

Kathleen turned on Yang. The wind blew the hair about her head like black snakes, giving her the look of an enraged Medusa. There was death in her eyes.

Yang staggered backward, terrified. He kept retreating until he was at the stern railing. Then suddenly he was overboard. For a few seconds his head was visible in the swirling maelstrom, then he vanished from sight.

"Get below!" Rowan yelled. "Now!"

Ben and Kathleen dove for the nearest hatch. The hatch cover slammed shut over their heads.

A surging mountain of white water was heading straight at the ship. Rowan stood at the helm clutching the wheel in a death grip. The wave reached them and the giant clipper ship clawed up its face, bow pointing at the sky. Higher and higher it went, being carried backward at the same time. The wave seemed to have no end. Then at last *Emerald Isle* crested, the bow began to fall, and the ship rushed down the eastern face into the turbulent sea.

* * *

The storm raged for hours. Everyone not needed on deck huddled below, in various stages of misery. But by early evening, *Emerald Isle* sailed into calmer waters, with clear skies ahead. She was undamaged.

In one of the aft staterooms, Megan tended to Li Fanfan, who had been forgotten in the desperate flight to freedom. The young Chinese girl was severely seasick.

"Well, this was quite a day for you, Miss Li Fanfan," Megan told her, wiping the girl's brow with a cool cloth. "Your first horseback ride, and now your first sailing journey. I'm glad to know your name at last."

"I want to die," the girl moaned.

"It will pass, I promise," Megan said. "I wonder what happened to Second Mistress," she mused. "We never saw her on the way out."

"She run away, I bet," Li Fanfan said. "She never like it there, even though she pretend."

"Neither did you, I think."

Later that evening, food was made available for those who felt like eating. After a small meal with Alex, Megan knew the time was at hand when she would have to face him alone, and come to grips with what had happened to her. She also knew that as a Connelly woman she was expected to be tough. Oh, from now on she would be polite company—socialize like before, laugh at jokes like before, be strong for her daughter. But she would never be the same. She would look at other people, especially women, from a different place now. A gauzy curtain had fallen, through which she saw crookedly. She had been taken violently, raped, and a crack in the earth had opened up, one that could never be closed.

Kathleen came to her cabin. She closed the door behind her and stood looking silently at her daughter in the dim glow of the oil lamp.

Megan sat, unable to look at her mother for a long moment, then finally raised her head. "Never ask me, Mother," she said.

"Pardon?"

"Never ask me," Megan repeated, raising her eyes at last. "Never ask me what happened after I was kidnapped."

Kathleen looked at her daughter's face, searching. "Very well," she said softly. But she knew.

"How did you know where to find me?" Megan said, asking the question that had gnawed at her since the desperate flight from Yang's compound.

Kathleen crossed the stateroom and took a seat next to her daughter. "To begin with, I found your knitting needles," she said softly.

Megan squeezed her eyes shut for a few seconds, face contorted. "Then you know I—"

"Did you, Megan? Did you smoke opium again?"

Megan nodded her head. "God help me, I did." Then she slumped against Kathleen and broke into sobs.

Kathleen held her daughter tightly. "It's all right, my girl. It's all right. I've never forgotten the sacrifice you made in exposing yourself to it the first time." She stroked the red hair. "But I have faith that you would never have sought it out again on your own. Did someone place it in your path?"

Megan nodded. She told Kathleen about the mysterious boxes and notes that had showed up at the restaurants, how she had first thrown the second one away, then retrieved it and stashed it away in the stable, and how she had finally succumbed to its temptation late one night. "Mother, I'm so sorry," she sobbed.

Kathleen let her cry. When she had collected herself sufficiently to speak again, Megan continued her story, telling her about finding the note in her saddlebags. "I suspected from the start it wasn't from Yuen Ling-Po, even though his name was on it," she said. "In any case, it was the last straw. I was determined to put a stop to it. I decided to follow the card's instructions, go into San Francisco, and confront whoever it was." She hung her head. "I guess I wasn't very smart. It was a trap. Oh Mother, I was trying to be like you!"

Kathleen tilted her daughter's head up so she could see her face. "I want you to promise me something. Stop trying. Being me isn't all it seems. If it wasn't for Ben, I would have been dead long ago."

Megan wiped her cheeks with the back of her hand. "So, how did you know where I'd been taken?"

"We put Hsien Lu to the task," Kathleen said. "He found out. He's not a man to refuse. But there's more to it than that. It became obvious that someone *wanted* us to know what happened to you. This whole thing seems to have been planned from the start to get us out of town in pursuit of you. And it doesn't end there. Danielle told me just before we sailed that she's convinced there's a connection between your kidnapping and this summer's stockholders' meeting. She thinks the timing is no coincidence."

Megan's eyes went wide with amazement. "Leatherwood?" she said.

"Could be," Kathleen said. "In any case, we're going to get to the bottom of it when we get back. But Danielle is going to have to handle company business by herself, along with Robert, until we return."

"She can do it," Megan said. "She's the best."

"Aye, that she is. Now, I have something for you." She pulled an object from her dress pocket. It was the *An Paidrin Beag* wrist rosary. "I believe this is yours. I'm afraid I wore it out on the voyage over and had to restring it. I decided to make a necklace out of it. Here," she said, leaning forward and fastening it around her daughter's neck.

Megan brushed the rosary necklace with her fingers. "I love you, Mother."

Kathleen rose and stepped away. "Now," she said, "Alex wants to be alone with you. He really isn't needed about the ship now. But I sense he's uneasy. He asked me to come see you first. He can be a bit clumsy at times, I guess. This, I think, is one of them."

Megan rose and retrieved a bucket of fresh water and a sponge. "I want you to wash me, Mother," she said, offering her the sponge. "I want you to wash away the filth of China. I want you to make me clean for Alex."

Kathleen took the sponge, looking at her daughter for long silent moments. Then she put the sponge down on the table beside the bucket. "I love you, Megan. I would give my life to take away the pain you've suffered. But this is something your husband should do." She walked to the cabin door. "I'll send him in."

Alex entered a few minutes later. He paused inside the doorway, looking at his wife. Kathleen had brought her one of her favorite dresses. Now she stood in the dim light of one of the cabin's oil lamps, shadows playing about her with the ship's gentle rocking motion.

Alex came forward and tenderly wrapped his arms around her. "Lass, I could hardly breathe knowing the danger you were in. I would have taken on all of China to get you back. You're so precious to me. I love you so much. And I'm so sorry for what you've suffered."

Megan felt the bravado she had kept about her for weeks began to crumble and fall away from her like a fragile shell. She fought for control, embarrassed, and pulled away slightly from her husband's embrace. She raised her eyes to him, tears wetting her cheeks. "Oh, Alex. I'm forever broken."

Alex put gentle hands on Megan's head. Her coppery-red hair glowed in the lamplight. "Nay, lass," he said softly. "You're the Angel's daughter. You can't be broken." He stroked her hair lovingly, as Kathleen had done. "You can never be broken."

After a few minutes in his embrace, she pulled away gently and sat down. Then ever so slowly, she pulled her dress down over her shoulders, baring herself to the waist. Picking up the sponge from beside her, she held it out to him. "Wash me, husband," she said. "Make me clean for you."

He took the sponge.

She removed her dress completely and let it fall to the floor.

Alex proceeded to wash his wife slowly, tenderly. Megan had bruises on her neck and thighs, and faint scratches around her breasts. Alex said nothing about them, but continued gently washing, sponging over her breasts, her stomach, her thighs, until he had reached her feet. He picked up each one and washed it thoroughly, as if reluctant to be done with his task. Finally, he put the sponge down, and looked at Megan, uncertain of what to do next.

She rose and went to the bunk on one side of the room. There she stretched out her still-magnificent body, tossing her hair about her shoulders. In the glow of the lamp she looked like a goddess.

Alex went to her, removed his clothes, and lay down beside her. He pulled her to him and held her close, hands roving lightly over her shoulders. She didn't relax for a long time. When at last he felt her soften to his touch, he rolled her onto her back. He brushed his fingers lightly over her full breasts, feeling her nipples become erect in response. He kissed her ardently around her face and neck, and slowly ran his hand down over the silky mound between her legs.

She stiffened and began to tremble. "Oh, Alex," she sobbed. "I thought I could--" She didn't finish.

"It's all right, love," he whispered into her hair. "It's all right. Whenever you're ready. You choose the time." He gently stroked her breasts, content to lie beside her as she wept uncontrollably into his chest.

Megan's tears gradually subsided, and for a long time she and Alex were entwined in silence. Finally she spoke. "Parmenter raped me," she said, barely audible.

"I know."

She began to tremble again. "Alex," she said, crying, "I cleaned myself the best I could."

"What he did doesn't change my love for you. You are my perfect woman. I want you now. I'll want you tomorrow. Until my dying day."

Megan closed her eyes and drifted off to sleep, wondering how he could possibly have known.

8.

The following morning, Megan stood on the deck with Alex at her side, as *Emerald Isle* plowed eastward through calm seas. They had been inseparable since emerging topside an hour earlier. She leaned back into his chest and held his arms around her firmly, sunlight playing off the golden strands in her red hair.

A hesitant Li Fanfan approached them. The teenage girl seemed lost on the vast deck, though her color had improved, her seasickness having slackened somewhat.

Megan didn't move away from Alex, but held out her arms in welcome to the girl.

Li Fanfan bowed low. "Honorable Megan, I greet you."

Megan smiled. "Come here, dear one," she said. Li Fanfan didn't move, so Megan pulled the girl to her.

She resisted at first, unsure how to act among barbarians.

Alex pulled back a bit and Megan put her arms around the girl. She could feel her stiffness and sense uncertainty. "I'm afraid I've neglected you," Megan said. "I'm so sorry. I owe you more than I can ever repay. You risked your life for me. I shall spend the rest of mine trying to make up for it. Now," she said, taking the girl's chin in her hands and lifting it up, "the first thing you must learn is to address me simply as 'Megan'. I would consider it a favor, and I'm not feeling particularly honorable right now, anyway."

The girl bowed again. "Yes, Honor—yes, Megan. It shall be as you wish."

"And have done with the bowing. That's not necessary or required in American society." She looked at the girl closely. "You look frightened."

Li Fanfan's eyes widened slightly. "Megan, your mother scare me. She call down rage from heaven."

Megan smiled. "Well, maybe. We'll never really know. That wave was probably coming anyway. I've learned, though, never to underestimate her. Don't worry; she'll warm to you. Just stay away from her when she gets like that."

"I stay far away, Megan," the girl said, looking down the deck to where Kathleen stood.

"Don't be afraid of her. Mother will reach out to you before long. I hope you don't regret your decision to come with us."

Li Fanfan looked out to sea. "I leave nothing behind but hard times, Megan. I not sorry I came."

"Is there anything you need?"

"When we reach America, I send letter to mother. Tell her where I am. Say someday I bring her to me. Can you send letter, Megan? This possible?"

"Yes," Megan said. "I have an old Chinese friend in San Francisco I can entrust with the job. He'll see that it gets there." She looked at the girl, an impish smile playing about her face. "Hmm. We can't let you run around all alone in your new country. You need looking after. And I know just the person for the job."

She sent Li Fanfan below after a while to see if the girl could keep some food down. Then she sought out Hsien Lu, whom she found standing on the quarterdeck. After she greeted him warmly and thanked him for his service, she said, "Old friend, I have a request. Perhaps you will find it pleasant. Li Fanfan is all alone now. She needs someone to keep her company, keep her safe until she's settled in. I'd like you to see to her welfare. Would you do this for me?"

For the first time ever, Megan thought she detected a hint of embarrassment on the tough warrior's face.

After a moment's hesitation, he said, "Yes, Megan, I will perform this service for you gladly."

Wary of his reflexes, Megan resisted the urge to poke him in the ribs. "Oh, come now! I hope it will be more than a service. You could use a bit of softening up, you know; you're much too serious. All this lopping off of heads and such. Female companionship could only do you good." She couldn't decipher his expression. But she knew he would do it.

Kathleen approached them. "Alex, bring Megan below to the main hold. All the crew that can be spared is gathered there." She turned to her daughter. "They gave up a lot to bring you back, Megan. It's time to thank them."

Alex escorted Megan to the vast main hold amidships. There were over 150 men waiting for them. When they entered, the men broke into a lusty cheer that went on and on until Alex finally raised a hand.

A reluctant silence settled over the big room. Alex put a gentle hand on Megan's back and pushed her forward.

Megan stood apart, looking out over the throng. She searched for words. "I—I can't believe what you did for me. You left your homes, your families, for weeks. You fought so hard. I know some of you are injured. You could have been killed; you might not have come back. All because—all because I—" She couldn't go on. "I'm so ashamed." She felt Alex's arm around her. "What can I say to them?" she whispered to him. "Nothing I can say is enough." She broke off, eyes brimming with tears, and buried her face in his chest, feeling hopelessly inadequate.

Then from the crowd of men she heard a single, strong tenor voice. Someone began to sing *Rose of Shannon*:

On Shannon's banks there is a rose
Of countenance so fair,
Her beauty has no equal
No treasure can compare.

As he sang, several other voices jumped in on the chorus.

My name I long to give her
To claim her for my own
But no man can possess her
This queen without a throne.

More and more joined in. By the time they got to the third verse, all 150 of them were singing loudly. Megan could only rest her head on Alex's chest and listen in silent wonder.

* * *

Tobias Parmenter was a marked man. And he knew it. As he sat hunched in a corner of a Victoria waterfront bar, he realized he hadn't thought through all the possible consequences of his newfound wealth.

Things hadn't gone at all as planned. His South Seas getaway hadn't materialized. Within what seemed like hours of Megan's sale, Jardine, Matheson had put a clamp on human traffic leaving the island. Rather than appeal to the populace for help in the righteous apprehension of a wanted criminal, his former employers had gone right to that most effective of Hong Kong motivators, money. There was now a considerable price on his head. Posters with his likeness had swiftly appeared seemingly at nearly the same time all over the island. And there wasn't anyone with anything that floated who didn't covet the reward. Such efficiency and speed, he knew, could only have been effected with the assistance of William Mercer. And if the colony administrator was involved, then British troops were after him as well.

He didn't dare venture outside town in hopes of locating a remote cove and a boat owner ignorant of his fugitive status. Traveling outside Victoria had always been risky for Europeans. But now word of his profitable transaction with Yang had spread, and the amount he had received grew with each successive telling. Every cutthroat, cutpurse, brigand, lowlife, mugger, and opportunist coveted his treasure. They knew he had it—somewhere. He was watched, and he was sure greedy eyes were on him wherever he went. Because of the danger, he dared not venture into isolated areas of Victoria, and thus was forced to try to hide in plain sight.

To that end, he had done his best to change his appearance. He had shaved his face bare, cut his curly black hair, and donned clothes no seaman would wear. Putting on one of the large conical bamboo-weave hats favored by the Chinese, he walked with head down, and tried his best to look inconspicuous. For a European, that wasn't easy. He knew it was just a question of time until someone shoved a knife in his back, thinking he might have at least some of his treasure on him. Somehow he had to bide his time until things cooled down enough so that he could find a way off the island.

Now, as he sat morosely in a corner of the bar, ruminating on the burden his treasure had become, he once again imagined that everyone who came in was glancing his way. He had seen one of the wanted posters with his face on it two doors down the street. He nursed his rum and glanced furtively around the room. *It isn't even a good drawing,* he thought. *The least they could do is hire a competent artist.* He had deliberately chosen a table with a view out the dusty window onto the street. He tilted his head up to drain the last of the rum and felt a chill run through him. Four British soldiers were standing in the street. They were engaged in conversation with a barefoot peddler.

He glanced around. The path to the back door was still clear, but he couldn't be sure more soldiers weren't waiting there. He started to sweat as he assessed his chances for avoiding the encounter altogether, when he became acutely aware of someone standing nearby. He turned his head away from the window just as a slender, thirtyish Chinese woman slid into the seat in front of him. He stared at her in consternation, reflexively backing away in his chair. "Who are you and what do you want?" he said, one eye on the soldiers in the street.

"No time for talk," the woman said. "It is only moments before the soldiers find you. If you want to escape them, you must come with me. I can hide you."

Parmenter stared at her, wide-eyed with confusion and near panic. *She knows who I am!* he thought. That wasn't good. He did a lightning-fast appraisal of the woman. She wore expensive clothes, but her silk sheath dress was worn and dirty. She was quite attractive, he thought, though her appearance had a hard look. There was a weariness in her dark eyes. Nevertheless, she sat with regal bearing, and he thought he could see arrogance in her expression. Her lips were pursed in impatience, and she drummed long fingernails on the table.

"You must hurry," she said. "No time to doubt. Come!"

He glanced at the street and saw to his horror that the peddler was pointing directly at the bar where he sat. The soldiers' eyes followed the pointing finger. Then they began to move toward him. He was out of options. "Lead on," he said, swiftly rising to his feet.

The woman walked quickly to the back exit, with Parmenter in close pursuit. She led him out into a junk-filled alley, and broke into a run. It soon became obvious she was in better shape than he was. He struggled to keep up with her as she twisted and turned through interconnecting alleys. Twice he called her to a halt and bent over, hands on knees.

"You can rest soon," she prodded him. "If you want to stay alive, keep going. Move!"

They ran on, dodging lines of hanging laundry, trash bins, rusty bicycles, and the harangues of back alley residents who resented their noisy passage. It was a steady uphill all the way, and by the time the woman finally halted, Parmenter was utterly spent, gasping for breath. The woman seemed no worse for the experience, and curtly ordered him through a shabby door into a nondescript building. It looked no different than dozens of others around it, except for having a deserted air about it. Having come this far, and without strength to object, he wordlessly obeyed.

He walked into a dingy, dark room that was laden with the odor of a long series of occupants. There was a packed-dirt floor and walls covered in places with tattered and faded posters. Two low sleeping mats occupied opposite sides of the room. A small cooking brazier filled with charcoal was on the floor near a scarred table and two chairs. On the table were a teapot, cups, and various utensils.

Parmenter sank into a chair, too weary for further examination of the room's contents. Hot and gasping for air in the humid atmosphere, he removed his jacket and hung it over the back of his chair.

The woman poured tea from the teapot into one of the cups, and offered it to him.

He took it without drinking, but he could feel that the cup was warm. The tea was obviously still hot. It seemed she had been expecting company, perhaps him. "All right," he said, "who are you? I want straight talk, and I want it now."

The woman sank into the other chair and regarded him coolly. An imperious expression settled on her features. "For a man on the run from everyone, you are very demanding," she said.

Parmenter's eyes never left hers as he reached down and withdrew a large knife that was strapped underneath his left pant leg. Slowly he raised the knife, then with a lightning move, slammed its point into the table between them. He left the knife quivering slightly as it stuck upright inches from the woman's hands. "And for a woman alone with Tobias Parmenter, you're careless with your life. If you know me, you know my reputation. If I don't hear something from you that pleases me, I just may slit your throat."

To his surprise, the woman didn't flinch, but merely smiled at him. "You don't want to add murder to your list of crimes," she said. "Though I don't doubt it is already there—along with the rape of the barbarian woman."

Parmenter's features twisted in surprise. "How do you know about that?" He pulled the knife out of the table and pointed it at her throat. "Talk."

The woman picked up the teapot and filled her own cup. "You will treat me with respect. I am Mei Li Kang, Second Mistress to Lord Zhao Yang." Despite her impoverished surroundings and tatty appearance, she imbued the words with power and pride. She didn't tell him that after she had seen First Mistress smashed by the heavy gate, she had fled Lord Yang's compound in terror as her world had crumbled around her.

Parmenter looked at her in silence for a moment. Then he broke out in laughter. "Then, woman, you are Mistress of Nothing. Yang's body was found washed up on the breakwater yesterday. A little the worse for wear, I hear. Guess the typhoon blew him in."

Mei Li Kang's eyes glittered with affront. "You lie." But it was the truth and she knew it. She had already heard, and was playing the last bluff available to her.

"Suit yourself," Parmenter said. "But if he wasn't dead, I'd have to wonder what you're doing here."

Mei Li Kang seemed to fold in on herself ever so slightly. "There is no denying it," she said softly, looking away. "Still, I must survive. I can hide you."

"So that's it. You want me to pay you to hide me."

Li Kang gathered her dignity. "Why not? It is an honorable bargain. I know you can afford it."

"I'll think about it."

"While you do, please do not refuse my hospitality. Have some tea."

Parmenter looked at his teacup, then at hers. "I haven't seen you drink any," he said quietly.

"It is rude for the hostess to drink first."

Parmenter shoved her cup closer to her. "Drink."

"Of course." Li Kang picked up her cup and did so.

Parmenter watched in satisfaction as the woman took a swallow of the tea. Then he picked up his cup and drank. The thin, lightly flavored water the Chinese called tea had never been to his liking, and he took only a short sip. "So, you can hide me out for a while. That doesn't solve my problem of getting off this accursed rock."

Li Kang smiled. "One problem at a time. Now relax, finish your tea. I will go out and obtain more food." She started to rise but Parmenter reached across the table and grabbed her wrist.

"It wouldn't surprise me if it was *you* set those troops on me at the bar," he said. "How do I know you're not going to bring British soldiers right back here and claim the reward?"

She looked at him with contempt. "Why would I do that now? I could have done so earlier. No, collecting the reward for your capture is not honorable. Now, release me, if you wish to eat tonight."

Parmenter grudgingly released her, glaring at her in distrust. "You'd better come back alone," he growled.

Wordlessly, she left. He looked at the remains of his tea for a moment, then poured it out onto the dirt floor. He turned away from the table—and his head reeled. A wave of dizziness swept over him. He fought to remain upright, grasping desperately at the edge of the table. But it was no use. He pulled the table over on top of him as he sank down to the floor, and blackness.

Some indefinite time later, Parmenter drifted back into consciousness, fighting to clear away the fog enveloping his mind. Slowly, he became aware of the rustling of clothes nearby, and felt hands purposefully roaming over his body. Blinking hard and trying to focus, he struggled to move his limbs, but they refused to cooperate. He realized his pockets were being searched, and he was pretty sure he knew who was doing it. His mind was rapidly clearing, but he decided to feign unconsciousness for a bit longer.

The hands lifted away, and he heard a low curse of exasperation. He opened his eyes and saw Li Kang's feet nearby. Her back was turned to him as she searched the jacket he had taken off earlier. It wasn't for nothing he had survived life among the most notorious, backstabbing brigands on the seas. Li Kang hadn't figured on his iron constitution, and that he had poured out most of the tea. With the stealth of a panther, he rose from the floor and wrapped a muscular arm around her throat.

She gasped and fought him wildly, but there was no escape. He didn't see the knife he had stuck in the table earlier, but he kept a small dagger concealed under his left arm. He drew the dagger and held it to her throat, letting the point stick her slightly. "You have a strange idea of honor. Tell me, Mistress of Nothing, what makes you think you could get away with this?"

He was greeted with a volley of curses and then an attempted bite. He whirled her around and smashed a fist into her jaw. Li Kang flew backward and bounced off the wall, but she came up, panting and bleeding from her mouth, with his other knife in her hand. She glared at him for a moment, then lunged. He easily sidestepped the thrust, caught her arm in a viselike grip, and squeezed until the knife fell from her hand. Then he put an arm underneath her chin and shoved her back against the wall.

"You poisonous bitch, I ought to kill you right now," he said.

She bared her teeth in a chilling smile. "You need me," she rasped.

He tilted his head and looked at her with curiosity. "Why?"

"Because without me you'll never get off this island alive. And I can make it happen."

Parmenter eased his arm off a bit. "How?"

"My cousin owns a ship. He sails day after tomorrow. I can get you on board. With your treasure."

Parmenter looked at her with suspicion. "Why should I trust you now? You just tried to steal it. Not that you would have found it on me."

She wrenched away from him, rubbing her jaw. "Because you have no choice. You won't last another twenty-four hours on the run."

He backed away from her. "I saw you drink the tea. But you weren't affected by it. How did you do that?"

She smiled, crossing her arms. "My cup was coated with an antidote to the sleep medicine. Pouring the tea made it dissolve and mix with the tea, making the tea harmless to me. But I didn't count on you being able to recover that quickly."

"I haven't survived more than twenty years at sea by luck. I took only a small sip and poured the rest out. Funny thing, I didn't trust you. And I still don't."

"Then let's agree on that," she said, "and strike a bargain of mutual distrust. We can do each other good—as long as we understand each other."

Parmenter smiled. "You know, you're my kind of scum. I think I understand you. Just make sure *you* understand that if you cross me one more time, I'll slice you into sharkbait."

She moved a step closer to him. "The trip will cost you, of course."

"I figured. How much?"

"We'll bargain with my cousin. But one thing you need to know right now. I'm going along."

"Hmm. Why?"

"There's nothing here for me now. My life is gone. Lord Yang is dead, and I made too many enemies." She walked to the open doorway and stared out across the city spread out below her on the hill. "Besides," she said softly, "I want revenge. Third Mistress must pay for her betrayal."

"Who?"

"Li Fanfan, former Third Mistress of Lord Yang. On her head are the death of First Mistress, and the barbarian invasion of Lord Yang's compound. Because of her, I am penniless and homeless. She has shamed me. *Me*, a woman far above her station. I will be revenged."

"How do you know you could ever find her?"

Mei Li Kang offered a slight smile. "Because I know where she went. She rode out of Lord Yang's compound in the company of the barbarian woman and her rescuers. I have been told she was taken aboard their ship, and sailed with them. I was also told the barbarian woman was from the

American town of San Francisco. I will go there, and there, I am sure I will find Li Fanfan."

Parmenter snorted in derision. "You're wildly optimistic, lady. America is bigger than you can imagine." A chill settled over him. "Wait a minute. Where is your cousin's ship bound for?"

"San Francisco," she said.

"The deal's off! I'm damned if I'll sail out of here right to Megan Daley's hometown. I'd be signing my own death warrant." The memory of three days earlier exploded in his head. He had watched from hiding as the war machine that was *Emerald Isle* smashed her way out of Victoria Harbour, sweeping aside every threat to gain the open sea. As the big clipper ship had pulled away from the dock, he had gotten a brief glimpse of a small black-maned woman on the deck. That, he was sure, was the legendary Angel, the woman whom the savages of California said couldn't die, the woman who seemed to leave a trail of dead adversaries in her wake. Now that he had had her daughter, he had no wish to ever get within one hundred miles of her.

Li Kang looked out the doorway again, a bemused expression on her face. "I see soldiers working their way up the hill. I wonder who will find you first, them or some local trash?"

Parmenter went to the doorway and peered out. She wasn't bluffing; there were indeed British soldiers roaming the hillside. His flight with Li Kang had apparently been reported. His back was against the wall, and he knew it. He drew a deep breath and let it out slowly. Unbidden, the memory of his rape of Megan Daley unfolded in his mind. How sweet it would be to ravish her again . . . . He turned to Kang. "All right, get me aboard as quick as you can. But let's be clear. I don't trust you or your brother or anyone on board that ship. I'm going to stick like glue to you for the whole voyage. I'm going to be your damned partner! If any evil befalls me, you're going down too. Count on it. Your life is in my hands. Got it?"

Mei Li Kang merely smiled, an unsettling expression that did nothing to allay his fears.

Long after nightfall of the following day, Parmenter was smuggled aboard a tired-looking three-masted schooner, along with his treasure. It would cost him fully one-quarter of it to make the voyage, of which he had no doubt Li Kang was getting a sizable percentage. The ship sailed for San Francisco the following morning. He was safely off Hong Kong Island. But he couldn't shake the conviction that he was sailing straight into the jaws of Hell.

* * *

Danielle often stood on the cliff top in the fading light. From her right hand hung a brightly glowing lantern. She was sometimes there for over an hour, and Bridget would fall asleep at her feet. For more than a month, she and Bridget had made a daily trip to the edge of the bluff behind her home. There she would stand as long as her legs would hold her and her growing belly upright; then she would sit. Robert was with them sometimes; other days he watched from the porch. He had bought her the biggest spyglass he could find, so she could search far out to sea. She already knew what to look for when she would finally spot *Emerald Isle*'s tall masts.

"We shall fly a red banner from the mainmast if Megan's aboard, daughter," Kathleen had whispered to her just before the clipper pulled away from the dock in San Francisco. "Red for red hair. Look for the banner."

When she was there late, when the light began to wane, when she could no longer see through the spyglass, she lit the lantern. And each time, before she turned away for home, she grasped the lantern by the base and raised it high over her head, held it aloft until her arms ached. *See the light, sister. Here am I. Let me guide you home.*

On a warm late August day, Danielle stood once again on the blufftop, staring out to sea in the sunlight of early evening. She had left Bridget with Alex, and watched alone. She fretted more and more about the five-year old as Megan's absence grew in length. So far Bridget had held up remarkably well. She was in fact one tough little girl, proving once again that the blood of the Angel flowed in her veins. Danielle knew Kathleen would be proud to see the same iron-willed determination she so often demonstrated manifested in her granddaughter. But she wondered how much longer Bridget could keep up the brave face. The girl had grown increasingly restless in the last three weeks. She had trouble sleeping and had insisted on sharing a bed with Danielle, a practice that had exiled Robert to the downstairs sofa. He hadn't complained, but Danielle knew he wasn't happy. Bridget also now and then unexpectedly broke down in tears, clutching Danielle like she would never let go, then wiping her face and jutting out her lower jaw in a display of stoic fortitude that made her resemble a miniature Kathleen.

Danielle knew there was nothing she could do except comfort Bridget as best she could. Some days she felt bad that she fell short of filling the girl's needs, as her belly grew larger with each passing week and strange moods came and went. Carrying a child was affecting her in ways she wasn't prepared for. For the first time in her adult life she didn't always feel in control of herself, and it bothered her greatly.

Now she stood looking out to sea for what seemed the hundredth time. The lantern was by her feet, ready for the coming darkness. She had been there an hour when Robert came and urged her to come in. She refused. He knew better than to insist, and so put a jacket around her shoulders and went back inside. She barely noticed.

Danielle picked up the spyglass from the long grass that waved around her feet in the fitful breeze, and put it to her eye. She waved it slowly back and forth, scanning the horizon. On the third pass, she stopped. There was something out there. No, it was a trick of light, no more. Then she looked harder, pushing her eye tightly against the eyepiece. It was not a trick of light. Something *was* there, wavering in the haze. She wiped her brow and pushed her hair aside, straining to make out the shapes. Then she could see them. Three very tall masts. Below them a long dark hull. Her heart began to hammer in her chest. No other ship she knew looked exactly like that. It was *Emerald Isle*, and she was coming in.

Danielle waited, pacing back and forth as the ship drew closer. She had to see the mainmast; she had to know before she ran for the house. After nearly half an hour, the big clipper ship was close enough for her to tell. Hardly daring to breathe, trying desperately to steady her trembling hands, she trained the spyglass on the top of the mainmast.

A red banner was flying.

Danielle snatched the lantern from the ground and ran for the house. "Bridget!" she screamed.

Lantern glowing beside her, Danielle stood on the pier with Bridget and Robert, watching the magnificent, streamlined shape of *Emerald Isle* glide into the harbor in the waning daylight. There was just enough light left for the ship to safely maneuver to the pier. Trembling with anticipation, Danielle paced back and forth, shoes thumping along the thick wooden planks. Robert hoisted Bridget up onto his shoulders to wave to the ship as it eased toward them. They could make out figures clustered along the starboard rail.

When the ship was about one hundred yards out, Danielle picked up the lantern and, supporting it by its base, raised it high over her head. She, Robert, and Bridget stood in the circle of light cast on the darkening pier. *Here I am sister*, she thought. *I lit the lantern every night you were gone. Now come to the light. Here is your sister. Here is your daughter. Here is your home.* She held the lantern aloft until her arms gave out. Then she turned and gave it to Bridget. "Light your mother's path, little one," she told her.

They could see Megan waving from the rail, standing beside Kathleen, Ben, and Alex. She looked about ready to jump over the rail and swim for shore, but did not as the pilot brought the giant clipper ship slowly, delicately in alongside the pier. Hawsers were thrown out to the dockhands, and the aft gangway was run out. Nearly three months after she had been so brutally taken, Megan was home.

Bridget bolted up the gangway at top speed, firmly clutching the lantern. Halfway up, she set it down, and flew into her mother's arms. Everyone else stood back, letting them embrace. After long moments, Megan raised a tear-stained face and, smiling broadly, beckoned Danielle forward.

Danielle started up the gangplank, but a few steps from Megan her knees buckled, and she collapsed, sobbing. After all that Megan had been through, surprisingly it was her sister who came apart now. Megan hadn't seen Danielle cry since she was a young girl. Still clutching Bridget tightly, she came quickly forward and bent down to embrace her.

"It's all right, sister," she said soothingly. "I'm all right, and I'm home now." She put a loving hand on Danielle's face and raised it to look into her wet gray-blue eyes. "Thank you for taking care of my baby." She lifted up her hair and wiped Danielle's cheeks. "Now we shall take care of yours together."

Danielle nodded silently and struggled to her feet. She looked up as Kathleen, Ben, and Alex descended the gangway. A look of sorrow settled on her face as Kathleen approached and embraced her warmly.

"Oh, Mother, we lost the railroad," she said, barely audible.

"Don't blame yourself," Kathleen said. "If that's the price we had to pay to get Megan back, then I say it was worth it. Speak no more of it tonight. Tomorrow you can give me the details, and we shall set about establishing the connection between that and Megan's abduction. I'm quite sure there is one. Now, in the days ahead Megan will sorely need the strength she is used to from you. Give the burden of the railroad over to me, and set about comforting your sister. She went through a lot, some of which she refuses to tell me."

"I will, Mother." She looked around and was somewhat startled to see a small Chinese woman standing nearby. She looked scared. "But who is this?"

"Oh, my manners are slipping," Kathleen replied. She strode over and took the hand of the new arrival. "Danielle," she said, leading the woman to her, "this is Miss Li Fanfan. We are deeply indebted to her. She was a true friend to Megan during her captivity, and aided us greatly in getting her back. In fact, without her assistance, it might have taken much longer than it did. She asked to come with us, and we didn't hesitate to take her."

Li Fanfan bowed low to Danielle, who curtsied in return. "And this is my husband, Robert," Danielle said.

"You are woman from country called France," Li Fanfan said. "I hear so much about you. Your mother say you most intelligent woman."

Danielle smiled. "Sometimes."

"Please, Dan-yel, you teach me speak barbari—uh, American tongue better?"

"It will be my pleasure, Miss Li Fanfan. Between Megan and myself, I'm sure we'll have you speaking like a native in no time. And you're welcome to stay with either Megan or us as long as you like."

"I've asked Hsien Lu to look after her for a while," Megan said.

Danielle noticed Hsien Lu standing nearby, and walked over to him. "*Mon ami*," she said, embracing him for a long moment. "Knowing you, I can't wait to hear your stories from this expedition. You must be our guest for supper tomorrow, you and Li Fanfan both."

"It will be my pleasure, Honorable Danielle," Hsien Lu said.

Danielle and Robert went aboard to thank Captain Rowan profusely, then the entire party climbed aboard the big carriage Danielle, Robert, and Bridget had arrived in.

Li Fanfan squeezed in uncomfortably between Hsien Lu and Megan, who held Bridget on her lap. The crush of white people around her made her nervous. *Now I am irrevocably in the company of barbarians*, she thought. *It appears now that they will not eat me, but they are most strange. They are fond of touching each other, and openly show their most intimate feelings. I would like to learn more of why this is so. I shall ask many questions of Honorable Megan. And her mother—aiee, such power radiates from her! I must work hard to win her favor. The Warrior Hsien Lu seems wise in the ways of these people. I will stay close to him, if he will let me.*

It was thoroughly dark by the time the big carriage pulled up in front of Alex and Megan's house. Megan sprang from her seat and sprinted up the steps to the porch, where she turned to face the rest, a radiant smile on her face. "I'm home!" she said. She spread her arms wide as Bridget flew at her again, then put her down as Alex came up, lifted her off the porch, and carried her through the doorway as if she were a new bride. Inside, he looked at her tenderly as she reclined in his arms, her hands around his neck.

143

"Never again," he said. "You're never going anywhere without me again. You're more precious to me than gold, Megan. Nothing could replace you. I love you, and I want you by my side always."

She buried her face in his neck. "And so it shall be," she murmured.

He put her down gently, and, with Bridget holding her hand, Megan began a slow walk around the house, drinking in the sensations of being home again. Upstairs and down she wandered, looking, touching, feeling. She finally stopped at her bed, where she sank slowly down and ran her hands back and forth across the bedspread. She smiled at Bridget as the girl jumped up beside her. "You'll sleep with us for a while, if you wish," she told her. "Would you like that?"

"Yes, Mama," Bridget replied. "I sure would." She put her arms around her mother. "Oh, Mama, I knew Grandma Kathy would bring you back."

The buzz of conversation and movement in the house slowly faded away. Exhausted, Danielle left with Robert, promising to return in the morning. Ben and Alex sat in the parlor sharing a bottle of brandy, while Kathleen roamed around the house, seemingly at a loss for something appropriate to do. At eleven o'clock, Megan came into the parlor and signaled Alex to come to bed. He bade goodnight to Ben and went upstairs with her, where he found Bridget soundly asleep in the middle of the bed. Her favorite doll was clutched tightly underneath her chin.

It was nearly one o'clock in the morning when the silence of the parlor was broken by the faint sound of footsteps on the wooden plank floor. A table lamp dimly lit the room, just enough to reveal Kathleen's still figure seated on one end of a sofa. She turned her head at the sound of the footsteps and saw Megan standing in the doorway, faintly outlined by a hallway lamp.

"I couldn't sleep," she said.

"I couldn't either," Kathleen replied, smiling. "Come join me."

Megan walked over and sat down next to her. She looked at her in silence for a moment, then put her arms around Kathleen's neck. "Mother, I was so foolish."

Kathleen shushed her with a gentle hand to her lips. "No. You were my daughter. You conducted yourself like a true Connelly woman. And I've never been more proud of you."

They sat together in the dim light for a while, content to hold and touch each other. Then Megan reclined, putting her head in Kathleen's lap.

Kathleen softly stroked her daughter's hair, watching the slow rise and fall of her chest. "Do you remember," she said, "the first time you were stolen from me, when the Indian took you that winter night in the Sierras, so long ago?"

Megan nodded silently.

"Such a long time," Kathleen mused. "Seventeen years. You were nine. When that savage bashed me over the head and ran off with you, after killing your father, I was nearly mad with grief. Then I was just plain mad. I was determined that he was going to have to kill me too if he wanted to keep you. And he couldn't do it. I dared him to plunge that spear into my chest, and he couldn't do it. I learned something that day, and I've carried it with me ever since. I learned that if I looked someone in the eye and didn't back down, didn't give up, I could bend people to my will."

"You might have died several times over, Mother," Megan said.

"And then," Kathleen continued as if Megan hadn't spoken, "Alex stole you all over again, at least your heart. Then he came back for you, even after I threatened him with a gun. How foolish I can be! He's such a wonderful addition to the family. I'm proud to have him for a son-in-law." She fell silent, but continued to stroke Megan's hair.

Megan thought she was through, but then Kathleen started again.

"And now this happens," she continued. "Once again, you were stolen. And why? For profit? For revenge? I will know. By all that's holy, I will know. And someone will pay."

"Please, Mother, let it go," Megan said. "I'm back, I'm safe, but I'm weary. I wish we could all just relax a while and wait for Danielle's baby. Go back to the Senate and be a leader. Let it go."

"I can't, daughter. I can't let it go. You were grievously wronged. You were taken and sold into slavery. I fought for your life there in the Sierras seventeen years ago. I fought for you again years later when that same savage attacked me for the third time, and I killed him. And I will fight for you now. Someone has come after this family again. And I will know who."

Kathleen spoke no more, and Megan lay in the darkness listening to her breathe. She knew her mother well. She heard the familiar iron in her voice. And she knew what was coming. Whoever was involved in her kidnapping had better put their earthly affairs in order.

Megan had finally gone upstairs for good sometime in the night, but Ben had had to come to the parlor at 3 a.m. and take Kathleen to bed. Even so, the next morning she was up before everyone, impatiently pacing in the kitchen, bristling with nervous energy. Ben had to get her out of the house and take her for a walk along the bluff top to calm her down.

"Let Megan sleep as long as she needs to," he told her as they strolled along the footpath through the grass. "Don't rush her on this investigation."

"Very well," Kathleen said, clearly frustrated at the delay. "Bridget and I will find something to do for a while."

Megan finally came downstairs just before one o'clock in the afternoon. Clad in a soft robe, she settled into a high-backed chair in the parlor and partook of some rolls and tea that Kathleen brought her. Kathleen then sent for Danielle and Robert. By two o'clock everyone was gathered in the parlor.

Though the house belonged to Megan and Alex, Kathleen dominated any meeting, no matter where she was, and it was no different this time. She was given the high-backed chair usually reserved for Alex, and sat waiting for everyone to settle in. When she was sure she had their attention, she began.

"So, Danielle, what was Stanford's offer this time?"

Danielle consulted her notes. "Cash for shares of Sierra and Western stock at their high market value over the last six months, *plus* a gift of ten shares of Central Pacific stock for each share of Sierra and Western sold. Our stockholders increased their railroad shares tenfold in this deal, in addition to getting top price for their Sierra and Western shares."

"Yes, but the Central Pacific shares aren't worth a damned thing," Ben put in.

"No, not now," Robert said. "And while there's no shortage of skeptics who think they'll never reach the Nevada border, I'm not one of them. I think they're going to succeed in a big way, and the value of those shares is going to skyrocket. We'd all make a great deal of money." As soon as the words were out of his mouth, he knew he'd said the wrong thing.

"I don't *need* more money!" Kathleen said hotly. "They stole our railroad. I want it back."

"Sorry," Robert said quietly.

"Now," Kathleen continued. "I think Danielle's correct that there's a connection between Megan's kidnapping and the events that led to loss of our railroad. It seems all too obvious that we were meant to learn where she had been taken. Someone maneuvered us out of the country for a while so they could pull off this theft. I'm open to suggestions as to whom."

"Leatherwood's at the top of my list," Ben said.

Heads nodded in agreement around the room.

"Danielle, you were here. What do you think?" Kathleen said.

Danielle stroked her chin, a thoughtful look on her long Gallic features. "He certainly took advantage of your absence. But did he initiate the events that caused it? I simply don't know. If he did, I think he's only one layer of a bigger deception. I'm willing to bet there's someone else. Someone bigger."

"One of the Central Pacific's Big Four?" Alex put in.

"Could be," Robert said. "Though there's no evidence they're directly involved at present. But if they do turn out to be behind it, I'd vote for Huntington. The man's got the soul of a shark. And he's a master at creating layers of false trails and confusion, at least in company books. If he's created a deception, it'll be a tough nut to crack."

"We're getting ahead of ourselves," Kathleen said. "I think we ought to start at the bottom and work our way up, if we can."

"What do you mean?" Robert said.

"Let's start with the reintroduction of the opium into Megan's life," Kathleen replied. She noticed out of the corner of her eye that Megan hung her head. "The notes, the pipes. Who put them in her path? I think I saw who planted the note in her saddlebag. I don't know who he is, but if I see him again"— she paused, her face darkening—"I'll know him. Ben and I will stay here until we get this matter sorted out. The ranch will run itself. Let's see if we can find the busboys from the restaurants. If we can get hold of them, maybe we can find out who put them up to it."

Li Fanfan settled into a spare bedroom in Megan's house, spending her days in amazement at the barbarian world and all its trappings. In the evenings, she would meet in the parlor with Hsien Lu, who patiently explained in Chinese the meaning and purpose of some of the things she saw. Often her eyes were big with wonder.

Kathleen assigned Alex to look for the substitute hay delivery boy, unaware he was also one of the restaurant busboys. Alex would be joined by Hsien Lu, whose services Yuen Ling-Po had graciously extended. They began their search at the two restaurants where the boxed opium pipe had shown up. The busboys hadn't been seen at either place since the incidents, but Alex was able to get a good description of their appearance. When he described the second boy to Kathleen, her eyes lit up.

"That's him," she said. "That's the boy that came with Reno to deliver the hay!"

"Are you sure?" Alex asked.

"Sure enough to call Reno in for a talk. Have Hsien Lu invite him over for some lemonade."

The next day, Reno sat in the cool parlor of Megan's house, fidgeting with his cap and trying not to look scared witless. An invitation to a private talk with the Angel was a pleasure he would rather forego. But there was something in the expression of the big Chinese man she sent to fetch him that made it clear he had better not refuse.

"So," Kathleen said, pouring him a generous glass of lemonade, "what was this boy's name?"

"I believe it was Hiram, ma'am," Reno said.

"And just how is it he showed up to help you that day?"

"Well, Jimmy took sick, and he brought Hiram along to stand in for him."

"How convenient," Kathleen said.

Reno twisted his cap and took a long drink of lemonade, glad the Chinese man wasn't present for the interrogation. "Well, that's just it, ma'am, Jimmy didn't *look* sick. He showed up first thing in the morning, said he couldn't work that day, and that Hiram would take his place. I didn't have time to ask questions. We had hay to deliver."

"Is Jimmy in the habit of being sick?"

"No ma'am, never knowed him to be sick before."

"Hmm. Tell me," Kathleen said, refreshing his glass from a pitcher, "where can we find Jimmy?"

Alex and Hsien Lu stood in the dark interior of the haybarn. Stripes of sunlight came through the boards of the walls, lighting up the dust in the air and casting zebra lines of illumination on the lanky youth before them. Jimmy was tall and broomstick-thin, with too-short pants held up by red suspenders. He had a shock of unruly reddish-brown hair over his forehead, a prominent nose with an arched bridge, and a jaw that came to a point. Alex thought he looked like a hick, which in fact he was.

"I want answers, Jimmy," Alex said. "How did Hiram take your place? It seems you weren't sick."

Jimmy looked at the scowl on the face of the Chinese man standing next to Alex. He licked his lips in nervousness. "Well, ah—he, ah, he showed up day before, and offered me a twenty dollar gold piece if'n I'd lay off for a day. Well, I couldn't turn that down." He looked in desperation at the men. "Could I?"

"Weren't you curious about why he wanted to do that?" Alex asked.

"He, ah, he said I wasn't to ask no questions. So I didn't."

Alex sighed in disgust. "Have you seen Hiram since?"

Jimmy shifted from one foot to the other. "No sir. You want me to look for him? I swear, I'd know him if I see him!"

"Another pair of eyes wouldn't hurt," Alex said. "Tell you what, find him and you'll earn a $100 reward. That goes for you too," he told Reno, who stood nearby. "He may go back to restaurant work. I suggest we fan out and visit every restaurant around the bay. This could take some time, so let's get to it."

A week later, a tired-looking three-masted schooner slipped into San Francisco harbor just before sunset. No one paid much attention to the nondescript ship, a frequent visitor to the city. And there was no one around when, long after dark, two furtive passengers disembarked. Tobias Parmenter wasted no time slipping into the deeper shadows. And Mei Li Kang was soon another yellow face among the anonymous masses on the dark streets of Chinatown.

9.

Alex and Hsien Lu, aided by Jimmy and Reno, fanned out around the bay, going from one restaurant to another. Not wanting to call attention to themselves, they didn't announce their intentions to the restaurant managers, but merely took coffee or tea and observed for a while.

Two weeks passed. Alex heard nothing from the other searchers. Danielle reached her eighth month of pregnancy. It continued to be troublesome, and her doctor ordered almost continuous bed rest. Megan visited her almost daily, and usually brought Li Fanfan with her. The awed Chinese girl had fallen into servant behavior, and sometimes had to be forcibly corrected by Megan when she scrambled to wait on others.

"I appreciate your willingness to serve," Megan told her one day. They were once again in Danielle's house, at her bedside. "But this is America. No one needs to be a servant here unless they choose to. And then they are paid for their duties. I don't want that for you."

"But Honorable Megan, I owe great debt to you! I work in house, pay off debt. Please, I serve."

"You owe me nothing. Let's call it even. And please drop the 'Honorable Megan' stuff."

Li Fanfan hung her head and sorrowfully looked at the floor. "Yes, Megan," she said softly.

"Hmm," Megan mused. "I can see we need to work on your self-confidence. If you're going to be around Connelly women you'll need to quit acting like a servant, and start acting more like you own the world. Now, I must ask you, has Hsien Lu been treating you well?"

"Yes, Megan, he—he kind to me." She frowned.

"But?"

"Megan, he scare me. He most fierce warrior."

Danielle chuckled. "There's nothing unusual in that. He scares most people. But you can trust him with your life."

"And perhaps," Megan mused, "you will have a softening influence on him."

Later, when Li Fanfan was out of earshot, Danielle looked at Megan with a bemused expression. "I wonder if we should be playing matchmaker. After all, Hsien Lu doesn't work for us. He's just on loan."

"Yes, I know," Megan replied. "But they'd be good for each other. Ling-Po will certainly never do anything about it. So," she said with a saucy smile, "it's up to us. Could be fun." Her expression changed. "How's the baby doing?"

Danielle sank back on her propped-up pillows. "Holding its own. The doctor said I almost lost it at the stockholders' meeting. I do feel pain some days, pain that doesn't seem right. And I'm very tired. But I'm only about a month from delivery. If I can just hang on a while longer . . . ."

Megan reached out and took her hand. "Dear sister, I haven't forgotten that you were there with me when Bridget was born, and I was so scared. I'll be here whenever you need me. I'll move into your bedroom until the delivery if I have to. Just say the word. We'll be strong together."

Danielle smiled. "Maybe I'll take you up on that." She gently squeezed Megan's hand. "I love you, sister."

In early September, Alex finally got the break he was looking for. He was in his stable grooming Shamrock when Reno came riding hard up the rise to the bluff top. The boy reined his horse to a halt in a cloud of dust at the stable entrance.

"Found him!" he said, jumping down. "Hiram's washing dishes in a little restaurant on the south bay."

Alex stopped brushing the big stallion and approached Reno. "You actually see him?"

"Sure did," Reno said proudly.

"Did he see you?"

"No. I hid my face behind a menu soon's I saw him. I'm pretty sure I got out of there without him spotting me."

"Good work. I want you to be ready to take Hsien Lu and me over there first thing in the morning."

The following morning, the three of them stood outside a small restaurant on the waterfront in the southern part of San Francisco. Like some other structures along the water, it was actually a converted ship's hull. Land had been precious even in the city's infancy, and filling in of the bay had begun at an early stage. Abandoned ships—a legacy of the gold rush days—had been deliberately run aground and leased out as stores and hotels, and the bay filled in around them. As filling continued further into the bay, some of the ships were left a considerable distance from the water. This one, however, was still at the high tide line.

Alex eyed the restaurant. "I'm going in to make sure he's there," he said to the other two. "I'll try to flush him out. You two take up your positions like we discussed." With that he climbed the front steps and entered.

Alex let his eyes adjust to the dim interior light, then took a table. He ordered coffee and waited. After about ten minutes, a boy emerged from the back room to clear nearby tables. It was Hiram, Alex was certain. As the boy paused to pick up dishes from the table next to his, Alex leaned over close to him. "Megan Daley sends her regards," he whispered.

Hiram whirled on him, eyes wide in shock. He backed up, stumbled, and dropped the load of dishes he was carrying. Amid the thundering crash of shattering china, he bolted for the door.

Reno saw Hiram come flying out of the restaurant and launch himself off the top step. Hiram's mouth gaped as he simultaneously hit the ground and saw Reno in his path. He whirled left and fled down an alley on the port side of the restaurant ship. He got about four steps before he skidded to a halt in the dirt. A big Chinese man with a grim expression on his face and a large saber in his right hand stood in his path. Terrified, he spun around to flee, but found his escape blocked. He stood trembling and mute in the alley.

Alex approached him, fury on his face, until he was just inches away. "Boy, you've got some things to answer for. And there's someone anxious to meet you. You're coming with us."

As he sat in the parlor of Megan's home, Hiram was sure his life had come to an end. Around him were several people, any one of whom, he was sure, would cheerfully kill him without thinking twice. Megan Daley, or the man he now knew as her husband Alex, the murderous-looking Chinaman behind his chair, Ben Wilson—any of them would do it. But the person he feared most was right in front of him. The Angel had him now, and she was in a rage.

Kathleen, dressed in black, strode back and forth in front of the boy, arms folded, occasionally shooting lethal glances his way. She was content to let him stew for long moments. After an uncomfortable silence, she spoke without looking at him. "Do you know my reputation, young man?" she said in an icy voice.

Hiram managed to croak out a reply. "I—I know what people say about you."

"And what do they say?"

"The savages over in the Sierras, they, uh, they say you can't be killed."

"And what else?"

Hiram was sunk into depths of misery he had never experienced. "I've heard people who cross you end up dead." Tears were beginning to form in his eyes. "Mrs. Wilson, are you going to kill me?"

Kathleen stopped pacing and approached him. She bent over and placed her hands on the arms of his chair. The gaze of her sky-blue eyes bored into him. "You'll never know the hell my daughter went through because of the events you set in motion. The heathen who bought her as a *slave* is dead. His number one mistress is dead. So is a fair number of his household army. But I'm not going to kill you. Yet. The only reason you're still alive is because I want some answers only you may be able to provide." She backed off and leaned against a desk in front of him, arms crossed. "And if I like what I hear, maybe you'll see tomorrow. If not--". She looked at Hsien Lu.

That look was all that was necessary. Hiram crumbled. "What do you want to know?"

Kathleen gave way to Megan, who stood before him, green eyes blazing with anger. "This is a simple question. I want to know who paid you to place that note in my saddlebag. I don't suppose he'd be stupid enough to give you his real name, so you can just tell me what he looks like. We'll start with that."

Hiram was sweating. No matter what he did next, he was going to lose. He decided to concentrate on surviving the moment. Then he'd take his chances with the mysterious man who hired him. "Well, Mrs. Daley, he was a little shorter than average, kind of stout, thick-necked, with ruddy cheeks that got red when he was upset. Not much hair, just some dark fringes over his ears. He had thick lips that he pushed out sometimes. It kind of made him look like a fish. Usually had a couple days' growth of beard. Had some spectacles he put on for reading. Didn't dress real well. And—and he told me some wild tale about coming out alive from some scrape he got in with you before. Something about a warehouse getting blown up."

Megan looked at Kathleen, eyes widening in a dawning realization. "My God, it's Othniel Wanamaker."

Eli Leatherwood luxuriated in his elegant new office on rails. As president of the Sierra and Western branch of the Central Pacific Railroad, he hadn't hesitated to have a car built that he thought befitted his new status as a railroad baron. He wasn't a big one yet, but that would come, he was sure. For now, this would allow him to come and go on the rails with style. He even had plans to have the car pulled by the Central Pacific's *Governor Stanford* locomotive itself out to rail's end in the Sierras to personally inspect track-laying progress. Charlie Crocker probably wouldn't want him there, but, well, he'd find some way to soothe the CPRR construction chief.

His office on wheels was truly magnificent. Why, it probably rivaled anything the Big Four had, he was certain of that. Leather couches and chairs, crystal lampshades, brass fittings, polished oak. In fact, there was only one blot of imperfection in the entire place. And he was looking at it.

Othniel Wanamaker was once again sullying his beautiful leather guest chair. He had told the loathsome little man to stay away. But now, long after dark, the soiled creature had once again invaded his domain. That made Leatherwood nervous; it meant there was probably bad news. "So, what is it this time?" he said, resting his chin on his steepled fingers.

Wanamaker shifted in the chair. "Alex Daley and that big Chinaman been makin' the rounds of the restaurants in town. Ain't too hard to figger out what they're lookin' for."

Leatherwood remained calm, but inwardly he was churning. "Well, that's nothing we didn't expect. The Wilsons and their daughters are a smart bunch. They're probably trying to work their way up from the busboys. They can't trace them to you, can they?"

"Naw," he said, "there's no way." He didn't tell Leatherwood his ego had gotten the better of him, and though he hadn't told the boys his name, he had made the mistake of regaling them with tales of his survival from the previous encounter with the Angel and her family.

"What about the letter?"

"Likewise. I had it made in Chinatown. No names exchanged."

Wanamaker looked entirely too uncomfortable for Leatherwood's liking. "Hmm. I'm not satisfied. You know where the busboys are?"

"Yeah, sure."

"All right. Here's what you'll do. Get to them as fast as you can. Tell them to get out of town. Way out of town. To Nevada or somewhere. Make it permanent."

Wanamaker rubbed the stubble on his chin. "I'll need motivatin' money."

Leatherwood reached into a drawer, withdrew an envelope, and shoved it across his polished desk. "Here it is. Get them out of town. And then join them."

Wanamaker looked uneasy. "I dunno. I don't cotton to bein' in Nevada come winter. And it's gonna start showin' up in another couple of months."

Leatherwood leaned forward in his chair, face a rigid mask. "If you stay in this town, and I think you're a security risk, I'll get rid of you myself. Do you understand me, Wanamaker?"

Wanamaker took the envelope from the desk and stuffed it into his coat pocket. Then he slowly rose from the chair, a mixture of indignation and fear on his bloated features. "Yeah, I understand," he said hoarsely.

Leatherwood rose. "You got your revenge. I got what I wanted. Your part is done, and you've been well paid. Don't come back here. Ever."

* * *

Tobias Parmenter hadn't relaxed the entire first week he was ashore in California. At first, he had planned to ship out on the next available vessel bound for the South Seas. But the more he looked around, the more fascinated he was with the energy and optimism around him in the new state. Compared to that, the prospect of living in the South Seas seemed boring now. He'd miss the excitement of society on the frontier. Too, it had taken a quarter of his ill-gotten treasure to get him out of Hong Kong. With some of what he had left, he didn't doubt California offered excellent opportunities for investments that would not only restore what he had lost, but perhaps even increase it.

He wasn't fool enough to hang around San Francisco. Too great a chance he'd be recognized. So the second day in port, he'd headed off to Sacramento and started asking questions. He discovered gold mining wasn't the place to invest his money. It was clear from what he heard that the easy pickings were gone. It was going to take investments in equipment to make money now. And that was too chancy. He hadn't the patience or knowledge for ranching, and that would raise his profile entirely too high. No, he needed a growing enterprise where his money could work quietly. And in Sacramento the talk of the town was railroads. To hear the locals chatter, the transcontinental railroad was the greatest thing ever to hit civilization. Its western arm, the Central Pacific, was gobbling up lesser railroads in California right and left. He'd heard the Sierra and Western had recently joined the fold. The potential for growth was said to be enormous, and most of the people he talked to lamented they didn't have any real money to invest in the new enterprise.

But *he* did. Here was something he could quietly sink some money into and perhaps reap enormous profits a little farther down the road. Not wishing to try riding a horse—an experience he cared little for—he hopped aboard a train and rode up into the Sierras to rail's end. There he saw a sight such as he had never witnessed. Spread out below and beyond him on the mountainside were thousands of men. Most of them were Chinese. He was amazed at the energy with which they tore at the earth. A vast field of bobbing pickaxes, shovels, saws and hammers flashed in the sunlight, as the workers graded roadbeds, felled trees, built trestles, and blasted cuts out of rocky precipices. The noise thundered off the mountainside. In all his years at sea, he had never seen anything to compare with it. The vibrancy, the sheer insane optimism of the stupendous project took irrevocable hold on him. When he returned to Sacramento, after being assured of the confidentiality of his transaction, he invested a chunk of his treasure in Central Pacific stock.

Deep in Chinatown, Mei Li Kang festered with resentment. And with every passing day it grew. She was disgusted with the barbarian world she had entered. In China she had been a woman of class and privilege. Here she was nothing. Her attempts to establish herself in a position she considered appropriate to her noble lineage had come to naught. Her money would keep her alive, but it wouldn't buy her status. It seemed even the Chinese here had succumbed to the barbarian ways. Some of them actually sneered at her! It just wasn't the proper order of things. Worse yet, maintaining the luxurious quarters she knew she deserved was using up her share of Parmenter's passage money fast. She faced the disturbing prospect of having to *work* before long, something she had never done in her life. *Oh blast it*, she thought, *this is all the accursed Li Fanfan's fault!* When she got her hands on the traitorous little peasant, she would wring her slender neck, and delight in throttling the life from her.

And she already knew where the girl was. Mei Li Kang was glad that, as in the old world, money bought information in the new world as well.   She had paid for knowledge as to where Megan Daley lived, and confirmed that Li Fanfan was living with her. They had been seen together in Chinatown. She would watch, and she would wait. And when she saw them, well, she had a delicious idea. Li Fanfan was a country girl, a bumpkin, subject to all manner of superstitious beliefs. It would be fun to throw a little scare into her before she killed her. She smiled at the prospect.

Then, when the deed was done, she would have to see to the means to maintain the lifestyle to which she was accustomed. She was certain any Chinese man of power and influence would value her as a mistress. Indeed, she had already heard much about one such man, a successful merchant named Yuen Ling-Po. Unlike China, merchants in America were respected for their accomplishments. And he more than most. Yes, she would have to wangle an introduction before long. Such a man would surely appreciate her.

* * *

Everyone in the parlor of Megan's house except Hiram was speechless at the boy's revelation. Megan sank into a chair in disbelief. Kathleen looked at Ben in consternation. And Hsien Lu's expression darkened.

"I thought he was dead," Megan finally got out.

"So did I," Kathleen said. "Apparently he isn't. That is, if it really is him."

"It must be," Megan said morosely. "Why would anyone else do this? He must have revenge on his mind. But I haven't heard a word from him or about him since he tried to blow up our railroad trestle, with me on it, and we blew up his warehouse instead. Last I knew, his freight business collapsed, and he left the gold rush country. That was, what, four years ago? There's been no word of him since."

"Megan," Kathleen said, "It's disturbing to think about, but he must have been watching you for some time. He had to have known your routine to get the box placed at your table in your favorite restaurant. And he must have watched you almost constantly every time you went into town to be aware of where you were when you changed restaurants."

Megan shuddered. "So the creepy little weasel was watching me from the shadows all the time."

"It would seem so," Ben said. "We don't yet know how his revenge crusade, if that's what it was, became connected to your kidnapping, and the loss of our railroad."

"I don't think he organized all of that himself," Kathleen said. "He hasn't got the brains or the money to pull it off. He had help. Intelligent, well-financed help. I'm sure of it."

"Do you remember what I told him when we blew up his warehouse?" Megan said.

"Yes," Ben said. "You told him that if he ever threatened our family again, he'd find himself on a ship bound for Shanghai, never to return to these shores."

"That was pretty much it."

"This is all very well and good, but we have to find him first," Kathleen said. She turned back to Hiram. "Do you have any idea where he might be, young man?"

"No ma'am," Hiram said. "We met in a different place every time. I wasn't to see him again after the last time."

"Mother, I know what I told him last time," Megan said. "But couldn't we just forget about him for a while, and concentrate on getting our railroad back? I don't like to see us chasing all over San Francisco looking for the little rat. It doesn't make us look good."

Kathleen's face darkened like a thundercloud, but she glanced at Ben, who nodded his agreement. "Very well. I think it's a good idea. Let's concentrate on the big issues first. I want to confer with Danielle and Robert, and see if we can uncover a money trail. It took money to pull off Megan's kidnapping. It had to come from somewhere, and likely not from Wanamaker. She turned to Hiram once again. "And you, young man, you're on retainer, as of now. In other words, you're working for us. Any objections?"

Kathleen's expression told Hiram he'd better not object. "No ma'am."

"Good. Now, we're going to stash you somewhere, and I want you to stay low. We'll give you money for food and lodging. If anyone asks you about this meeting, you were never here. I'm not taking any chances on you accidentally tipping off Wanamaker that we're onto him. And if you see or hear of anything that can help us, you're to report it to us immediately. You'll be watched," she warned, glancing in Hsien Lu's direction. "Try to disappear, and I'll send Hsien Lu after you. And he'll find you. That wouldn't be pleasant. Got it?"

Hiram gulped, and nodded silently.

"And as for Othniel Wanamaker," she continued, walking to the window and looking out toward the city, "I have a feeling that eventually he may come to us."

The day after the meeting with Hiram, Megan felt she needed to get away, and suggested to Li Fanfan they take a trip into Chinatown. The teen girl was enthusiastic.

"Oh yes, Megan! I wish see Chinatown very much. See what Chinese do in your country."

"Good," Megan said. "I'll leave Bridget with Danielle, and we'll make a day of it, just us girls. We'll do some sightseeing, some shopping, find a good restaurant. And I think there's a circus in town."

They set off in a carriage occupied by the two armed escorts who accompanied Megan whenever she left home now. The morning fog had burned off, and the polished carriage wheels gleamed in the brilliant sunshine as the horse strode along at a rapid clip. They were soon in Chinatown. Megan and Li Fanfan strolled leisurely through the area, going from shop to shop. Megan had Li Fanfan try on some Western clothes, but the girl was clearly uncomfortable with how she looked, and Megan didn't press her to take them.

"Perhaps later," Megan said with a smile. "Now, how about some lunch? I'm famished."

They found a small restaurant where Megan decided to be adventurous with Chinese food. Li Fanfan now had the upper hand, as she guided Megan through a menu of items unfamiliar to the American woman. Megan took her advice and tried egg flower soup and sweet and sour shrimp, which she enjoyed.

"Different than China," Li Fanfan said, savoring the taste, "but still good."

After a leisurely meal, they strolled along the boardwalk looking in shop windows, tailed closely by Megan's bodyguards. They eventually paused at one that featured paintings of Hong Kong and Victoria. Li Fanfan couldn't take her eyes off of them.

"Homesick?" Megan asked, coming over to stand beside her.

"Some," the girl answered. "This not home. But I not sorry. Look," she said, pointing through the dusty window, "in this painting I see walls of Master Yang's compound." She shuddered. "Bad things go on there."

"Well, he's dead now," Megan said comfortingly. "Him and his evil mistresses. Come on; let's get back to the carriage. It's getting late."

She turned away, but Li Fanfan lingered, staring at the painting. Dark memories churned through her consciousness. She began to feel a prickling on her neck and an increasing dread. Forcibly looking away from the painting, her eyes shifted to one side. She gasped and began to tremble. Beside the painting, from the darkened interior of the store, a malevolent visage was glaring out at her. Putting a hand to her mouth, she recoiled in horror and stumbled off the boardwalk. The disturbing image faded back into the shadows.

Megan had turned to urge her to come along when she saw the distraught Chinese girl backed up against a hitching rail and shaking. She rushed forward and put protective arms around her. Li Fanfan was pale. "What is it? What happened?" Megan said. "You look like you saw a ghost."

Li Fanfan buried her face against Megan's shoulder. "I did," she murmured.

Megan paced in her parlor as Li Fanfan sat huddled in a chair. She had fetched the girl some tea and tried to comfort her, but she was still shaken, and Megan was trying to downplay the encounter. "Are you so sure of what you saw?" she said. "The light was rather dim in that store."

"I sure," the girl said, barely audible.

Megan was tempted to add that all Chinese looked alike to her, so how could Li Fanfan be sure it was Second Mistress, but thought better of it. "I mean no disrespect, dear, but I don't believe in ghosts. If it *was* Second Mistress you saw, it was no ghost. It really was her. How or why she came here, I can't imagine. The most important question, though, is what is she up to?"

"You go to look for her, Megan?"

"Hmm. No, I don't think so, not right now. We have bigger things to take care of. But it seems clear she was trying to frighten you, so you won't be going into town alone like we thought you might. When the time is right, perhaps I'll ask Hsien Lu to go in to look around. *That'll* put the fear of God into her."

Ben, Kathleen, and Robert gathered around Danielle's bedside. Her delivery was near, and she continued to be confined to bed.

"Are you in pain, dear?" Kathleen asked her.

Danielle rested both hands on her enormous stomach. "Now and then. I haven't had a good night's sleep in longer than I can remember. I'm just very tired, and as joyous as this occasion is, I'll be glad when our baby finally comes. Was Megan so much trouble to carry?"

Kathleen chuckled. "No, she was easy. All the trouble with *her* was in the growing up." She leaned forward, staring intently at her adopted daughter. "You're scared, aren't you?"

"Yes," Danielle said softly.

"Well, I have a present for you. I've sent for Mrs. Grady to come over from Sacramento."

Danielle's mouth fell open in surprise. "The midwife who helped us when Bridget was born?"

"Yes. I expect her tomorrow. She'll stay until you deliver. And Megan and I will be here with you too."

Tears glistened in Danielle's eyes. "Thank you, Mother."

"Now," Kathleen said, reaching out to pat her hand, "I know you're tired, so we'll keep this meeting as short as possible. Ben and I think we need to move without further delay on investigating Central Pacific's records. We'll be looking for information that might help us get the railroad back, and we think Robert's the natural person to do the investigating. He's got connections in San Francisco that might get him on the inside. But we'd like your permission. This is a critical time at your house. He really should stay close by, and if you say so, he'll wait until after your delivery."

"No," Danielle said firmly. "I want him on it now, if he's willing. We can send someone to fetch him when the time comes, and he can be here quickly."

Kathleen looked skeptically at Robert.

"No," he said. "I'd have to go to Sacramento to Central Pacific headquarters to examine the books." He rose and went to Danielle, putting his arm around her tenderly. "There's no way I'm getting that far away from you until our child is born." He took Danielle's hand and squeezed it gently. "When I do go though, it won't be easy. Collis Huntington's a master at creating confusion and false trails in company books. It's going to take some real digging to find anything of significance."

"Mother, you also need to get over to Sacramento as soon as possible," Danielle said. "You've got to talk to the leased parcel owners at Milepost Thirty-one. It won't be long until Leatherwood discovers The Sierra and Western right of way includes two parcels that were leased for five years, if he doesn't know already. Those leases are about to expire. You need to renegotiate them now, or buy them outright if you can."

"We've thought of that too, Danielle. Ben leaves tomorrow for just that purpose," Kathleen replied. "I'm not going either, with you about to deliver. Business negotiations may not be my strong suit right now anyway. But I'm *so* grateful for your advice that we lease those right of way parcels in *our* names, and not the railroad's. That could turn out to be our ace in the hole."

"It won't be if the leases expire and you can't renew them. You can expect the Central Pacific to move aggressively to acquire them. I'd give a thousand dollars to be there when they find out," Danielle said.

"Maybe you will, daughter," Kathleen said. "By the way, have you heard about Leatherwood's fancy new railroad car? Apparently, he's playing the role of railroad baron to the hilt. If we ever establish a connection between him and Wanamaker, I'll burn that car down around his ears."

Leaving Danielle to rest, Ben, Robert, and Kathleen went downstairs to the parlor. Kathleen sank into a chair with a cup of tea and put a hand to her head.

"I'm continually amazed at the greed and viciousness of the Big Four," she said. "They already own most of the track in California. They won't stop until they have it all. We've always striven to keep our rates low and fair. But they rape the public with outrageous fares, and if they hold a monopoly, it will only get worse."

"Undoubtedly," Robert said. "They don't hesitate to do whatever it takes to gain their ends, even Stanford, and he was governor. Despite their lofty status, I prefer to think of them as distinguished scoundrels. Remember how they swayed the vote on the bond issue on the San Francisco ballot in '63? The bonds were to provide $600,000 to the Central Pacific. Stanford didn't take any chances. He sent his brother Philip to the polling places in a buggy laden with sacks of Central Pacific gold. Philip threw gold by the handful among the voters. No surprise the bond issue passed."

"Then there was the phony geology report," Ben said. "The Big Four had the state geologist in their pocket. He submitted a report to the federal government that the Sierras began twenty-four miles west of where they actually start, and Abe Lincoln bought it. The money awarded for flatland construction was $16,000 per mile, and for mountains, $48,000. Those twenty-four extra miles of phony mountain construction netted the CP another million dollars in government subsidies."

"It wasn't the first time they used a doctored map," Robert said. "Huntington lied and used bribery to submit a work route map to the Secretary of the Interior showing the CP building from the California-Nevada border all the way to Salt Lake City. That ignored the clause in the Pacific Railroad Act that limited them to building only 150 miles east of the Nevada border."

"Gentlemen, this is all very interesting," Kathleen said, rising. "But it's late and I grow weary of such talk. I think I'll retire." She rose and walked away, then stopped and turned. "I almost forgot to tell you. Megan went into Chinatown with Li Fanfan yesterday, and the girl swears she saw Second Mistress behind a shop window."

"What?" Ben said, astonished. "How could *she* possibly be here? I would have thought her dead, or still somewhere on Hong Kong Island. Li Fanfan must be mistaken."

"I'm not so sure," Kathleen said slowly. "The girl thought it was a ghost, but Megan thinks it really was her. Call it woman's intuition, but I think she may be right. I can't imagine why she'd be here. Alex is pretty upset. It was all Megan could do to keep him from charging into Chinatown looking for her. And if *I* ever see her," she said darkly, "I'll strangle her myself." She turned to walk out of the room. "Hmph," she called over her shoulder. "First Othniel Wanamaker pops up, now her. Who else is out there?"

Five days later, Ben stood on the front porch of the massive Spanish mission-inspired ranch house that was the centerpiece of the 20,000-acre Eire Ranch. He and Kathleen had begun the ranch in the late 1850s with money from Kathleen's huge gold strike. Located outside of Sacramento, the ranch encompassed five acres of fruit trees near the house—plums, cherries, apples, and apricots. The rest of the vast spread was devoted mostly to grazing land for large cattle herds, but there were smaller areas planted in wheat, oats, and alfalfa.

He was expecting company. After making a fast trip over from San Francisco, he'd sent word to the two property holders at Milepost Thirty-one, requesting their joint presence at the ranch as soon as possible. Such was the regard for the Wilsons in the Sacramento Valley, as well as respect for the power they wielded, that invitations were rarely declined. As he looked down the curved gravel driveway that led up to the house, he saw that this time was no exception. At the head of a cloud of dust, a carriage carrying two men exited from the long dirt road leading up to the driveway. A high-stepping carriage horse gracefully pulled the vehicle around the arc of the drive and slowed to a halt in front of Ben.

"Nice horse," Ben observed.

"Ain't she a beauty?" the driver said, alighting to the ground and stepping forward to rub the horse's neck. The animal's well-brushed mane fell on its polished coat, gleaming in the sunshine. "Yep, bred for the carriage, and well worth the money."

"I'll have my stable hand see to her while you're here," Ben said, motioning to a teenage boy standing nearby, who came forward and gently led the horse and carriage into the shade of a huge oak tree spreading its limbs near the west corner of the house. "Good to see you, Earl," he said, extending a hand to the driver. "And you, Mort." He shook hands with the other arrival.

The driver looked at him intently. "Your message sounded kinda urgent," he said. "Lucky we could both come over right away."

"Thanks for being so prompt," Ben said. "Yes, I need to talk with both of you. Come on inside." He led them into the large corporate boardroom off the parlor. A long table with upholstered leather seating for twelve dominated the room. Large ferns flanked a big window that overlooked the orchards. Polished wooden panels covered the walls between bookcases and display shelves that ringed the room. Ignoring the table, he bade the two men sit in wing chairs in one corner.

Earl Bodine, the driver, was a fiftyish man with a heavy build, a full head of black hair sprinkled with gray, and white sideburns. Piercing dark eyes looked out from his strong-featured, square face, which was clean-shaven except for a beard along the chin and lower jaw line. He was a Mormon who'd made a good strike in 1852 at Mormon Island and retired to the life of gentleman farmer. It had been his luck, like that of his companion Mort, to have purchased a plot of land which in part sat astride Ben and Kathleen's later railroad route to Placerville.

The other man in the room, Mort Sampson, was tall and scarecrow-thin, with big ears and a long sharp nose. He'd been a storekeeper in Tennessee who came out to seek his fortune in the gold rush, but, like so many others, had arrived too late. Despite the fact the easy gold was long gone, he knew opportunity when he saw it, and set himself up in business as a purveyor of mining supplies to later arrivals who had less sense.

"Sorry to hear about your losing the railroad, Ben," Earl said, "real sorry. I'm sore aggrieved to see the Big Four muscle in on what you built."

"Thanks. Has anyone from the CP contacted you about your parcels?" Ben said.

"Not me," Mort said.

"Me neither," Earl said. "Do they know?"

"It seems they don't, probably because the parcels are leased in our names," Ben said. "The lease payments don't run through the company books. But it won't be long before they discover it. Danielle has always kept a tight rein on the books, and she's still Chief Financial Officer, but that could change. If Collis Huntington gets a look at them, and he will at some point, he'll figure it out. Nothing gets past him."

"So why'd you call us in, Ben? You want to negotiate a new lease?"

Ben inhaled deeply and let it out slowly. "No. Gentlemen, we want to buy your parcels."

Bodine stroked his chin beard in thought. "Hmm. I thought it might come down to that someday. You got revenge on your mind?"

"Something like that. We built the Sierra and Western. It's our railroad. We want it back."

"Well, I heard the buyout from Central Pacific was real generous," Mort put in. "Why not take the money and be done with it?"

Ben gave him a hard look. "You ever meet my wife?"

"Sure, Ben, lots of times. You know that."

"Then you know Kathy won't back away from this. It's not in her nature. Money's not the issue here. We want every bit of leverage we can get hold of. Owning property the Sierra and Western tracks run right through is a start. Will you sell?"

"Suppose'n the CP was to make us a better offer?" Mort said. "Maybe we should see what they have to say."

"From what I've already seen them do, they just might find a way to acquire your parcels through some legal manipulation, without paying you a cent," Ben said. "Unlike Kathy and me, you don't have the money and influence to fight back."

Bodine shot Mort a hard look. "Shut up, Mort. We have to do the right thing here. Folks don't come any better than the Wilsons. 'Sides, anything we can do to stick it to those greedy bastards over at the CP sits fine with me. I don't cotton to the high rates they charge everyone. Hell, Ben, I'll sell."

"I'm for it," Mort said. "We go way back with you and the Angel. This is no time to stop. Make us an offer."

Ben did.

Eli Leatherwood barely got one foot on the dark gravel-covered ground as he stepped down from his railroad car when Othniel Wanamaker slithered out of the darkness and grabbed his arm. He looked down in shock and revulsion at the little man and reflexively pulled away. "Don't touch me!" he said. "What in hell are you doing here? I told you never to come back." Even in the darkness, Leatherwood could see that Wanamaker was visibly agitated.

"Somethin's goin' on," Wanamaker said, grabbing the lapels of Leatherwood's expensive suit. "I can't find the busboys."

Leatherwood grabbed Wanamaker's arms and spun him around, slamming him up against the railroad car. "What?"

"They done disappeared, both of 'em," Wanamaker said in a frantic whisper. "I went to where they were workin', and they ain't there no more! Their bosses said they just up and vanished."

"Relax. They probably got tired of working there and quit."

"No, it ain't that way. Word has it somethin' scared one of 'em bad. This is the Angel's doin', I know it."

Leatherwood seized Wanamaker by the collar and jerked him away from the railcar. "You get a grip on yourself! This is probably nothing. You hear me? Now get out of here and lay low or get out of town. Now! I see you again, I'll shoot you." He gave Wanamaker a shove and watched the disreputable little man shamble back into the darkness. Breathing deeply and smoothing his hair, he leaned against the railcar, lit a cheroot and tried to regain his composure. A feeling of dread crept over him. Despite what he had told Wanamaker, he had a feeling the man was right. The busboys hadn't disappeared for no reason.

He had heard Megan Daley was brought back, apparently in good health. He never doubted Kathleen Wilson would pull it off. *Not that that will satisfy her,* he thought. *Hell hath no fury like that woman scorned. I'd pity Satan himself if he crossed her.* He didn't doubt the Angel had gotten hold of the busboys. Wanamaker would be her next target, and with his low intelligence, it was only a question of time until he screwed up and the Wilsons found him. And that would lead them directly to Eli Leatherwood. That was something he couldn't allow to happen. The answer was clear, and he'd always figured it might come to this: Wanamaker had to go. Permanently.

10.

Midwife Elizabeth Grady was in residence at Danielle's house by September 14th. But she arrived with her right arm in a sling. "Fell off a horse ten days ago," she told Kathleen. "The arm's fractured up high, and my other shoulder's kind of messed up too. I'll probably need some help with the delivery."

Grady had overseen Bridget's birth. Kathleen trusted her completely, and knew Danielle would welcome a familiar and knowledgeable presence at her bedside for the delivery. Kathleen was paying her generously to stay as long as needed.

Grady had been only too happy to accept. "I'll consider it a working vacation," she told Kathleen. "It's been too long since I've spent some time on the coast." On arrival, the sturdily built gray-haired woman went directly up to Danielle's bedroom.

Danielle welcomed her warmly. "I'm so glad you're here," she said, smiling, as she reached up to embrace her. "You were so steady at Bridget's birth. I'll feel better with you in the room."

"Your mother tells me you've had a rough time of it with this baby," she said, gently pushing Danielle back onto her pillows. "Well, let's see how you're doing." She pushed Danielle's nightgown up under her breasts

167

and put a practiced left hand on her swollen belly. For long silent moments she moved the hand slowly up and down the sides of Danielle's abdomen, probing, sensing, eyes seemingly focused on something in the distance. Finally, she took her hand away, pulled the nightgown back down, and smiled. "Good, good. Now, rest while I visit with your mother."

Danielle gave her a faint smile. "I will. And thank you again for being here."

Grady squeezed her hand as she rose, then turned and walked slowly downstairs into the parlor where Kathleen and Robert were waiting.

Kathleen immediately noticed the sober expression on her face. "Something wrong?"

Grady sank into a chair next to Kathleen and looked at her and then Robert. "The baby's dropped down. But it doesn't feel as if it's in the right position."

Kathleen put a hand over her mouth in dismay. "Are you sure?"

"Not completely, so I didn't tell her. But I thought I felt the head up high. We really won't know until birth. But we should be prepared for trouble."

Kathleen sighed. "That's getting to be a habit."

Two days later, Danielle rose in late morning and walked into an adjoining room to relieve herself. She did so, and was about to return to her bed when she felt a surge of moisture down her inner thighs. She clutched the wall for support as a wave of dizziness swept over her, and looked down. The floor beneath her was wet.

Megan and Kathleen were sitting on Megan's porch in the autumn sunshine—Li Fanfan had gone into town with Hsien Lu—when Bridget came tearing through the tall grass between the houses. Overcome with curiosity about childbirth, she had gone to Danielle's.

"Mama!" she cried. "Aunt Danielle broke. Mrs. Grady says come right now."

Megan leapt to her feet. "Her water broke. Let's go!" She took off at a run, with Bridget on her heels. Kathleen called into the house for Ben and Alex, then dashed after them.

The whole party thundered up the stairs to Danielle's bedroom, only to be headed off by a vigilant Mrs. Grady at the bedroom door. "For Heaven's sake, get back!" she scolded. "She doesn't need a frenzied herd milling around her bed. She's having contractions, but we could be in for a considerable wait, so I suggest you all go downstairs, pour yourself some tea, and settle in. I'll send Robert down if there's news."

Properly admonished, they did so, though unhappily. And they waited. Three hours passed. Then four. At five hours, Megan and Kathleen began pacing. Danielle continued to experience contractions, now about ten minutes apart. At hour six, Ben broke open a fresh bottle of Irish whiskey, pouring a shot for himself and Alex. He offered a glass to Kathleen, but she shook her head.

At the seventh hour, Robert came down the stairs and announced Danielle's contractions were increasing. "They're coming about eight minutes apart and getting stronger. Danielle's asking for Megan and Kathleen. Mrs. Grady says come on up."

Megan and Kathleen rose and headed up the stairs, Megan leading with Kathleen close behind. At the top, Kathleen realized she was being followed, and turned around to find Ben and Alex at her heels. "And just where do you think you're going?" she chastised. "This is women's work. Now go on, the both of you, and take care of Bridget until we send for you. Shoo!"

Ben looked at Alex, and shrugged. Putting an arm around his son-in-law, he led him back down the stairs. "Well," he whispered, "we put them in this position, so I guess we'd better leave the consequences to them."

Upstairs, Kathleen and Megan hovered around Danielle's bedside. Robert sat near her head, holding her hand and occasionally wiping her brow with a cool wet cloth.

"How are you holding up, daughter?" Kathleen said.

"Just fine, Mother," Danielle said, attempting a reassuring smile and squeezing her mother's hand.

Kathleen cocked her head and studied her daughter's face closely. "Liar," she said. "Now don't you worry. Nothing will go wrong. You've got three strong women here to help."

"And my man," Danielle replied, tears glistening in her eyes. "He's here too."

"And I'm staying all the way," Robert said.

"Another contraction," Mrs. Grady called out as Danielle winced. She consulted her pocket watch. "She's speeding up."

Over the next half-hour, contractions became steadily stronger and longer lasting. Danielle showed increasing signs of distress. Perspiration plastered her chestnut hair against her forehead, and she uttered a series of low moans.

Robert looked at Mrs. Grady in anxiety.

Grady washed her hands and arms using water from a basin on a dresser, and instructed Megan and Kathleen to roll up their sleeves and do the same. "You can't be too clean for a new baby," she told them. "I may need both of you before it's over."

The contractions increased to only minutes apart. "This baby's coming," Grady said. "Everyone in position. Danielle, knees up, legs apart. Robert, you've got to be her steady rock. Keep hold of her hands, and keep wiping her brow. Talk to her. Megan, I want you to help her with her breathing, just like she helped you with Bridget. Mrs. Wilson, I want you down here with me. Now," she said, "Danielle, push harder with the contractions."

Danielle began pushing, resting between contractions. Robert kept her face cool, wiping the perspiration away. Ten minutes of intense effort left her exhausted.

Grady leaned over and slowly inserted the fingers of her left hand into Danielle's vagina, gently probing increasingly deeper. "Megan, keep her focused on you," she said.

Megan bent over her sister. "Danielle, look at me. Right here," she pointed, "at my eyes. Look at me, right here!" She moved close so her emerald-green eyes were only inches from her sister's face.

Danielle stared up at her, tension written on her Gallic features.

"Danielle, I need more pushing, if you're up to it," Grady said.

Danielle gathered her waning strength and pushed hard as Megan counted out the duration for her. Then again.

"She's not fully open," Grady said. There was silence for a moment, then Grady called out, "Danielle, stop pushing."

Danielle knew immediately something wasn't right. "What is it? What's wrong?" she said, gasping with exhaustion.

"It's a breech," Grady said. "The baby is coming out backward. This is what I'd feared. I wasn't sure when I felt your stomach two days ago, so I decided to wait and see. It's all right, Danielle," she said, soothingly, "we can fix it."

"What do we do?" a worried Robert asked.

"The baby has to be turned around for proper delivery, and it has to be done *now*. Coming out backward could result in damage to the baby's brain. And with this bum arm, I'm not a good candidate. One of you has to do it," she said, looking at Megan and Kathleen.

Megan closed her eyes and went rigid, her jaw muscles clenched. Then she opened her eyes, the fire of determination plain to see. "I'll do it," she said firmly.

"Let me see both of your hands," Grady said. She looked them over and shook her head at sight of Megan's long, manicured fingernails. "No, Megan. You might scratch or cut with those nails."

Kathleen, who had formed the habit of keeping her fingernails trimmed short in her gold panning days, met with Grady's approval. "Besides, your hand and arm are smaller. Are you up to it?" she said.

"Aye," she said, voice rock steady. "For my daughter, anything."

"Come, I'll guide you," Grady said. "But first, wash your hands and arms again extra good."

Kathleen did so. "Megan, roll up the sleeves of my blouse," she said. The job was done in seconds, and Kathleen knelt between Danielle's legs. "Danielle, I'm here for you, as I have always been," she said, her amazing sky-blue eyes fixed on Danielle's.

"Good," Danielle said, voice distorted with fear. "Oh God, Robert, I'm scared. Hold me."

Robert put his arms around her shoulders, entwining his fingers into hers.

"Now," Grady said to Kathleen, "reach in and push firmly on the baby's bottom."

Kathleen inserted her right hand into Danielle until she could feel the baby. She pushed. "Nothing's happening," she said, voice tense.

"Harder. Don't be afraid; we have no choice."

Kathleen redoubled her efforts, and this time felt the tiny body slowly begin to move upwards into Danielle's womb. She kept pushing.

Danielle cried out in pain and arched her back. "Aahhh! Mother, it hurts."

"Kathy!" Robert whispered urgently, eyes wide.

"Keep going," Grady advised. "You need room to turn it around."

Kathleen pushed until her arm was inside her adopted daughter nearly up to her elbow.

"Mother," Danielle moaned. Tears streaked her cheeks. "It hurts. Please hurry."

Kathleen looked at Grady.

"Now," Grady said, "feel around, become aware of where the baby's head is."

Kathleen did, struggling to keep her composure in the face of Danielle's pain, and at the experience of being so deep inside her daughter's body. Her hand encompassed the placenta and then the uterine cord. "I have it," she said after a few moments.

"Does it feel like the cord's free of the baby's head and neck?"

"Yes."

"Okay, put your hand behind the baby's head and neck and gently ease it downward. Put your left hand on Danielle's stomach and push in

171

coordination with your inside hand. When you feel the head move a bit, switch your hand to the legs and push them upward. Gently, gently."

"Oh Mother, please hurry," Danielle whispered. Then she passed out.

Kathleen did as she was told, sweat dripping from the end of her nose. After a couple of agonizing minutes, she announced, "Okay, it's in position now."

"You're sure?" Grady said.

"Aye."

"All right, slowly withdraw your arm."

"She's passed out!" Robert said in a near-frantic tone.

"That's okay," Grady said, motioning Kathleen out of the way. "She should come around soon."

A few minutes later, Danielle stirred into consciousness with a moan. Her contractions resumed, and continued for nearly another hour, leaving her exhausted. Then her eyes flew open. "It's coming!" she gasped.

"I see the head," Grady said calmly. "Here it comes."

Kathleen put her hands out and the infant, a boy, slid into them. But he made no sound.

"Hold him face down with one hand underneath his stomach," Grady said. "Gently pat his back a few times."

Kathleen did, and after a few gentle thumps, she was rewarded with an intake of breath and a weak, gurgling cry. After a few seconds, it strengthened.

"Well, his lungs are working," Grady said. She massaged Danielle's stomach for a few minutes, and the placenta was ejected, along with some blood. "That's normal," she told a worried Robert, who turned pale. Then she cut the cord and tied it off with heavy sewing thread as Kathleen cleared the baby's mouth and nasal passages, then lovingly washed him in warm water. When she was done, she wrapped him in a soft cloth and placed him in Danielle's arms.

Danielle burst into tears of joy.

Robert was crying too, with relief. "Well done, love," he said, brushing the hair back from Danielle's forehead. "Very well done."

"A grandson at last," Kathleen said with a sigh. "The cost was almost too great. Danielle might have—" She left the thought unfinished.

"Yes, she could have," Grady said. "We still have to be mindful of bleeding from her womb. I strongly advise bed rest for her the next few days."

Robert slumped in a chair in the corner, looking pale and awestruck. "Love," he said slowly to Danielle, "I'm astounded at what you just did."

A bit later, Kathleen paced back and forth in the parlor downstairs, scowling. She had sent Bridget upstairs to view the new baby so she could talk with Ben and Alex. Despite the safe arrival of her new grandson, she was furious.

"Danielle might have died," she said. "Or the baby. Or both of them. I blame this on all the worry that's burdened her this summer resulting from Megan's kidnapping. It all started with that. I've watched a happy, confident woman filled with joy at the prospect of motherhood reduced to a fearful shadow of herself." She stopped pacing and looked at Ben. "And someone is going to pay."

Upstairs, with Robert gone to pour himself a stiff drink and Mrs. Grady busying herself with cleaning up the room, Megan eased into bed beside Danielle, who was lovingly regarding her new son. She tenderly embraced her sister and gently brushed back a strand of chestnut hair that had fallen across her face. "You did good, sister. This family needed a son," she said. "Welcome to motherhood."

Danielle leaned her head against Megan's. "I'm so glad you're here with me. I wouldn't want to have done it without you."

"This is our time," Megan said softly. "This is the time when we celebrate what we can do that men can't. When we claim, if only briefly, the throne of life, as the bringers of new generations." She leaned close and kissed Danielle on the temple. "Be proud of what you've done, Danielle," she whispered. "Be proud, and nurture your son."

"I will call him André Terence Bradshaw," Danielle said softly. "André in memory of my father, and Terence in memory of yours."

* * *

Robert Bradshaw leaned back in the hard wooden chair and rubbed his face in exhaustion, then turned up the oil lamp on the desk beside him. He'd been poring over selected Central Pacific books in a small hotel room in downtown Sacramento for four days. One thing in his favor was the fact that the Sierra and Western Railroad was now a wholly owned subsidiary of the Central Pacific. Though the Big Four had succeeded in underhandedly acquiring the railroad, they had unwittingly given him, as a holder of significant stock in the company and as its legal counsel, access to the Central Pacific books. Still, he didn't want to call attention to his activities. Huntington must have been distracted by the feverish pitch of Central Pacific construction to have neglected replacing him already. He didn't want to give him a reason to do it. So rather than search at the

Central Pacific offices, he'd generously bribed a clerk to let him take the books off the premises in the evening.

His fear that Huntington would make things tough to decipher proved correct. No trail through the books could be followed for very long. Every time he thought he was onto something, it fizzled out into a dead end. Columns of figures didn't always add up. Moreover, construction costs looked ridiculously padded compared to what he knew of railroad building through Ben and Kathleen's line, even allowing for the challenges of the Sierras. He was sure the Big Four were grievously overcharging the government on construction contracts. The profits that must have generated didn't show in the books. The costs of supplies appeared inflated too, and wages for labor were embarrassingly low. It was hard for him to believe that Congress had accepted all of this at face value, but Robert knew they had. He pored over lists of investors, some of whom he didn't doubt were fictitious. Thinking there might be a clue among the names he could check on later, he laboriously copied the lists into his legal ledger.

On the fifth day, weary and discouraged, he was about to close the last of the books he'd borrowed when he came across a section containing financial data he hadn't seen before. What he found there stunned him. He copied down as much of it as he could, returned the books, and took the next riverboat back to San Francisco the following morning.

Three days later, still weary but excited, Robert gathered with Danielle, Ben and Kathleen, and Alex and Megan in the parlor of the Daley house. A legal ledger containing his voluminous notes was in his lap. He took a long drink of iced tea as everyone else looked expectantly at him.

"Danielle tells us you found something," Kathleen said. "We're ready to hear it."

Robert put down his glass of tea and opened the ledger. "Yes, I found some things that surprise me. Whether any of it will do us any good remains to be seen." He looked around the room at the waiting faces. "The Central Pacific is broke."

There was a brief silence in the room as the news sunk in. Looks of doubt and surprise settled on the assembled faces.

"Broke?" Ben finally managed. "They've been gobbling up every railroad in California for the last few years. That took money, no small amount of it."

"Yes, and they've been doing it with smoke and mirrors, and borrowing from Peter to pay Paul," Robert replied.

"They got a big loan from the U.S. government in '65," Ben said. "Over one and a quarter million in U.S. bonds[9], I think, for work they did in '64. What happened to that?"

"They got it all right, but they'd already borrowed against it before they received it. There's no question building the railroad across the Sierras is swallowing a staggering amount of money."

"The monetary conversion rate doesn't help, either," Robert continued. "Federal aid comes in paper money, but partly due to the Civil War, it doesn't inspire a lot of confidence. The paper money brings just 57 cents on the dollar when it's converted to gold."

"I remember something else that went sour," Ben put in. "When Judah was surveying the route across the Sierras, he predicted a railroad through there would earn at least $100 million hauling cordwood from the forests along the right of way. That revenue never materialized."

"Huntington's not too fond of Judah's judgment," Robert said. "I came across a note from him to Hartford complaining that he felt Judah often saw dirt where there was stone on the Sierra route."

"So they're broke," Megan mused. "I don't know where they came up with the money to acquire our railroad."

"There's more, and worse," Robert said, flipping the pages of his laboriously written notes in the ledger. "I came across a list of investors who supposedly purchased Central Pacific stock. I did some cross checking at City Hall in San Francisco yesterday, and I could find no evidence of any of them. I'll wager they don't exist."

"Phony investors?" Alex said. "What good would that do?"

"It builds false confidence in the public," Robert said. "People think the public is buying into the Central Pacific, and they're more likely to follow suit. But those people don't exist, I'm sure of it. And I'll also bet one of the Big Four, probably Crocker, is going to end up with those shares supposedly owned by ghost investors."

"What a disgusting mess," Megan murmured.

"You haven't heard the worst," Robert said. "Crocker's set up a corporation called the Contract and Finance Company. He's patterned it after the Credit Mobilier.[10]

"Oh God," Kathleen murmured, putting her head in her hands.

---

[9] Actually $1,258,000.

[10] The corrupt Credit Mobilier was set up in 1863 by Thomas Durant, one of the prime movers in the construction of the Union Pacific Railroad. It became one of the great bonanzas of the 19th century in terms of putting money into the pockets of Union Pacific insiders. The ensuing scandal reached all the way to Congress and the White House.

"I don't know about this," Megan said. "Please fill me in."

"It's simple, slick, and devious," Danielle said. "The railroad sets up a wholly-owned company to physically build the railroad line. It then awards the construction contracts to that company, in effect awarding business to itself. But it doesn't stop there. The railroad directors outrageously pad construction costs, dramatically increasing their profits. So they award themselves inflated contracts, then pocket the difference between actual costs for construction and claimed costs. The directors and some investors eventually get rich, and the government is robbed."

"What astounding greed," Megan said. "It makes me sick."

Kathleen had gotten up during Danielle's explanation, and was pacing the room. "So they're broke. That means they're vulnerable. They've got to keep building aggressively to keep federal money flowing in. Hmm. They're using primarily Chinese laborers now, aren't they?"

"Over 6,000 of them," Robert said.

"I wonder what the Big Four's reaction would be if construction suddenly ground to a halt," Kathleen said to no one in particular.

"Panic, I reckon," Ben said.

"I have no doubt," Kathleen said. She turned to Megan. "Daughter, I may have worn out my welcome with Yuen Ling-Po. But you still enjoy a good relationship with him, I believe."

"Burned your bridges again, Mother?"

"I got a little crazy when you were taken. Can you blame me? I'm afraid I said some things to him I can't take back. So I want you to pay him a visit."

Oh," Megan said. "What are we going to talk about?"

"Mutiny," her mother said darkly.

* * *

My fortunes are improving, Mei Li Kang thought as she walked down the streets of Chinatown dressed in a new *cheongsam.* Her hair was done with great care in the traditional fashion, her nails newly painted and polished, her makeup and lipstick perfect. With patience and a little of her dwindling money spread in the right places, she had finally wangled an audience with the merchant Yuen Ling-Po, one of San Francisco's most prominent businessmen. Now as she strode down the boardwalk in the mid-morning sunshine to meet him, she tingled with excitement. *Such a man is sure to recognize my value,* she thought. Through the proper contacts, she had presented herself as a woman of noble lineage, sophisticated and intelligent, with a record of faithful service to a man of wealth and power. She had made it clear that a man of Ling-Po's stature would doubtless benefit from an alliance with her. Anxiously she had waited for three days for an answer. Then it had come: an invitation to tea. She felt vindicated. She would not have to suffer the humiliation of work after all! She would go and she would conquer, with her charm, her polished manners, her skills of command. And then—then she would be in the position of power she coveted, the better to torment the wretched Li Fanfan, and perhaps even wreak vengeance on the barbarian Megan. Just the thought of it quickened her steps as she neared Yuen Ling-Po's residence.

Megan was once again in Yuen Ling-Po's elegant quarters above the shabby storefront in Chinatown. Though she had returned to his home several times since her first visit nearly six years earlier, she still looked with wonder on the magnificent Oriental furnishings around her. She sat again on the same silk sofa with its bird of paradise motif, surrounded by the beautifully carved folding screens of polished teak, the fine hand-painted ceramic vessels perched atop lacquered tables and cabinets, the stunning hand-woven rugs on the shining wood floors.

Leaving her bodyguards downstairs, she had brought Li Fanfan up with her, and the young girl sat primly beside her, silent and subservient, as an ancient servant woman poured tea. *That elegant tea service itself is probably a priceless antique*, Megan mused. The doddering old woman struggled to pour tea into the hand-decorated cups without spilling. Megan recognized her as the cantankerous guardian of the front door who had tried so hard to turn her away that dark night years before when she had come, desperate for success, longing to prove herself. When she had struck the bold agreement with Ling-Po that provided the workers to build the Sierra and Western when no one else would. When she had bravely smoked opium for the first time to prove her commitment to the deal, and it had taken its hold on her.

The gray-haired old Chinese woman finished pouring the tea, and Ling-Po curtly dismissed her. She shuffled off, hunched over with age.

Megan watched her go with sympathy, despite the clear memory of the woman berating her so vociferously. She leaned closer to Ling-Po. "Who is that poor old woman?" she whispered.

"Ancient crone is Venerable Mother," Ling-Po said in the pidgin English he sometimes favored, despite his total mastery of the language.

Megan was aghast. "She's your mother?"

"Yes," the old Chinese merchant said, puffing on a long-stemmed pipe. "She is overdue to meet ancestors. Maybe I hasten her along someday."

"You would treat your own mother this way?"

Ling-Po shrugged. "She does not complain."

Grimacing, she sat back on the sofa. She knew it was useless to rush discussion of business with the man, so she and Li Fanfan sat in silence for a few minutes, sipping their tea as Ling-Po filled the room with aromatic smoke from his pipe. Finally he seemed inclined to speak.

"Li Fanfan, Hsien Lu treats you well?" he asked.

"Yes, Venerable Master," said the girl.

"Good. I have instructed him to get to know you better. Female companionship would benefit him. I hope to see you together now and then as you become acquainted with Western ways. Meanwhile, I am glad you continue in the company of Honorable Megan. She is a good woman."

"Yes, Venerable Master," Li Fanfan said softly, clearly awed by the power emanating from the merchant, even after living in Lord Yang's household for a time.

"Now," he said, turning to Megan, "your mother sent word that you bring a new business proposition to me."

"Yes," Megan said, feeling infinitely more confident than during her first negotiation with the wily old man years earlier. "As you may be aware, we lost our railroad—the very line built by the workers you provided—to the Central Pacific. It was done in a most underhanded fashion, and almost certainly precipitated by my kidnapping. We want it back."

Ling-Po stroked his goatee while puffing on the pipe for a moment, then spoke. "Yes, I was informed of your most unfortunate troubles. I was sorry to hear of it. The criminal Yang was well known to me. I am glad he is gone, especially since it was at your mother's hand. I never doubted she would bring you back. Now, how may I be of service to you?"

Megan spent about ten minutes outlining what Kathleen had in mind. "Can you make it happen?" she concluded.

Ling-Po was silent for so long Megan thought he wasn't going to answer. He appeared lost in thought, eyes seeming to see something elsewhere, smoke from his pipe drifting upward. Then at last he slowly put down the pipe and looked at her again. "Yes. Now let us negotiate compensation for such an event."

Over the next half-hour, Megan and the old Chinaman parried and thrust, advanced and retreated, as they worked their way slowly toward a mutually beneficial arrangement. When at last they both seemed satisfied, Megan rose and bade her goodbye. "Representatives from our legal office will forward the proper papers to you within two days. And now we must be going." She and Li Fanfan, who bowed low to their host, went to the stairs leading down to the first floor. She motioned Li Fanfan to go first.

The teen girl was about halfway down the stairway when she stopped abruptly, hand frozen on the railing. She was face to face with Second Mistress.

Mei Li Kang's features seemed to turn to stone, then twist into a malevolent, sick smile. In the dimly lit hallway, she did not see Megan looming above.

Li Fanfan shrieked in fear and fell backward.

Megan stopped dead at the girl's cry. Her eyes widened in shock as she recognized the figure at the base of the stairs. Without a moment's hesitation, she launched herself into the air. "You evil bitch, I'll kill you!" she screamed, clawing at Li Kang's throat in fury as she crashed into her, driving her to the floor below.

"Barbarian cow!" Mei Li Kang bellowed in Chinese, trying to rake Megan's face with her nails. The two women staggered erect and tottered around the small entryway, a screeching, flailing, tangle of hatred. Stumbling, they exploded through the front window out onto the boardwalk in a hail of shattered glass, just as Megan's bodyguards burst in the door.

Megan snapped Li Kang's head back with a solid punch to the chin, but the Chinese woman recovered and chopped at Megan's neck with the edge of her hand, stunning her just long enough to break free. Li Kang sprinted away down the boardwalk, one of Megan's bodyguards in hot pursuit. But displaying the same speed evident in her flight up the hillside of Victoria with Parmenter, she soon put distance between herself and her pursuer, and was lost in the street crowds.

Megan stood swaying and panting as the remaining guard put a protective arm around her. "I'll say one thing," she said, wiping a trickle of blood from the corner of her mouth, "that woman can run."

By this time, Yuen Ling-Po had descended the stairs and stuck his head out the doorway at the commotion.

Megan explained who the woman was.

"But I was to entertain her this afternoon!" he said in astonishment.

"She was looking for a new meal ticket," Megan said, bitterness in her voice.

Ling-Po looked at Li Fanfan, who was seated on the boardwalk, still trembling from the encounter. "I will send Hsien Lu for the woman's head," he said.

"No," Megan said. "Leave her to me. This is personal."

Three blocks away, Mei Li Kang huddled inside an empty warehouse, hiding in the deep shadows behind planks leaned up against a wall. Panting and sweaty, she gathered her torn clothing and tattered dignity about her. Her chance for the life she knew she deserved was gone. There were not enough funds left to wait for another opportunity. And the barbarians would be looking for her now. She would have to flee San Francisco. But to where? Seething with hatred, she fingered the knife strapped to her thigh. *The barbarian Megan will pay,* she vowed. *I swear by my ancestors, she will pay with her life.*

"Well, I see you made the headlines again, daughter," Kathleen said, flopping down the latest edition of the *Alta California,* the same newspaper that had carried the news—in big, boldface type—of Megan's bout with opium several years earlier.

Megan looked at the front page.

Heiress in Chinatown Brawl
Megan Daley in Ruckus
Outside Opium Den
Celestial[11]Escapes Capture

"Well, at least I kept *you* out of the headlines this time," Megan replied tartly.

Kathleen sank into an armchair. "That paper doesn't miss a thing," she said. "Sometimes I wonder if they have reporters following us around, just waiting for an incident. Well, I blame myself for the example I've set. Your temper is no worse than mine." She sighed. "I suppose it comes with the blood." Rising, she went to her daughter, sitting beside her on the sofa. "How's your neck?"

Megan rubbed the back of her neck. "Pretty sore. She chopped me hard."

Kathleen put a gentle hand on her thigh. "I wish you'd quit trying to be me."

"I can't help it, Mother," Megan said softly. "I'm a Connelly woman, like it or not."

"Aye. And it could get you killed, sweetheart. You know, it's not such a great thing, being me. I can think of three occasions when I might well have been dead if not for Ben. And it was mostly because of my temper.

---

[11]   In that era, Asians were commonly referred to by westerners as "celestials".

I don't want that for you. Alex might not always be around to bail you out of danger." Kathleen lovingly stroked her daughter's hair. "Oh, you *are* my daughter, God help you. I know, more than anyone, the price you paid to get Ling-Po to provide the workers for the railroad. It still pulls at you, doesn't it? The opium?"

Megan glanced down at her lap, then away, unable to look at her mother. "It's there, Mother. I keep it deep, I keep it down. But it's there. And it always will be."

Kathleen pulled Megan's head onto her shoulder and put her arms tenderly around her headstrong daughter. "I know. I know. But together, you and me, we will never let it see the light of day again. I love you so much, my girl. I would give my life for you."

Mother and daughter sat together in silence for a long while, taking in each other's warmth and love, taking strength from the rhythm of each other's breathing. Finally, the hour having grown late, Megan got up, excused herself, and went upstairs to bed.

Kathleen thought about retiring too, but her eyes fell on Robert's ledger lying on a table. She had been studying it off and on all day, probing the notes for something that could give her leverage to get her railroad back— and possibly provide a clue to who financed Megan's kidnapping.

She had paid particular attention to the list of investors Robert had hurriedly copied down, looking for names she knew, people she could hope to question. As a powerful state senator, she had some authority to call people to account. So far she had seen few names she recognized. But now as her fingers ran down the list again, she grew weary and discouraged. She was about to give up for the night when something abruptly stopped her and caused her to back up on the list. Her fingers ran a few names back up the page, and stopped. She stared at the name, breath catching in her throat. Then she ran her fingers back and forth across it. With the sixth sense she had always seemed to possess in matters concerning her daughters, she knew it was no coincidence. Her fingers trembled on the page as they framed the name: *Tobias Parmenter*.

11.

Later the next morning, Kathleen met with Robert and Alex. Megan was upstairs with Bridget, safely out of earshot.

Kathleen looked at Robert, an expression of barely-controlled rage on her face. "How old do you think that list of names is?" she said.

"It's recent," Robert said. "Though the page itself isn't dated, it immediately follows a page that is. That page is dated three days after Megan's return. To answer your unspoken question, no, I don't think the list was made before her kidnapping. The section of the book it's in appears to be very recent. And so do the transactions it records."

"So Parmenter's really here," Kathleen said.

"Or was, recently," Robert replied.

Kathleen got up and began pacing, her long skirt rustling slightly in the quiet parlor. "I can't believe it," she muttered. "Has he got a death wish?"

"If he does, I'll fulfill it," Alex said.

Kathleen turned to face him. "Only if you find him before I do."

"Do you think we should tell Megan?" Robert said.

Kathleen looked at Alex, eyebrows raised.

Alex shook his head. "No. Not yet, not unless we confirm Parmenter's still in the area. She's still agitated over Yang's mistress popping up. I don't want to upset her further."

"First the mistress, now Parmenter," Kathleen said in wonderment. "I can't believe they'd come here." She stopped pacing, eyes suddenly wide. "You don't suppose they came over together?"

"Could be," Alex said. "More likely than coincidence. But why?"

"I can't imagine," Kathleen said. "But let's all be on the alert. We seem beset by a gathering of evil."

Elijah Leatherwood tried hard to remain calm as he looked at his visitor. The man before him in his railroad car was another he had hoped never to see again. He was just too dangerous to have around.

Tobias Parmenter's face twisted into a cruel smile at Leatherwood's unease. "You're sweating, Eli," he said mildly. "I might get the idea you're not glad to see me."

"Frankly, I'm not," Leatherwood said, mustering the best glare he could manage. "There's no reason you should be here. What's done is done. You did your job, and you were well paid for it."

Parmenter grinned. "Better than you know."

Leatherwood felt a prickling of fear on his neck. He didn't like unexpected consequences from his plans cropping up. "What do you mean?"

Parmenter looked supremely smug. "Megan Daley. Just about the sweetest piece of tail I ever had. What I wouldn't give to do her again."

Leatherwood gasped. "You raped her? Your instructions were to deliver her unharmed!"

Parmenter laughed. "Do you really think I could sail all the way to China with her aboard and not have her? To tell the truth, she's lucky the crew didn't have her too. I kept them off her, though I damned near had a mutiny on my hands. Don't worry, she didn't have any marks that showed when I delivered her to Yang."

"I'm sure she was grateful," Leatherwood replied with bitter sarcasm. "Now, I told you to never come back. Why in hell are you here? I thought you'd be in the South Seas, lying in the sun."

Parmenter shrugged, then ran a hand through his curly black hair. "Quite simply, I'm bored."

"Looking for something to do, eh? Hang around these parts long enough and you could get yourself killed."

Parmenter smiled again, a cold, merciless expression. "I crave excitement. Got anything that needs doing—that pays?"

Leatherwood gave him a long look. Then he spoke, slowly. "Actually, I do. I'd like to get rid of somebody. Permanently. You'd be well paid."

"Tell me."

Leatherwood told him. Then, with firm instructions to Parmenter to never, ever, darken his door again, he watched, heart thumping, as the man faded into the darkness outside his railcar.

So, Megan Daley was raped, he thought. He knew he was in for it now. The Wilsons would stop at nothing to find out who brought that about. Would he someday have to send an assassin after Parmenter? And what then? He could almost feel the noose tightening around his neck.

Megan guided her big stallion carefully through the silent crowds of yellow-skinned men who lined the Central Pacific tracks as far as she could see. Shamrock's coppery-colored flanks shone in the morning sunlight, his breath visible in the crisp mountain air.

Resplendent in an emerald-colored cape, matching plaid wool skirt, and polished calf-length riding boots, her dark red hair brushed to perfection, Megan smiled but said nothing as she rode past.

Alex rode close behind on his bay, a rifle across his saddle, watching the faces of the assembled masses. He knew it was Megan's show, as it usually was with the Connelly women. But he was used to it by now.

Megan had waited three weeks after the meeting with Ling-Po, while the vastly influential old merchant got the word out to the thousands of Chinese laborers toiling across the Sierras. Then she and Alex had traveled to the mountains by riverboat and rail, the horses accompanying them. They had waited two more days at the foot of the mountains, then received word that all was ready.

Kathleen had a long talk with Megan before she and Alex departed for the Sierras. "Stay quiet but firm, daughter," she advised. "Don't needlessly antagonize anyone, like I would. But don't back down either. The rest I will leave to the negotiating skills you've so admirably displayed with Ling-Po."

She turned to her son-in-law. "Alex, I'm sending four of our best bodyguards along with you, but I want you to make any decisions regarding her safety. And you stay glued to her side."

Alex put an arm around Megan and gently caressed her shoulder. "You know I will, Mother. Count on it."

Now, as Megan rode through the army of Chinese laborers, an amazing sight followed behind. The little yellow men laid down their tools and sat on the ground.

Alex looked up the hillside above them and could see the tall figure of Charles Crocker's feared Chief of Staff, the man the Chinese roustabouts referred to as "One Eye Bossy Man", James Harvey Strobridge. Strobridge had lost an eye while inspecting a delayed black powder blast at Bloomer Cut, an 800-foot long trench laboriously blasted through a mound of fiendishly hard aggregate rock. The patch he wore over the empty eye socket only served to make him look even more intimidating. Now Alex could see him glaring down at them with his one good eye. Strobridge had a reputation for driving workers relentlessly, mercilessly. "Men generally earn their money when they work for me," he once said in severe understatement.

It was not an easy thing for the Chinese to disobey the man. Yet, as Megan passed by and waved her arm in a horizontal motion away from the tracks, they simply walked away from their tasks, sat down, and took tea.

Above them, Alex saw Strobridge send a man running away uptrack. He had no doubt the runner was sent to fetch Crocker. Indeed, the messenger returned in ten minutes accompanied by a mountainous figure of a man carrying an ax handle. Alex knew immediately it was Crocker; no one else was likely to be that big.

Crocker propelled his 260-lb. bulk down the slope with alarming speed and strode up to Alex and Megan, ax handle gripped firmly in one meaty fist. He raised the shaft and pointed it at Alex, who dismounted at his approach. The mounted bodyguards were a few yards off, discreet but watchful.

"What in thunder are you doing?" he spat.

"My wife has new instructions for the workers," Alex replied.

Crocker turned red. "The hell you say! These are *our* workers. I want them back at work. Now!"

Alex gripped his rifle firmly. "If you can get them back to work, do so."

Trembling with rage, Crocker turned and strode to the nearest seated Chinese. Bellowing and waving the ax handle threateningly, he waded into the masses, shoving and kicking.

No one moved. After a couple of minutes of fruitless bullying, Crocker extricated himself from the crowd and again approached Alex. "What's this all about?" he said, moving to within inches of Alex, eyes burning with anger.

Though he didn't have Crocker's bulk, Alex was several inches taller, and as always when Megan might be in danger, in no mood to back down. "Just a little demonstration of our power," he said.

Megan rode up slowly on Shamrock. The horse snorted and seemed to glare at Crocker. "Tell Huntington we want our railroad back," she said, green-eyed gaze boring into him.

"You are trespassing!" Crocker yelled. "I'm ordering you off Central Pacific land right now. Get moving."

"I don't think we're trespassing," Alex replied. "The government grants the C.P. alternating sections along the right of way. By my calculations, this particular section is still federal. Besides, as significant C.P. stockholders, we arguably have a right to be here anyway."

By this time, Strobridge had come down the slope and joined Crocker, his single eye glaring murderously at the idled masses.

Crocker turned to him. "Get 'em back to work, Stro," Crocker said. "I don't care how."

But even though Megan was no longer moving forward, the work stoppage was. In the distance, like a quiet wave, the Chinese were walking away from the unfinished railbed.

"Get her out of here," Crocker ordered Alex. "She is at risk."

Alex cocked the rifle and pointed it straight at Crocker. "Make a move against her, and I'll blow your head off," he said, iron menace in every word. Then he signaled Megan, and together they and the bodyguards slowly rode off, the Chinese sitting in their wake like a vast flock of silent birds.[12]

Megan and Alex rode with the bodyguards back to their camp. It was early October, and sunlight could not chase away the chill in the air. Megan dismounted and turned Shamrock over to one of the men. "That was the last night I'm sleeping in that tent," she told Alex. "It was below freezing this morning."

"I'm with you," Alex said. "Let's break camp and go back to Sacramento."

"Do you think the strike will hold?" she said.

"I don't know," Alex mused. "Crocker will set Strobridge on them like a rabid dog. We'll see how much influence your old friend Ling-Po has. But any delay at all will send Huntington into fits. The C. P., like the Union Pacific, is paid by the mile of track laid. It was already a

---

[12]   In 1867, Chinese railroad laborers did indeed strike the Central Pacific.

mismatch; the U. P. is laying track Hell-bent for leather out on the plains, where it's mostly flat. Meanwhile, the C. P. measures progress through the Sierras sometimes in feet per day. Every day's delay costs them not only thousands of dollars, but also in the race to claim land. The more track laid, the more land awarded. And land is wealth and power. Make no mistake; Huntington will move heaven and earth to get the Chinese back on the job."

But the strike held. Not only held, but word reached them that some of the Irish laborers, who made up a large percentage of the remaining track layers, were walking off the job as well, in sympathy for Kathleen's Irish birth.

Megan and Alex settled in in Sacramento, sending regular dispatches back to San Francisco, where Kathleen and Ben were doting on Bridget and their new grandson.

Two weeks passed, and then Megan received a communique from Collis Huntington that she was to meet him at his offices at precisely noon on Friday. It was more of a demand than an invitation. After a moment's thought, Megan fired back a note that she would be happy to meet with him—on neutral ground. She suggested the Occidental Hotel downtown.

Huntington waited two days, then accepted.

Megan and Alex were at the hotel early. She wanted to be seated in the meeting room's best and biggest chair before Huntington got there, to claim the high ground.

But she wasn't early enough for Collis Huntington.

She found him already seated in the room's most impressive chair. He was alone.

Collis P. Huntington made his start in Sacramento as partner in a hardware store with his future fellow member of the Big Four, Mark Hopkins. Earlier, upon first arriving in the gold fields, he had shoveled gravel for all of one morning before deciding he had thoroughly wasted his time. He thereupon set himself up as a trader in hardware, and together with Hopkins, was soon dominating the gold rush country market in shovels, blasting powder, and other mining supplies. In appearance, he had a high forehead, a straight high-bridged nose, and a full beard. He looked faintly like Ulysses S. Grant. He liked to boast that no one had ever bested him in a business deal. A newspaperman of the time described him as "ruthless as a crocodile", and meant it as a compliment. Although Stanford was by far the most publicly visible of the Big Four, in reality it was Huntington who ran the Central Pacific.

"Lass, it looks like he's already staked out the high ground," Alex whispered.

"Watch me get it right back," Megan said softly, walking into the room.

Huntington did not rise. Instead, he fixed her with a severe look. "Sit down, Mrs. Daley."

"I would, but you're in my chair," Megan replied sweetly.

Huntington glared at her for a moment. Then the faintest flicker of respect registered on his face. Even he could not resist this challenge to his chivalry. He slowly rose, buttoned his coat, and stepped away from the chair. With all the polish of the most refined gentleman, he offered the empty seat to her. "Of course. My mistake. Please be seated."

Megan nodded in gracious assent and settled into the high-backed leather chair as Huntington pushed it forward. Alex stood behind Megan as Huntington sank into another chair, looking a bit ruffled.

The railroad magnate scowled at Megan. "Mrs. Daley, let us get right to the point. I don't know what power you have over our Chinese laborers, but I want you to call off this strike immediately. Surely you realize that as holders of significant stock in the Central Pacific, you're damaging your own interests with this action."

"Our financial resources are extensive," Megan replied. "Greater than your own. The threat to our stock value is of little consequence to us."

"Then I urge you to consider your family's reputation and good will," Huntington countered. "The people of this state are eager to see the transcontinental railroad completed, and begin receiving the great tide of prosperity it will bring. You are standing in the way."

"You overstate the case," Megan said. "Most of the prosperity will fall into the hands of you and the rest of the Big Four. As for our reputation, my mother built her businesses on a foundation of honesty and fair play. She has never overcharged for services rendered. She also enjoys great popularity in the senate. The people of California will not quickly abandon her."

"I think they will," Huntington said coldly. "Your family stands in the way of the future."

"There is your own reputation to consider," Megan said. "I wonder what the public would think if my mother were to outline in the senate just how much Charles Crocker's Contract and Finance Company resembles the corrupt Credit Mobilier?"

Huntington turned red, and Megan knew she'd gotten to him. She followed with another sharp thrust. "And I wonder what they would think if they knew some of your investors in fact don't exist?"

Huntington's eyes widened ever so slightly, then the master manipulator recovered, his expression turning stony. "If your mother spreads that lie on the floor of the senate, she will regret it."

Megan leaned forward in the chair. "Give us back our railroad, Mr. Huntington."

"The Sierra and Western was legally acquired in a transaction approved by your own stockholders," Huntington said. "Why should we?"

Megan's Irish temper was rising. "That transaction was approved by a minority created by unusual events ultimately traceable back to my kidnapping."

Huntington's expression didn't change. "So you say."

Megan exploded. Jumping to her feet, she slammed her hand down on the polished table. "I paid the price for that deal!" she screamed. "I was taken by force!"

Huntington's eyes widened in shock. "I'm sorry. I didn't know."

Alex took hold of Megan's arms as she seemed on the verge of launching herself at the railroad baron. "Let's go, lass. We're wasting our time here." He forcibly edged her toward the door.

"The strike goes on!" she shot at Huntington as Alex pulled her through the doorway. She fought him so hard her feet were off the ground. Out in the hotel lobby, Alex loosened his grip and turned her to face him, ready to comfort his obviously distraught wife. He knew how hard it must have been for her to admit she had been sexually assaulted.

But brushing the hair away from her face, she smiled and winked at him. "How was that?" she said. "Pretty good?" Then she turned on her heel and walked out.

Alex sighed. "Connelly women," he muttered.

* * *

Othniel Wanamaker was pulling up stakes. It was time to get out of town. Word was out on the street that someone was looking for him. He had no idea who it was, but figured it to be someone Kathleen Wilson had sent. He shuddered at the thought that it might be Hsien Lu, Yuen Ling-Po's right hand man. That one, he knew, was not only relentless but merciless, and wouldn't hesitate to take his head off if instructed to do so. He grimaced and put a hand to his neck at the thought, rubbing the scratchy three-day old growth of beard. Yes, it was time to go elsewhere. Perhaps south. There was a scam he'd run in San Diego once before that might see him through the winter. Enough time had passed that it might work again.

So on a chill Wednesday morning, in the seedy flat he occupied on the edge of Chinatown, he packed his bag, ruminating sadly as he did so on how little there was to put in it. *A lifetime of hard work summed up in a suitcase,* he thought. *Always figured I'd have more to show for it. Times were fat once a few years ago, when I owned Pacific Freight. Then those damned Connelly women—Kathleen and her daughter Megan—they destroyed it. Well, I had my revenge. Megan Daley paid big time. Now it's time to cut and run before I pay.* He lifted the bag off the lumpy bed and exited the room for the last time.

Downstairs on the boardwalk, he looked nervously this way and that. Right away, he had the feeling someone was watching him. But with no one suspicious in sight, he shuffled off toward the waterfront. He didn't hear the footsteps of someone falling in behind him.

Wanamaker made his way along at what was for him a quick pace, head turning frequently in apprehension. A growing feeling that he was being followed made sweat break out on his creased forehead. Wanting to get to the harbor as quickly as possible, he took a shortcut he knew well, through a long alleyway. The scratch of his worn boots in the dirt was uncomfortably loud; the scuffle of rats in piles of debris as he passed made him jump. He wiped a sleeve across his brow and kept going, eyes fixed longingly on a patch of sunlight at the far end of the alley.

He didn't make it to the sunlight. As he passed a wooden door hanging slightly askew on its hinges, a brawny arm wrapped around his throat and he was dragged into darkness.

He was flung to the dirt floor of an empty warehouse. Dust filled the air around him, sending him into a fit of coughing. Slowly his eyes adjusted to the dark. Someone was standing silhouetted against the narrow shaft of light streaming in around the door. He slowly got to his feet—and his mouth fell open in shock. "You! You're supposed to be in the South Seas!"

Tobias Parmenter chuckled, an oily, evil sound. "Surprise." From underneath his coat he withdrew an enormous knife. "Eli Leatherwood sends his regards." His eyes went cold. "You're a dead man, Wanamaker!" Parmenter advanced on him.

Othniel Wanamaker knew he had failed to get out in time, and his life was over. Reflexively, he backed up against the wall behind him, resigned to his fate. "I knew somebody was following me the minute I set foot outside the boarding house," he said softly. The light was not so dim that he couldn't see the slight look of confusion on Parmenter's face.

"Huh? I wasn't following you." That was as far as he got.

The door behind him creaked open, and Hsien Lu stepped into the room.

Parmenter whirled and backed up two steps, knife at the ready. "Who in Hell are you?" he said in surprise.

Wanamaker knew he was doubly dead now.

"Get out of here," Parmenter said, pointing the knife. "This isn't your business."

"The man Wanamaker is my business," Hsien Lu said. "I have need of him. You will leave."

Tobias Parmenter had never backed down from anyone, and he had the scars of battle to prove it. On the high seas as a cabin boy at twelve, he had survived on guts and cunning. He had never shunned any work that would build his strength, and had seldom lost a shipboard wrestling match. He had learned knife fighting in alleyways from Bangkok to Copenhagen. He feared no one, and couldn't resist a challenge. So he didn't back down now, when he should have. "Last chance, Chinaman," he said, grin vanishing.

Hsien Lu didn't move, standing with his feet wide apart, arms at his sides. "If you do not leave, I must kill you," he said softly.

Parmenter made a swift backhand swipe with the knife, swinging it in a vicious arc. He wasn't close, as Hsien Lu effortlessly dodged away.

The two men circled each other. Parmenter went on the attack, but he couldn't make solid contact. It maddened him that Hsien Lu hadn't even reached for his weapons, a dagger at his belt and his saber. They continued to circle wordlessly in the dust, Parmenter thrusting and faking, but cutting only empty air where Hsien Lu had been an instant before. Parmenter was using every trick of hand to hand combat he knew, every sneaky move he'd picked up in years of mutinous brawls and street fighting.

And he was losing.

He connected with a swinging forearm smash to Hsien Lu's chest, an impact that would have staggered most men. He might as well have attacked an oak tree. Hsien Lu countered with a lightning chop to the forearm, and Parmenter felt his whole arm go numb. He fell back against a wall and dodged a split second before Hsien Lu's fist blasted a hole through inch-thick boards where his head had been. Parmenter edged away, wary now, a look of increasing desperation on his face. There were half a dozen times his opponent should have gone down but hadn't. Knowing he had few chances left, he grew increasingly reckless. He fought on, smashing and slicing, to little effect against Hsien Lu's glacial calm. Finally, he lunged straight at the shorter man, knife aimed for the throat. Hsien Lu deflected it, but the blade cut a thin line across his collarbone and upper chest.

Hsien Lu ignored the wound and smashed the heel of his hand into Parmenter's breastbone. Then in a shockingly fast move he drew his saber, whirled it in an arc, and chopped Parmenter's head from his shoulders. It tumbled to the ground, the first hint of shock registering in the eyes. It was followed by the heavy thump of Parmenter's headless body crashing into the dust.

Hsien Lu turned to Wanamaker, who cowered in a corner stunned at what he had seen.

Wanamaker closed his eyes and lowered his head. "Just make it quick. Please," he whispered.

But instead Hsien Lu reached down and pulled him roughly to his feet. "The one known as the Angel wishes to see you," he said. "And she will."

Li Fanfan was upset to see that Hsien Lu had blood on his clothing and hands when he entered the parlor of Megan's home, where she had been anxiously waiting. "Honorable Warrior, you are injured!" she said, approaching him and sinking to the floor at his feet, head down. "Let me attend to your wounds."

"It is nothing," Hsien Lu said.

"Please, Master, let me do so," Li Fanfan replied, earnest pleading written on her young features. She looked at him in anguish, then lowered her gaze to the floor once again.

"I will attend to it," he said, then glanced up. Kathleen was standing behind the girl, wagging her finger at him, a silent scold on her face.

He scowled at Li Fanfan, but Kathleen could see it was all bluster. "Very well. You may do so." Again he looked at Kathleen, who raised her eyebrows in expectation. "And—and I am most grateful."

Kathleen watched them with quiet pleasure, the little Chinese girl and the gruff warrior, as Li Fanfan tenderly cleaned and dressed Hsien Lu's wounds. Hsien Lu looked uncomfortable at first. At one point the girl scolded him gently to hold still as she secured a dressing. He was momentarily taken aback, but then gave her, just for a moment, the faintest of smiles. Kathleen was thrilled. The big warrior could crush the teen girl without half trying. And yet, she had touched him. She had penetrated his tough shell with the gentle lance of her heart.

Kathleen left them talking quietly with each other, and went into the next room, where Ben and Robert were entertaining their unexpected guest.

Othniel Wanamaker slumped in a chair, a thoroughly cowed and discouraged lump of humanity. He was still shaken by the sight of Parmenter's head lying several feet from his body. He had expected the same fate all the way to Danielle's house, but Hsien Lu had not so much as looked at him. He could tell, though, that any escape attempt would result in his rapid demise.

Now he sat in Danielle's parlor, wondering how long the Wilsons would keep him alive. He was sure it wouldn't be long. He felt a prickling on the back of his neck, and turned.

The Angel was staring at him.

Kathleen approached him slowly, arms crossed. The gaze of her sky-blue eyes bored into him. She stopped in front of him like a cobra ready to strike. "Othniel Wanamaker," she said slowly. "It's been a long time. When we last met, I believe I had a gun in your face. Your status with us has not improved."

Wanamaker said nothing.

Kathleen walked away, hands clasped behind her back, then turned to face him again. "It would seem someone wants you dead," she continued. "No surprise there, so do I. I can guess who the other is, though. Doubtless the person who funded and planned Megan's kidnapping. I know *you* didn't. You haven't got the intelligence for it. Care to tell me who it was?"

"No."

Kathleen came forward, leaning over until she was just inches from Wanamaker's face. "The only thing keeping you alive is the thought of getting useful information out of you. If I get some, I may decide to spare your miserable hide. If not . . . ." She left the deadly implication hanging in the air.

Wanamaker shifted uneasily in his chair. "I'm dead either way, I figure. So I'm damned if I'll give anything to you Connelly women, after what you done to my business."

Kathleen sighed. "By the way, we have the busboy Hiram too. He's been most cooperative." She left, motioning Robert to follow her.

"I need some fresh air," she said, leading Robert out onto the porch. They stood in the darkness, feeling the ocean breeze wash over them. "What are we going to do with him?" she said.

"I don't know," Robert said. "We have no authority to hold him captive. But we can't let him go either."

"How about if we just wrap him up tightly and throw him off the cliff at high tide?"

Robert smiled. "The thought is attractive, I must admit."

"I want information from him," Kathleen said, "and I don't much care how we get it. We can probably hold him a few days. What's he going to do, run to the police? I don't think so. He probably also realizes that whoever sent Parmenter after him may send someone else. If he leaves this house, he's a hunted man, and he knows it. No, let's entertain Mr. Wanamaker a while longer."

"Are you going to tell Megan about Parmenter?" Robert said.

"When the time is right," Kathleen replied. "When the time is right."

Robert glanced into the room through the window behind them. "I see Hsien Lu is letting Li Fanfan tend to his wounds."

"Yes, with a little encouragement from me," Kathleen said. "There's hope for him yet. I actually saw him smile at her."

"You're kidding."

"It's true. I think, though he wouldn't admit it yet, something is growing between them."

* * *

Eli Leatherwood had heard nothing of either Wanamaker or Parmenter, and that suited him fine. Wanamaker was likely dead by now, he thought, and so also the thread connecting him to Megan Daley's kidnapping. Yes, he had struck at the Wilsons and gotten away with it, and his life was the richer for it.

Now he was a busy man with important decisions to make. So he was too occupied with his railroad baron pretensions to notice the headlines above a small item on page four of a three-day old edition of the *Alta California.* Had he done so, he might not have slept so well that night. For on the lower right edge of page four, nearly unnoticeable beneath an advertisement for *Dr. Morpheus's Miracle Elixir,* the following headlines appeared:

Missing Sea Captain Found Dead
Tobias Parmenter, Believed Involved with
Daley Kidnapping, Discovered Decapitated

* * *

Mei Li Kang regarded her new surroundings with satisfaction. She was once again, in her estimation, in a station somewhat befitting her noble lineage. True, being madam of a mobile brothel might be considered by some to be a disgrace. But she was surrounded by barbarians anyway, and what did they know about dignity and the privilege of class?

Nothing, she thought as she sat in the cheaply elegant parlor she had set up in one end of the boxcar containing her brothel. *They are ill mannered and vulgar. But there is opportunity here all the same. With my breeding and intelligence, it should not be hard to rise to the top.*

She had fled San Francisco in terror after the encounter with Megan, hearing on the street that Yuen Ling-Po had set the assassin Hsien Lu on her trail. She was still bitter over the lost opportunity to become mistress to the wealthy merchant, and dismayed to learn that he was allied with the barbarian Megan and her family. But fearing for her life, she went to Sacramento, and there decided to go into business for herself. She had just enough money left to start a modest enterprise. But it had to be, of course, one that would provide her with a position of authority, one from which she could command others.

She took a rail trip into the Sierras, saw the great masses of workers pushing the rails across the mountains, and knew opportunity when she saw it. First, she leased a railcar that had formerly been used as a rolling dormitory for laborers, then had it converted inside into two levels of rooms, outfitting it with modest furnishings. Then she had scoured Sacramento for the best prostitutes, and offered them more than they were used to. She got fifteen women, five of them Chinese. When all was ready, she had the converted dormitory hauled out to near track's end and pushed onto a temporary siding.

Business was brisk from the start, and Li Kang sat in her parlor and counted her profits. With money in her pocket again, she had the resources to resume her old hobby—the concocting of poisons. But she was also thinking. She saw the means to make her burning desire for revenge come true. There was one addition to her stable of soiled doves that would put the perfect cap on her operation—that wretched little peasant Li Fanfan. True, the girl was no longer a virgin, but she should prove most attractive to the weary laborers. Oh, how she relished the day she could put the little plotter in her place! No doubt the girl's newfound alliance with the barbarian Megan had given her a puffed-up sense of importance. It was time to remind her of her proper station in life. And whatever it might be, it was certainly beneath that of the former Second Mistress to Lord Zhao Yang.

Yes, she would have to find a way to get Li Fanfan under her power. And then—ah, then the barbarian Megan would surely come to rescue her, and when that happened she would kill the troublesome woman. She fingered the dagger strapped to her thigh in anticipation. *And if she should bring the assassin Hsien Lu along,* she thought, *I will have to poison him, so sorry. And this time I will not fail.*

12.

Megan was in her Sacramento hotel room reading the day's newspaper when Alex returned.

There was a sad look on his face. "Bad news, lass. They've broken the strike."

"What?" Megan said, rising. "After only three weeks?"

"Aye. I don't know how he did it, but Crocker got them back to work."

Megan stepped forward and embraced her husband, putting her head against his chest. "Darling Alex, I've failed."

Alex looked down at his wife, stroking her head gently. "Nay, lass," he whispered. "You did what you set out to do. You got the workers off the job. And that hurt the Central Pacific badly, never fear. What happened after that was never under your control." He raised her face to his, bent his tall frame down, and kissed her tenderly. "You are the most amazing woman I know," he said, smiling warmly. "I love you."

Megan sank her head back against his chest. "Mother wouldn't have failed. She would have made the strike last much longer."

Alex pressed her to him again, hands caressing her back. "No, lass. Your mother didn't have the power to begin the strike. You did. If you

197

were like her, I wouldn't love you as much as I do. Your mother is—well, one of a kind. But I'm glad you're not her."

"Sometimes I want to be like her," Megan murmured, "but most of the time I don't. I just wish I could do what she does."

"What you do is quite amazing enough for me," Alex said softly. "It was you I wanted, not your mother."

"Thank you, Alex," Megan replied, so softly he could barely hear her. "You remind me every day how lucky I am." She kissed him tenderly, then slowly pulled back. "I suppose we'd better go back home. But first I want to make one more visit to Collis Huntington."

Megan didn't bother to seek an appointment with Huntington, or meet him on neutral ground. She was sure they'd find him in his offices. The man was rumored to have no life outside of working on the Central Pacific books.

She was right. When she and Alex walked boldly into his surprisingly modest office in downtown Sacramento, they found him behind his desk, scribbling away.

He looked up at their entrance, and glared at them. "Well, Mrs. Daley, I didn't expect to see you here. I'm sure you've heard Charlie Crocker has got the Chinese back on the job."

"Yes, we've heard," Megan replied.

"That strike cost us dearly," Huntington growled. "But not fatally. Nevertheless, I won't forget it. Your family has made powerful enemies."

Megan approached two steps closer, green eyes locked onto his. "So have you. My mother wields enormous influence in the senate. And her memory is equal to yours, I assure you."

"I don't have time for idle chatter, Mrs. Daley. What do you want?"

"I just wanted to give you something to think about before we leave town. You see, as far as the Sierra and Western Railroad is concerned, we still have one more card to play. You'll be hearing from us. Good day, Mr. Huntington."

Megan got the shock of her life when she walked into her house and found Othniel Wanamaker sitting in one of her best chairs like a fat toad. "You!" she yelled. She snatched up a heavy brass candlestick and charged him, with Alex right behind. "You bastard!" she screamed.

Ben flew into the room from the kitchen and grabbed her around the waist three feet short of Wanamaker, who had thrown up his arms and was cowering in the chair. "Megan, don't do it," he said. "Calm down. Calm down."

Trembling with rage, Megan fought him for a moment, then twisted away as he loosened his grip.

Ben took the lamp and gently pushed her at Alex. "Mind her, Alex," he said.

"What is he doing in my house?" Megan said, panting with anger, fists clenched. If looks could kill, Wanamaker would have been reduced to a cinder then and there.

"Mr. Wanamaker is our guest," Kathleen said, entering the room.

"Guest!" Megan said, incredulous.

"In a manner of speaking," Kathleen replied calmly. "We've been trying to get information from him as to who planned and financed your kidnapping. He hasn't told us. Yet."

"I don't care why he's here, *Mother*. I will not have this vermin in my house."

"That's your and Alex's decision, Megan. Actually, he's free to leave any time he likes. Legally, we can't hold him. But he never had it so good. A roof over his head, and three square meals a day."

"Yeah, just like beef bein' fattened up for the slaughter," Wanamaker said.

"You're plenty fat enough to kill right now," Megan said coldly. She turned to Kathleen. "If you want to keep him around, fine. But he will not be in my house. Let him sleep in the barn."

"Aye," Alex put in. "The barn it is for this trash. But what if he runs off?"

"Not likely," Ben said. "Mr. Wanamaker is a hunted man. Strangely enough, we may be the only reason he's still alive."

Alex moved Wanamaker out to the barn while Kathleen took Megan upstairs to her bedroom. Gently she broke the news that Parmenter had returned, and was now dead.

Megan hung her head, holding her arms tightly about her as if suddenly chilled.

"I'm sorry to break this news to you, daughter," Kathleen said softly. "Parmenter was apparently hired—by whom we don't know—to eliminate Wanamaker. Unfortunately for him, he found him at the same time Hsien Lu did."

Megan shuddered. "I can guess what happened."

"You guess correctly," Kathleen said. "Parmenter lost his head."

199

Megan sat in her parlor, Bridget firmly ensconced on her lap. Alex had gone next door to update Robert on the strike.

"I missed you, Mama," Bridget said, putting her arms around Megan's neck.

"I missed you too, little one," Megan murmured softly in her ear. "It was hard to sleep so far from you."

"I watched Aunt Danielle's baby for her," Bridget said proudly.

"Did you now?" Megan said. "Such a big girl you're becoming!"

"Aye, that she is," Kathleen said as she walked into the room.

"Now, it's late, and time even the biggest of little girls should be going to bed," Megan told her.

Bridget pouted, an expression so reminiscent of her mother that Kathleen smiled. "Do I have to, Mama?"

"Yes, I'm afraid so."

"Can I sleep with you and Papa tonight?" Bridget said, clutching her cloth doll tightly.

"Yes, of course," Megan said, lovingly brushing the black hair back from her daughter's forehead. "Now, get upstairs and snuggle in. Papa and I will be up soon."

Bridget reluctantly went upstairs. Kathleen settled into a chair next to her daughter, and fixed a penetrating gaze on her. "Do you feel better knowing Parmenter is dead?"

Megan grimaced. "Yes and no. It scares me that he was really here. I'm glad he's dead, but I wanted to see to it myself."

Kathleen put a hand on her daughter's arm. "*No*. You don't want that in your head. *I* don't want that in your head. Listen to me, my girl. I still have flashes of memory that come to me quite unexpectedly. Blowing that Indian apart with the Sharps. Plunging the knife into him, hearing his death wail cut off." She stopped and put a hand to her forehead, suddenly breathing deeply. After a moment she regained her composure and looked up. "I don't want that for you, Megan."

"You survived, Mother."

"Not intact," Kathleen said, looking away. She was silent for a long moment, then spoke again. "A little bit of me died on Carson Pass with your father in 1850. A little bit more of me died with that Indian up in the mountains. Part of me has been numb for years." She fell silent, looking down at her hands. "Don't wish to kill, daughter. You'll never be the same."

Megan got up and sat on the floor at her mother's feet. "You've carried such a heavy weight for this family, Mother. I don't think any of us really know the depth of it."

"Ben knows. Believe me, he knows." She put a hand to her head and massaged her right temple.

Megan's brow wrinkled in concern. "Have the headaches returned?"

"I'm afraid so, daughter. If it isn't my head, it's my neck." She sighed. "It seems like a lifetime ago. It was. And that Indian's big fist is still falling."

"Let me comfort you, Mother," Megan said, rising. She stepped around behind her, put her hands on Kathleen' shoulders and began expertly massaging her. Megan worked on her for a long time, and finally felt Kathleen relax beneath her hands. She looked in wonder at the small, slender woman so many called the Angel.

She's so big to so many, she thought. *She rarely lets her guard down, and then mostly to Ben. She's just human—and yet still a legend. That Indian might have killed her when he bashed her on the head and stole me. But she didn't die. We were condemned to death on Carson Pass, but she got us through alive. That time in the meadow, with the arrows flying in thick and fast, the Indian tried to kill her again, and failed once more. He tried yet again, that final confrontation in the mountain snows, and that time she killed him. How I wish I'd been there to see that, even though she nearly died.*

And the night the Angel legend started with that dying miner; what was his name? Taggart? Yes, that was it. I've never told her, but I was peeking around the bedroom curtain that night, awestruck as she took on the appearance of an angel, convincing that fading old man he had entered heaven. To this day, I swear there was an unearthly glow around her, something I've never seen before or since. That night, at least, she really was *an angel.*

And I am her daughter. Dear God, help me to be worthy, and yet not like her.

Megan stopped when she realized Kathleen had fallen asleep. But at that her mother stirred.

"Promise me one thing, daughter," Kathleen murmured sleepily. "Let me handle the resolution of what happened to you. If it comes to dangerous ends, I'm better suited for it. Stay home and take care of Bridget. She is our future."

Megan said nothing.

* * *

Eli Leatherwood had finally gotten the news that Tobias Parmenter was dead. When he heard that the body had been found in two pieces, he put a hand to his neck in revulsion. What a horrible way to go. If the Wilsons ever figured out his connection to Megan Daley's kidnapping, they'd send someone after him too, never doubt it. *Maybe the same someone.*

Worse yet, the news about Parmenter hadn't mentioned anything about Wanamaker. Had Parmenter done the deed? An uneasy premonition in his stomach told him Wanamaker was not only still alive, but in the cold clutches of the Angel herself. *Better polish up my alibis,* he thought. *I may need them. Well, Wanamaker can sing like a canary. I'll deny it all, and let them prove it if they can.* But the thought did not comfort him.

Meanwhile, he was living the life of railroad baron to the hilt. He was seldom seen in his San Francisco financial headquarters offices. His plush railcar spent less and less time on Sierra and Western tracks, and more time on Central Pacific tracks in the Sierras. He'd fallen in love with railroad building. The sight of thousands of laborers hacking, blasting, drilling, and grading their way across the mountains stirred his blood. It was the most magnificent enterprise he had ever seen, and he longed to be a greater part of it. He was all too aware that even though he was president of the Sierra and Western, he was still just the Big Four's puppet. And they could dismiss him any time they chose to do so. It particularly grated on him to be under the thumb of Collis Huntington, whom he detested. The man considered himself a wizard of business, but Leatherwood was sure that an experienced financial professional like himself could outmaneuver a former storekeeper any day of the week. *And twice on Sunday,* he thought smugly. No, it wouldn't do to continue to be at the mercy of the Big Four. He would either transform them into the Big Five, or found his own railroad empire. And to do that, he had to own the Sierra and Western outright. Then, with his financial connections in San Francisco, he could fund expansion of the railroad throughout Southern California, and then east across Nevada and Arizona, and on across Texas, which was still hungering for a railroad after having lost the transcontinental route. So he was developing a plan.

At present, his railcar was on a siding not far from the track layers' current base camp. But he was not alone. Outwardly, it incensed him to share the siding with a mobile brothel, but he had been unable to resist the lure of its temptation, and he'd quickly developed a taste for Asian whores. Some of them had amazing skills. The madam, Mei Li Kang, was a smooth sort with the charm of a child and the soul of a reptile. He made a mental note that she might someday prove useful.

* * *

Megan paced back and forth in her parlor, hands clasped behind her, very much like her mother would do. Occasionally she glared at Wanamaker, seated in a rather uncomfortable wooden chair before her. For long minutes she paced silently, letting Wanamaker squirm.

Finally she spoke. "Do you remember, Mr. Wanamaker, what I told you last time we met?"

Wanamaker clenched his jaw and said nothing.

"Let me refresh your memory, then: 'Never cross a Connelly woman.' I told you on that day that if you ever had anything more to do with threatening our family, you'd be put on a ship bound for China, never to set foot on American shores again. Coming back to you now?"

Wanamaker remained silent.

Megan walked up close to the shabby little man, looming over him in her best Kathleen impression. "Do you know," she said slowly, "what happened to me because of what you put in motion?"

Wanamaker finally spoke. "No."

"Let me fill you in," Megan said frostily. "I was nearly assaulted by a crew of swinish sailors, raped by their captain, sold into servitude in Hong Kong, stripped naked, humiliated by arrogant, hostile women, subjected to all manner of attempted re-education, and nearly forced to submit to sex with a Chinese gangster old enough to be my grandfather. Not to mention separated from my daughter and husband for weeks. And all because you were hell-bent on revenge! Well, you got your revenge. I hope it was worth what it's going to cost you. Because now you're going to pay the price. Again. And I'll tell you this: Danielle nearly lost her baby because of my kidnapping. If she had, I would have put a bullet in your fat hide the moment I saw you. Count on it."

Wanamaker at last reacted, getting slowly to his feet and glaring at her. "So stop jabbering and do it," he said. "I got nothin' to live for."

Megan's breath caught in her throat. She had been looking away but turned back to gaze at him strangely.

"What's that look for?" Wanamaker said.

"That's the same thing Ansel Platt said four years ago after his failed attempt to wreck our railroad nearly killed me." She turned away again. "Just before he jumped from the trestle to his death."

"You mean before your Chinaman threw him off."

"No," Megan replied. "None of us touched him. It was his choice." She began pacing again. "And now it's decision time for you, Mr. Wanamaker. We're not going to kill you. You can put your mind at rest about that. Frankly, that would be too easy an out for you. Besides, you're not worth a bullet. And I don't want the memory of your blood on my hands. No, I see a cruise in your future. What your destination will be is going to be up to you."

Li Fanfan looked with admiration at Danielle's baby boy. "Honorable Danielle, I hold him please?" There was earnest desire in her voice.

"Yes, of course," Danielle replied, smiling and handing the baby to her. She had given up trying to get the girl to drop the "Honorable".

The teen girl smiled at the baby. "I wish for baby of my own," she said wistfully.

"It would be good to have a husband first," Danielle said, half in jest. "How are you and Hsien Lu getting along?"

"Such a good man I never see," Li Fanfan said softly. "When we are together, he always make sure I safe. I would trust him with my life, Honorable Danielle."

Danielle put her hand over Li Fanfan's. "That's a good start. I think your instincts are correct. Megan and I both owe our lives to him."

Li Fanfan carefully handed the baby back to Danielle. "How I make him want me?"

"Just keep doing what you're doing. I know he seems tough, but he's got to be vulnerable somewhere. When you find that point, meet his needs there. Compliment his weakness with your strengths. And you do have them. It didn't take long to see that."

San Francisco's Pier Six was wet with dew in the pre-dawn darkness. Patches of fog lingered across the black harbor water. A small group of silent figures, some carrying lanterns, walked quietly down the pier toward its end. The group consisted of Ben, Kathleen, Alex, Megan, Hsien Lu, and Wanamaker. As they neared the end of the pier, a small rowboat tied to a piling became visible. It bobbed gently in the swells rolling in to shore. A silent, cloaked figure sat at the oars. He looked up from under a hood at their approach.

Ben looked down at the mysterious oarsman, nodded solemnly in greeting, then back at Wanamaker.

Kathleen separated herself from the group, stepped to the edge of the pier planking, and turned to face them. "The time has come, Mr. Wanamaker. Out there," she gestured over her shoulder, "are two ships. Both sail with the tide. Both belong to Wilson-Connelly Shipping, so I can be sure of their destination. One will take you to Río de Janiero, Brazil, where you'll be put ashore, penniless, to survive as best you can. The other ship will take you to Shanghai, China, where you'll be taken into the interior to work as an indentured servant the rest of your life. In Río you have a chance. In China there is no chance. Your destination is now in your hands." She paused and approached him, eyes sparkling in the light of the lanterns. "For the last time, Mr. Wanamaker, who was it?"

Wanamaker looked sadly at the rowboat and the macabre-looking oarsman waiting for him, then back at Kathleen. "Always figured you'd kill me," he said.

Megan stepped forward. "I'll never forgive you for what you did to me. But the truth is, Mr. Wanamaker, life has punished you—and will continue to do so—far more than I can with a bullet. No, the greatest punishment I can devise is for you to go on living."

They waited. Nearly a minute of silence dragged by, broken only by the faint slap of water against the pier pilings. Then Wanamaker spoke at last. "It was Leatherwood."

Megan hung her head, an expression of sadness on her face. "I always thought he was a weasel. But I didn't imagine he would do this."

"I did," Kathleen said, cutting her off. "From the start."

"There's more," Wanamaker said, surprising them. "I know how you can get your railroad back."

The group talked softly for about fifteen minutes on the pier, then all watched as Wanamaker was rowed out to the Río-bound ship by the hooded oarsman, a sad, resigned expression on his face. His chubby figure became increasingly hard to see in the dim light from the lanterns, then was finally swallowed by darkness and fog.

"He looked like a condemned man being rowed across the River Styx by Charon," Megan said. "The hooded oarsman was a nice touch."

"Something I couldn't resist," Ben said, flashing a faint smile of satisfaction in the darkness.

"Think he'll last long in Río?" Alex said.

"One never knows," Kathleen replied.

"If he ever sets foot in California again, I'll put a bullet between his eyes," Alex said, voice cold as ice.

No one disagreed.

It was nearly two a.m. when the party returned from the waterfront, so Kathleen ordered a good night's sleep, then a meeting at noon the next day in the big conference room in Danielle's house.

When noon came, no one was missing. Even Bridget was there, sitting in a chair in the corner combing the hair on her doll. Danielle left her baby in the care of a housekeeper. Everyone was eager to discuss the surprising revelation Wanamaker had left them with. Hsien Lu was there as well. At first he had stood back against the wall as a servant might, but Danielle had firmly ushered him to a seat at the table. His expression barely changed, but Kathleen, watching him closely, could tell he was pleased to be seated as an equal. Li Fanfan stood silently and primly behind him, ready to attend to his every need. Megan hadn't made much headway on rooting out the girl's ingrained subservience, but where Hsien Lu was concerned, she was content to let it go.

Wanamaker had confirmed that Leatherwood had provided the money to bribe the busboys, and supplied the elaborate opium pipes. "I was just tryin' to embarrass your daughter," he told Kathleen on the pier, as if that would make his offense less heinous. "I never figured on her gettin' kidnapped and shipped out. That was all Leatherwood's idea."

"You could have stopped it at any time," Kathleen had told him coldly. "But you didn't. You didn't have the guts to do the right thing."

Wanamaker had continued, revealing that Leatherwood had also hired and paid Parmenter. Events had then followed exactly as Leatherwood had hoped. To be sure, Danielle's pregnancy crisis was unexpected, but Leatherwood was there to pick up the pieces. He had delivered, as promised to one of the Big Four (which one even Wanamaker didn't know), the Sierra and Western Railroad. The Big Four, in turn, had anointed him President of the line.

But then Leatherwood had gotten greedy. Being president of the line wasn't enough for him; he wanted his own railroad. He wanted to be equal to the Big Four. As a member of the Sierra and Western board, he had been aware of the two privately owned sections outside of Sacramento on the Sierra and Western line. He had tried to buy the sections when the Central Pacific acquired the Sierra and Western, but the Wilsons had beaten him to it. He knew the pressure the Wilsons would undoubtedly put on the Big Four by levying toll fees to cross the sections, toll fees so high it would make it impossible to operate the railroad at a profit. The sections couldn't be bypassed by building around them; it was the Wilsons' good fortune that local topography made that impossible. And so there they would sit, Leatherwood knew, and with the Angel's legendary (and foolish, in his opinion) generosity, she would probably rebate the toll fees back to Sierra and Western customers. "And that will make her more popular than ever," he had told Wanamaker. "Well, popularity never put money in my account. It's opportunism that counts. Johnny on the spot and Devil take the hindmost, that's the ticket."

So, using established connections in San Francisco, he had quickly put together a group of wealthy investors whose ambitions nearly equaled his own. Then he had journeyed to see Huntington. He knew better than to bother with Stanford. Stanford was merely a very prominent figurehead.

Huntington had been greatly vexed at the news about the two sections owned by the Wilsons along the Sierra and Western line.

"I don't need to tell you what the Wilsons will do," Leatherwood had prodded him.

"Indeed," Huntington said, his scowl deepening. "I suppose this is the other card that Megan Daley said she had to play. They'll levy exorbitant toll fees against us, making the Sierra and Western a money-losing proposition."

"Precisely," Leatherwood said, steepling his fingers for effect.

"That strategy will backfire," Huntington said. "The Wilsons will be regarded as obstructionist and greedy by the people of California, who are eager to see railroads in their state."

"Not when Kathleen Wilson rebates the toll fees back to the customers, which she is almost certain to do, perhaps to the extent that freight rates will once again in effect equal the low fees she was charging them originally. She'll be seen as the very soul of generosity, and her popularity will only increase. I don't need to spell out what will happen to yours."

Huntington ground his teeth, then stuck out his lower lip. "Such a scenario is unacceptable, though I care not a fig for my popularity. I leave such concerns to Stanford. But then, you didn't come all this way just to tell me bad news. I presume you think you have a remedy?"

Leatherwood smiled. "Indeed I do."

Kathleen looked around the room. "Let me get this straight," she said as she sat in the big green wingback chair at the head of the conference table. She directed the comment at Robert. "Leatherwood put together a group of investors and plans to make a proposal to the Big Four to buy back our railroad?"

"If Wanamaker understood him correctly," Robert replied, running fingers through his thick brown hair.

"But why?" Megan chimed in in frustration.

"Greed and ambition, I reckon," Ben replied. "I always had the feeling he had dreams of something bigger, and given the opportunity, he'd go after them."

"He wasn't *given* the opportunity," Kathleen said bitterly. "He created it. At the expense of my daughter."

"My question still hasn't been answered," Megan said. "Even if Leatherwood convinces the Big Four to sell the Sierra and Western to his group, how can he make it work any better for him? He still has to cross our sections and pay toll."

207

"Maybe not," Robert said. "He may be planning to acquire the sections via eminent domain."

"What does that mean?" Megan said.

"Taking private property for public use," Robert replied. "He'd offer a take-it-or-leave-it purchase price, undoubtedly not a very good one, to us for the sections. If the courts sided with him, we'd have to accept it, and the sections would be his."

"But why couldn't the Big Four do the same?" Kathleen said.

"Because with Stanford out of the governor's office and Crocker out of the legislature, they're not part of any public government entity," Robert said. "Leatherwood is."

They all looked at him blankly.

"Eli Leatherwood sits on more boards of directors than just our own," Robert went on. "He's also chairman of the board, and a major benefactor of, the Placer County Water District. It isn't too much of a stretch to imagine him pressuring the district to go after our sections on the pretext that dam building is necessary there for flood control purposes, thus eventually pursuing their acquisition through eminent domain, if necessary."

"That sounds awful flimsy," Ben said. "Could he really make that work?"

"Maybe," Robert said, rubbing his neck in thought. "It all depends on how much public fear he could whip up on the flood control issue versus the loss of the railroad line. The line does run adjacent to a stream that swells seasonally from mountain snowmelt. It won't be easy; Kathleen's generosity has built up a lot of good will. But it *could* happen. Besides, right now all he has to do is convince the Big Four he could do it."

"I can't imagine the Big Four letting go of the Sierra and Western for any reason," Kathleen said.

"The weight of public opinion might be one reason," Robert said. "They probably realize we'd rebate the toll fees back to the customers, making them look greedy."

"They *are* greedy," Kathleen said, "but few seem to realize it yet."

"Too, Huntington likes to boast no one has ever gotten the best of him in a business deal," Robert continued. "His pride just won't allow him to pay the toll fees. Even so, he would never consent to the deal unless Leatherwood threw in some kind of ironclad partnership arrangement, something that would guarantee the Central Pacific some measure of future control and income. I don't know how that would work, but I do know this: if Leatherwood's group ever gains control of the Sierra and Western, we'll never get it back."

"Maybe we should let it go," Ben said quietly.

"My daughter put her life in peril for the Sierra and Western," Kathleen said, cold fury in every word. "She did something that got inside of her and changed her forever."

No one spoke, though everyone in the room knew what she meant.

Kathleen walked slowly to the window and rested a hand on the sill, looking out at the foam-flecked ocean waves in the distance. She put her other hand to her head for a moment and seemed to sway ever so slightly. Ben noticed and started toward her just as she turned to them. Her face was pale. "Megan paid for that railroad," she said, her voice a hoarse whisper. "And I will never give it up."

Weary of discussing the fine points of Leatherwood's possible deal, the party retired to the parlor. Evening had fallen. The oil lamps gave a dim light to the room. Everyone, Ben included, was waiting for Kathleen, who had left the room, to call the next move. She was the unquestioned matriarch, but now, as she had grown older, only to the extent that Ben let her be. He was the power behind the throne. If he saw she was overextended, he would rein her in. And she would listen, if reluctantly, as she always had.

Megan sat in a soft chair, sober and quiet. "Ben," she said, finally breaking the silence, "Mother was pale as death when she turned from that window."

"I saw it," Ben said, standing a few feet away. "I don't know what that was. And was it my imagination or did she seem unsteady on her feet just for a second?"

"It wasn't your imagination," Danielle said, an expression of unease on her French features. She idly twisted her long chestnut hair with one finger. "Ben, has she said anything more lately about her neck pain?"

Ben let out a heavy sigh. "Yeah, she has. And in the last month there've been some headaches." He paused, then continued. "She didn't want me to tell you."

"So like her," Megan said. "She never wants to let on she has a weakness." She got up and went over to Ben, placing her hands over his. "Ben, please get the doctor out here tomorrow."

"I will. I'll go out to the stable right now and tell Robby to have my horse saddled and ready early in the morning. I'll ride into town first thing and get him." He went to the front door, took his jacket from the coat rack, and walked out.

He had been gone just a few minutes when Kathleen came back into the room. Megan recognized the look on her face, a look she had last seen years earlier the night Kathleen decided to go into the Sierras after Two Moons, the Northern Paiute Indian who tried for years to kill her. It was a look of rage that made Megan shudder.

"Mother, what are you about?" Megan said, crossing her arms across her chest.

"I'm going after Leatherwood, daughter. He's going to pay for what he did to you, to us."

"Mother, you're not going to do this. You're too old."

Kathleen's eyes blazed. "Don't tell me that! As long as there's breath in this body, I'll protect what's mine. It's going to get dirty, Megan. I didn't raise you for this. In fact, I've done everything I could to keep you and Danielle from it. I'm not going to stop now. You let me handle this."

For perhaps the first time in her life, Megan walked over and got in her mother's face. "No."

Kathleen's eyes widened slightly. "No? No? You will not tell me that, Megan!"

Megan was doing her best to keep her Irish temper in check. "No," she repeated quietly, putting a hand on her mother's arm. "If I have to hogtie you, you're not going after Leatherwood."

Kathleen pulled away from her, breath coming heavily. "Get away from me." She backed away across the parlor floor. "I'm going to find that bastard and I'm going to kill him! Do you understand?" She was terribly agitated now, fists clenched, trembling.

Danielle was near tears. She turned to Robert, who had been standing in the background. "Robert, please do something."

Megan turned to Alex, who thus far had remained silent. "Alex, go get Ben. Now."

Kathleen swayed slightly, face contorted in a mixture of rage and confusion. "No!" she screamed. "No, I'm going! You can't stop me!" She started to walk across the parlor floor toward the front door. But after three steps she came to an abrupt halt and suddenly clutched her head with both hands, eyes wide in shock and pain. Her mouth opened in soundless agony, then her mouth trembled and she uttered a tortured sound. "Ben," she gasped as she sank heavily to the floor.

Everyone was frozen in shock for a second, and then all except Megan rushed to her. Megan ran frantically for the front door and flung it open. "Ben!" she screamed into the darkness. "Bennnnnnnn!"

13.

The small, frail-looking woman lay still, deep in the softness of her bed. Her black hair, usually combed to perfection, fanned out on her pillow in unruly chaos. Her eyes were closed; only an expression of pain on her face and the slightest rise and fall of her chest gave evidence she was alive.

Figures mingled and crossed paths around her bed, silent, stricken, and aimless. Periodically two of them would brush together, mumble hushed words of vague comfort, then pull apart and drift away.

Kathleen had not regained consciousness since collapsing the evening before. It was now late morning. A haggard-looking Megan paced the bedroom, chewing on her rosary beads. Danielle sat in a corner, running her own beads slowly through her fingers, lips moving in silent supplication. One of the housemaids brought in a tray with tea and coffee. It was ignored. Ben slumped in a chair at Kathleen's bedside, his unshaven face a mask of weariness. He had scarcely left the chair since he had carried Kathleen's limp form up the stairs the night before.

Downstairs the mantel clock chimed the noon hour. Megan knelt at Kathleen's bedside and gently took hold of her right hand. "Mother," she called softly as she had periodically throughout the night, "wake up.

Open your eyes, Mother. Please open your eyes." She kept trying for another minute, but there was no response. A single tear rolled down Megan's cheek as her head sank against her chest. Ever so slowly, she rose and motioned Ben to join her at the foot of the bed. She leaned close to him, her back turned to Kathleen. "I think we'd better send for Father Higgins," she whispered.

Ben sighed heavily and rubbed his neck. Summoning the priest for last rites was something he'd been putting off. "Yeah, okay," he said reluctantly. "Just to be on the safe side. I'll send Robby out right away." He started to walk toward the stairs.

"Ben!" Megan whispered urgently behind him. He turned, saw Megan's eyes gone wide, and followed her gaze.

Kathleen's eyes were slightly open.

Ben was at her side in an instant, kneeling close to her face. He put a gentle hand on her cheek. "Kathy, can you talk? Can you hear me?"

Kathleen slowly turned her head to look at him as Megan knelt at the other side of the bed and burst into tears of relief.

"Oh, Mother, I thought we'd lost you," she sobbed.

Kathleen's mouth opened as she tried to speak, and failed.

She tried again, her forehead wrinkling with the effort. A spark of anger flared in her eyes as she was still unable to speak. *What happened?* she mouthed silently.

Ben softly brushed the hair back from her face. "We don't know, love. But I want you to just take it easy. Don't try to talk anymore for now. We've sent for the doctor. He should be here any minute. I know it isn't easy for you, but for once in your life, just rest." He leaned over and kissed her delicately on the forehead. "I love you," he whispered, gazing into her half-closed eyes.

Her lips formed the words, *Where's Danielle?*

Danielle, weeping too much to talk, leaned over from the other side of the bed and hugged her gently.

How long? Kathleen mouthed.

"About fourteen hours," Ben said. His face twisted into a grimace, lips in a tight line. "Dear God, we were afraid you weren't going to come back to us."

Water, she said with her lips.

Thirty minutes later, Alex and Robert arrived with the doctor. Ben gave the man a severe look. "Took you long enough."

The doctor said nothing as he put his bag on the floor next to Kathleen and sat down.

Alex, appearing winded, sank into a chair. "He wasn't at home. We had to scour Chinatown for him."

Ben gave him a skeptical look. "Is he sober?"

"He is now," Robert said.

"I see she's awake," Alex said. "Thank God."

"How about it, Doc," Ben said, frowning. "You up to looking at her?"

"The cold night breezes do wonders for a muddled head," the doctor said. "I must admit I was feeling no pain when your son-in-law found me. But I'm sober as a judge now."

Ben gave him a hard look.

"Okay, bad joke," the doctor said. "I'm fine. Now get out of the way and let me do my job."

The doctor spent about ten minutes talking softly to Kathleen, running his hands gently around her head and neck, prodding here and there, and checking her reflexes and vision. Finally, he gave her hand a squeeze, rose, and walked over to Ben. "Let's go somewhere and talk."

Ben, Alex and Robert headed downstairs to the parlor with the doctor, leaving Megan and Danielle with Kathleen. They would not have left her side anyway.

Ben started to offer the doctor a glass of brandy, thought better of it, and sank heavily into a chair. "So, Doc, what was it?"

The doctor looked fleetingly at the bottle of brandy, then ran a hand through his silver hair. "I'm not completely sure," he said. "We know so little—nothing really—about what goes on in the brain. She does have a stiff neck. So a likely possibility is a brain hemorrhage."

"A what?" Alex said.

"A burst blood vessel in her head."

"How serious is that?" Robert said.

"Damned serious. It could have killed her. Another one might."

There was silence in the room for long uncomfortable moments.

Finally, the doctor spoke again. "I know what you're thinking. It's too soon to tell if she'll have lasting damage. Her pupils and reflexes look okay, so I'm betting she's going to improve. She might make a complete recovery. We'll know more in the days to come."

"How do we care for her?" Ben asked.

"Complete bed rest for at least three weeks," the doctor said. "For nourishment, start her out with water, then go to thin soups, and only after that, solid food. Don't try to build up to that too fast. She'll need care close at hand around the clock." The doctor paused and ran a hand through his hair. Then he continued. "I'll tell you this, Ben. I've heard

213

tales about some of her exploits. Hard to believe as some of them are, I reckon from what I know of her, they're true." He leaned forward in his chair. "Those days are over. You can't let her go running around risking her life anymore. And you've got to keep her temper in check. That's about all we can do to guard against another one of these attacks. In any case, this was a warning. The next one could leave her crippled. Or it could be fatal. From now on, count every day as a blessing."

Ben looked at Alex. He didn't have to say anything.

Kathleen surprised all of them by making a steady improvement. Two days after the attack, she was talking again. Four days after, she was sitting up in bed. And one week later, Megan came into the room and caught her standing up by the window. At the two-week mark, she showed no trace of illness at all. Megan practically had to sit on her to keep her in bed.

The late afternoon sunlight streamed across the Pacific as the fiery globe made its way toward the horizon. Megan laid back in a recliner, eyes closed, soaking up the faint warmth the sunlight brought. Her red hair was a blazing corona around her face. She wore a white knit sweater close about her throat, long sleeves rolled up at the wrists. A burgundy wool skirt offset the sweater.

Alex looked at his beautiful wife. She appeared asleep, but he knew she had been listening to him carefully. "It's up to you and me now," he said. "Ben should stay with Mother, and Danielle has her baby to care for. Someone needs to go to Sacramento and spike Leatherwood's plans to acquire the Sierra and Western. Not to mention bringing the bastard to account for your kidnapping." Alex was silent for a moment, seething with anger. "If I don't kill him first," he said, more to himself than Megan. "We can take Hsien Lu with us, if he's willing. So what do you say? Are you with me?"

After a couple of seconds of silence, Megan turned and looked at her husband.

Alex looked into his wife's emerald-green eyes. They were alive with the fire of a Connelly woman, burning with a ferocity he had seen before only in her mother's eyes the night she had driven him from Eire Ranch at gunpoint after learning Megan was pregnant by him. Even in his wife, the intensity of that look nearly made him shudder.

Megan put her hand over his. "When do we leave?" she said.

* * *

Eli Leatherwood walked back to his plush railcar with a spring in his step. He had left Collis Huntington's office thirty minutes earlier. Everything was proceeding according to plan. Before long the Sierra and Western would be his. To be sure, his group of investors would have a stake in it, but he had structured the deal so that he had controlling interest. Ah, the intricacies of high finance! He loved the game. *And I play it so well,* he thought smugly. Getting the best of Huntington wasn't easy, but he had done it.

Huntington had agreed to the sale, and brought Stanford on board, though the latter was at first reluctant to part with his new acquisition. But Leatherwood had made the deal too good to pass up. The Big Four would receive ten per cent of Sierra and Western profits for the next two years. They would profit and not have to lift a finger to get it, and they wouldn't have to deal with the two sections owned by the Wilsons. Leatherwood, having observed the success of the Big Four in gouging their customers, would make sure there *were* profits. He would also have those two years to wrest those two privately owned sections from the Wilsons. If he couldn't, ownership of the Sierra and Western reverted to the Central Pacific. If his profits didn't reach a certain level, ownership also reverted. And at the end of four years, if ownership hadn't reverted, the Big Four could exercise an option to buy back the railroad at fifty cents on the dollar of stock value, if its value was less than that of Central Pacific stock. Leatherwood was supremely confident his grandiose plans for expansion throughout the southwest, across Texas, and into the Deep South would prevent that from happening. The area was dying for a railroad, and still smarting from losing the transcontinental route. All it would take was a man of vision to provide them one. A man like himself.

Yes, a real railroad baron, he thought as he climbed the steps to his railcar. *All I need is two more signatures.* He unlocked the polished oak door, swung it open, and went inside. Two steps into the luxurious interior he abruptly stopped. The high-backed leather chair behind his desk was turned around, its back to him. And there was someone in it.

The chair slowly turned. Leatherwood's breath caught in his throat; he felt a chill on his suddenly moist skin.

Megan Daley was sitting in his chair.

It had been years since he'd seen her up close, and under other circumstances he might have appreciated that she was as stunningly beautiful as ever. But the look of menace on her face precluded that.

He heard the door click shut softly behind him. With a feeling of dread he turned—and his heart started to pound. Standing next to the door was the most fearsome-looking Chinese man he had ever seen. His right hand rested on the hilt of a large saber. Leatherwood knew at once this was Yuen Ling-Po's feared right-hand man, Hsien Lu.

Megan rose from the chair, green eyes cold as glacier ice.

Leatherwood didn't get to the top rank of San Francisco moneymen without acquiring poise under pressure. He recovered just long enough to sputter, "What are you doing in my office?"

"Othniel Wanamaker sends his regards," Megan said.

"Who?" Leatherwood said blankly.

"Feigned ignorance will do you no good," Megan replied. "Wanamaker told us everything."

"I don't know what you're talking about."

"No matter," Megan said. "I didn't expect you to admit it, scum that you are."

Leatherwood turned red. "You're trespassing. What do you want?"

Megan stepped around the desk and walked past him to the door. "Just thought we'd pay you a little visit to let you know we're in town. We'll see you again soon." With that, she and Hsien Lu went out, but not before the Chinese man gave him a murderous look.

Alex and Robert watched from the shadows across the street from the Central Pacific's Sacramento headquarters. It was their third day observing the comings and goings of Central Pacific personnel. They were looking for a promising target, and would choose carefully.

With Kathleen recovering in San Francisco, Alex and Megan had journeyed to Sacramento with Robert and Hsien Lu. Alex had at first been reluctant to stay behind as Megan went to confront Leatherwood, but he knew she could not be safer than being with Hsien Lu. He also didn't want to risk losing his temper and killing the man right in Sacramento. Robert had come to provide his legal expertise, if necessary, in penetrating the Central Pacific's tangled business dealings.

They had a surprise companion. Li Fanfan had insisted on going along. No one thought it a good idea at first, but Megan had softened to her pleas. It was obvious she wanted nothing more than to be with Hsien Lu, whom she followed about like an obedient puppy whenever he was around. Hsien Lu didn't seem to mind; in fact Megan had observed him to now and then make tender gestures to the girl. Once in Sacramento, however, Li Fanfan was instructed to stay in her hotel room, out of the way.

Kathleen had, predictably, made efforts to get up and make the trip herself, but Ben had literally pushed her back onto the bed. "You're not going," he said firmly. "In fact, you're going to do nothing but rest until the doc says differently. If I have to tie you to the bed, that's the way it's going to be."

Kathleen glared at him, but for the first time in her life, she was secretly glad someone was restraining her.

"Give this to Megan," Ben advised. "She's up to it. You know she is; you raised her."

"Very well. Bring her to me, please; I want to talk to her. Bring Bridget too."

The three met in late afternoon. Megan sat attentively by her mother's bedside, holding Bridget in her lap, as Kathleen firmly instructed her to keep her head.

"We Connelly women have a short fuse," Kathleen said. "Thank God Danielle balances us out. I've never seen her blow up. She seems to have infinite patience. But you, my girl, are too much like me. Now, you are going over there to expose Leatherwood for what he is, and bring him down, and destroy this deal he's cooking up with the Big Four. Not to kill him. Just do the job, and come home to Bridget." She squeezed Megan's hand, then looked at her granddaughter.

"What do you think, Bridget? Will you be okay without your mother for a while?"

Bridget smiled, and turned around to face her mother. "Go get our railroad back, Mama."

While Megan and Hsien Lu went to put the fear of God in Leatherwood, Alex and Robert had set up camp unobtrusively outside the Central Pacific offices. They had yet to stay late enough to see Collis Huntington leave; the man must virtually live in his office. But now, on the third day, they saw a mousy-looking, bookish young man emerge from the offices in early evening and head off down the boardwalk.

"He'll do," Robert said. "Let's follow him."

They fell in behind him a few yards back. The man walked two blocks, then, as they had hoped, went into a restaurant. They waited outside a couple of minutes, then went in after him.

Mouse Man was seated alone at a corner table, perusing a menu. His bowler hat was on the table. He was dressed in a white shirt with buttoned turned-up collar, and bow tie. A brown sweater vest overlaid the shirt underneath his cheap jacket, which was too short at the sleeves. He was clean-shaven except for a small mustache, and wore gold wire-frame glasses.

Alex and Robert walked casually over to his table. "Mind if we join you?" Robert said.

The man blinked owlishly at them through his glasses. "What? Who are you?" He looked around the restaurant. "There's no shortage of unoccupied tables. What's wrong with them?"

"The view is better from here," Alex said, settling into a chair. Robert did the same.

"I'm calling the manager," Mouse Man said.

"I wouldn't do that," Alex said quietly. He had fished a twenty-dollar gold piece from his pocket and was slowly flipping it across his fingers.

The man eyed the gold piece with undisguised interest.

"Pick anything you want from the menu," Alex said. "We're buying."

Mouse Man visibly relaxed. "Since you put it that way, by all means stay," he said. He proceeded to order the most expensive item on the menu when the waiter appeared.

After the waiter left, the man leaned back in his chair and fixed his visitors with a penetrating gaze. "All right, who are you?"

"Not important," Alex said. "We want information, and we think you can give it to us." He slid the gold coin across the table and under the man's napkin.

"Information? About what?"

"The president of the Sierra and Western, Eli Leatherwood, has constructed a deal with Collis Huntington to purchase the railroad. We want to know the details, specifically what he needs to complete the deal. We don't think the agreement is finalized yet."

"I know nothing of such a deal," the man said curtly. "And in any case, Mr. Huntington's affairs are no concern of yours."

"I'm afraid they are," Alex replied. "We have a strong interest in the outcome of that deal."

"I would never betray Mr. Huntington's trust," the man said, bristling with indignation.

Alex looked at the ring on the man's left hand. "You have a family," he said. "How well does Huntington pay you for your loyalty?"

The man's face flushed red. "You're trying to bribe me!"

"No doubt about it," Robert said calmly. He pulled a flat wallet from his inner suit pocket and held it close to his chest so no one else in the restaurant could see it. He opened the cover. Inside was a sizable stack of money, crisp and new. "Five thousand dollars," Robert said. "It can be yours."

Mouse Man sat back in his chair, stunned. "Is it real?"

"Yes, it's real," Robert replied. "We can make it gold coins if you prefer."

The man squirmed in his chair, gripped by inner turmoil. "It would take me more than two years to earn that," he said quietly.

"The information we want can only help Collis Huntington," Alex said. "He's about to enter a deal in which, in the long run, he'll undoubtedly be betrayed."

The man looked down at his lap. "Eli Leatherwood is a crook. Mr. Huntington should have nothing to do with him."

"Then help us eliminate him," Alex said. "Help Mr. Huntington from making a mistake. He'll never know who did it."

Mouse Man was silent. The waiter came, put his supper on the table, and left. The man picked up his knife and fork and let out a heavy sigh. "Tell me what you need," he said.

* * *

Mei Li Kang reflected smugly that her spies in Sacramento had proven most effective. They had alerted her, as she had hoped, to the arrival of Megan Daley and her husband. The assassin Hsien Lu was with them, as expected, but oh! the joy!—so was the traitorous little peasant, Li Fanfan. It was all too perfect. Her spies let her know where the party was staying, and she watched and waited. When the time was right, she would strike.

* * *

Three days after the initial meeting with Mouse Man, Alex and Robert met with him again, this time in a private place where they could talk unobserved.

"Okay," he said when he was satisfied they weren't being watched. He then gave them the details of the deal Leatherwood had hammered out with Huntington.

"Leatherwood will get the best of that deal," Robert said. "Too many open-ended conditions. Is it finalized yet?"

"No. Leatherwood needs the signature of all of the Big Four. He's got Huntington and Stanford. He's going to head into the Sierras to the railhead to get Crocker's signature. Crocker will sign; he won't go against Huntington. That leaves Hopkins, and that presents a problem."

"Why?" Alex said.

"Because Hopkins is where he usually is. In New York, raising money."

"How is Leatherwood going to overcome that?" Alex said.

"A fast dispatch rider was sent out about ten days ago to get word to Hopkins. The rider took the train out to rail's end, then rode fast to where the Union Pacific is laying track out on the plains. He rode the Union Pacific rails back to Omaha, then lit out for New York to bring Hopkins back. They're expected to arrive at the Union Pacific railhead in two or three days. There Leatherwood plans to meet him and get the final signature."

Alex appeared lost in thought for a moment, then recovered. "Has Leatherwood left for the Sierras yet?"

"I don't think so."

Robert slipped the man an envelope. "Well worth the price," he said.

Mouse Man opened the envelope, quickly examined its contents, and seemed satisfied. "We never met," he said, and vanished into the street crowds.

In the lobby of their hotel that evening, Alex and Robert met with Megan and Hsien Lu, and revealed Leatherwood's plans. "We need to put a round-the-clock watch on him," Megan said. "We can't let him get that last signature."

"I agree," Alex said. "Where's Li Fanfan?"

"I left her upstairs in the room," Megan replied. "She said she was tired. As a matter of fact, so am I. Let's turn in."

"I will take the first watch on Leatherwood's railcar," Hsien Lu volunteered.

"Very well," Megan said. "Come upstairs with us and get your coat."

But when they entered the doorway to their room, they halted in shock. The room was a mess. Two lampshades were on the floor. Tables were overturned, and pillows strewn about.

And Li Fanfan was gone.

Megan looked around the room in a daze. "I should never have left her alone," she fumed, eyes brimming with tears. She turned to Alex, who was staring at the mess. "She must have put up a fight. But who could have taken her? And why?"

"I have an idea," Alex said. "It's a wild one, but the only one that makes any sense."

"Who?"

"Try Second Mistress," Alex replied. "She's got the motive. She hates both of you."

Megan put a hand to her head, eyes widening in surprise. "Could that celestial bitch be here?"

"She could be," Alex said. "Word had it from Yuen Ling-Po that she fled San Francisco a while back. She could have come here."

"We've got to find her," Megan said. "She's capable of anything."

"We can't do a worthwhile search at night," Alex said. "Let's try to get some sleep, and we'll start in the morning."

They were up early. Megan had slept hardly at all. As they descended the stairs to the lobby, Megan noticed a look of quiet rage on Hsien Lu's usually impassive face. *I pity anyone who gets in his way today,* she thought.

They split up and fanned out across the frontier town for four hours, then met again in the lobby at noon. No one had had any luck uncovering clues to the whereabouts of Mei Li Kang. They ate a quiet lunch. No one felt much like talking. They were preparing to head out again, walking toward the lobby doors, when, much to their surprise, Mouse Man burst in and bumped right into them.

"What are you doing here?" Alex said. "I didn't expect to see you again."

"I've been looking for you," he said, panting with exhaustion. "I took a chance you'd be in the best hotel in town. Glad to see I was right. I have urgent news."

They looked at him dubiously.

"Look, I figured out who you are. That changed things. I'd do anything for the Angel." He took a deep breath. "Leatherwood left Huntington's office about three hours ago. He has the sale documents, and he's headed for the railroad station."

* * *

Mei Li Kang looked with smug satisfaction at her bound captive. "So, you treacherous little commoner, at last you are mine."

Li Fanfan sat in a chair in the cheaply elegant office of Li Kang's mobile brothel, hands tied behind her back. The two men who had taken her had not been gentle. She had bruises on her forearms and wrists, and a scratch on her left cheek. Her hair, usually so neat abut her head, was tangled and messy. The tracks of dried tears were visible under both eyes.

"All that has happened to bring me to this low estate among barbarians began with your treachery," Li Kang was saying. "You let the *gweilo* know that the barbarian Megan was in our hands. You made plans to let her family into Lord Yang's compound. You were ready to betray everyone that had given you food and shelter, and a decent and honorable life."

"There was no honor in being torn from my family and sold to a stranger," Li Fanfan murmured.

"Such is the way of things," Li Kang said. "You should have been grateful to be taken from your peasant surroundings and given a life of privilege among women of noble descent such as myself. Instead, you betrayed us. You were unworthy. Now I will remind you of your proper station in life."

"You have signed your death warrant," Li Fanfan said. "I will be rescued, and you will die."

"I do not fear your cow bosom slut mistress!" Li Kang spat, lifting her skirt to reveal the dagger strapped to her thigh.

"It will not be her," Li Fanfan replied. "Master Hsien Lu will come for me. You cannot stop him."

Li Kang stepped away from the table she had been leaning against and crossed the room to stand directly in front of Li Fanfan. "If the assassin comes here, I will be ready. I have made a new batch of octopus poison, my favorite. You know how good I am at such things. He will not survive. And now it is time to begin your re-education."

She seized the girl roughly by the arm and led her out of the room and down the central hallway of the converted railroad boxcar. They passed two doors and entered the third doorway. In the room were a table with oil lamp, a woven area rug, and a bed.

Li Kang shoved the girl toward the bed. "Sit," she ordered. From a pocket she produced a pair of handcuffs, untied the ropes that bound the girl, and began to shackle Li Fanfan's left wrist to the barred headboard of the bed.

"No!" Li Fanfan cried, struggling to pull free.

Mei Li Kang slapped her hard. "Silence!" Then she finished securing her to the bed and stepped back. "Someone will come soon with food and tea. I suggest you accept it. You will not get more if you do not. Then your re-education will begin." She went out, shutting the door firmly behind her.

Li Fanfan sat on the edge of the bed in the dim glow of the oil lamp. She began crying, great tears rolling off her cheeks and falling onto her lap. "Oh Master Lu," she sobbed, her small body shaking, "please find me soon. Please."

14.

The railroad station was six blocks from their hotel, but Alex, Megan, and Hsien Lu started running. Robert decided to stay behind to further investigate Huntington's arrangement with Leatherwood.

After running nearly two blocks, they managed to flag down a passing carriage, and piled into it. "Don't spare the horses," Alex urged, and the carriage driver accelerated down the dirt street.

"But what about Li Fanfan?" Megan yelled in Alex's ear above the rumble of the horses' hooves. "We can't abandon her. I feel responsible. We've got to look for her!"

"I don't know what to tell you, love," Alex said. "We know what we have to do as far as Leatherwood's concerned. We can't do two things at once. I promise you we'll search for her at the first opportunity."

Megan blinked back tears but said nothing more.

They were at the depot in five minutes. A quick search for Leatherwood's plush railcar proved fruitless. Alex went into the station and talked with the ticket agent. Several minutes later he came out with a grim look on his face. "The ticket agent says Leatherwood pulled out two hours ago," he told them. "His car was being pulled by the *Governor Stanford*."

Megan paced back and forth on the wide, heavy planks of the station platform, arms crossed tightly across her chest. "What are we going to do?" she said. "We'll never catch him on horseback."

Alex looked around the depot at the empty tracks. All was silent in the afternoon air. "There's only one thing we can do," he said.

Megan walked up close to her husband and looked up into his broad, slightly freckled face. "What?"

Alex gazed into Megan's green eyes and saw the fire of determination there. "Steal a locomotive."

She looked at him closely, searching to see if he was serious. He was. "Can you run it?" she said.

"Well enough, I think. It was wise of your mother to have me apprentice for six months on Engine 84 with Henry Marshall, the Sierra and Western's first engineer. I'm no locomotive engineer, but I can make it go."

Megan looked around. "But there aren't any here."

"There will be. I checked the schedule when I was inside. There's a train due in at 4:10. It must be the afternoon run from Placerville. If it is, it'll be scheduled for a quick turnaround back. It's probably Engine Number 75, a 4-4-0[13]. She's a real beauty. I've ridden in the cab a few times."

Megan looked back at the big depot clock above the doors. "That's more than an hour away. Leatherwood's going to have a tremendous head start."

"Yes, but he doesn't know we're chasing him. I doubt the *Governor Stanford* is pulling very fast. And the ticket agent said Leatherwood is known to occasionally make a stop at a mobile brothel that sits on a siding out near where the track layers are working."

"Let's use the time to prepare," Megan said. "It's going to get cold before long. We're not dressed for the mountains. We need our coats from the hotel."

"I will retrieve them, Megan," Hsien Lu said. He had been standing by, quietly listening.

"Dear friend, you're not a servant," Megan said. "I'll go back for them."

"I don't want you out of my sight in this town, lady," Alex said. "Let him go if he's willing."

---

[13] The 4-4-0 designation meant there were four wheels under the front "truck" behind the cowcatcher, four drive wheels, and no wheels under the cab.

Megan turned to Hsien Lu and grasped his broad shoulders tenderly. "Old friend, what agony you must be feeling, with Li Fanfan missing. Instead of being with us, you should be searching for her."

"My first duty is to you, Megan," Hsien Lu said.

Megan whirled to Alex. "Oh, Alex, please let him go look for her!"

"But where?" Alex said. "We haven't a clue where she is."

"What we need to figure out is where Mei Li Kang is," Megan said. "Find her, I'll bet we find Li Fanfan."

"She will seek her own kind," Hsien Lu put in. "Wherever there are great numbers of Chinese, there she may be."

"Wait a minute," Alex said, eyes widening in revelation. "The ticket agent said something about the brothel being run by a Chinese woman. You don't suppose it's her?"

"I'd bet on it!" Megan said. "It's just the sort of thing that would appeal to her. It would give her money, power, control—all the things she craves."

Alex turned to Hsien Lu questioningly.

"I agree," he said. "It could be her."

"Then the three of us will go," Alex said.

Hsien Lu made a quick trip to the hotel and brought back their coats, hats, and gloves. Megan went inside the depot and bought what food was available and brought it out in a sack. They all sat down on benches outside the depot and waited.

The time for the Placerville train's arrival came and went. Megan got up and began pacing again. "Of all the days for it to be late," she muttered.

Finally, at four-thirty five, they heard a faint rumble and saw a plume of smoke in the distance. Two minutes later Engine Number 75 rolled into the depot, pulling three passenger cars and two freight cars behind its tender. The big drive wheels gradually slowed their revolutions and the massive mainrods connecting them eased their back and forth motion as Number 75 rolled to a stop in front of the station amid clouds of hissing steam and black smoke pouring from her stack. Like a chained beast, she sat awaiting fresh commands from her engineer that would bring her back to full, pulsating life, streaking across the rails once again.

From the bench, Megan eyed the big locomotive with appreciation. "I'd forgotten how beautiful she is," she said over the hiss of escaping steam.

"Aye," Alex said, "that she is. She can catch *Governor Stanford*." He watched as passengers stepped down from the cars and freight was unloaded.

225

"When do we make our move?" Megan said.

"Soon," Alex replied. "As soon as the cars are empty, the engineer will disconnect, and take the locomotive and tender up the track to the water tower, there." He pointed to a big tank sitting on a sturdy platform about one hundred feet north of the station. "He'll take on water. From what I can see, the tender still has a good supply of coal, so he won't need that. After filling up with water, he'll take her over to the turntable and get her pointed the opposite way. Last, he'll bring her down past the depot on the parallel tracks, then switch tracks and back up to connect with the train he just brought in. Then he'll be ready to pull out. We've got to make our move before he gets onto that turntable. If he gets the locomotive turned around, we'll be facing the wrong way to head into the Sierras, and I don't fancy chasing Leatherwood running backward. We've got to hope the engineer and fireman leave the locomotive at some point, or find some way to get them off it."

They watched as the last of the freight was off-loaded onto the broad station platform. The fireman climbed down from the locomotive cab and stepped between the tender and first passenger car. They heard a clanking sound, and the locomotive and tender pulled away from the cars and eased forward to the water tower. The fireman walked along behind.

The engineer brought Number 75 to a halt beside the water tower, climbed up on top of the locomotive, and removed the cap of the water reservoir. The fireman pulled on a rope attached to the water spigot to move it into position, then pulled hard on another rope. A valve opened in the water spigot and water gushed down into the locomotive.

"Let's go," Alex said, rising from the bench. "We're not going to get a better opportunity." He, Megan, and Hsien Lu walked slowly down the platform toward the locomotive, forming a plan as they went. When they neared the back of the tender, they separated, Alex and Hsien Lu walking casually around the far side of the engine, while Megan headed slowly for the side nearest the water tower.

"You know what to do, love," Alex told her.

"Don't worry, husband. He's mine."

Megan walked up alongside Number 75. The beautiful locomotive gleamed in the sunshine. The hub and spokes of the big 60-inch drive wheels were painted bright red, with a narrow band of white trim around the wheels. The connecting rods shone. Ornate gold filigree ran around the margins of the polished oak cab. The glass windows of the cab were clean, as were the French cut glass panes in the big lantern on the front of the engine. All was polished, painted and shining, a rolling example of loving care. Megan was taken with its beauty, despite herself. *It's truly a beautiful machine,* she thought. *But I have work to do.*

Megan walked beside the locomotive, swinging her skirt back and forth. It didn't take her long to catch the eye of the fireman, a tall, gangly youth who looked to be in his late teens.

The boy, who had returned to the cab with the engineer while the locomotive filled with water, gazed down at her with admiration. "Afternoon, Miss. You like my locomotive?"

Megan flashed a dazzling smile as she peered up, shading her eyes from the sun with her hand. "Oh, yes, very much! I would *so* love to see what it looks like up in the—whatever you call it."

"The cab? Why sure, Miss, I reckon you could come up for a look."

The engineer turned from his gauges and frowned. "I don't like no women in my cab."

The young fireman was dismayed. "Aw, c'mon, Ed. We ain't goin' nowhere right now. Just for a few minutes?"

The crusty old engineer gave him an acerbic look over his wire-rim glasses and thrust out his beard-stubbled chin. "All right, for a few minutes. Make sure she don't touch nothin'!"

The youth's grin nearly split his face. He stretched an arm down toward Megan helpfully. "Come on up, Miss. Mind the steps, and watch your skirt don't brush against anything greasy."

Megan grinned back at him and climbed the ladder to the cab. Near the top she appeared to need help and reached out a hand. The youth eagerly took it and pulled her up.

"Thank you," Megan said brightly. "My, you're strong!"

"Well, ma'am, I've shoveled a powerful lot of coal," he said, blushing.

Megan decided to try an overture to the engineer. "What a magnificent machine. It must take great skill to run it."

But he was immune to her considerable charms. "It does," he said gruffly. Then he climbed atop the locomotive's boiler to check the water level.

Megan turned back to the fireman. "How do you make it go?" she asked.

"Well, ma'am, it's like this," he said, and proceeded to explain, nearly falling all over himself doing so. He was helplessly in the grip of her powerful allure.

At one point she leaned close to him as he demonstrated something, enabling him to smell the perfume she had made sure to apply to her neck as she approached the engine. She straightened up and tossed her hair.

"My, it's hot in this cab!" she said, unbuttoning the top two buttons of her blouse and pulling it open a bit, revealing two inches of creamy smooth cleavage.

"Yes ma'am," the youth gulped, unable to take his gaze away.

"What's your name?" she said.

"Ah, uh, Jordy," he stammered.

"You're so kind, Jordy. I don't know how to thank you."

The youth blushed again. "Well, ma'am, maybe we could, uh—have dinner sometime."

The engineer climbing back into the cab interrupted him. "We're about full," he said, ignoring Megan. "I'm going down and shut off the water. Gotta use the facility anyway." He jerked a thumb at a privy sitting near the water tower. "You secure the cap." He started off down the ladder, then turned back. "And before I get back, I want her gone."

"Aye aye, cap'n," Jordy said, giving the engineer a mocking salute that went unseen. He turned back to Megan. "Ma'am, it sure has been a pleasure to meet you. I'd—I'd like to see you again sometime. You suppose we could?"

"I'm sorry," Megan said, holding up her left hand, "but as you can see, I'm married."

Crushing disappointment settled on the youth's face.

"In fact, maybe you'd like to meet my husband. He's standing right behind you."

So smitten was he, so completely held in thrall by her green-eyed gaze, he hadn't heard Alex and Hsien Lu creeping up the ladder behind him. A dawning realization that she wasn't kidding made him whirl around.

Alex was standing right in front of him, arms crossed. "I'm her husband."

Afraid at first that he'd crossed the line with a married woman, he started to stammer out an apology, then recovered. "I didn't—what—what do you want?"

"We want this locomotive," Alex said.

Jordy's eyes grew wide. "Well, you can't have it!"

"We can."

Any thought Jordy had about shouting an alarm was quashed by the sight of a fearsome-looking Chinese man who ascended to the cab, saber drawn.

"Wha—what do you want me to do?" he stammered.

Alex's trained eyes swiftly looked over the gauges, especially the vertical glass tube that showed the water level in the boiler. It read full. "Looks like we're ready to roll. Okay," he said, turning back to Jordy, "I want you to go and switch us over to the transcontinental track. This man will accompany you to make sure you do it right."

Jody gulped. "You're taking it into the mountains?"

"You got it. Now get moving."

Jordy descended to the ground along with Hsien Lu and walked about fifty feet to the track switch. Alex and Megan watched from the cab as Jordy threw the switch and the rails slid over, lining the locomotive up on a new track.

Megan put her hand on Alex's arm. "Are you sure you want to do this? Stealing a train is no small offense."

Alex squeezed her hand. "This is a Sierra and Western locomotive. Has been for four years. As far as I'm concerned, she's ours anyway. But I don't want to get you into anything you're not willing to accept the consequences for. You okay with this?"

Megan turned and grabbed a coal shovel that was leaning against the back of the cab. She slammed it into the pile of coal at the front of the tender, and scooped up a shovelful, then turned to Alex, her face a mask of intense determination. "Let's do it."

Alex smiled and lifted the butterfly doors at the front of the firebox. Megan threw the coal in. "Hang on to something," he told her. He released brakes and jerked the throttle lever hanging from the cab ceiling. A surge of power rumbled through the big locomotive. The huge red drive wheels spun in place for a second or two, then gained traction. The locomotive began to roll.

Just as they neared the switch, the engineer shot out of the privy, clad in red long johns, pants around his ankles. "Jordy! What the hell!" he roared. Then he gaped in astonishment as he saw his locomotive rolling away. It rumbled past the switch and Hsien Lu hopped aboard. Black smoke erupted from the stack as Alex opened the throttle. Number 75 surged forward and streaked east toward the Sierras.

Li Fanfan sat disconsolately on the bed. She was resigned to her fate. Food had been brought to her—rice, steamed vegetables, and tea—and she had eaten, though reluctantly. Attendants had come, unshackled her, taken her clothes off, and dressed her in a plain cotton shift, then reshackled her to the bed. She had no thought of resisting. There was no fight left in her.

An hour after the meal, Mei Li Kang entered the room. She was not alone. There was a man with her. Li Kang smiled at Li Fanfan. "Time for your first lesson," she said, and turned to the man. "Did I not tell you she is fresh and delectable?"

"You ain't wrong," the man said. He was a burly Irishman, clean-shaven, with long sideburns and thick reddish-brown hair. "I like the handcuff. Always did like my women chained." He started toward the bed.

Mei Li Kang settled into the room's only chair as the man began to undress.

"You ain't leavin'?" he said, astonished.

"She is new. I want to see how she does."

The man hesitated for a moment, then shrugged. "Suit yourself, lady. Don't make no never mind to me." He finished undressing, then motioned Li Fanfan to stretch out on the bed. Numbly, she complied.

He climbed astride her, grabbed her cotton shift, and pulled it up around her throat. He whistled in appreciation. "Wow. Not a mark on her. Nice high tits too, like a girl's. He hesitated. "Say, just how old is she?"

"Old enough," Mei Li Kang said.

"Whatever you say, lady." He grabbed her left breast and began to squeeze. "I'm gettin' hard already. Might as well get to it." He spread her legs, put on a condom Li Kang had given him, and plunged into her roughly.

Li Fanfan was determined she would not cry, would bear the humiliation stoically. She turned her head to the side, and saw Li Kang smiling sadistically at her. She turned the other way, her face to the wall.

The man didn't take long. When he was finished, he rested his heavy bulk on her for a couple of minutes.

Li Fanfan felt like she was being crushed.

Finally he lifted himself off her and began to dress. "A nice one," he said to Mei Li Kang. "Don't talk much, though."

"She will talk more as time goes by," Li Kang said.

The man left. Mei Li Kang walked over to the bed where Li Fanfan was still stretched out, and looked down at her. "First lesson," she said. "Prepare yourself. There will be more."

The *Governor Stanford* eased into the rail siding at dusk. Eli Leatherwood stepped down from his railcar and walked casually toward the mobile brothel directly ahead. *Plenty of time for a stop here,* he thought. *Hopkins isn't due in until late tomorrow. And I can see Crocker late in the morning. Think I'll spend the night here.*

He walked up the steps to the entrance and went inside.

Mei Li Kang greeted him in the small parlor. "Mr. Leatherwood!" she gushed. "How very propitious to see you."

"Oh? Why?"

"I have a new girl, fresh from China. Young, inexperienced. And," she whispered conspiratorially as she leaned close to him, "I think she's a virgin!"

"This I've got to see," Leatherwood said. "Lead on."

Mei Li Kang took him down the hallway to the third room. She motioned Leatherwood in.

Inside he saw a small Chinese girl lying on the bed. One wrist was handcuffed to the headboard. She did not meet his gaze.

"What's with the handcuff?" he said.

"She's a mean one," Li Kang said. "She might attack you."

"She doesn't look mean."

"Do not be deceived. Best she stay chained up."

Leatherwood slipped Li Kang a large-denomination note. "Very well. I may spend the night."

Li Kang smiled as she closed the door. "As you wish."

Once Engine Number 75 cleared the Sacramento railyard and Hsien Lu had climbed atop the locomotive and secured the water reservoir cap, Alex pulled the throttle wide open and left it there. With only the tender to pull, the big locomotive streaked along the tracks at nearly sixty miles per hour. A thick plume of black smoke erupted from her stack and trailed behind. Megan stuck her head out the cab window and exulted in the thrill of the big machine pounding along. Her glorious red hair blew about in the windstream. The connecting rods between the massive drive wheels flashed in the sunshine, a blur of motion beneath her. The vibration of the great machine went through her body from head to foot in an exhilarating continuous wave. "This is wonderful!" she shouted above the din.

"Enjoy it while you can," Alex said. "We've got work to do to catch Leatherwood. And when we do, things may get rough. You may wish you hadn't come."

"You know me better than that," Megan replied. "I belong by your side, wherever that takes me."

Alex grinned. "I wouldn't have it any other way. Now, grab a shovel. We've got a hungry engine to feed."

Megan shoveled coal until she was dizzy. Alex spelled her, then Hsien Lu took over. Alex nearly had to rip the shovel from his hands a while later; he wouldn't admit to being exhausted, though he was.

They made a gradual ascent toward the mountains. After a couple of hours, they began to pass through country dotted with scattered pine trees. Soon patches of snow appeared in shaded areas along the tracks and out across the hills. Alex closed the cab windows and Megan buttoned up her coat. Hsien Lu stared impassively at the tracks ahead, his face a mask of stone.

Night fell upon them. Alex, unfamiliar with the track, slowed Number 75 considerably as they thundered through the dark hills. Megan got into the bag of food she had brought from the depot, and passed out portions of bread, cheese, and sausage.

Heat from the firebox kept the cab warm, although they periodically had to turn their bodies, as it was hot on the side facing the firebox, and cold on the side facing away. Megan soldiered on, doing her share of shoveling. Her face and clothing became smudged with soot and coal dust, and her hair was tangled, but she didn't care.

About seven o'clock, she begged for a stop to relieve herself, so Alex brought the engine to a halt, and they stepped to the ground and did so. As they climbed back into the cab, Alex eyed the boiler water level tube. It read just above half full. "We used up a lot of water speeding along for so long," he said.

Megan peered at the gauge. "That much?"

"Yes. Locomotive are thirsty creatures. It's one of their drawbacks. I don't know where the water towers are on this line, so we're going to stop and fill up at the first one I see, regardless of the delay."

"But we can't!" Megan cried.

"You know what can happen if the water level in the boiler gets too low."

Megan shuddered. She knew all too well; she had been told about it the day she nearly died on Engine Number 84 as it thundered down through the hills from Placerville out of control. "Yes," she said. "The locomotive will explode. And so will we."

Alex eased open the throttle lever, and Number 75 began to roll down the track once more, its big lantern flickering a brilliant beam of light into the darkness ahead.

Eli Leatherwood stirred from his deep sleep to a pounding on the door of his room. He turned over, mumbled something unintelligible, and tried to go back to sleep. He felt cheated. The whore had been a dud. All efforts to engage her in conversation had failed; for all he knew she didn't even speak English. She didn't seem to know anything about sex, and she certainly wasn't dangerous. Once he had slapped her in frustration over her unwillingness to do what he wanted. Mostly she had just lain there, silent. Nevertheless, he had spent himself inside her twice before his tool gave out, and he had sunk into an exhausted slumber. About all the real satisfaction he got out of her was having a warm body in bed next to his, though even then she had edged as far away from him as she could. Once he had awakened in the middle of the night to hear her crying softly.

The pounding on the door wouldn't stop. Finally he shouted, "What?"

"Get up, Mr. Leatherwood! You better get out," Mei Li Kang's voice sounded through the door. "Trouble is coming."

He was suddenly alert. "What trouble?" he said, pulling up his trousers as he stumbled to the door. He jerked it open. "What trouble?" he repeated.

"I went for my morning walk," Mei Li Kang said. Then she proceeded to tell him what she had seen. She had walked a short distance through the woods to the edge of the ridge they were on, where she could look down the mountainside. She could see the railroad track as it switchbacked its way up the mountainside. In the early morning light two switchbacks down, a locomotive was pulled up underneath the water tower located there.

She saw one person step down, and a second one climb atop the locomotive. The figure on the ground swung the water pipe into position, and the locomotive began to fill. As she watched, a third figure, a woman, emerged from behind the locomotive. Her heart skipped a beat.

The woman had long red hair.

With a dread certainty, she knew almost at once who the woman was. There was no mistaking the barbarian Megan, even at that distance. The way she carried herself was undeniable. Mei Li Kang looked more closely at the other figure atop the locomotive. She knew a Chinese man when she saw one. It almost certainly was the assassin Hsien Lu. She didn't know who the other man was, but it didn't matter. All her carefully prepared bravado suddenly deserted her. She fled into the trees in terror.

Leatherwood stared at Li Kang, wide-eyed in fear. "Are you sure?"

"Yes. They're coming for me. I must prepare."

"You? They're after me!"

"No, it's *me* they want," she insisted.

A growing suspicion dawned in Leatherwood's mind about his chained prostitute. "Who *is* that girl? Never mind. I'm getting out of here." He grabbed the rest of his clothes from the floor and fled. If Megan Daley and her husband had tracked him here—and he could think of no other reason for them to be here—then Wanamaker must have told them everything, including news of his pending deal to buy the Sierra and Western. They had to be here to prevent him from getting those last two signatures—or much worse.

He burst out of the brothel's front door, clearing the four steps to the ground and landing on the hard-packed soil, then took off at top speed for the *Governor Stanford*. "Fire it up!" he screamed to the engineer. "Fire it up! Get us out of here!"

As he reached the locomotive cab, the engineer was just getting to his feet. He had refused to go into the brothel, labeling it a "den of iniquity", and Leatherwood would not let him sleep in his precious railcar, so he had spent the night on the floor of the locomotive cab. At least he had been warm; he had kept a small fire stoked in the locomotive firebox all night. He looked down at Leatherwood sleepily as the man vaulted up into the cab. "What are you on about at this hour?" he said.

"We've got to get out of here!" Leatherwood shouted. "There's another train just down the hill. There are people on that train that want my hide. How soon can we move out?"

"Well, it'll take a little time," the engineer said. "We got some fire in the belly, but we need more steam pressure than we got."

"Give me a shovel!" Leatherwood shouted. "We've got to get going in no more than five minutes." He snatched up a coal shovel. "Open the firebox door. I'll see to the coal, you see to the steam."

The engineer shrugged and turned away. Leatherwood started shoveling coal like a madman. His expensive clothes got dirty, but he took no notice. He had been shoveling for ten minutes when he heard the rumble of another locomotive in the distance. He whirled around. A black column of smoke was moving up the hill in the still morning air.

"We've got to go now!" he shouted at the engineer.

"What about my fireman?" the engineer said in astonishment. "He's still sacked out in that damn whorehouse."

"Forget him! Back this train up now and get back on the track."

"I can't!"

Leatherwood pulled a gentleman's derringer out of his inner vest pocket and pointed it at the engineer's head. "I'm your new fireman. Move this train. Now."

The engineer gave him a long look, then slowly reached down and released brakes. He put the train in motion and it slowly backed up on the siding until it sat on the main track. Leatherwood sprang to the ground, threw the switch, and climbed back into the cab. The *Governor Stanford* began to move slowly away.

"We ain't gonna have top speed yet," the engineer shouted above the noise.

"Give me what you've got," Leatherwood said. The locomotive, pulling its tender and Leatherwood's fancy railcar, steamed ahead in the only direction left for him to go—deeper into the Sierras.

Alex brought Number 75 around the last switchback and up onto the ridgetop. About two miles ahead, he could see a column of smoke. "That's got to be him!" he shouted over the locomotive's roar. "It won't be long now."

"Look," Megan said, pointing, "that must be Li Kang's brothel."

"I reckon so," Alex said. "But we've got a train to catch."

Megan stepped in front of her husband and grabbed him by the arms. "Listen," she said, "Li Fanfan is very likely in there. Have you forgotten she made it possible for you to rescue me? We already owe her more than we can ever repay. We've got to go in there and look for her."

Alex looked up at the smoke in the distance, torn by indecision.

"Leatherwood will keep," Megan said. "Sooner or later, he's going to run out of track. If we have to follow him all the way to Omaha, we'll get him."

Alex took one last look at the smoke, its point of origin getting farther and farther away, then sighed. "Okay. You're right. We'll check." He brought Number 75 to a halt opposite the brothel.

Hsien Lu was the first one to step down onto the ground. "I will go in first. If Mei Li Kang is present, there will be treachery."

"All right," Alex said. "We'll give you ten minutes. Then I'm coming in. Megan, you're to stay outside with me."

Hsien Lu walked slowly toward the brothel. All was silent until he got about ten yards away. Then the door suddenly slammed open and a frenzied horde of humanity—prostitutes and their clients—burst out in various stages of dress and headed at top speed for the trees. Megan looked them over from the train as they ran, but she saw neither Li Fanfan nor Second Mistress.

Hsien Lu went into the brothel. There was no sound from inside. He drew his saber and walked warily through the small parlor. He saw no one. He went down the hallway. The first room was empty. So was the second. He slowly opened the door to the third.

Li Fanfan was chained to the bed, staring at him. "Master! A trap!" she screamed.

Hsien Lu's lightning reflexes went into action. His saber arm came up as he whirled in a crouch.

Mei Li Kang had appeared at the end of the hallway seemingly out of thin air. She was visible for an instant, then disappeared into an open doorway.

Hsien Lu charged the doorway like an enraged rhino, saber ready. The instant he entered the doorway, Mei Li Kang hurled three tiny poisoned metal darts at him. His saber intercepted two, but the third got through and buried its point in his chest.

Hsien Lu pulled the dart out immediately, but he knew it was already too late. He could only hope his strength would last long enough to see Li Kang's head tumble from her shoulders. He moved toward her as she swiftly backed away, pulling a dagger from beneath her skirt and smiling insanely at him.

Li Fanfan pulled frantically at the handcuff chaining her to the bed. There was precious little space between the cuff and her wrist, and the skin there was already chafed. Now she yanked again and again, willing herself to ignore the pain. In a panic, she pulled as hard as she could, leaning all her weight into the effort. The bed slid across the floor, and she braced her foot against it to hold it in place. She pulled again and cried out in agony as her skin tore open and blood spattered the sheets.

"Master!" she cried, "Master!" She kept pulling, the flesh of her wrist torn and bleeding. It moved slightly within the cuff. Screaming in torment, she pulled yet again, teeth clenched, willing her hand to compress. Blood flowed, but she kept pulling, would not give up. Then the cuff suddenly slipped over the bulge of her thumb. She was free.

She fell on her back, then staggered upright, cotton shift stained with crimson. She stumbled out the door and ran into Li Kang's office, snatched a ceremonial dagger from its display case on the wall, and ran into the hallway.

Mei Li Kang was just disappearing into the parlor. Screaming like a banshee from Hell, Li Fanfan charged Li Kang. Li Kang whirled at the scream just as Li Fanfan buried the dagger to the hilt in her abdomen.

Mei Li Kang sagged against the wall, mouth open in silent agony, then sank slowly to the floor, eyes wide with shock and disbelief.

Li Fanfan looked down at her, hatred twisting her features. "This is America! You not own me. You not above me. I am free person!" She paused briefly. "American mistress teach me new word," she said, panting with rage. "BITCH!" she screamed, and slammed her left foot into Li Kang's ribs. The Chinese woman moaned and writhed in pain.

Li Fanfan ran to the room at the end of the hallway and found Hsien Lu on his knees, gasping for breath as his lungs tried to stiffen into immobility. He was staying alive through sheer force of will.

She knelt in front of him just as Alex and Megan burst in the door. Upon hearing Li Fanfan's screams, they had come running.

"He is poisoned," Li Fanfan said.

"Your wrist!" Megan said, aghast at the sight of Li Fanfan's blood-covered arm.

"Wrist can wait," Li Fanfan said. She eased Hsien Lu onto his back and bent over him, putting a hand under his neck to tilt his head back. Placing her mouth tightly over his, she pinched his nostrils shut and breathed deeply into his mouth twice, then placed one hand over the other, palms down, on the base of his sternum and pushed hard several times. She went back to his mouth and breathed into him twice more, then repeated the chest compressions. Long minutes dragged by as she breathed the breath of life into him again and again, her small body the only barrier separating him from death. Her tears fell on his face. Alex and Megan looked on in helpless silence. After nearly twenty minutes, Hsien Lu reached up a hand and squeezed Li Fanfan's arm. He began breathing on his own, and his color improved.

"Will he live?" Megan asked.

"Yes, I am sure," Li Fanfan said wiping away her tears. "He is very strong. Octopus poison most times kill in minutes. But not him. Now he must rest for while. I look after him."

"Where's Second Mistress?" Megan said.

Li Fanfan looked at her with grim satisfaction. "Down there," she said, pointing down the hall. "I kill her."

Alex stood up. "Megan, we've got to go. We'll have to leave him here."

Megan nodded reluctantly. "Okay. But one thing first." She reached under her dress and tore a strip of cloth from her chemise, then wrapped it around Li Fanfan's ruined arm. "This will help until it can be treated properly." She stood up and looked at the girl. "You are so brave. Take good care of him." Then she and Alex walked out the door.

"I want to see her body," Megan said. "The scum deserved what she got."

"If you must," Alex said.

They walked into the parlor. The bloody dagger Li Fanfan had used was still on the floor. There was more blood all over the Oriental rug in the middle of the room. But of Mei Li Kang there was no trace.

Hsien Lu was able to sit up after thirty minutes. He slowly moved so his back was supported by a wall. He regarded his rescuer with a smile, then frowned when he noticed her bloody arm bandage. "You are injured," he said.

"I pulled out of the handcuff," she said in Chinese.

He gingerly unwrapped the cloth strip. His eyes widened when he saw her wrist. "It is a noble deed you did for me," he said softly.

"I would give my life for you, Master."

"You must not talk so," he said. He looked at her wrist again. "These wounds are deep. I fear they will always show."

"I will wear them like a badge of honor," she said quietly.

"Come, let us treat your wounds properly," he said.

She helped him get unsteadily to his feet and they went down the hall into Li Kang's office. Li Fanfan found some balsam fir gum, good for treating cuts, and some soft cloth. Hsien Lu sat her down, treated her ravaged flesh with the balsam fir gum, and tenderly wrapped the cloth around her wrist. When he was done, he smiled at her and stood up. "Honorable Li Fanfan, a woman who would do what you have done is to be treasured," he said softly in Chinese. "I would wish you by my side always."

She was speechless. No one had ever addressed her as "Honorable" before, not even when she was Third Mistress to Lord Yang. But she dropped to her knees before him, tears streaking her face. "Master, it cannot be," she replied in Chinese. "I have been defiled in this place. I am unworthy. You must not shame yourself by remaining in my company."

Hsien Lu looked down at the girl, face alive with admiration and tender regard. "Stand up, Honorable Li Fanfan. You have proven your worth beyond measure. Such a woman can never be defiled. You are never to get on your knees to me, or to anyone else, again." He pulled her up.

She looked up at him, eyes shining. "Yes, Honorable Hsien Lu. If you would have me, I would be so pleased to be by your side forever."

He put his arms around her and drew her close. She rested her head on his chest, felt his strong heart beating, and at last gave herself up to his loving embrace.

Locomotive Number 75 streaked away from the brothel toward the mountains. Alex had the big engine running flat out again. Without Hsien Lu, more burden was placed on Megan for coal shoveling, but she didn't complain.

"Leatherwood got a big jump on us," she shouted over the pounding of the wheels and the hiss of the big pistons driving them. "Do you think we can catch him?"

"Yes," Alex said, though he could see no smoke ahead. "We'll catch him if I have to run this locomotive on bare ground."

They soon began a steady ascent, and Alex was forced to back off on the throttle. The hills and valleys became continuous, the switchbacks frequent. They ran along terrifying precipices at dizzying heights, with mountain streams rushing along hundreds of feet below them. The mountainsides were thick with evergreens. Ahead, snow-capped peaks towered in serene majesty.

"Sometime when we aren't in such a hurry, I want to take this route again. It's magnificent," Megan said.

They steamed along for an hour, Number 75 belching a great plume of black smoke into the clear mountain air as the locomotive climbed steadily. Alex spotted a trace of smoke in the air ahead. "Could be him," he said. They sped around a curve and a long flat valley came into view. A meandering stream ran through it, with the tracks going alongside. And below them, Alex could see the *Governor Stanford* just entering the valley floor. "There he is!" he shouted at Megan. "About three minutes ahead." He opened the throttle a notch. "Let's get him."

Eli Leatherwood's smug satisfaction that track's end was less than ten miles away was shattered by a glance behind him. The locomotive carrying Alex and Megan was rapidly descending to the valley floor. They were only minutes back now. "Open her up!" he yelled to the engineer. "We've got company." *I've got to reach Crocker,* he thought. He figured that Crocker, especially after the strike engineered by Megan Daley, had no love for either her or her family. The construction boss would surely protect him, if he could get there. And who would challenge a 260-lb. man wielding an ax handle?

The instant 75 straightened out on the valley floor, Alex jerked the throttle wide open again. Seventy-five erupted with fire and smoke and surged forward in pursuit.

"We need to catch him before he exits the valley!" Alex shouted above the roar. "I don't fancy trying to do it on the curves and grades that are sure to follow."

"How's our vital signs?" Megan shouted in his ear.

Alex's eyes swept over the gauges. "Everything looks good. Plenty of water, steam pressure's good. She's running at peak efficiency. I

239

wonder how *Governor Stanford* is doing?" Seventy-five thundered across the valley floor, her red-spoked drive wheels flashing in the morning sunlight.

Leatherwood looked behind him with growing panic. They were gaining! He turned on the engineer in frustration. "Can't you get any more speed out of this bucket?"

"No way!" the engineer shouted. "She's full out now. But more'n that, we got a bigger problem." He tapped the glass tube indicating boiler water. The water level barely registered. "We need water, bad. There's a water tower at the end of the valley. We gotta stop there."

Leatherwood paled. "No time! That locomotive catches us, I'm a dead man."

"We're both dead men if we don't stop," the engineer shouted. "We don't get some water soon, this engine's headed for Kingdom come!"

Leatherwood shot a glance over his shoulder. Seventy-five was now only about two hundred yards back. He turned around and pointed the derringer at the engineer's head. "I'll take my chances. You don't stop, got it?"

"An engine can't run without water!" the engineer screamed. But Leatherwood's pistol didn't waver. The *Governor Stanford* sped across the valley floor, with 75 close behind.

"Not long now!" Alex shouted. They were closing fast.

"He doesn't seem inclined to stop and talk," Megan said.

"No."

"What are you going to do?"

"I don't really know at this point," Alex said grimly.

The gap between the locomotives shrank rapidly. Seventy-five roared toward the back end of Leatherwood's luxury railcar. Only fifty yards separated the trains.

Thirty yards.

Twenty.

Ten.

"Hang on!" Alex shouted. Seventy-five's cowcatcher surged forward like a giant spear and smashed into the rear of the railcar just as the two locomotives flashed beneath the water tower.

In the cab of *Governor Stanford*, the engineer staggered from the impact and confronted Leatherwood. "You want to die, that's your business. I ain't going with you." He stepped to the edge of the cab platform and descended to the lower step. Leatherwood could do nothing; shooting him now would make no difference. As the locomotive rounded a curve, the engineer jumped and did a tuck and roll, tumbling onto a patch of long grass and brush beside the tracks. When he stopped rolling, he pushed himself up on one elbow and tipped his hat to Leatherwood's retreating figure, a final salute to a man he was sure was headed for certain death.

The locomotives exited the valley floor in deadly embrace and began to climb again, slowing as the grade grew steeper. Alex could see curves ahead. He eased off on 75's throttle but she remained attached to the railcar, embedded in the undercarriage.

"What now?" Megan said.

"Looks like we're locked to the back of Leatherwood's car," Alex said. "I'm going to try to climb over and get aboard. I'll show you how to use the throttle to slow us down if necessary." He did so, then climbed out of the cab and began to make his way along the narrow catwalk alongside the boiler. The locomotives roared around dizzying curves on narrow roadbeds blasted out of the granite mountains at great cost in both money and lives. Alex could see sunlight gleaming off water hundreds of feet below.

Aboard *Governor Stanford*, Leatherwood fought a rising panic. The locomotive was beginning to make strange noises. The boiler water level tube read empty. He looked back and could see Alex Daley making his way along the side of the trailing locomotive, a murderous expression on his face. Leatherwood didn't know what to do. Then he realized the valise with his sale agreement—the one he still needed two signatures on—was in his railcar. Frantically, he began to scramble back across the coal tender.

The locomotives lurched around a sharp curve, still locked together. Leatherwood lost his balance and fell into the coal pile. He got up, his expensive clothes marred by black coal dust. He lurched across the tender and fell through the open doorway of his car.

The *Governor Stanford* exploded.

A thousand pieces of intensely hot metal blew outward in all directions. A hailstorm of shrapnel slammed into Leatherwood's wooden car, shredding the upper half in a maelstrom of flying splinters. The bulk of the railcar deflected the metal fragments enough to blow them over Alex and 75, but the concussion of the blast blew Alex loose from the boiler catwalk and flung him against the front window of 75's cab. Megan screamed in fright as Alex, dazed and bleeding, looked at her through the window. She reached around it and helped him back into the cab.

"I'll be all right," he gasped.

Seventy-five was still pushing, a cascade of sparks coming from the mangled mass of the *Governor Stanford* as it shrieked along the rails. On the track ahead, the smoking remains were slowly being forced off the tracks. The remnant of the ruined engine finally was pushed off to the side by 75's forward motion. But it was still hooked to the coal tender. The tender jackknifed and, seemingly in slow motion, overturned on the tracks. It in turn took the blasted hulk of Leatherwood's railcar over with it as it twisted loosed from 75's cowcatcher. The smoking, shredded wreck screeched along the rails for fifty yards before the trains ground to a halt. Alex managed to get upright long enough to close the throttle and set brakes on 75.

Megan wiped the blood away with a handkerchief. "I'm going after him," she said.

Alex was too dazed to protest.

Megan gave Alex her handkerchief to stanch the bleeding on his forehead. Then she grabbed an ax from its bracket on the cab wall and climbed out onto the boiler catwalk. Seventy-five was still vibrating with energy, black smoke pouring from her stack, even though she had at last come to a halt. And she was *hot*. Megan gingerly grasped a narrow handrail and edged forward as quickly as she could. At the front of the engine, she carefully made her way down the cowcatcher to the ground.

Leatherwood's car—what was left of it—was lying on its right side, poised on the edge of a terrifying drop down a narrow gorge hundreds of feet deep. Megan cautiously climbed up onto the wreckage. Smoke from the shattered *Governor Stanford* drifted around her, sending her into a fit of coughing.

She moved forward slowly along the now horizontal right wall, picking her way around a jumble of overturned furnishings. She didn't see Leatherwood's fancy desk, and figured it had been ejected into the gorge.

Nor was there sight of Leatherwood. She thought he must have been ejected too. Then toward the front of the car she saw a thick silken drapery cord hung tautly over the edge of the car. It was far thicker than a drapery cord needed to be, another example of Leatherwood's vain display of ostentation. A large knot in the cord was wedged tightly in the crack of a splintered plank. She moved closer and peered over the edge.

At the other end of the cord was Leatherwood.

He was hanging on in desperation. From his left wrist a leather valise dangled by a thin rope. There was nothing beneath him but several hundred feet of thin mountain air. He heard the noise of Megan's approach, and looked up to see her standing over him, ax in hand. "Good God, help me!" he rasped. "Look what you've done. Pull me up!"

Megan knelt at the edge of the shattered car. She looked down at him dispassionately, as one might regard an annoying bug just before crushing it underfoot. "What *we've* done?" she said. "And what have *you* done, Mr. Leatherwood? You stole our railroad. And that was the least of your crimes. What you did to me is unforgivable."

"Please, have mercy!" he shouted. "I can't hold on much longer."

Megan stood up and grasped the ax handle in both hands. "Don't worry. You won't have to."

"Megan, don't do it!" Alex shouted from 75. He had made his way out onto the catwalk and was clinging to the handrail, clutching his head.

She gave no sign of hearing him.

"He's not worth it!" he yelled. "He's not worth the burden. Don't do it!"

Megan ignored him. She looked down at Leatherwood, green eyes devoid of pity. An expression of rage settled on her Irish features.

Leatherwood saw her transformed, and for a moment it was like he was looking at the Angel. "Look!" he shouted, holding up the valise. "These are the sale papers. I'm letting them go!" He slipped the rope off his wrist, and the valise went spinning into the void.

Megan raised the ax over her head. "Follow it to Hell, you bastard."

"No!" he screamed, "you can't do it. You won't!"

Alex was shouting again behind her.

"I was kidnapped," Megan said. "Torn from my daughter. From my husband. Raped. And all because of your greed!"

"You won't do it," Leatherwood pleaded, eyes bulging. "You won't let me fall. You're not Kathleen. You're not the Angel."

She looked down at him. There was death in her eyes. "I am the Angel's daughter."

Megan swung the ax.

It hit the cord dead on, but only a few strands parted. She swung again. More strands parted. The cord began to give way under its load. Leatherwood watched in horror as the cord gradually parted, then his face took on a look of resignation.

It was still there when the last strands broke, and he dropped into the void, still looking at her.

Megan, wide-eyed and shaking with rage, stared until she saw his body impact far below. Then she tossed the ax after him. *"Never* cross a Connelly woman," she whispered.

She stood, seemingly frozen, swaying slightly, trembling. Alex was suddenly beside her. He put his arms around her and slowly led her down off the car onto the ground, then up the steps to the cab of 75. Megan sank onto the cab floor, back against the wall. Alex put 75 in reverse, and they began the long journey to Li Kang's brothel. They did not speak the entire way.

Number 75 pulled up beside the brothel around noon. They picked up Hsien Lu and Li Fanfan, and Megan could see that there was a change between them. She smiled her approval, then turned serious. "Did you find Mei Li Kang?"

"No," Hsien Lu said. "A trail of blood led into the woods, but there we lost it. There is no doubt she was badly injured, but not enough to kill her, unfortunately."

"If she lives, she will turn up again someday," Li Fanfan said. "She does not forget. Or forgive."

It was a long, silent and sometimes cold ride back to Sacramento. Going backward put a chill wind in their faces, and even the heat from the firebox couldn't overcome it completely. It was also a hungry ride; Megan's sack of food was empty.

Number 75 finally rolled into Sacramento at two a.m. Alex parked the locomotive at the outer limits of the railyard, and did his best to shut it down properly. No one else was about to question them, so they faded into the night.

Megan sweet-talked the night clerk into getting them some food from the hotel restaurant kitchen, which they quickly devoured. Then they all went upstairs to their rooms and collapsed into sleep.

* * *

News trickled slowly across the Pacific to the good citizens of San Francisco that in Hong Kong, a well-known Chinese gangster named Lord Yang had met a tragic end, and that his chief mistress was dead as well, along with a goodly number of his household security force. Nor did it become commonly known in California for some time that Yang's other mistresses had vanished, and that the American pirate Eli Boggs and his entire naval force were wiped out by a tsunami that arose with mysterious and terrifying swiftness. On the streets of San Francisco itself, some knew of the baffling and sudden disappearance of a shabby character named Othniel Wanamaker. Others had read the newspaper story of the discovery that prominent sea captain Tobias Parmenter, once in the employ of Jardine, Matheson, had been found beheaded. And nearly everyone was aware of the tragic death of renowned San Francisco financier Eli Leatherwood in a violent railroad accident deep in the Sierra Nevada Mountains.

But the connection that no one made was the fact that all of these people had, at some point, crossed the path of the Angel or one of her family.

* * *

Late morning sunlight shone through the hotel window on Megan's red hair where it fanned out across her pillow in silken glory. She stirred sleepily and opened her eyes.

Alex was dressed and sitting in a chair, looking at her. "We need to talk," he said quietly.

She pushed herself upright, brushing back her hair. "Give me a few minutes." She went into the next room and emerged minutes later, looking more awake. She went to the bed and sat on it, waiting for him to speak.

"What you did yesterday really shook me," he said.

"I know."

"I wish you'd heeded me. As much as I hated him for what he did to you, I would have preferred not to have his death on your hands. It should be on mine."

"You were in no condition to do it. I saw the ax and—and something came over me. I couldn't stop myself."

"That something was your mother, Megan."

"No," Megan replied. "I'm not her."

"That was a pretty good imitation of her."

"Not so good. Or I wouldn't feel like I do now." A solitary tear fell down her left cheek, and her face twisted in anguish. "Oh Alex, what have I done? I don't know how to live with this."

Alex came over and sat beside her, putting his right arm around her waist. "Now you know why I didn't want it to be you. Don't worry, your mother will help you learn how to live with it."

Megan wiped away tears with the back of her hand. She turned to look directly at him. "I want to feel like a woman again. I'm ready now. Make love to me, Alex."

Alex looked into her eyes, and sensed her quiet desperation. He nodded and put his hands on her smooth shoulders and slipped her nightgown down to her waist. Then he kissed her gently, softly, on the forehead and

245

raised a hand to envelop one of her large full breasts, squeezing the nipple between thumb and forefinger.

She put her head on his shoulder. He could feel her trembling with need. For long minutes he stroked her back as she put her arms around him.

Alex pushed her slowly down onto the bed and pulled her nightgown completely off. He brushed the red hair back from her forehead as she smiled up at him. He got up and undressed, then stretched out beside her. His fingers caressed her throat, playing over the little hollow at the base. She put her head back at his touch and closed her eyes. He moved his hand down over her right breast, and could feel her pulse pounding. He gently massaged her breast for a few minutes, then lowered his head and took her hardened nipple into his mouth.

She gasped as he flicked her nipple with his tongue. A fine mist of perspiration dampened her forehead.

She began breathing more deeply as he ran his left hand down over her smooth stomach, then she gave a little "oh!" as it covered her silky mound. She opened her legs to him, and he began massaging between her legs, running his hand up and down, over her inner thighs, up to her stomach, but always back down to the delta of red hair. All the while his mouth never left her breast.

She gripped his hand and pushed his fingers down into her opening. He followed her lead and began probing deeply. She took hold of his wrists with her hands and squeezed hard, harder than he'd ever known her to. Megan arched her back and opened her mouth in silent ecstasy, let him know without words that she was ready to receive him.

Alex removed his hand, kissed her mouth ardently, and climbed on top of her. Lifting himself up, his rigid member found her moist opening, and he buried his entire length within her.

She gasped. Then her hands clutched his head fiercely, as if she wanted to tear his hair out. Alex thrust harder and harder into her. She disengaged from his mouth and probing tongue to put her cheek next to his, moaning "yes, yes, yes" over and over. Megan shuddered violently as the orgasm seized her, quickly followed by Alex's own. Waves of bliss swept over them as they melted into one being for long glorious moments.

When the tidal wave at last receded, Alex, aware once again of how heavy he was on top of her, lifted off and turned over on his back.

But she needed his closeness still, and quickly turned over, stretching out on top of him, the big pale globes of her breasts spread out against his chest. Both reluctant to let go of the other, they lay there for a long time.

She did not speak, content to feel him beneath her. But after a while, he could sense the wetness of silent tears against his chest.

He looked down at his magnificent, volatile woman. *I wonder what those tears are for,* he thought. *Joy? Remorse? I won't ask her this time. Yes, she is the Angel's daughter, so much like her mother. She has her mother's temper, and can be tough as nails. Yet she is different. She's vulnerable, not an impenetrable tower of iron, like Kathleen. No, this one—this one needs me. And she tells me so. I thank God for that. It's a full time job, keeping her out of trouble. But I'll gladly spend the rest of my life doing it.*

Alex softly stroked her red hair, and marveled at the woman he had been given. A woman of raging strength and soft vulnerability, of wild impulses and steely determination. A woman of tears, and fire.

Epilogue

The late October sunlight shone on the faces of three women as they sat on the shore of the great ocean. It shone on the faces of their men. It shone on the faces of their children. And it shone on the golden sand on which they reclined, breathing in the ocean air.

Megan looked over at her mother. Kathleen was clad in a thick off-white sweater and tan wool skirt, her lustrous black hair, now showing more than a little gray, in sharp contrast as it fell across her shoulders and down her back. "How are you, Mother?" she said.

"By God's grace, I'm having a wonderful day," Kathleen said, smiling. "What more could I ask for than what I see around me now?"

The men, Ben, Alex, and Robert, were trying their luck at surf fishing, standing with rubber hip boots amid the rush of incoming waves, flicking their poles out over the white foam. Danielle reclined in a beach chair nearby, holding her sleeping baby to her chest. Bridget played in the sand in front of them.

"Think they'll catch anything?" Megan said, looking at the men.

"Probably not," Kathleen said. "But it really doesn't matter. They're having a good time." She turned and looked at her daughter, a sudden smile lighting up her Irish face. "What was it again old Huntington said when you confronted him in Sacramento after disposing of Leatherwood?"

249

"'Take your railroad and be damned.' Or something like that. He wasn't going to be burdened with our toll fees. Nothing came of our stealing the locomotive, since there was a prevailing opinion it was ours anyway. And nothing came of Leatherwood's death after the engineer of *Governor Stanford* testified as to what Leatherwood forced him to do."

"He never saw you swing the ax."

"No. As far as he knew, Leatherwood was thrown into the gorge when the car overturned. And that's where the story will stay." She paused for a moment, then spoke again. "Which one of the Big Four do you think Leatherwood was working with? Crocker? Huntington?"

"No, I'm guessing it was Stanford. He's the glory-seeking one. But we'll never really know." Kathleen put a hand on her leg. "A nasty business, daughter. I wish you hadn't been involved."

Megan rested her head on her knees and looked out to sea. "It was my job, Mother." She smiled at a sudden thought. "Li Fanfan's wedding was truly special, wasn't it?"

"Yes, it was," Kathleen said. "And Yuen Ling-Po, the old snake, giving the bride away. Even *I* liked that. She and Hsien Lu make a wonderful couple. They compliment each other so perfectly. I hope they're together forever."

Megan said nothing in reply, silent for a moment. Then she turned her face to Kathleen. "I worry about you, Mother."

"That will do you no good. What will be will be. I don't worry about you. Not anymore. I did constantly when you were a teenager. What a fright you gave me sometimes! But you've been tested. And found worthy." She paused and picked up a handful of sand, letting it sift through her fingers. "You're ready. The Connelly women are in good hands." She gazed at Bridget playing with sand and bucket. She looked like a miniature Kathleen. "Kathleen Junior, that one," she said, smiling.

"Aye," Megan said. She's so like you it's enough to make me believe in reincarnation."

"Except I'm not dead yet," Kathleen said. "But the day is coming, daughter, when I won't be here."

Megan frowned. "Not having you here would be like the Rock of Gibraltar suddenly disappearing, Mother. It's hard to imagine."

Kathleen smiled again. "Don't fret, daughter. All things pass away." She continued to sift the sand through her fingers. "This sand was once rock. Over millions of years, time and tide wore it away." She looked out over the sea. "We are sand on the shore of time, Megan. The tide we call life carries us where it will. We can only struggle against the current, and pray we can keep our heads above water." She stopped, and for a moment,

Megan thought she was finished speaking. Then she continued. "The doctor says I'm living on borrowed time. I do count each day as a blessing. As for you, you'll have challenges ahead. Mei Li Kang is doubtlessly still out there somewhere, full of hate and lusting for vengeance. Raise Bridget to claim her birthright as my granddaughter. She will need it."

"I will, Mother. You can count on it. But maybe she'll have some help."

Kathleen looked at her questioningly.

"I think I'm pregnant."

Kathleen leaned over and hugged her daughter. "Are you sure?"

"Pretty sure. I've had morning sickness the last three mornings."

"Have you told Alex yet?"

"No. I'll tell him tonight." She turned her attention to Bridget, who was exulting in the freedom of the seashore. The black-haired five-year old picked up handfuls of sand and tossed them into the air.

"Look, Mama!" she cried.

Megan stood up and spread her arms wide, throwing her head back to catch the breeze as the great sun struck her red hair in a fiery blaze. "Throw it again, daughter," she said, smiling broadly. "As high as you can."

Bridget scooped up a double handful of sand and threw it high. A puff of breeze caught it and carried it down the beach. The golden sunlight streaming in across the wide water struck the sand, and the tiny flakes of minerals in it—quartz, micah, pyrite, and gold—flashed and sparkled in the clear afternoon air.

About The Author

B. J. Scott includes Irish and Scottish immigrant blood, as well as Cherokee, in his heritage. A former college instructor and professional photographer, he holds Bachelor's degrees from Washington State University and Brooks Institute. He lives on the Central Coast of California with his wife and two sons, where he is currently in the planning stages of the third book of the Angel Trilogy, Legacy of Angels.